Right Where You Left Me

also by holly caste

Golden Bay Beach Series

Anything Rae Touches

Fragments of Gray

Right Where You Left Me

HOLLY CASTE

LN
P

Right Where You Left Me
Paperback Edition

Love N. Books Press
An Imprint of Wolfpack Publishing
1707 E. Diana Street
Tampa, FL 33610

www.lovenbookspress.com

Edited by My Brother's Editor

Paperback ISBN 979-8-89567-711-7
Ebook ISBN 979-8-89567-710-0

This one is for the millennials, elder emos,
Y2K baddies, and nostalgia queens.

dear reader

Hey! Thanks for picking up my book! Before you dive in, please check out the trigger warnings:

Explicit language, detailed sex scenes, innuendos among teens, alcohol & marijuana use, illness/hospitalization, grief/death. This might be triggering for some readers. I purposefully did not include detailed information on this page to savor a major plot point. However, if you'd like to know more info, please go to the "More Trigger Info" at the end of the book.

playlist

"Swing, Swing" by The All-American Rejects
"stranger" by Olivia Rodrigo
"Feeling This" by Blink-182
"Scared of Loving You" by Selena Gomez and benny blanco
"Lose Control" by Teddy Swims
"You and Me" by Lifehouse
"crushcrushcrush" by Paramore
"MIDDLE OF THE NIGHT" by Loveless
"Kids in Love" by Mayday Parade
"right where you left me" by Taylor Swift
"Goodbye to You" by Michelle Branch
"Boston" by Augustana
"I Love You, I'm Sorry" by Gracie Abrams
"First Date" by Blink-182

Right Where You Left Me

CHAPTER ONE

PRESENT

2024

MEN ARE IDIOTS.

Particularly the one in front of me, kneeling on one knee as he extends his hand, showcasing a stunning diamond ring.

Warren and I have been dating for seven months, are still living in separate apartments, and in that short amount of time, I have never once expressed that I wanted to marry him. Yet here we are, frozen in the middle of my parents' holiday party with at least a hundred sets of eyes on us as Warren asks, "Will you marry me?"

A knot twists in my stomach as my lips mold into a fake smile. "Um…"

A bright flash from a professional photographer blinds me for a second, and when I blink back into focus,

I spot dozens upon dozens of phones being held up, recording this moment.

The waitstaff is already passing around tall champagne flutes filled with Dom Perignon. The string quartet paused their Christmas medley minutes ago while Warren gave his lovely speech before presenting me with the ring. There's not a sound in this renovated ballroom, the guests holding their breath as they watch me sweat under the glow of the chandeliers.

My heart pounds.

I'm about to look like the biggest asshole ever.

I lock eyes with my brother, Trent, and his fiancée, Lucille, and both of their faces drop.

I think that's when the rest of the crowd gets the hint of what my response is going to be.

Mom's heels clink against the marble tile, lasers shooting out of her eyes as she makes her way toward me, wrath spilling out of her pores. With every step she takes, her spine gets more rigid, even though she's wearing a false smile, just like me.

"Why don't we step outside?" I reach for Warren's arm, getting him up off the floor. The second he's standing, I yank him through the French doors, stepping outside into the courtyard.

Conversation erupts as soon as we shut the door, and I can't make out the exact words of the murmurs, but I have a feeling I know what's being said.

"Ivy—" Warren starts, but I put my hand up.

"Just give me a sec."

Shutting my eyes, I take deep breaths as I pace around the gray stone pavers. Brisk air brushes against me, but I'm too heated to be impacted by the cold.

Pinching the bridge of my nose, I try to gather my thoughts as they race a mile a minute, but I can't. The only thing I can say is, "What the fuck was that?"

"I thought that's what you wanted, Ivy."

"What on earth would make you think that?"

"You told me you wanted more commitment from me!" Warren snaps.

"Yeah, as in, I don't want you to fuck your secretary! Not propose to me in front of both of our families when we haven't even been dating for a year!"

He flings his head back, the warm-white Christmas lights hanging above us brightening his hardened features. "That was one time! I hooked up with her one time in the beginning of us getting together because I didn't think we were exclusive. I thought we were past all that, Ivy."

Crossing my arms over my chest, I suddenly sense the chill in the air. I'm at a loss of how to respond, because we did work through whatever that fluke moment was with him and his secretary, and I did, in fact, state that I was past it.

"We've only been together for seven months," I say, my voice softening.

"And?"

Our gazes connect. As I admire him in his Armani suit with his slicked-back hair, a vise grip around my lungs strengthens. I chew the inside of my cheek, knowing that if he were truly the man I wanted to marry, I wouldn't be having any sort of negative bodily reactions like this.

"Babe." Warren steps closer, running his hand down my biceps in an attempt to warm me. "You know this is it for us. This is what we're supposed to do." At the same time, we both glance through the French doors and into my parents' ballroom. I'm surprised no one's face is smashed up against the glass panes, trying to eavesdrop. Instead, the music is back, people are mingling, and hors d'oeuvres are being passed around. "This is our life, Ivy. We're supposed to marry someone within our social circle. What does it matter if we've been together for seven months or seven years if we're going to get married in the end?"

"I don't want that kind of life, Warren. I fought really hard to get out of it. I left Maryland right after high school and only returned for obligatory get-togethers. Boston became my home ever since I attended Harvard. I only agreed to date within 'our social circle' because my mother had been on my case about being single and in my thirties, so I shut her up by going on a few dates with her friends' sons."

His hand slowly drops. "So you've been with me just to get her off your back for a little while?"

"No. I wouldn't have stayed with you this long if I didn't like you."

"But you don't love me."

"I do."

"Not enough to marry me."

The only sound that comes out of me is my shallow breaths, turning into small wisps of fog as they're greeted by the bitter air.

"Have you ever loved anyone that much?" Warren asks, not in a taunting way, but in an earnest attempt to know me better.

The answer freezes on my tongue—an answer that I'd rather not acknowledge. So instead, I reply, "You deserve to be with someone who wants the same life you do. I'm not that woman."

He nods, his shoulders stiffening. "I hope one day you're able to fully love someone, Ivy."

The tone felt endearing, but the words scraped against my skin.

Swallowing down my unwanted emotions, I take a few steps back. "You should get back in there."

"Where are you going to go?"

I shrug. "I'll figure out my next move. But you should go back inside and let all of them comfort you by setting you up with someone better." I try to make light.

"You could get some comfort too." Warren points toward the door, gesturing to the large crowd that will undoubtedly rush the both of us, wanting to know the outcome.

"I'm okay with being the villain in this story."

He gives one more nod before turning to go inside. As he enters, I can hear the muffled sounds from the party get louder, but it's quickly stifled when the door shuts.

Darkness shrouds me as I back away from my childhood home, moving further into the acres of manicured landscape that we've casually called our backyard.

Tonight will be yet another reason I'll hate coming back to this place. I *knew* I shouldn't have gone to the holiday party and just flown in on Christmas, but Mom insisted I had to be here because she had invited my now ex-boyfriend's family.

I bet she put Warren up to this.

She just can't wrap her head around my wanting to break free from the lifestyle she had always dreamed of as a little girl. We're oil and water in human form.

A shiver runs down my spine as the cold bites the tip of my nose.

I need to get out of here, but I need to get my phone first.

Sneaking around the side of my parents' old-money brick mansion covered in my namesake, I make my way through the staffing door. A few workers are chatting, leaning their body weight against the countertops, but the second they spot me, they snap to upright positions with panicked looks on their faces.

"I need you to do me a favor," I say, going to the small

blonde girl who appears terrified that I'm about to scream at her for taking a break.

"Sure," she responds in a mousy voice.

"You know who Trent is? My older brother?" I ask, even though I've never met this girl before.

"Um..."

"Tall guy with the same dark hair as me—we kinda look alike?"

"Yes!" The brunette next to her snaps her fingers when she makes the connection of how similar Trent and I look.

"Amazing," I say to her. "Find him, tell him to grab my purse, and meet me in my bedroom."

I can't risk having him meet me in here. There's a high probability that either of my parents will come into this back room to chastise one of their staff about something senseless.

They both nod their heads and start to leave.

"Thank you!" I whisper-yell to them, and they smile, grateful I acknowledged their efforts before they disappear down the hall and into the ballroom.

Sneaking out of the opposite door as if I'm a teenager once again, I tiptoe my way toward the back staircase that leads to my old bedroom and is far away from the side of the house where all the festivities are going on. No one would have a reason to venture over to this end.

Lurking up the stairs and eventually toward my room, I scurry into the only place that has ever felt like home in this mammoth house.

Rushing, shutting the door behind me, I go to let out a sigh of relief, but the air gets trapped in my chest.

My safe haven is gone.

Every single item that stood frozen in time for years, never touched or glanced at aside from when I make my forced bi-yearly family visit, is packed up.

Stacks and stacks of boxes with all my belongings encompass the space. My old posters have been taken down, a discolored outline on my teal-painted walls showcasing where they're supposed to be hung. Every trinket, book, CD, down to the last butterfly clip, is shoved into a box.

A lump grows in my throat, my eyes burning.

Sure, I don't tear up when I end things with my boyfriend and publicly reject his proposal, but *this*?

These four walls held me when no one else did.

I might not like coming here to deal with my parents, but it would've been nice to know they were having strangers pack up my shit. I could at least mentally prepare. Or, hell, I could've done it myself if they were so eager for yet another spare room to fill their egos with.

"Heads up, Mom's on a warpath," Trent quietly says as he enters with my purse in hand. Closing the door behind him, his face twists when he notices my room is in boxes. "What the hell?"

"Oh, so I guess Mom didn't have your shit ready to ship out the second you told her you were going to propose to Lucille?" I snatch my bag, displacing my anger for our mother onto him.

He shakes his head. "My room's still intact. She's actually been bugging me to start going through it before the wedding."

"Nice to see she gave you your year-long engagement to get your crap out of the house." I fish for my phone, and the second it's in my palm, I start searching for flights back to Boston. "She didn't even wait to hear me give Warren an answer before she had the housekeepers touch all my belongings. If she were smart, maybe she would've thought that one through and realized I'm a flight risk and the probability of me saying yes to anyone is slim to none."

"What's your plan?"

"For life or for getting out of here? Either way, the answer is, I'm going to wing it and figure it out."

"Are you coming back downstairs?"

"Absolutely not." My scarlet nails furiously tap on my phone, trying to find the soonest way out of here. "I'm grabbing a flight back home."

"It's two days before Christmas. Everything's going to be booked. The airport's going to be insane."

"It is what it is."

Trent sighs, his head tipping back as he stares up at my ceiling. "What should I say when they start asking where you went?"

"Say nothing. You don't know anything. I could be unpacking these boxes in here for all you know."

He chuckles, and my attention snaps from my phone and onto him.

"What are you laughing at?"

"It's just funny that even after all these years, and even though we're in our thirties, we're still sneaking around Mom and Dad's back."

"I guess there are some things we'll never grow out of."

We've grown apart in adulthood. It's mainly my fault. I separated myself from the memories that live in this town. Trent got pushed away as well. We got accustomed to the space, carrying on as different people doing different things with our lives.

Yet, standing in this room, conspiring on how to deal with our parents, seems all too familiar and, in a strange way, comforting.

I think he feels it too because he cracks a smile. "Text me when you get back to Boston," he says, backing toward my door.

"I will."

As soon as he leaves, I immediately secure the next flight I can catch—which isn't for another four hours and has a connecting flight with a three-hour layover, but that pain-in-the-ass traveling sounds a helluva lot better than swallowing my pride and going back to the party.

Once the ticket is paid for and I order an Uber, I know I should leave before my chances of running into Mom get any higher. But my masochistic heart can't leave this room without knowing how it once looked. My fingertips graze the cardboard boxes wrapped in thick packing tape.

Even if I wanted to empty everything and shake all the remnants out on my floor, I couldn't because I have nothing to pierce it open with.

My shoulders begin to round, giving up the hope of seeing a singular item from my past. Not that it would be particularly healthy for me to get sucked back into that time in my life, but there are still a few memories that I cherish, and I wouldn't mind using some happy thoughts to mentally escape this epic fail of a night.

Starting to part ways with my belongings, I spot one stray box off to the side that hasn't been taped shut. I nibble on my bottom lip, knowing I should leave this room—and this house—altogether.

But that pull—the same pull that I've felt in the center of my chest whenever I think back to *those* days—makes it hard for me to walk past. My heart has been guarded by a corroded, chain-link fence, weeds and ivy strangling the metal, barely letting the smallest of gestures sneak through the tiny spaces.

I used to be sentimental, wanting to capture every moment by means of collecting movie ticket stubs, cheap jewelry, and bottle tops.

But that was before.

My heart hammers, knowing my Uber driver is probably pulling up to the iron gates in front of my parents' estate.

Maybe I'm about to do this to try to make myself smile on a shitty night. Or maybe I'm about to do this to make my heart hurt even more. Either way, on impulse, I dive to the floor and open the cardboard.

The immediate sight of Lindsay Lohan on the cover of my *Mean Girls* DVD makes me grin, remembering how much I loved this movie. Filtering through the rest of my belongings, not really sure what I'm searching for but knowing I haven't found it yet, I rifle through my Paramore CD, a stained Coach wristlet, an empty Four Loko can—which God knows what reason I decided to keep—and faded Warped Tour tickets.

When my fingers come in contact with a men's Blink-182 shirt, my pulse stops.

The more I clench onto the shirt, the more it feels as if the cotton is burning a hole through my skin, incinerating my bones until there's nothing left of me but dust and ash. A stinging sensation fills my eyes, but I force myself to keep it together.

Swallowing around the clog of emotions in my throat, I place the shirt to the side and spot the last item at the bottom of the box that the tee was hiding. My old chrome pink Canon digital camera.

A wave of nausea rolls around my stomach in an all too familiar way, one that I haven't felt in years.

It's bound to be out of battery, but that doesn't stop me from shoving it in my purse.

I should leave it here.

I should leave it tucked away in this box, never to be seen again.

But I know there are pictures on here that I don't want to completely delete out of my memory. As much as I have sworn to myself that I never want to travel down this turbulent memory lane, I can't let go.

It's the reason I just turned down Warren.

It's the reason I've never settled down.

It's the reason I've never wanted to come back to Maryland.

In the twisted depths of my wilted heart, there has always been a part of me that has never been able to let go of *him*.

CHAPTER TWO

I'M NOT sure what's worse, going to a mall two days before Christmas—back when online shopping didn't exist—or being stuck in an airport for two days at Christmas. Regardless, I can now confirm that they both suck.

The airport is swamped, people bustling every which way in a frenzy. The overwhelming sounds of rolling luggage, crying children, and people loudly speaking into their phones fill my ears. It's an overload to the senses as I pass by the gates, restaurants, and shops.

Since I left all my belongings in the hotel Warren and I were staying at, I'm traveling with nothing on me but my purse. I'm sure Warren will drop my suitcase off to me when he gets back. It won't be a big imposition, seeing that we only live five blocks away. Which, let's face it, should've been another warning sign for him that I didn't want to get married. If I wasn't willing to uproot myself to move five fucking blocks or invite him to live in my space, what made him think I was ready to get hitched?

Shaking off my annoyance, I roam into one of the many gift shops. The last thing I want is to sit on a plane, another airport during my layover, and then a second plane wearing this fancy holiday dress and high heels, which are squeezing my pinky toes. So I opt to purchase overpriced navy-colored sweatpants and a sweatshirt. *I heart Crabs* is embroidered on the dark cotton right across the chest. Fantastic.

"Will that be all?" the cashier asks.

"And these." I place slippers and a small tote bag on the counter. As the cashier continues to ring me up, my gaze flits around the store, seeing if I need anything else. Noticing a phone charger on the display next to me, I grab it, even though I should let my phone die so I don't have to keep reading Mom's passive-aggressive texts or hit ignore each time she calls. Directly next to the colorful wires are packages of double-A batteries. The digital camera in my purse practically screams at me to get the batteries, and without talking myself out of it, I take them and hand them to the cashier.

Bad idea, Ivy.

Bad fucking idea.

Ignoring the loud voice in my head, I carry on with my decision and make my purchase.

Hours tick by, and I've since changed my clothes and found a new home at one of the airport's sports bars. It's dim in here, but the huge TVs make up for the lack of light.

It's crowded, every seat taken, and several people stand next to their luggage. Luckily, I found a cushioned stool directly in front of the bartender about forty-five minutes ago.

Nursing my pinot noir, the man seated next to me attempts to make small talk for what feels like the hundredth time, clearly not getting the hint that I have no interest in speaking with him.

"Going to see your family for the holidays?" he asks.

"Nope." I stare at my almost-empty glass and not at

him. If I ran into him on the plane, I wouldn't even recognize him.

"Traveling to see your…significant other?" He tiptoes around asking me if I'm single.

"Considering I just publicly rejected his proposal a few hours ago, I'm going to say no."

"Oh, wow, I'm sorry—"

"Don't be." With tired, heavy eyelids, I glance over at him, noticing his features for the first time. He's older than me, in his mid-forties, and probably shouldn't be poking around a woman's romantic life, considering he has a gold band around his ring finger. "I never fully loved him," I state, mirroring Warren's statement to me.

I hope one day you're able to fully love someone, Ivy. Fuck him.

Taking another sip of wine, my head dizzies a bit, and that's when I realize I'm definitely tipsy.

The man doesn't know how to respond, so he goes back to watching the various sports being played on the different TVs, while I go back to my solitude.

"You a hockey fan?" The man breaks the silence and points toward the game being shown behind the bar.

"No."

"Too bad, I'm a die-hard fan."

For the love of God, shut up.

He continues as if I'm engaged in this conversation. "The Cobras are my favorite," he states about the professional hockey team. "It's too bad Paxton Rhodes had to retire after his injury at the end of the season last year. He was incredible to watch. One of my all-time favorite athletes."

My wine glass is glued to my lips as I pour every last drop down my throat, hoping it does more than give me this slight buzz.

Thankfully, the man gets a notification on his phone,

which causes him to stand up. "I have to head to my gate." He picks up his duffel, slinging it across his shoulder. "It was nice talking to you."

"Was it?"

He opens his mouth to say something, but then shuts it. With a curt nod and tight-lipped smile, he's off.

Letting out a puff of air, I rest my forearms on the bar and let my head hang while I wait for my turn to get on a plane.

The interaction with the man, as simple as it might've been, irks me, causing a prickly sensation under my skin. The combination of exhaustion and red wine has my thoughts spiraling down a rabbit hole.

My mind jumps from the man, then back to Warren's parting words.

I hope one day you're able to fully love someone, Ivy, repeats in my mind over and over again as if stuck on a loop.

I did love someone. I loved someone so much that when it ended, it hurt so excruciatingly bad that it forced my heart closed, becoming locked up ever since.

My nails tap against the empty glass, a temptation gnawing at my insides. I twitch, fighting with myself not to act on the one thing I want to do right now. But Warren's words get louder and more hurtful, slicing the little parts of me I keep tucked away from the world.

Screw it.

Fishing for my batteries and my digital camera, the pounding in my chest warns me how horrible of an idea this could be. Do I really want to reopen this wound with the possibility of my pain gushing all over, spilling into every aspect of my life?

Sweat forms as I slip the batteries into the side of the camera, knowing that when I look through these pictures, everything will come flooding back to me: the memories, secrets, and him—what could've been and what almost was.

Despite my better judgment, I turn it on, the black screen lighting up. Breezing through the first few photos, a nostalgic feeling hits me as I see myself hanging with random people in college dorms.

Then the next image appears.

It's all I need for my heart to sink into my stomach while bile races up my esophagus, the taste of burning pinot noir lighting my throat on fire.

It's a picture of us.

Happy. His lips pressed against my cheek as he took the selfie. I know exactly where we were when he snapped the image. It was mere minutes after I made the biggest mistake of my life.

Placing the camera aside, I pinch the bridge of my nose, forcing my feelings to stay trapped inside.

Sighing out a shaky breath, I curse myself for doing this. Hating myself for looking at these pictures. Hating myself for bringing this camera with me to begin with.

But most of all, hating myself for still allowing Paxton Rhodes to have my heart.

CHAPTER THREE

paxton

2004

September

THE TASTE of Becca's cookies-and-cream-flavored lip gloss still lingers on my tongue an hour later. At least, I think that's her name. Either way, I really need to get this disgusting taste out of my mouth. Had I known her lips were covered in that crap, I might've held off, but instead I chose to seize the moment with a hot cheerleader, bypassing any notice of her smelling like sugary plastic.

Probably not the smartest idea to make out with her under the bleachers on my second day at East Valley High School, considering I just moved here, but I've done worse.

I wipe my mouth with the back of my hand one more time for good measure, then walk inside our new apartment. It's a tight squeeze for a two-bedroom in an apartment complex, but it's nicer than anything I've ever had.

"How was school?" Uncle Jeff asks, hearing me enter even though his back is turned while he rearranges his outdated desktop computer on a small desk.

"It was good. Nothing major to report." I drop my backpack off my shoulder and let it fall to the floor by the door. "Need help?" I mosey over to him, taking a look around my latest home.

Our living room acts more as a multipurpose area with our couch, TV, a narrow wooden table we have our quick meals at, and now a computer desk. The kitchen is small, just enough space to walk in and grab what we need, but not enough to do actual cooking—not that either of us is good at that. Our apartment is nothing extraordinary and probably a little too cramped for most, but I feel so lucky to live here.

"Nah. Just moving shit around to see where I like it." When he attaches the keyboard and gets the desk looking how he wants it, he stands tall and puts his hands on his hips, surveying the space. "Looks good. I think this is gonna be a great move for us. Hopefully, the last one."

For all intents and purposes, Uncle Jeff is my parent. My sperm donor of a father took off before I was born, and things with Mom, well, she was in and out of my life just as much as our cash flow was. We moved a lot, sometimes staying in shelters or motels. It wasn't until I was nine years old that the courts got involved and placed me in foster care when they found out through my school that Mom had left me alone for several days while she went off doing God knows what, and I haven't seen her since.

Neither of my real parents gives a shit about me. That's why I consider Uncle Jeff a better parent than either of them.

I don't really know how Uncle Jeff found out about me or my situation, considering I never met him before he became my guardian, but I wasn't in foster care for too long until he took over.

He doesn't have a large stream of money, but his kindness makes up for any financial lack tenfold. I'm forever grateful he opened his door for me when he didn't have to at all. We've apartment-hopped a bit as he struggled to find a decent-paying job, but he just got a new job as a maintenance worker at a local hospital, and this recent move seemed like the right one.

Uncle Jeff was hesitant to place me in yet another school with a new group of kids, but I've done it so many times that I'm used to it. He's sacrificed so much for me, even using his savings on my hockey equipment a few years back, so I don't mind getting moved around one more time if it's for the sake of him finding a job he actually likes and will pay him what he deserves.

"Yeah, I like it here," I say, going to the fridge to grab two Arizona Iced Teas. As I pass him one, he gives me a wide smile. "Why do you have a creepy grin on your face?" I jokingly back away, making him laugh.

"I'm glad you're enjoying East Valley."

My stomach dips, wondering if he found out about me making out with Becca. Not that it matters or that he hasn't caught me in more compromising states. But what's causing me to sweat under his stare is the thought of him finding out about Becca and thinking I'm going to make her my girlfriend—because there's no way in hell that's happening.

"Okay…"

"I have some exciting news that I think will make you like East Valley even more."

Twisting off the cap to my drink, I take a sip, waiting for him to continue.

"Have you heard of the Pelicans?" Uncle Jeff asks, the

lines around his hazel eyes becoming more pronounced the more he grins.

"Uh, you mean the best tier one travel hockey team? Yeah, everyone in Maryland knows who they are."

"I got a call from them earlier." He glances at his dark-blue Nokia cell phone lying on our small wooden table that's pushed up against one of our living room walls. "The coach saw you playing in a game with your old high school and was blown away. Took him a little while to track us down, but he wants you to try out for the team. They have a scholarship position open and think you'd be a perfect fit."

My jaw drops, and the iced tea in my hand nearly does the same, but I come back to life just in time to catch it. "Holy fucking shit!" I choke out in disbelief, my heart racing at the speed of light.

Uncle Jeff bellows a laugh. "I was hoping you'd have that reaction!"

"You're serious? You're not messing with me?"

"I'd never joke around about something like this. You better go check your hockey bag to make sure you have all your gear from the move. We leave in a half hour."

"Wait, I'm trying out today?"

"Yep." Uncle Jeff beams. "You better go hurry and check," he says, hitching his thumb over his shoulder to gesture toward my new bedroom.

Without a second thought, I'm darting into my room, scouring my hockey bag to double-check I have everything. The grin on my face goes from ear to ear as my bloodstream bursts with excitement.

Never in my life has something lined up so easily. This feels too good to be true. I don't get opportunities like this knocking on my door. I either need to work my ass off to get to the finish line or watch from the sideline, seeing everyone else have an easier time than me.

Doubt creeps up the back of my neck as I zip my bag after doing a final check. All the voices in my head telling me that things like this don't happen to me try to bring me down. But as I stand tall, my hockey stick firmly seared to my hand, I know I'm not going to fall for the hesitation that's brewing in the back of my head.

I don't know much in life, but I know I'm a damn good hockey player for a fourteen-year-old, and the best fucking travel team in the state is about to see how awesome I am.

CHAPTER FOUR

I DON'T KNOW what happened.

I mean, I *do* know what happened—I just don't believe it.

I've been pinching myself, waiting to wake up from this awesome dream because it all seems unreal. But here I am, officially a player on the Pelicans.

The guys on the team are cool, even though they all go to Windsor Prep. Go figure, all the kids on the best travel team are rich kids. But despite my assumption, thinking they'll be pompous assholes, they're pretty down-to-earth and love hockey just as much as I do.

I hit it off with my teammate, Trent, pretty immediately, both of us cracking jokes to each other during my tryout. In fact, he's going to pick me up for the game tonight since Uncle Jeff is working overtime. Trent invited me over to his house early so we can work on our wrist shots and eat dinner before the game.

Peering out the window, I glance down at a black Audi—the one I was told to look out for—pulling up to the front of my apartment complex. Grabbing my gear, I lock up, then head outside to Trent.

His dad gets out, rounding the car to greet me. "Hi, Mr. Rhodes."

Before I can answer, the back seat window rolls down, and Trent pops his head out. "That's our driver, Henry."

"Driver?" I glance over at the man I assumed was his dad.

"I swear I'm not a dickhead rich kid, right, Henry?" Trent assures me when it becomes very evident just how much money he comes from and how vastly his world differs from where he's picking me up right now.

Henry laughs. "That's true."

"You needed a ride, and I don't have a license yet, so Henry's helping me out," Trent adds to ease my hesitation.

Slowly nodding, I turn to Henry. "Hey."

He smiles, taking my gear from me and putting it in the trunk as I hop in the car, the scent of fresh leather instantly invading my nostrils. Usher's "Yeah" plays on the radio, but Trent starts speaking over the music. "Tonight's gonna be sick. We're definitely winning the game."

"Hell yeah, we are," I say, loosening up as Henry puts the car in gear.

"I was gonna order us a pizza for dinner. Is that good?"

"Yep, I'm good with anything." I'm not picky when it comes to food. I had days where my stomach growled far into the night, so as long as there's something in front of me to eat, I'm not complaining.

We bullshit for the fifteen-minute car ride until we pull up to iron gates. My eyes go wide as I watch Henry enter numbers on a keypad, getting the gate to open to the huge estate.

"Dude," I speak lowly. "We live two totally different lives."

I feel as if I'm in the middle of a movie set, passing a fountain as the car casually parks in the rounded driveway directly in front of a gigantic brick mansion.

Trent chuckles. "It's not all it's cracked up to be."

In a state of shock, I follow him inside, unable to fully process that this is my teammate's home. My body stills, noting the marble flooring and concerned that if I move an inch, I'll somehow knock over the line of pillars with ostentatious flower displays on top. A chandelier that costs more than a year's worth of rent hangs over a grand staircase, and there are countless rooms to either side of me. It even *smells* rich in here, like some fancy lady perfume.

"Trent, is that you?" A woman's voice travels out of one of the rooms next to us, her heels clicking on the floor as she appears. Her hair is tightly pulled into a bun at the top of her head, and she wears a black dress and a thin, shiny black sweater over her shoulders. "Oh." Her dark-blue eyes land on me, judgment pouring out of them but quickly hidden by a facade of generosity as she gently smiles. "Who's this?"

"This is Paxton, the newest team member," Trent says. "Pax, this is my mom."

"Nice to meet you, Mrs. Hartwick. Thanks for letting me hang out here." I extend my hand, trying to act fucking cordial and shit, and she places half of her fingers in my grip, giving me a dead fish handshake.

"Trent, honey, Dad wants to see you in his study. I'll show your teammate around and have him meet you in your room shortly."

Trent huffs but does what he's asked, and his mother waits until he's disappeared to talk to me. "So… Patton—"

"Paxton."

"I'm sorry, I must've misheard Trent." She laughs it off. "Where are you from?"

"Uh." That's a convoluted question. "I live in East Valley with my uncle," I say, opting for the simplest answer.

Her head tilts to the side. "Your uncle? What about your parents?"

"They're kicking around somewhere." I shrug, not wanting to feel the heat of her judgment.

"I see." She drops her mask, showcasing her true feelings toward me as she takes in my appearance, her face twisting in disgust as her eyes linger on my worn Vans, ripped jeans, and Blink-182 T-shirt with a long-sleeve shirt underneath. Her attention travels up to meet my hardened gaze as my jaw sets in anger.

I don't give a fuck what you think of me, lady. You're still not better than me because you have money.

"Come on, Pax," Trent calls from upstairs, allowing me to get away from his mother.

Breaking the rising tension, I skirt around her and go to where Trent is. Once I'm on the second floor and we round the hallway, Trent whispers, "Sorry. My mom can be a bit of a bitch."

My brows shoot up in surprise at his admission. "I wasn't going to say anything, but now that you mention it…"

He laughs as he leads us to his room. "Don't worry, she's not around much. She's usually at important functions and dinners or hanging with other bitchy moms where they pretend they're doing a service to the community and their husbands' businesses, but really they're just gossiping."

I snort. "What does your dad do for work?"

"He's a chief financial officer. Just like my grandfather

and great-grandfather." He rolls his eyes as if that's what's lined up for him as well.

"So it's just the three of you living here?"

"Four. I have a younger sister. Do you have any siblings?"

"Nope." A familiar sense of loneliness settles around my bones. "Just me."

I'm reminded once again of how different our worlds are.

CHAPTER FIVE

MY CONAIR STRAIGHTENER sizzles as I run it through my bangs, trying to side-sweep them across my face. "Swing, Swing" by the All-American Rejects plays through my stereo as I continue to take my time getting ready. We're going to another boring dinner with another boring business partner of Dad's.

Of course, Trent gets out of it because he has a stupid hockey game, but *I* have to suck it up and listen to old people talk all night.

A loud knock on my door startles me, and I miss burning my forehead by a hair—literally.

"Ivy." Mom opens the door, not waiting for me to open it.

"What?" I ask, placing my straightener on my dresser and turning the volume knob down, quieting the song before spinning around to glare at her.

"We're leaving for dinner in ten minutes. We can*not* be late."

"I know."

"I'm serious, Ivy. I already sent up Stella to tell you to hurry up, but apparently that wasn't enough, and I needed to come up here myself," Mom says about our housekeeper. "Finish whatever you're doing to your hair and meet us downstairs." She starts to leave but glances back at me, her face contorting in disgust. "And for the love of God, wipe off some of that black eyeliner. I can't wait for you to be done with this phase."

"It's not a phase, Mom!"

Ignoring my comment, she says, "Ten minutes." Then promptly spins on her extra pointy heels and clanks down the hallway, leaving my door open.

When I hear the sound of her heels disappearing down the stairs, I put the volume back up so I can finish listening to my song.

Staring at myself in the mirror, I fixate on my eyeliner. It doesn't look bad at all. If anything, it makes the blue in my eyes stand out even more, and the rest of me looks perfectly presentable by Mom's standards: a gold bubble dress with gold ballet flats.

With the clock ticking, I hurry up and do the rest of my hair. After squeezing gel into my palms, I ball up the ends of my hair, scrunching everything aside from my bangs. I hear Trent calling out to someone. I can barely make out what he's saying over the guitars flowing through my speakers, but just the sound of his voice builds resentment inside me.

I bet I wouldn't be excused from dinner if I played hockey.

As I release the fist in my hair, an unfamiliar voice comes from behind me.

"This is one of my favorite songs."

My body twists at the sound of a deep voice complimenting my music taste. My stomach is instantly bombarded with butterflies when I spot a boy slightly older than me hanging in my doorway. His brown hair is long, pushed over to one side of his forehead, while the ends stray out around the base of his neck. The longer I stare at his hazel eyes and endearing smile, the harder my heart pounds. He's wearing a black Blink-182 tee with a gray long-sleeve shirt under it.

He stares back, and that's when I realize I've been gawking at him instead of talking.

"Yeah, the All-American Rejects are the best," I say, as my brain searches for more words to keep him here longer. "Are you one of Trent's friends?" I internally cringe at how stupid that question was because, obviously, he's my brother's friend and not some guy breaking and entering to tell me he likes my music.

"Yeah, I just started on the team a few weeks ago, and your brother was nice enough to take me under his wing." He takes a step closer, and I'm pretty sure I'm about to die of a heart attack. "I'm Paxton." Another step, another second I'm closer to dying from his hotness.

"I'm Ivy."

"You got a cool room," he says, glancing over at my corkboard with pictures of me and my friends, some movie tickets, and other random items push-pinned into it, then to my bookshelf and massive CD rack, and over to my Fall Out Boy poster. "Your mom is okay with you hanging that up?" He points to the large image of boys who are tattooed and are wearing eye makeup.

"You must've spent more than thirty seconds with her," I joke.

"I met her for the first time about a half hour ago."

"My condolences. And no, she's not a fan of my walls, but I do it anyway. She's got to pick her battles with me, and band posters have fallen to the bottom of her priorities."

Paxton chuckles. "You're a little bit of a rebel. I like it."

My insides go haywire, as if Pop Rocks filled up my bloodstream. I'm usually crowned the family's black sheep, but hearing Paxton call me a rebel does something to me that I've never experienced before.

"Do you go to Windsor Prep with your brother?" he asks.

I shake my head. "No, I'm only twelve—but I'm practically a teenager," I abruptly add, knowing that if he's on my brother's hockey team, he's probably the same age, fourteen.

It's nothing new to have one of Trent's friends over, but usually, none of them are interested in talking to me, and I'm not interested in them either. But something about Paxton makes me never want to stop staring at the way his hair is messily tousled.

"Do you have a MySpace?" I blurt out the question, and he nods. "I do, too. Technically, I'm not allowed to—my mom doesn't know—but it's not like she checks on my computer or anything." I gesture to my Mac desktop sitting on my whitewashed, wooden desk. "But you could add me if you want. I'm in Trent's top eight. Or at least I should be."

His lips tip upward. "I'll look for your profile when I get home after the game." Suddenly, his nose crinkles as if he just got a waft of something bad. "What's that smell?"

The moment he asks, I get all my senses back and can smell it too. The scent of something burning fills my nostrils, and when I put two and two together, I gasp. "My straightener!"

Spinning around, I rush to the end of my dresser to unplug the cord. Lifting up the straightener in a panic, there's already a burn mark in the wood and melted eyeliner pooling around it. *Mom's going to kill me if she sees this.*

Needing to figure out how to fix this, I quickly go to move the straightener to the other side of my dresser.

"Ow!" Paxton winces as the top of his hand gets scorched by the hot clamp.

"Oh my god! I didn't see you—"

"I was coming over to help—"

"I'm so sorry!"

"It's all right."

"Do you want ice?"

"No, I'm good." His non-injured hand holds on to where I accidentally hurt him, and he holds it to his chest.

"You should run it under cold water at least."

"I will. I was actually on my way to the bathroom." He reaches out and plucks the straightener from my grasp. "But first, let's put this away before you inflict any more damage."

As he gently places it on the heat-resistant mat, which is where I should've put it to begin with, blood rushes to my cheeks. "I'm really sorry," I emphasize. "Did I just ruin your chances of playing in the hockey game tonight?"

"Nah, I'll be fine." He smiles through whatever pain he might be feeling. "And hey, now I'll always remember you." He lifts up his hand, a bright red mark scarring the space under his knuckles. "A guy never forgets the first girl who burned him," he says, chuckling, making it okay for me to laugh along with him even though I feel like a complete idiot.

"Ivy, Mom sent me in here—" Trent pauses in my doorway, his gaze shooting between me and Paxton.

The moment Paxton realizes my brother is here, he darts to the opposite side of the room so fast it almost makes me second-guess that we were standing in close proximity.

"Uh, Pax, I said the bathroom was the *third* door on the left," Trent states.

"Sorry, I heard the music coming from Ivy's room and

got distracted," he says, shoving his burned hand into his jean pocket.

"Oh, okay." Trent's curiosity fades at Paxton's remark. "For future reference, we don't hang out with my sister."

"Hey!" I interject.

"Not my fault you're boring."

"Says the guy who uses sports as his sole source of entertainment." I cross my arms over my chest, and I spot Paxton fighting back a smile.

"Whatever." Trent resigns our little argument. "Mom's gonna have a meltdown if you're not downstairs in thirty seconds." Then he turns to glance at Paxton. "I'll be in my room. We're gonna leave for the game in a little bit."

With that, Trent goes back down the hall, leaving me and Paxton alone once again. Both of us know we need to get going, but we both linger for a beat.

"I gotta head out," he announces. "But I'll see you around, Rebel."

My mouth parts into a wide smile as I watch him leave.

The sound of my new nickname echoes inside my head.

Rebel.

I think that's my new favorite word.

CHAPTER SIX

PRESENT

THE RISING sun beaming into the airport wakes me up. Yawning, I stretch, uncurling my limbs that have been scrunched up in one of the chairs while I waited for my second flight.

"Last call for flight eighty-three to Boston," a flight attendant says over the intercom, springing me into action.

Panic flurries through my bloodstream as I rush over to the flight attendant with my ticket in hand, ready to scan.

I can't believe I was in that deep of a sleep that I almost missed my flight!

Once I'm boarding the plane, my muscles begin to relax when I realize there's still a line of people slowly inching toward their seats. Since it's a short flight, this plane is smaller with only two seats on either side.

Making my way toward seat 12D, I run my fingers

through my hair because I'm sure it looks a bit of a mess. My gaze bounces around, glancing at the passengers, and as I get closer to my seat, I spot a man sitting in 12C, the aisle seat, though I'm unable to make out his face due to his baseball cap shielding it as his chin points downward.

When I finally reach my seat, the man lifts his gaze, and the second our eyes lock, my heart stops.

The blood in my veins turns to ice, and all the air gets sucked out of my lungs.

Time freezes for what feels like an eternity.

But when I note the look of pure shock on the face before me, time starts ticking again.

Since I was eighteen, I've imagined what it would be like to stand in front of Paxton Rhodes again. There were endless scenarios. One where I would repeatedly kick him in the balls while I screamed at him, another where he'd see me out somewhere while I was wearing a stunning dress and laughing with my friends while my husband graciously kissed me on the cheek and Pax would have regret looming over his head for the rest of time, and of course one scenario where we'd reunite and I'd tell him everything and he'd sweep me up in his arms, declaring me as his one true love.

Out of all the scenes, storylines, and movie plots that my mind conjured up, I never *ever* once thought the universe would force us next to each other on a plane while I ran away from Warren and my family because I'm an asshole who can't get close to anyone.

I glance down at my ticket, checking the seat number.

I check it a second time.

And a third.

"Do you need assistance?" a flight attendant asks from behind me, appearing out of thin air.

"No, I just..." I do a quick scan of the plane, seeing if I could switch my seat, but it's packed.

The only empty seat is the one directly next to Paxton.

He rises so I can get into my seat, his tall stature towering over me.

Holding my breath, the fibers of my muscles constricting, I rigidly sink down into my fate.

He sits back down, and I check over my shoulder, getting lost in those familiar hazel eyes for a millisecond as Paxton stares back at me. His lips curl upward into a sexy smirk.

"Hey, Rebel."

Air comes flying out of me in a very obvious way, those two words like flames licking my nerve endings. My body reacts in a way it shouldn't, tingles erupting from my chest in a rush of anxiety and excitement.

Wetting my lips, ignoring the heat creeping up my neck, I make sure my voice hides any emotion as I blandly reply, "Pax."

I try not to notice how much manlier he looks than the last time I saw him. Sure, I've unfortunately seen him on TV or scrolling on social media, but I never took the time to appreciate how buff he's gotten since he was twenty. The man on the news wasn't the Paxton I knew, so I paid no mind because he's essentially a stranger, another athlete I had no interest in learning about.

His legs shift as he focuses on the back of the seat in front of him.

My jaw sets tight, every cell in my body getting overwhelmed with tension, knotting my muscles together until the entire length of me hurts.

Both of us pretend to listen to the flight attendant as she does her safety spiel, and by the time I rip myself out of my thoughts, I realize the plane is ascending.

The air between us thickens as Paxton continues to adjust himself, growing more uncomfortable.

"How—" He clears his throat. "How've you been?"

As if in slow motion, I gradually turn my head to look at him, my eyebrow arched as daggers shoot out of my eyes.

If there's one good thing I got from Mom, it's her death stare.

My nostrils flare as I debate how to answer such a fucking complicated question. But Pax doesn't get the privilege of knowing the answer. He doesn't get to know that I just dumped Warren, or even the good things that are happening in my life, like how much I love my job. The more I stare at him, the angrier I become that he would even try to do small talk with me.

"Shouldn't you be on a private jet or something? What the hell are you doing on a normal person plane?" I ask.

"I don't have a private jet, and I could ask you the same about not flying first class."

"I don't have my parents' money." That's one thing I want to make clear, not only with him, but anyone who knows my affluent upbringing.

He nods in understanding. "I booked a last-minute flight."

"Same."

We both rip our focus away from each other.

Minutes drag by, feeling like hours.

The heat of his body invades my space, making it doubly harder to breathe.

I could be nice and ask him about his massive professional triumph, or try to get to know this version of him. In fact, in a few scenarios I've played out in my head, we've had a lovely conversation as a final farewell, tying up our past so I could finally move forward.

However, for whatever reason, my brain is not willing to play out that scene and is opting for more of a destructive path.

"You look good." He breaks the silence.

"I look like shit, Pax," I snap, whipping my head to face him. "I ran out on my family's holiday party, this is my second flight of the night—or day, whatever the fuck time it is—and I'm wearing a sweatshirt that says *I heart Crabs.*"

His lips press together to fight back a smile, and I swear to God if he cracks one, I'm going to slap it right off his infuriatingly good-looking face.

"Can I get either of you something to drink?" the cheery flight attendant interjects with her rolling cart filled to the brim with drink options.

Alcohol. Every last drop of alcohol. "Water, please," I state.

"I'll have the same. Thank you." Pax smiles at her, and her cheeks turn a light shade of pink.

I'd only imagine that after all these years, he's gotten more popular with women, and when I watch the way the flight attendant brushes her arm against him as she hands me my water, my teeth grate together.

Jealousy unfolds inside me even though it shouldn't.

Pax never was and never will be mine.

The ice water does next to nothing to cool me down, but I pretend it does as we go back to being silent.

As we sit in the awkwardness of unspoken words, memories, and old emotions, my body grows accustomed to the tension as the flight carries on.

The pilot makes her announcement about the time and temperature in Boston as we prepare for landing. There's a shift in energy all around us as people begin to perk up, knowing we'll be able to get off the plane soon.

Paxton sits up in his seat and shifts over to look at me for the first time in an hour. "Do you live in Boston or—"

"Pax," I cut him off, the sound of defeat encasing my voice as his name falls from my lips. "Let's not do this.

We don't need to make small talk, let alone speak to each other at all. Our seats being next to each other was just a fluke thing. Let's just carry on as strangers."

He's unable to mask his disappointment, and for a split second, I want to go back on my statement and invite him into my world.

"Okay." He nods in agreement. "But you'll have to talk to me eventually."

I scoff. "And why's that?"

The look of disappointment is immediately wiped away by a mischievous smirk, letting me know that he's aware of something I'm not. "It'll be pretty awkward if we're both in Trent and Lucille's wedding party and you're giving me the silent treatment."

My stomach drops at the same time the wheels of the plane hit the tarmac. We all jerk in our seats, and my hands go flying out to stabilize myself, one of them gripping onto my seat and the other one falling onto Pax's thigh.

"I see you're coming around to the idea rather quickly," Pax teases as his gaze drops to his lap.

Yanking my hand away, my bloodstream fills with raging emotions. I grab my tote bag, searching for my phone so I can text Lucille so I can get a full rundown of the wedding party. She'll probably be overjoyed to share all her wedding details with me, and in hindsight, I really *should* have been a better soon-to-be sister-in-law and asked her all this shit as she was planning it.

My heart pounds as I continue to fish out my phone. Tilting my bag at an angle that Paxton can't peek in, I make sure he doesn't see my old digital camera buried at the bottom.

I curse myself for not being as close with Trent and not knowing that he and Paxton are still thick as thieves. I had always assumed they kept in touch here and there, but when Paxton went pro and his life got busier, I didn't think they remained friends to the point where my brother would ask him to be a groomsman, and I never had the guts to utter Pax's name, let alone ask Trent how Pax is doing.

"You can panic about it later, Ivy. It's time to get off the plane."

My attention drifts over to the empty seat next to me, then upward to where Paxton is standing, holding up the line forming behind him as he waits for me to step into the aisle.

"I'm not panicking," I mutter as I move to stand in front of him. "And don't act like you know me."

He leans in close, the amusement in his voice brushing up against my hair as he speaks, "Whatever you say, Rebel."

CHAPTER SEVEN

IVY HARTWICK.

The biggest pain in my ass. The woman of my dreams, and the one I let slip through my fingers.

I longed for the day when I'd come in contact with her again, even though I know she wants nothing to do with me.

I scoured the nation, making my way from mattress to mattress, date to date, hoping to find someone who remotely makes me feel the way Ivy did. But not a single soul has come close.

As we exit the plane in single file, my gaze drops down to Ivy's phone, which is lighting up with message after message from her mother.

How could you do this to me and your father?

Do you enjoy embarrassing me?

You better fix this. I'm telling Warren's family you'll be making things right by him.

Ivy can't swipe the messages away quickly enough, and she eventually gives up on doing whatever it was she pulled her phone out for and slips it into the pocket of her sweatpants.

I've imagined seeing her every way conceivable, but wearing tacky tourist sweats was something that never crossed my mind. But even with *I heart Crabs* across her tits, she still looks gorgeous.

I don't know how she manages to do it, but she's the only one who has ever stolen my breath purely by being in her presence.

"You're teetering on the edge of stalking," Ivy says over her shoulder as we hop on the escalator toward the exit that leads to the taxis and Ubers.

"You're done being stubborn and ready to talk to me now?" I quip.

"I'm not ready to talk to you. I was just informing you that if you're going to continue to follow me, I'll have to get one of those gentlemen over there to arrest you for stalking." She points to two cops standing near the exit as we step off the escalator. "And I'm not stubborn."

I let out a laugh. "Bullshit."

Ivy abruptly spins, strands of her long, dark hair whipping across her face as she looks at me with her sapphire eyes, slicing me in half. "Don't act like you know me."

Those words—the same ones she sputtered at me a few minutes ago on the plane—rip me to shreds. Because at one point in our lives, I knew her better than I knew my damn self.

"I used to know you *real* fucking well." My gaze drops down the length of her body in the way I knew she once loved and back up to see her dilated pupils. A smile tugs at my lips because, at the very least, I still know how to rile her up.

Hardening her features, she replies, "The key words were 'used to'—"

"Paxton Rhodes!" A small voice pipes up from the escalator.

Glancing over to where my name was called, I spot a boy no more than seven years old, his eyes wide, exploding with excitement as his father tries to calm him down. The grin on my face grows as I watch the boy bounce off the escalator and race toward me.

"I'm really sorry to interrupt," the father says, glancing back and forth between me and Ivy.

"You're my favorite hockey player ever!" The boy beams, causing passersby to glance my way.

I'm no stranger to being picked out in a crowd. Hockey fans know who I am, whether they love or hate the Cobras.

"Would you mind if he got a picture with you?" the father asks.

"Not at all!" I crouch down to get eye level with the kid. "What's your name, little man?"

"Joey!"

"Do you want to be a professional hockey player one day, Joey?"

He nods so fast his head might pop off.

"Well then, I have a secret for you," I state, feeling joy radiating off him. "No matter what, don't give up on yourself. If your dreams change, that's okay, as long as you're still following what lights you up and makes you happy."

"Okay!" he responds, as if he understands the depth of what I'm saying to him.

"Let's get a picture."

As I place my hand over his shoulder, smiling for his dad's phone, I catch Ivy out of the corner of my eye, witnessing this entire interaction. To my surprise, she didn't run off when she had the opportunity to. She stayed.

After shaking the dad's hand and saying goodbye to Joey, I shift my attention back to Ivy. For the first time today, she's gazing at me with something different than animosity.

"Does that happen often?" she asks.

I shrug. "Sometimes."

Nodding, she gets lost in thought as her emotions brewing behind her eyes morph back into hostility. Without a word, she heads toward the exit.

I'm right behind her, the cold air blasting my face as soon as we step outside. Chatter and blaring horns fill the lack of conversation between us.

"Do you need a ride?" I ask, knowing that my car service is scheduled to pull up any second.

"No. I'm taking a taxi," Ivy states, moving toward one.

"You never answered my question earlier," I call out, causing her to pause. "Do you live in Boston or are you visiting?"

Rolling her eyes, her shoulders drop in unwanted defeat. "I live here. What are you doing in Boston?"

"Visiting someone."

"Well, I'm sure your someone is awaiting your arrival, half-naked in the hotel room. Carry on with your day. I'll see you at Trent's wedding."

She goes to catch a taxi once more, but my response stops her.

"God, I hope not." I laugh. "I'd hate to see Uncle Jeff half-naked."

"Uncle Jeff?" Ivy's curiosity piques. "How is he? What's he up to—Wait, why is Uncle Jeff in Boston?"

I notice how she doesn't say *your* Uncle Jeff or just

Jeff. She says it as if he's her uncle too. That's how it always was, and I'm glad she's keeping it that way.

The taxi next to us leaves and is immediately replaced with a black BMW with tinted windows, and my phone buzzes in my pocket, letting me know it's my car.

"He got transferred to Massachusetts General Hospital," I state. "He's been diagnosed with ECD. It's a rare blood disease. There's a new treatment they're trying out, and his name was on the list." As I announce his illness out loud, emotions lodge in my throat.

Any overwhelming resentment Ivy has for me dissipates, and she's staring at me like she once did as a teenager.

"Oh my god, Pax, I'm so sor—"

"My ride's here," I cut her off as I step toward my getaway. I don't bother asking if she wants to hop in the car with me because even though she's looking at me with such empathy and claims that I don't know her, I do—and I know her stubborn, independent ass won't get in the car. "See you at Trent's wedding."

As soon as I shut the car door, there's silence. No more honking, talking, or yelling—but my thoughts are louder than ever. I try to escape them, making conversation with my driver, but the closer we get to the hospital, the only thing my mind can do is ping-pong between my anxiety over Uncle Jeff and the heartache over Ivy. I knew I'd see her soon. I just didn't realize how soon and that it'd be on the same day I'd be getting into Boston to take care of Uncle Jeff.

When I walk into the hospital, the scent of Clorox makes me wrinkle my nose. I pull the bill of my hat downward to cover my face as much as possible so no one recognizes me as I head to the hematology unit.

I made sure Uncle Jeff not only has a private room but the best fucking room this hospital has to offer. I've been on a press tour speaking about my recently retired lifestyle—which has been a hard enough pill to swallow—and haven't seen Uncle Jeff in a few weeks. But the moment we were contacted about this new treatment, I had him flown out to Boston and promised him I'd be spending the holiday season with him no matter what.

When I reach room 704, my stomach churns at the sight of him. I hate seeing him with an IV sticking out of his arm, the color drained from his face, and looking thinner than I've ever seen. But I push away the uncomfortable feeling clawing up my throat and enter the room as if nothing's the matter and we're living in our apartment again.

"Your Christmas gift arrived early," I joke.

Uncle Jeff turns his attention to me, and a smile pulls at his chapped lips. "I'm honored you finally graced me with your presence," he retorts.

"Should I autograph your hospital sock? Or maybe the bracelet, and we can throw off the nurses?" I note the couch next to the heater under the large window. It's where I'll be spending most of my time for the foreseeable future, but for now, I opt for the chair and pull it up next to his bedside.

"I don't want your autograph now that you're a washed-up player."

"Hey, I'm still worth a little something." My stomach dips, still not sure how to process my retirement. It wasn't by choice, as I tore my ACL in my last game of the season, which pushed me to retire. I thought I had a couple of years left in me. So now I have this blank slate, and after several months, I'm still unsure of what to fill it with. My entire adulthood, I lived and breathed hockey, and now that it's been ripped away, I'm empty.

After months of recovery, I decided to sell my house in Illinois—where I was living because of being on the

Cobras—and I put all my stuff in storage while I lived the nomad life, traveling around and seeing the world. However, Uncle Jeff's health shifted my plans.

"How was your flight?" Uncle Jeff asks, and now my body freaks out for an entirely different reason.

"It was…interesting."

He scoffs. "I have a feeling whatever the story is will be too much information for me."

"No, no, it's nothing like that." I scratch at the scruff on my face. "I ended up sitting next to an old friend."

"Who?"

The strumming in my heart increases as I say, "Ivy." I don't even need to say her last name or ask if he remembers because I know for a fact that he does.

His eyes light up, the most life I've seen flicker across his face in ages. "Ah. You mean the one that got away."

My mind shifts back to an earlier part of my life when I answer, "Yeah. The one that got away."

CHAPTER EIGHT

2005

November

MY EYES BURN from staring at the new flat-screen TV in Trent's game room. I swear this is all we've been doing since he got an Xbox 360 the day it came out. This has got to be the coolest room in his entire home: a pool table, arcade games, and the biggest stereo system I've ever seen. I'd never leave this place if I were him.

I ignore the ache in my thumb as I erratically press down on the buttons, trying to beat him in *Madden*.

"Fuck yeah!" Trent cheers as he kicks my ass.

"You dick." I toss the controller to the side as my friend gloats next to me.

We've been hanging out more, even outside of practices and game days. He invites me over to just chill and bullshit, which feels strange that I now have a regular spot to do that. I'm so used to people coming in and out of my life that I never really settled into a typical friendship. Everyone was just acquaintances, people I could talk with and maybe drink or smoke with if I'm bored. But I never had an actual best friend.

"Shit, we gotta leave for the game in like a half hour," Trent says after he does his victory dance, looking like a complete fool but making me laugh nonetheless. "I'm gonna make some pizza bagels before we leave. You want any?"

"Sure, thanks."

Something I appreciate most about Trent is that even though he comes from a wildly different upbringing than me, he doesn't act like he does. He could easily have a chef make us a pizza bagel from scratch, but he chooses to heat up the frozen meal himself, like the rest of us. And the very few times I've had him hang out at mine and Uncle Jeff's apartment, he didn't turn up his nose or assume he's better than us because he comes from money. He treats us as equals.

No clue where he gets that quality, though, because his parents are the complete opposite. His dad, Charles, is all right. He's quiet and not as outwardly turned off by me as his mother, Meredith, is, but I'm assuming he shares similar feelings as she does. If they were around more and their presence didn't get swallowed by their ginormous house, I wouldn't come over as often as I do.

"Hey, guys." A high-pitched voice comes from the doorway, and I note Ivy standing there with a dainty smile on her face. She's wearing her school uniform: a plain gray skort and a maroon polo with the words *Upper River Middle School* embroidered right above her heart.

"What's up?" Trent asks as he walks toward her to exit to go to the kitchen.

She shrugs. "Just bored and heard you guys having fun."

"We finished playing *Madden*. I'm going to make us pizza bagels before we have to leave."

"Can you make some for me? I'm going with Dad to the game later," she states. Henry usually drops us off early for warm-ups, and Trent's dad and Ivy show up just before the game starts.

"Make your own food," Trent playfully teases Ivy, but we all know he's going to make her pizza bagels too.

She scowls, giving him the finger as he passes by, and when he finally leaves, she focuses her attention on me.

"Hey, Rebel." I say her nickname that I coined last year as I glance down at the faint scar on my hand that she gave me the first time I met her.

Honestly, I don't know much about Ivy. She rarely hangs out with us, and not to be a dick, but Trent and I aren't really interested in having a thirteen-year-old girl play video games with us or join in on our mindless conversations.

But I do know that Ivy smiles every time I call her Rebel, and the look on her face is really sweet, so I keep calling her that.

"Hey, Pax," she replies as she moves across the room.

I catch the way her cheeks turn pink as she gets closer. I don't want to read into anything, but I think she *might* have a little crush on me.

I try not to make things awkward between us, keeping things cordial so she can't confuse any interaction as flirting. I don't have the heart to tell her she should set her sights elsewhere, not only because she's Trent's sister, but because she's in the eighth grade and I'm in the tenth, and, well, that's just plain weird.

"You excited for tonight? This is the game that'll get you guys into the playoffs, right?" She treads across the room and plants herself down on the couch next to me. The leather squeaks as she shifts around.

"Yep."

"You're definitely going to win." Ivy beams.

I chuckle. "I'm betting on the same thing."

There's a beat of silence between us, and it's a millisecond too long for my liking, so I start to clean up Trent's gaming system.

"Can I ask you something?" Ivy's voice comes from behind me as I put the controllers away.

"Go for it."

"If it's too personal, you can tell me to shut up."

My brows draw in tight. "Okay…what is it?"

"You didn't have any family at the past couple of games," she states, working her way up to her question.

"Yeah, my uncle was working and couldn't make it."

"What about your parents?"

There it is.

That's the question she was sitting on.

My chest tightens, but I brush it off. "Uh, they're not around. I live with my uncle."

Ivy gasps. "Like Jess from *Gilmore Girls*?"

Glancing over my shoulder, I spot her eagerly sitting on the edge of the couch, waiting for more information, and I can't help but laugh. "I guess? I never watched that show."

"Oh my god, you *need* to. It's my favorite! It's on The WB on Tuesda—" She abruptly stops herself, slamming her hand over her mouth, her face dropping in embarrassment. "I'm sorry, I didn't mean to talk about my show instead of your parents."

"It's all good. I'd much rather talk about TV than them."

"Did they…" She shifts uncomfortably in her seat. "Are they…your parents, did they…"

Abandon me? Forget about my existence? Disappear from my life?

Yes.

"Are they..."

"Spit it out, Ivy."

"Did your parents..." Her voice turns into a whisper when she says, "Die?"

"Nope. They're just assholes, so my uncle has custody over me."

"Oh." Her dark-blue eyes get wide with empathy as her mouth turns downward. "I'm sorry I was being nosy. I shouldn't have brought it up."

"Don't be sorry. I don't mind. I love living with my uncle. He's great."

"Will he be at the game later?"

I shake my head. "He's working again."

"So you don't have anyone coming to support you tonight?"

"He'll be there in spirit." I smile through the glaring observation she just made.

Although Uncle Jeff supports me to no end, I do sense his absence when he misses several games in a row. Even though I know the reason why he can't attend is to support us financially, it still feels bleak when I glance up at the stands and see no one—another reminder of the limited number of people I have in my life.

I just didn't think other people caught on to it.

But maybe Ivy is more perceptive than most.

"Do you miss your parents?"

Her question makes the lining of my throat swell. My parents are something I actively avoid thinking about on a daily basis.

"What the hell, Ivy, you can't ask him that!" Trent comes barreling in with two plates filled with pizza bagels.

"I was just trying to get to know your friend better," she snaps. "Do *you* ever ask him about his parents?"

"No, because if he wanted to talk about them, he would." Trent crashes the plates down onto the coffee table. "And I know how to mind my business and not ask invasive questions."

"Guys, it's fine," I interject before this gets out of hand for no reason. "I didn't mind you asking, Ivy," I say to her, then turn to Trent. "Let's eat. We have to leave soon."

We're neck and neck with the Tornadoes, tied at seven points. Coach calls a time-out, and we skate to the bench so he can go over the next play.

As he's finishing up giving us our plan of action, my gaze goes upward. Our team colors are black, white, and orange, which are the colors that fill the stands as we play at our home rink.

"My sister's such a dork," Trent says, shaking his head as he chuckles.

Following his line of sight, I spot Ivy cheering for us, head to toe in our colors. She's wearing an orange beanie with a pelican on it and a matching sweatshirt. There, on her left cheek, are two numbers written in black eyeliner.

Eighty-three.

My number.

When our eyes lock, she gives me a smile as she proudly shows me what she's branded herself with.

I've had my suspicions that she has a crush on me, but this doesn't feel like a ploy for me to get to notice her.

This is her letting me know she's here to support me.

Letting me know I'm not alone.

This is the first time I've realized that Ivy has a way bigger heart than I ever knew.

CHAPTER NINE

"YOU LOOK RIDICULOUS," Dad grumbles next to me in the stands as I take a picture of Trent and Pax on my disposable Kodak camera.

"I'm supporting my brother and his teammates," I say, rolling my eyes.

"Why did you only write Paxton's number on your cheek?"

"Because he doesn't have any family here to support him."

"Yes, I'm aware."

"Like, why is this even a big deal?" *God, he's so annoying.*

Dad doesn't respond, choosing to sip on his soda before speaking again. "You better wipe that off before we get home so your mother doesn't see eyeliner all over your face."

"I brought makeup wipes in my bag." I point to my silver sequin purse, which houses all of my essentials and also includes patent leather flats I'll be changing back into once we get into the car, so Mom doesn't have a heart attack if she sees me in Converse.

Dad's oblivious to those sorts of details. As long as I look presentable, he doesn't care.

Mom, on the other hand, only allows me to wear certain brands and dress in a way she approves because I'm "an extension of her" and all that crap.

I'd love to have a tight-knit mother-daughter bond with her. Whenever I watch *Gilmore Girls,* I dream of having a Rory and Lorelai type of relationship, but we're nowhere near that. We're the characters Lorelai and Emily to a tee. She loves the world of prestige, while I can't wait to escape all of its confines.

"Mr. Hartwick, long time no see," another dad greets mine.

I concentrate on the game while they schmooze and talk business. Dad works in finance, and from what I gather, he's fantastic at his job, which is why everyone is extra nice to him. I couldn't tell you the details of what he does because whenever he begins explaining it, my eyes glaze over and my head starts playing some Ashlee Simpson song.

"And how are you, Little Hartwick?" The man calls my attention to him. "I see you're cheering for Rhodes tonight." He points to Paxton's number on my cheek.

"Yeah, I figured my brother gets enough attention. Might as well focus on someone else," I reply.

"Judging by the way Rhodes plays, I can assure you he's going to be getting more than just your attention." He glances back over to the ice rink. "He and Trent are the star players."

"That they are," Dad agrees, getting sucked back into the game.

Paxton's skills are probably why Dad and Mom are okay with Trent hanging out with him so often. He's good—*really* good—and has helped Trent become a stronger player. The two of them are carrying the team, and it wouldn't look great if our parents exiled Paxton because he wasn't as wealthy as us.

Paxton makes a goal, and the whole crowd erupts into a cheer, excitement bursting out of everyone, knowing we're minutes away from making the playoffs as long as they can block the rest of the Tornadoes' attempts to tie the game back up.

"Can we see him better from here?" A random girl with a ponytail pushes her way into the narrow, empty space next to me on the bleachers, talking with another girl.

"Yes, there he is!" The other one points, squeezing her way in.

"Oh my god, Paxton's so hot!"

There's an ache in my gut as I glance over at the girls who are slightly older than me, but somehow come across like they have years of maturity over my head.

"The things I would do to get him to be my boyfriend." Ponytail girl continues gawking at him.

"I heard he doesn't do relationships. Just makes out or whatever."

"Or whatever." She shoulder-checks her friend, and the two burst into a fit of giggles.

They keep laughing as they gossip, talking about how they hope there'll be a party after the game and all the other girls they'll have to compete with in order to catch Pax's attention for the night. The more their conversation goes on, the more I sink into my seat, feeling like a complete idiot.

I didn't write Paxton's number on my face as a weird way to flirt with him, but I *did* want him to know I'm here for him.

How stupid could I have been to think he wouldn't

have anyone show up, and he'd be here all alone? He has them—all the girls who fawn over him.

He doesn't need me.

CHAPTER TEN

PRESENT

"BITCH, what is going on with you today?" my best friend and coworker, Zaina, teases me.

"I can't focus on anything." I dramatically drop my head onto my computer's keyboard, causing it to make a ton of beeping sounds.

Luckily, we're in the back office, so none of the patrons can hear us. We work in the heart of Boston at the Contemporary Art and Lifestyle Museum. I'm one of the lead curators at the museum, and Zaina is my exhibit designer. Quite honestly, this career is a dream come true. Aside from the fact that it's a culmination of my interests, I'm pretty incredible at the job, if I do say so myself. Although today I can't keep my head in the present.

"Did your Christmas vacation not go as planned?" Zaina asks, and I immediately wince. I haven't updated her on anything, and I'm lying to myself, claiming I haven't told her yet because this is my first time seeing her since I left for my Maryland trip, but in reality, I don't want to get into all the muddled details.

"It was a hot mess," I mutter, slowly sitting back up and staring at the row of *m*'s I accidentally typed into the search bar.

"Why?"

I wave her off and continue deleting the gibberish off my computer.

"Nope," Zaina says, spinning my chair around to face her. "I'm not letting you get away with this evasive crap. I can tell something's wrong. What happened?"

"Fine. But you're getting the CliffsNotes version," I say, crossing my arms over my chest.

"CliffsNotes sufficed in high school. It'll suffice now."

Looking at the perfectly tamed curls framing her dark brown eyes, I watch the expressions on her face change as I tell my shortened story. "Warren proposed to me in front of everyone, and I turned him down, dipped without saying goodbye, my mom's been blowing up my phone—basically threatening to have me excommunicated from the family—and to top it off, on the flight home, I sat next to the one and only guy I ever loved, who I haven't seen since I was eighteen, and of course I was wearing a shirt that said *I heart Crabs*."

Zaina's face drops as she begins to process everything I threw at her. She starts to open her mouth, but then closes it, and does it several more times while staring at me.

"Oh, the best part of this whole thing is that the guy was Trent's best friend growing up, and as we were getting off the flight, he dropped the news that he'll be one of Trent's groomsmen."

My best friend, the unfiltered woman that she is, starts bellowing a laugh so loud I'm sure the patrons on the next floor can hear. She pinches the bridge of her nose, holding in tears from her laughter.

"Why were you wearing a shirt that said *I heart Crabs*?" she asks, wheezing through her laugh.

"*That's* what you're focusing on?" I chuckle at the absurdity with her.

"I'm sorry." She collects herself, taking a breath while holding back a smile. "Who's the guy?"

"Paxton Rhodes."

Her head tilts to the side. "Where have I heard that name before?"

"He's an NHL player."

"You sure know how to bury the fucking lead!" Zaina nearly jumps out of her seat. "What is he doing in Boston? Did you invite him to your apartment yet? Are you guys back together?"

"Whoa. Chill." I put up my hand to slow her down. "There is no 'back together' because we were never together to begin with. He's visiting his uncle, who's receiving treatments at the hospital. And no, I'm not inviting him back to my apartment. I'm not planning on seeing him until Trent's wedding, where we'll awkwardly pose next to each other in photos and call it a night and never see each other again."

She snorts. "Have fun in your delusional world."

"I hate you."

Spinning back around to my computer, I ignore Zaina, grinning ear to ear, waiting for me to disclose more about Pax, and eagerly wanting to see how this all unfolds. But she'll be sorely disappointed because there will be no story to tell. I don't plan on reaching out while he's here —if he still is—and I'll only be engaging with him from a distance at my brother's wedding.

Nerves creep up my spine, jitters running through my

heart as I continue to convince myself that what I'm thinking is actually true.

Guilt has been tugging me at the seams, knowing that I should visit Uncle Jeff. The hospital is across the street from where I work. Truthfully, I'd love to see that man again. I always cherished our time together, and even though I haven't seen him in forever, it would mean a lot to spend my free time with him.

But the risk of bumping into my past again has been stopping me.

Ever since the plane ride, I haven't been sleeping—tossing and turning, trying to shut my brain off from thinking of Pax. It's taken years of pushing him out of my thoughts to get me to the point of being a functional human, and now that he's conveniently taking up residency in the forefront of my mind, I'm pissed.

The unearthed grief and anguish from when I was eighteen have been rumbling in my chest.

I had worked so damn hard to pack those feelings up in a box, never to be opened again, and I intend to keep it that way.

"You want to go to a yoga class tonight?" Zaina asks as we step out of the museum and into the frigid air, which stings the tip of my nose.

"I'll join next time. I'm wiped. I haven't been sleeping well," I state, glancing over her shoulder at Massachusetts General Hospital behind her.

"Okay." Zaina takes a step toward the west end parking lot. "I'll see you bright and early tomorrow."

"Have a good night." We give each other a wave and part ways.

Logically, I know I need to hop in my car and take the short car ride to my apartment, but as I walk toward the lot where my car is parked, my eyes won't stop looking at the hospital.

A rattling in my veins lets me know how much I want to check up on Uncle Jeff. I want to see his warm, familiar face. As a weight drops in my stomach, I know I also want to make sure he'll be okay.

Groaning, knowing my heart is going to win over logic, I move away from the parking lot and toward the hospital.

Even though the winter air is mirroring the fucking Arctic, my body boils under my puffy coat as the anxiety of a possible run-in with Pax sinks in.

When I get to the hospital, I head to the front desk to find out which room Uncle Jeff is in. I make sure to fix my hair in the elevator, because I'll be damned if Paxton sees me looking like a hot mess again.

When I step out onto the seventh floor, it's quiet aside from a few machines beeping and hushed conversation between nurses and doctors. There's an overwhelming scent of cleaning spray as I travel down the hall toward Uncle Jeff's room.

I hover outside his door, staring at the name Jeffery Rhodes, room 704. I listen for the deep resonance of Pax's voice to prepare myself, but I only hear the muffled sound of a TV.

Peering into the room, I see that Uncle Jeff is alone as he lies in his hospital bed with a medical gown on. My gut twists so hard it causes my eyes to burn when I notice he's hooked up to all sorts of machines. The creases in his forehead have deepened, and his eyes look sunken in. He's dropped weight since the last time I've seen him and looks pale under the fluorescent glow.

My heart plummets as the reality of what I'm witnessing hits me.

He's not okay.

Just as I'm about to cower away, unable to process another loss, his eyes catch mine, and his whole essence lights up. "About damn time you came to visit me."

A sigh flies out of my mouth, my shoulders dropping in relief when I realize his body might be failing him, but his mind hasn't.

"What makes you say that?" I cautiously tiptoe into his room.

The closer I get to him, the more I sense a wretch in the back of my throat aching to cry out. I don't know if I can stay, watching him in this state.

"I heard you had an interesting flight the other day." He smirks in a knowing way, easing my nerves.

I chuckle. "You could say that."

"Have a seat." He points to the purple vinyl chair near his bed, and I do what he asks, even though my feet are begging me to bolt. He studies my face, noting my forced calm expression, and states, "You hate being here."

"I hate seeing you like this."

"Don't treat me like I'm sick. I tell Pax the same thing. Tell me about you. I haven't seen you since you were a kid. Do you have any children of your own?"

I shake my head, ignoring the way my heart aches. "No."

"You married?"

"God, no. Every man I date is worse than the next."

"Yeah, we're not the best." He laughs, then changes the subject. "What about work? Are you doing something you enjoy?"

"I love my career. I'm a curator at the Contemporary Art and Lifestyle Museum, which is a short walk from here. Last year, I was even granted the Outstanding Leadership Award."

"I'm proud of you, Ivy." Uncle Jeff beams. "I'm glad you're finally getting some recognition."

"Thank you."

"I've always had no doubt you'd do well in life, despite the distress you were under the last time we saw each other."

My mind flips back to when I was eighteen and ran into him at the time I needed it the most. He's the only one who ever knew my secret, and the only one who promised me that no matter what, he'd be there for me.

"I feel horrible for never staying in touch with you." My unfiltered thoughts flow out of my mouth.

"You did what you had to do. I always knew that if you needed me, you'd find a way to reach out."

Tears prick behind my eyes, and I fight to keep them at bay.

"Heard you gave my nephew a bit of the cold shoulder," Uncle Jeff says, trying to shift gears.

I chuckle. "I might've been a little rude to him."

"He can handle rude. Don't you worry about him. Or me."

"Easier said than done," I state, noting the obvious of us being in a hospital room. I'm worried about the both of them. There's no stopping that.

"Well, for right now, you don't have to worry about us. Why don't you tell me more about what's been going on in your life?"

And I do.

We spend the rest of the evening catching up and reminiscing. Even though it's beyond awful that Uncle Jeff is in this condition, I'm grateful that he's re-entered my life, and I intend on it staying that way.

CHAPTER ELEVEN

2006

September

MY FORK SCRAPES against the porcelain bowl as I push around my carbonara pasta dinner. The chandelier overhead is set to the "evening lighting," and the centerpieces on our long, ornate dining table have switched to autumn flowers even though the weather is still hot enough to make us melt under the sun.

"How are you enjoying your dinner, Paxton?" Mom asks with an extra dose of sweetness in her voice so she doesn't expose her true feelings toward him.

"It's great," he says between bites, not waiting to finish chewing before he speaks. It makes me smile, which is the first time I have today since my second period class.

Mom forces a grin, then glances at the other end of the table to where Dad sits, and they have a silent conversation, which probably has to do with the fact that Pax doesn't have proper dining etiquette. How dare he.

"Why aren't you eating, Ivy?" Mom focuses her attention on me.

"I'm not hungry," I mumble, staring into my bowl as I speak.

"What's wrong?"

"Nothing."

"She's probably upset because some guy in school didn't notice her," Trent chimes in, instantly making me irate.

"What are you even talking about?" I snap.

"Is that true, Ivy? Are you getting upset over a boy? You know how stupid that is—" Mom starts to go on a tangent, but I cut her off.

"That's not it! Trent is just making crap up!"

"Language." Dad comes out of nowhere to reprimand me.

Sinking into my seat, my face heats up, sensing Pax looking at me. "I'm not upset because of a *boy*." I make sure that's perfectly clear so the guy diagonal from me doesn't think I'm pathetic.

"Then what is it?" Mom continues to probe.

"I got an eighty on my American Revolution test, okay? Everyone happy they have an answer?"

"That's why you're upset?" Trent scoffs. "Who the hell cares about an eighty?"

"*I* care about my grades. I want to be a straight-A student, unlike you." We bicker back and forth from across the table until I finally give up. "May I please be excused?"

"Yes," Dad says, at the same time Mom says, "No."

There's a second of silence as I glance from one end of the head of the table to the other. When neither of them indicates whose instruction I should be following, I get up and excuse myself without waiting for permission.

With my brows furrowed and shoulders slumped, I make my way upstairs to my bedroom. The walk seems endless as I pass room after room that are perfectly decorated but hold no life in them.

When I finally reach my room, I pop in a *Gilmore Girls* DVD and curl up under my covers, letting Lorelai and Rory get my mind off my sucky day.

Just as the episode ends, there's a knock on my door.

"I'm sleeping," I say, hoping Mom will leave me alone.

"You sound pretty awake for someone who's sleeping," Pax says.

As if lightning struck my spine, I'm immediately sitting upright, my pulse racing through my veins. "Pax?"

"Taking that as an okay for us to enter your room." With that, my door swings open, and in roll Pax and my brother.

"What are you guys doing?" The strumming in my chest grows stronger. Pax has only been in here once, when we first met, and if I knew he'd be coming back in, I'd straighten up and make it smell pretty.

It hasn't changed much in the past two years, aside from more pictures added to my corkboard and new books on my bookshelves.

"Pax thought we should come check up on you," Trent says, flinging himself horizontally across the foot of my mattress. Being nosy, his arms stretch over the edge of my bed, and he starts flipping through my CD binder that's lying on my floor.

"Why?" I nervously loop my hair behind my ears, watching Pax as he sits in the empty space between me and my brother.

Internally squealing, I try not to freak the eff out that Paxton Rhodes is currently on my bed. A swarm of butterflies takes off in my belly when I notice how close I am to him.

Close enough to feel the warmth of his body.

Tingles shoot through my bloodstream the moment I'm able to admire the flecks of honey that appear in his hazel eyes.

The sound of the *Gilmore Girls* theme song rips his attention toward my TV, and as the title pops up on the screen, he says, "Hey, isn't this the show you were telling me about?"

I bite back the biggest grin in the world because he remembered. He remembered me talking about my favorite TV show from a *year ago*.

"Um, yeah," I say flippantly as if it's nothing and not like my insides are currently melting into a puddle of mush.

"When were you guys talking about *Gilmore Girls*?" Trent asks, still looking through my CDs, probably to steal one or two for his own collection.

"Ivy was telling me about it a while ago," Pax says and then focuses back on me. "I came across it on TV once, but it was toward the end."

"You watched it?" My voice raises in surprise.

He shrugs. "Only the last five minutes. They talk fast."

"The mom is hot," Trent says.

"Ew, shut up." I kick his leg, but it doesn't bother him.

"So…" Pax interrupts us before we get into another bickering match. "You want to tell us what's really going on, Rebel?"

The way he's looking at me takes me aback. Like he's calling out my bullshit and won't stand for any more of it. Like he can *see* me.

"What…what are you talking about?"

"You're upset over an eighty?" Again, he gives me an expression that tells me I need to cut the crap and just tell him what's really eating away at me. But now that he's made it his mission to find out what's wrong, it feels extremely embarrassing that I've gotten upset over something so meaningless.

"Yeah. I want to go to Harvard for art history one day. I need my grades to be top-notch."

"Told you she's not going to open up to us," Trent says.

"I'm allowed to be upset over a freaking grade, Trent!"

"Okay, fair." Pax nods but doesn't give up. "So it's that plus something else that's got you so on edge."

I glance back and forth at the two of them, who have seemed to make themselves comfortable in my space, knowing that neither of them is going to pack it up and leave.

Annoyed, I let out a sigh and say, "It's dumb, mean girl stuff."

My brother whips his attention to me. "What happened?"

"It's not a big deal."

"What happened, Ivy?" Pax presses in a tone I never heard him use before, but my god, did it stir something inside me that I never knew existed.

Heat creeps up my face as I begin explaining, "I was talking with my friend, Cassidy, in the hallway about possibly trying out for the cheerleading squad next year, and these girls on the varsity team overhead and started making fun of me and saying all this horrible stuff."

"What'd they say?" Trent springs up.

"Who?" Pax demands.

"They were making comments about my face and

body," I say to my brother, then focus on Pax. "And you don't even know them. You don't go to Windsor Prep."

How I managed to make enemies within my first few weeks of my freshman year is beyond me.

"I know a lot of people at Windsor Prep. I go to parties with your brother all the time."

"Give me their names. I'll speak with them tomorrow," Trent states.

"*No*!" I snap. "Do you know how pathetic I'll look if my brother talks to them? I didn't even want to bring this up to you guys to begin with because it's embarrassing. Just leave it alone, let me be sad for the night, and I'll get over it tomorrow."

Neither of them is pleased by my response, but they stop pushing me to talk, and the three of us settle in silence. Trent goes back to my music collection while I stare at the TV, and Pax glances around my room.

After a few minutes, Pax breaks the quiet. "You know what I like to do when I'm having a shit day?"

"Play hockey," I say at the same time Trent says, "Hook up with a girl."

My brother's response makes me queasy. I don't like to picture Paxton that way, even though I've heard the rumors.

"Both true," Pax admits. "But you know what else I like to do?" he asks me specifically with a sweet smile on his face. I shake my head, unable to guess what's about to pop out of his mouth. "I hang out at the skatepark, smoke some weed, and listen to Blink-182. It makes everything better for a little while. And I think the three of us should go do that right now—minus smoking because we're in hockey season and I'm not gonna let you get high. But I still think it'll be fun if we go there."

My eyes widen, excitement pumping out of my heart. "Are you serious?"

"Hell yeah, Rebel." He gives my leg a little nudge, sending shockwaves throughout me.

"Which skate park?" Trent asks.

"There's one near my apartment."

"How will we get there? Henry won't drop us off there without telling Mom and Dad," I state.

The three of us concoct a scheme of sneaking out once we know Mom and Dad are asleep and calling a cab to meet us a little past our iron gates. The cooks and cleaning staff have all gone home, but we came up with a script just in case we bump into one—better safe than sorry.

Before I know it, the three of us are squished in the back seat of a cab, freedom humming around our bones.

"Wait, we don't have any skateboards," Trent points out.

"Oh, fuck, you're right!" Pax says, and the three of us laugh at how we didn't catch that one major piece of going to a skate park. "Hey, man." Pax taps the driver's shoulder. "Would you mind stopping at my apartment instead? It's only a few blocks from where we were going."

He silently nods, and jitters fill my stomach for a whole new reason.

Oh my god. I get to go to Pax's apartment!

CHAPTER TWELVE

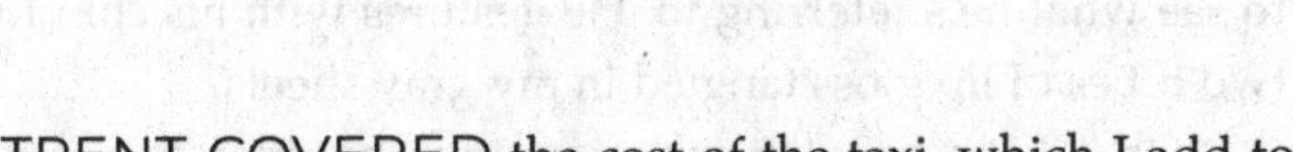

TRENT COVERED the cost of the taxi, which I add to the list of things I need to pay him back for.

"Hang tight for a sec while I grab my boards." I keep my voice low as we enter my home. "We gotta be quiet because my uncle's asleep."

"No, I'm not." Uncle Jeff pops up from the couch and turns on the lamp next to him. The way his eyes are half-open indicates that he definitely was asleep, and I most likely woke him. He takes a moment to let his vision adjust and then says, "Hey, Trent."

"Hi, Jeff. Hope you don't mind us stopping by."

"Not at all. Who do you have hiding behind you there?"

Ivy pokes her head between me and Trent. "Hi! I'm Ivy, Trent's sister." She pushes her way out and goes to sit down on the opposite end of the couch. "I heard a lot about you."

"You have?" Uncle Jeff gives me a quizzical glance.

"Well, sort of. I know you're raising Pax and that he adores you."

As Uncle Jeff beams, I shake my head and navigate

toward my room with Trent following. "Does your sister always try to befriend people she crosses paths with?"

"Nah, she's pretty selective in who she wants to talk to," Trent replies. "She can be a straight-up bitch at times."

Flipping on my light switch, my room looks like someone turned it upside down and shook it. There's shit everywhere—but at least it smells decent thanks to my Axe cologne. Pushing my sweatshirt on the floor out of the way, I search under my bed for my skateboards.

"I like your lip gloss collection," Trent says.

"What?" Yanking my boards free, I pop my head up to see what he's referring to. He gestures with his chin to two tubes of lip gloss tangled in my gray sheets.

"Oh." I smirk, glancing over my shoulder to make sure other sets of ears aren't on us. "I'll tell you about it later."

"Tell me who it was at least."

Standing up, I pass him one of my boards to borrow. "This girl, Lexi, from school. They must've fallen out of her purse."

"She your girlfriend?"

"Hell, no." I look at him like he's insane. "You know I don't do that relationship crap."

Trent shrugs. "Thought maybe she was the one who got you to change your ways." He can't even keep a straight face as he says that sentence, causing both of us to burst into laughter.

"Never happening, bro. In fact, I'm gonna need to start hitting up more girls in your school because I'm running out of options at mine."

The entire Pelican team, and now Ivy, go to Windsor Prep, and while I don't mind going to East Valley High School, it sometimes feels like half of my life is somewhere else.

Which is sort of how it's always been for me.

I never felt like I belonged anywhere.

I'm always waiting for people to bail on me or for me to get ripped away from my environment, which is why I don't do relationships. If people are always going to leave, what's the point? I might as well just have fun and see where that takes me than constantly be waiting for when a person is going to drop me like I'm nothing.

"I know a shit ton of girls for you." Trent grins. I sort of started him on the "fuck relationships" path, and he recently began getting with girls. He's even been coming to me for tips and advice—which, not to boost my ego or anything, feels really goddamn cool.

"Send them my way."

Smiling, we head back into the living room where Uncle Jeff and Ivy are still talking. When they spot us, they abruptly halt their conversation, and Ivy stands up.

"It was great meeting you," she says to my uncle.

"You as well."

"I'll be back later," I say as we make our way to the exit.

"Wait," Uncle Jeff calls after us. We all freeze as he rises, putting his hands on his hips. "I feel like I should be asking you where you're going and all that stuff."

"The skate park," I state the obvious, gesturing to my board.

"Don't get into any trouble. Especially if you're bringing Ivy along."

"Don't worry. Nothing's going to happen with both of us looking after her."

"Yeah, she's good," Trent adds, messing up her hair.

"Hey!" Ivy smacks his gut while Uncle Jeff gives me a nod.

The three of us walk a few blocks until we're finally at

the entrance of the skate park. There's a tall chain-link fence around the perimeter with a lock on the gate.

"It's closed," Ivy points out with disappointment wrapped around her words.

"Never stopped me before." I gently toss my board over, and Trent does the same. With an unspoken conversation between us, we know he's going to help his sister over, and I'll catch her on the other side.

Like I've done countless times before, my feet go between the gaps of the fence, as do my hands, and I eventually hoist myself over, dropping down onto the cement on the opposite side. Straightening my spine, I turn to look at a wide-eyed Ivy. There's excitement building with every breath she takes, but I can also sense the hesitancy as she looks at me for guidance.

"What are you waiting for, Rebel?"

She cracks a smile, and the sight of it makes my chest zing in an unfamiliar way. Pulling her dark hair into a ponytail, she prepares herself to break in, even though her side-swept bangs get in her face every time she looks down to see where she should put her foot. Trent is still on the ground behind her, just in case she falls, despite her telling him she didn't need him there.

But her gusto leaves when she gets to the top and pauses.

"Swing your leg over," I instruct.

"I'm gonna fall."

"No, you won't. I got you." Stepping closer to the fence, I reach my arms up, letting her know I'm not far away.

Her hands shake as she pushes through her fear, swinging her leg around. She slowly does the same with the other, but loses her balance as she struggles to figure out where to put her foot. "Pax!"

"You're good. Just take one step down and I'll grab you."

Doing what I say, she lowers herself slightly so I can reach up and hold her. My hands curl around her hips, and I gently bring her down so her feet can finally touch the cement.

The fence rattles as Trent is next to hop over, but the sound immediately fades when Ivy looks up at me, the streetlight overhead giving away the blush that's appearing on her cheeks.

"Thank you," she says in a breathy voice.

That weird feeling is back in my chest. "Yeah." I nod.

"You guys ready?" Trent holds my skateboard in his hand while he waits for me to pick up mine.

"Yep." As I retrieve my board, I shake off the strange feeling. "Let me show you guys what this place is all about."

Walking further into the skate park, Trent and Ivy are able to see just how huge this place is.

"This is sick," Trent states as he checks out the halfpipes.

This concrete utopia has become a regular stomping ground for me. It's quite different from what Trent and Ivy are used to. Walking further in, there are other misfits who hopped the fence, hanging around and killing time. I go to school with most of them and know the others just by spending my nights here. The familiar opening drumbeat to "Feeling This" by Blink-182 plays on someone's portable stereo. The smell of spray paint from someone painting graffiti mixes with the faint scent of weed.

"Hey, Pax," Blair, a girl who always chills here, says before lighting up a joint. "Who are your friends?" she asks, blowing out a puff of smoke.

"This is Trent and Ivy," I state.

Her eyes immediately zoom in on Trent. "Wanna

come hang?" she asks only to him, patting the empty space next to her as she sits on the edge of a concrete bowl, her legs dangling.

"Yeah," Trent says with an extra ounce of enthusiasm. He gives me a look, letting me know to get his little sister away from whatever might go down.

While he goes over to Blair, I scoop my arm around Ivy's shoulders, swinging her around and moving us in the opposite direction. "So how much of a skateboarder are you, Ivy?"

"I've never even stood on one."

"Perfect."

We pass by a few people doing tricks on their BMX bikes, and I watch as Ivy becomes enthralled by their swift movements.

"I'll give you a lesson on that next time," I joke, bringing us to an open space where no one can bump into us.

Placing my board down, I show Ivy where to place her feet, and as soon as she tries, the skateboard goes flying out from under her.

"You weren't kidding," I say, chasing after the board, hearing her giggles.

"Sorry." A coy expression paints her features when I stand in front of her.

"Nothing to be sorry about. I was exactly the same when I started." I line up the skateboard for her and extend my hands out. "Here, hold on to me for balance." She places her palms in mine, an immediate spark shooting through my bloodstream when her soft skin connects with my calloused edges. When she's steady, I ask, "Ready?"

Ivy nods, an amber glow from the streetlights creating a halo around her. A sense of satisfaction settles into my bones, knowing she trusts me. Gripping onto each other, I begin to walk so she can move. A slight breeze moves her dark hair, showcasing more of her face.

She laughs as I slowly pick up speed, and I can't help but laugh along with her. My heart flutters, enjoying this moment.

Enjoying Ivy's touch.

Enjoying Ivy's smile.

Enjoying being enveloped by Ivy's energy, hoping she's enjoying mine just the same.

CHAPTER THIRTEEN

October

TWO WEEKS AFTER THE SKATEPARK, there's a knock on the front door of my apartment. My brow quirks in surprise when I spot Ivy in her Windsor Prep uniform. It's different from her old uniform, with a white polo and a navy pleated skirt. Her lips pull into a smile as she clutches onto a plastic shopping bag.

"Ivy?" I stupidly ask as if it's not really her.

"Hey, kiddo, come on in!" Uncle Jeff calls from our kitchen-living room table, and as my head whips around to see him pulling out a chair for Ivy, she sneaks past me to join him.

"Were we expecting you?" I ask her.

As she sits down and places the bag on the table, she glances over her shoulder at me. "Uncle Jeff was."

"Oh, he's your uncle now too?" I tease, leaning my weight against the wall as I witness their interaction.

They completely ignore me while they go on with

their conversation. Ivy spills out the contents of the bag, and out come several pictures of me at my game this past weekend.

"This was when Pax stole the puck." Ivy showcases an image of me to Uncle Jeff. "And this was when he—"

"Wait, what is all this?" I interject.

Ivy looks up at me. "I'm here for Uncle Jeff, not you. Hush."

"Yeah, hush," he chimes in. "When you brought Ivy over a couple of weeks ago, the two of us got to talking, and she told me she'd take pictures of your upcoming game since I couldn't make it."

"I can finally put my new digital camera to use!"

The two go back to reliving my hockey game as I stand nearby in complete shock. My body makes the same unfamiliar sensation that happened when I was with Ivy at the skatepark, and my insides feel…warm?

When Ivy's finally finished giving Uncle Jeff a play-by-play, he offers her a snack and heads to the kitchen. As he prepares whatever half-assed snack presentation he can conjure up, I sit down in his chair.

"You didn't have to do this," I whisper to Ivy.

"I know. But I wanted to." Her deep blue eyes twinkle, and a tingling feeling in my chest radiates throughout me the longer I stare at her.

"Thank you."

She smiles. "Of course."

"How did you get here? I didn't see Henry's car."

"A taxi."

"Ivy! You can't ride in a fucking taxi by yourself!"

"You took a taxi here."

Uncle Jeff comes over with a tray of various bowls of chips.

"What's the big deal?"

"The big deal is that it's not safe!" I snap. "We're driving you back home."

"But—"

I point a finger at her. "Don't even think about arguing with me on this, Ivy."

"I agree with my nephew on this one, kiddo."

Ivy rolls her eyes. "Fine. In the future, I'll have Henry drive me."

Jolts of excitement and hope run through my bloodstream as I latch on to what Ivy is saying. "Future?"

She nods. "Yeah. Future."

Ivy kept true to her word, showing up at my doorstep every game Uncle Jeff missed so she could help fill in the gaps. Trent's even on board and gets on Ivy's case if she doesn't take a perfect picture of one of my plays.

I should've expected her today, seeing that this is our new routine, but it totally slipped my mind that she'd probably show up at my door today, considering Uncle Jeff isn't home. But Ivy doesn't know that.

"Uh, hey," I say to Ivy as she stands on the other side of the door like she has been for the past several weeks, wearing her uniform and carrying a stack of pictures, waiting to be let in. My stomach twists into knots as I glance at Alicia on my couch. We go to school together. She's kind of annoying but eager to score with a hockey player, so I stupidly seized an opportunity. "Uncle Jeff is working overtime tonight," I inform Ivy, turning back to face her.

"Oh, okay." Ivy takes a step back. "I'll come back another da—"

"No, stay." I reach out for her, my hand wrapping

around her tiny wrist and guiding her in. When she spots Alicia, her face pales, and I immediately pick up on her hesitation. Turning to Alicia, I say, "You gotta go."

"What?" Alicia's jaw hangs open in disbelief.

"Yeah, sorry. I forgot I had plans with Ivy."

"Are you kidding me right now?"

"Nope. My best friend's little sister takes priority." I gesture to my wide-open front door. "I'll see you at school."

A disgruntled Alicia glares at Ivy as she snatches up her purse, muttering curses under her breath as she walks past. She's sure to slam the door shut, causing Ivy to jump.

"You didn't have to do that," Ivy says.

I shrug, leading us into my small kitchen to grab a bag of red Doritos. "I don't like her very much anyway."

"So if you don't like her, then why did you invite her over?" Her brows crinkle in curiosity.

As I part my lips to tell her the truth, I sense my cheeks heating. The way her dark-blue eyes stare into mine makes my heart race. I suddenly change my mind, not wanting to stain her image of me, so I shove an orange chip in my mouth, and in between chewing, I say, "Math homework."

She squints, not buying my lie, but decides to drop the conversation. Scooting around me, she opens my narrow pantry and takes out a bag of Ruffles. "Do you truly see me as your best friend's little sister?"

"Well, you are. So…yeah," I say as I watch her place the pictures for Uncle Jeff on the table, then go to sit down on the couch—exactly where Alicia was sitting.

Opening up the Ruffles, she pulls out a chip, crunching on it as she leans back, getting comfortable. Because she *is* comfortable here. She crosses her legs, her skirt moving up a little, exposing her thigh. The heat in my cheeks is now spreading through the rest of me.

"But you don't see me as your friend?"

My attention immediately moves from her legs to her eyes, and when I notice how sad they look, my thoughts swiftly shift gears.

"Oh no, Ivy, that's not what I meant." I dart over to sit near her. "You are my friend. I guess I just always associated you as Trent's sister first." *Which is why you shouldn't have been glancing at her thighs, asshole.* "But we've never hung out, only me and you. It's either been us plus Trent or us plus Uncle Jeff, not us alone."

"You were hanging out with that girl alone, and you apparently don't like her very much," Ivy quips.

"I kicked her out for you."

"Because I'm your best friend's little sister."

"And because you're my friend."

Our gazes lock. Ripples of warmth flood my insides the longer I stare at her unique, sapphire eyes, and I *know* my body shouldn't be feeling anything remotely close to this.

"Cool Ranch Doritos are so much better than Nacho Cheese," she says, thankfully breaking the tension.

"Well, it was a nice friendship while it lasted," I tease. "Guess I'll have to kick you out too. You know where the door is."

She ignores my comment. "You'll have to buy a bag of blue Doritos if I'm going to be hanging around more often," she says, while continuing to snack on the chips in her hand.

"I'll see what I can do."

"I'll take that as a yes, which I'm incredibly thankful for because my mom refuses to put them on our grocery list."

"Because she knows Cool Ranch is the lame flavor or

because she's a bitc—" I bite my tongue, not meaning to outwardly insult her mother, but Ivy obviously knows what I was about to say.

"It's all right, you can call her a bitch. She is one."

"She's not the most..." My face scrunches as I search for a polite term.

"Kind? Compassionate? Likable?" Ivy opts to finish my thought. "I can go on if you want. I've got a list of nice adjectives that my mother lacks."

I chuckle. "The few times I've seen you two interact, I can tell you guys butt heads a lot."

"You've got no idea."

Leaning back, I let myself become more comfortable, allowing my legs to outstretch. Our feet are almost touching. If either of us moves, we'll bump the other. I like being this close to Ivy. I've never noticed how sweet she smells until now.

"She's tough on Trent too, but not in the same way she is with me," Ivy says, stopping my mind from spiraling into thoughts that definitely should not be popping into my head.

"Yeah, I've noticed." My brain reenters the chat. "Why is that?"

"Who knows?" Ivy shrugs. "She expects me to be prim and proper and fall in line with her lifestyle, but it just doesn't suit me. And the rest of the women who are a part of the Colonial Dames—all bitches."

"What's the Colonial Dames?"

"They're a stuffy, privileged, special society vowing to uphold the country's history. But in reality, they're kinda like a cliquey sorority for old people. The society is just an excuse for them to get together and gossip. They have luncheons, fancy events, and all that boring stuff."

"And your mom is expecting you to be a member one day?"

"Yep. I'm destined to be a Dame."

"Nah." I smile at her, and her line of sight lands on my lips. "You're a rebel."

A rosy color paints her cheeks as she fights back a grin. My stomach flips at the sight of her becoming bashful, but I know I shouldn't read into how my body reacts around her.

Because at the end of the day, Ivy is still my best friend's little sister.

CHAPTER FOURTEEN

PRESENT

A LOUD KNOCK on my apartment door has my eyes shooting open.

"Ms. Hartwick." A voice comes from the other side. "Ms. Hartwick, you've got a delivery."

Becoming more alert, I recognize that it's Clint, my doorman, knocking on my door. Unsure of why he's dropping something off for me, I hurry to grab my powder blue robe, wrapping the plush fabric around me as I make my way out of my bedroom.

My apartment is nothing spectacular, but it's mine. My one-bedroom, one-bathroom, and living room-slash-kitchen open floor concept has my mark all over it. Hues of cool colors are painted on the walls, with random photographs I've found at thrift stores hanging up. My taste has matured and is not as chaotic as it used to be, with simplistic decor dispersed around my space. As I walk into my living room, I pass by the large windows overlooking the city street and go to my front door.

"Sorry to wake you," Clint says. He's a stocky man, always wearing a newsie cap. "You had three large boxes delivered." He gestures to the right of him, and I poke my head out to see what he's talking about, considering I didn't order anything.

The moment I spot the boxes, anger blasts through my bloodstream.

I know exactly what's in those boxes and who sent them.

"Thought they'd be too heavy for you to carry, so I brought them up for you." Clint places his hand on his now-empty dolly.

"You didn't have to do that. I got it from here," I say as nicely as possible to not displace any of my temper onto him. "Thank you."

"Anytime, Ms. Hartwick." He whistles a cheerful tune to himself as he leaves down the hallway and toward the elevator.

I'm left alone with three cardboard boxes with my childhood address typed on the return label. Mom's latest fuck-you tactic must be mailing me my belongings, finally ridding me of her house. Bright and early on a Saturday morning, no less.

The muscles in my arms strain as I struggle to get all three boxes into my apartment. Out of breath, I plop the last one right beside the door, unable to carry it further into my space.

I haven't even had coffee yet. My brain can't process going through any of this.

Bypassing the boxes and my unopened luggage that Warren dropped off while I was at work the other day without any communication, I make my way into my kitchen to get my day started with a caffeine kick. The throbbing in my head reminds me I had one too many margaritas with Zaina last night at a new dive bar she found. Thankfully, we'll be able to sweat out most of the alcohol later today in yoga.

I wasn't planning on going out, as I'd been stopping by to see Uncle Jeff at the end of my workdays this past week, all the while successfully avoiding Pax. But when Uncle Jeff realized it was a Friday night, he told me to get out of the hospital and go have some fun.

I might've had a little too much fun trying to drink away any thoughts of his nephew, and now I'm left with a hangover I definitely wouldn't have if I were still in my twenties.

Grimacing at the new clutter in my living room, I let the warm, dark roast hit my tongue, waking me up even more.

My teeth grinding together, I search for my phone to text Mom. She's laid off trying to guilt me into marriage, and all has been quiet on her end for several days.

As I go to open my phone, it immediately buzzes with an incoming FaceTime. My muscles tense for a brief moment, expecting a conversation with Mom, but when I spot Lucille's name across the screen, I loosen up a tad.

"Good morning, Ivy!" Lucille's blond ringlets are up in a ponytail, and her face is a little rosy as if she just finished working out.

"Morning." I take a sip of my coffee once more.

"I'm just checking in with my bridesmaids to make sure you're all set for our winter getaway the first week of February."

"Yep, I'll be there the whole time, Friday to Monday." Luckily, I was able to take off from work, and the drive is only a couple of hours north of me.

"Perfect! I'm so excited!" Her smile sparkles, and I'm truly so happy that she's this overjoyed to be marrying my brother.

They've been together for three years, and even though I don't see Trent often, he's never been more smitten with someone. Lucille has been making an effort to build a relationship with me ever since they got engaged, and I appreciate her for it.

"It's cute you're calling it a winter getaway instead of your bachelorette party," I say.

"Yeah, I wanted to do something different, and since I love skiing and ice skating, I thought this would be a fun idea. The resort is *huge*. It's like a mini-town with tons to do. Plus, it's not technically a bachelorette party since Trent and the guys will be there too."

"What?" I put my mug down on the counter.

"Did I not give you the details? It must've slipped my mind. I'm sorry. My head is in a million places with wedding planning." Lucille props up her phone on what looks like a bathroom vanity and fixes her hair as she talks to me.

"No, it's okay. You don't need to apologize. I'm just surprised, that's all." If she could hear my heart thumping against my ribcage, she'd know I'm way more than surprised. I nibble on my bottom lip as she continues to talk.

"Trent and I figured we're past the crazy bachelor and bachelorette party phase, and we wanted to do something together. We'll still sort of be separated, the guys will be on the first floor of the cabin, and the second floor will be for the ladies." She wets a washcloth and begins cleaning her face, thankfully not noticing the nervousness that's tightening my muscles. "And there'll be lots to do, so we're not going to be together for *every* activity."

"Cool," I manage to squeak out. Immediately clearing

my throat, I fix the register of my voice. "It-it sounds cool —great." My rising panic makes me fumble over my words.

"Okay, now for the reason I really called." Lucille tosses her cloth to the side and looks directly into the phone. My stomach drops at what might come out of her mouth. "I know we're not super close, but we are going to be sisters very soon, and I wanted to check in to see how you're doing after everything that happened with Warren."

"Oh." My shoulders drop in relief.

"I wanted to give you some time to process and not bring it up right away, but if you need someone to talk to, I'm here."

"I appreciate that, but I'm totally fine."

"Are you sure?"

"Yep. Not a single tear has been shed."

It sounds cold, but it's true. The chain-link fence around my heart doesn't let anyone in—certainly not men. Whenever I had to end it with a guy, I waited for the tears to come or the feeling of sorrow, but nothing ever happened. Well, aside from when I was a teenager. But since then, I've been able to not get attached and keep it moving. Maybe there's a heartbreak for them, but not for me.

"All right…" Lucille eyes me suspiciously, as if I'm avoiding telling her the truth. "Well, if you need anything, call me."

"I will." I smile at her kindness. "Thanks, Lucille."

"I'll see you soon!"

And the panic is back. "See you soon."

The moment we hang up, anxiety pumps through my heart. My fingertips tingle at the thought of being under the same roof as Paxton for multiple days.

I try to breathe and bring some rationale into my brain.

At least we'll have the entire wedding party as our buffer. Nothing outrageous will happen with that many people around. I can keep it together for an extended weekend.

CHAPTER FIFTEEN

THE SCENT of incense blends with the musk of sweaty yoga mats as Zaina and I finish up our Saturday afternoon class.

"I'm pretty sure I fell asleep during shavasana." Zaina yawns, rolling up her sage-green mat.

"So *you* were the one who was snoring!" I tease.

She gasps. "I was not!"

"Relax, I'm messing with you. If you were snoring, I would've kicked you."

"I can always count on you to give me a swift kick in the ass."

The two of us grab our belongings and bundle up to brace the cold. She's headed home to get rest before her Tinder date tonight, while I'm headed to my place to stand under a hot shower until I shrivel up, then spend the rest of the evening reading a romance novel.

"Let me know how your date goes," I say, walking toward my car.

"I'll give you all the dirty details on Monday." She gives me a wink as we part ways.

My teeth chatter as I sit in my Honda, hoping that the

warm air will start blasting soon. Before I can pull out of the lot, my phone buzzes, signaling a text.

UNCLE JEFF

Any chance you can stop by today?

Worry wraps around my bones, considering he'd been adamant about not visiting him on the weekend because he "doesn't want someone who is young and healthy to spend all their free time with a boring, old man in a hospital." He gave me clear instructions to have fun on my days off work and not stop by unless necessary.

We exchanged numbers, and he promised to message me if he needs anything. Now that he's asking me to come visit, I have a horrible feeling in my gut that it is necessary that I get there as soon as possible.

ME

On my way.

Driving to the hospital, my mind bounces from horrible thought to horrible thought.

Does he have bad news to tell me? Did his treatment fail? Did they tell him he only has a few days left?

All of these grim questions follow me until I'm finally standing in front of his hospital bed. Before either of us begins to speak, I do a quick scan of his face to see if he appears any worse or is in distress.

"What's going on?" I ask. All Uncle Jeff does is smile at me. There's not a sound between us until someone suddenly comes barreling in—

"What's wrong, Uncle Jeff?" Pax asks, out of breath, as if he ran up the stairs instead of waiting for the elevator.

Pax does a double-take when he sees me, the tension in the air instantly thickening when our eyes lock.

"Nothing's wrong." Uncle Jeff finally speaks. "I just

thought it was about time the two of you stood in the same room together."

My mouth hangs open. "You sneaky old man."

He begins laughing at the apparent friction between me and Paxton. The way his cheeks redden with joy makes it hard to be pissed at him.

"You told me something was wrong," Pax snaps.

"No, I didn't," Uncle Jeff corrects him.

Pax fishes his phone out of his pocket. "You sent me a text that said, 'Come quick.'"

"Exactly. Nothing in my message said that there's something wrong. You assumed that on your own." His smug grin has the corners of my mouth turning upward.

"Well, when you're on the last leg of treatment and I get a message like that, I'm obviously going to think the worst." Pax runs his hand through his shortened hair, blowing out a stressful puff of air.

I notice how every muscle in his body is tight with anxiety, and it makes my heart sink. As much as I'd like to act as if he's no one to me, I know Uncle Jeff's diagnosis must be eating him alive. For the first time since fate forced us together on the plane a few weeks ago, I have the urge to talk to him and see if he's okay.

The more he stares at Uncle Jeff, the more a hint of a smile appears. "You're such an asshole," Pax says to him with a choked chuckle.

"I don't remember you being a meddler back in the day," I tell Uncle Jeff.

He shrugs. "I have fewer things to keep me entertained as of late. So what do you say the two of you hang out here in my hospital room and catch up? Or Pax, maybe you can take her out for a bite to eat?"

Paxton's attention shifts as he glances down at the shiny floor as if preparing himself to speak. When he's ready, he focuses his gaze on me. Those captivating hazel eyes are dangerously close to luring me in when he asks, "Do you want to get some lunch?"

"I have to go home and shower. I just got out of a yoga class."

Goddammit. As I say those words, I suddenly realize I probably look like a disaster—once again.

I run my hand through my slick hair, adjusting my ponytail to tuck in any flyaways.

"Okay. Dinner?" Pax asks.

No is dancing on the tip of my tongue. The urge to blow him off and keep pretending as if he doesn't exist is tempting, but I know we'll be in close proximity soon with Trent and Lucille's winter getaway and their wedding, so I might as well rip the Band-Aid off.

"Fine," I state.

"May I pick you up?"

"You may not." I haughtily grin up at him, and his jaw tics with frustration. Seeing him annoyed at my response is quite satisfying. "I'll meet you at O'Donnell's at six. It's a restaurant a few blocks over. Look it up." Turning my attention to a delighted Uncle Jeff, I state, "I'm only doing this for you."

He nods. "Have fun."

I give him an exaggerated eye roll before exiting his room.

The same teenage giddiness I used to harbor begins to simmer in my chest, as much as I don't want it to. The past two times I saw Paxton, I was caught off guard and clearly not looking my best.

But tonight, I'll make sure every inch of me is flawless.

CHAPTER SIXTEEN

paxton

IT'S SIX FIFTEEN, and still no sign of Ivy.

I'm not surprised, though. I'm half expecting her to stand me up.

But even though fifteen minutes have passed and I have low hopes of her showing up, I make myself comfortable in a booth at O'Donnell's, planning to close the place down waiting for her.

Scrolling on my phone, I move past sports articles with my name in the headlines. Being forced into retirement has shaken my foundation. I feel like a kid again with nothing to cling to except Uncle Jeff. The thought of his illness makes the lining of my throat thick with emotion, not wanting to imagine the void I'll feel if his treatment doesn't work.

I have the guys on the team and Trent, but everyone gets busy with their own lives, and rightfully so, because I did the same.

A weight settles on my shoulders, wanting to reconnect with Ivy but knowing there's a big chance she won't want to. I don't blame her. Things got messy when we were younger, which I was always fearful of, and because I blurred the lines, I lost the best person in my life.

"Hey." The sound of Ivy's voice has my heart jolting.

My head snaps out of my phone, and my insides immediately go haywire at the sight of her. She takes her time removing her coat, letting my gaze linger over her body.

It might be January, but she obviously didn't dress for the weather, and I can't help getting a glimmer of hope that she dressed for me.

My thoughts instantly shift to ones I know I shouldn't have as I take in her black heels with her sheer black tights. Her tight, off-the-shoulder dress hugs every curve in a shimmery burgundy color. Gorgeous loose curls cascade down her chest, and her eye makeup makes the blue hue of her irises stand out.

"Hi—hey," I stammer, getting up to greet her, and she slides into the seat across from me. It's an awkward exchange, and I don't miss the way she fights back a smirk, glad that I'm flustered. As I sit back in the booth, she nonchalantly flips her hair off her right shoulder. "I wasn't sure if you were going to show," I state.

"I had my doubts too. How many more minutes were you going to give it before you left?"

"I would've waited all night for you, Ivy." My voice deepens with sincerity.

Our eyes lock, and I don't dare look away.

I'm telling the truth.

I would've waited until they locked the doors, and even then, I'd probably stand outside waiting for her to appear.

"Can I start you off with something to drink?" Our waiter appears, forcing Ivy's line of sight off me.

"Pinot noir, please," she states.

I order another water, and the waiter nods before disappearing.

"Never thought you'd turn into a wino," I tease, trying to get her comfortable with me once more.

Her eyebrow arches. "Oh? And what type of woman did you think I'd turn out to be?"

"The same pain in the ass as you've always been, minus the wine. I envisioned you with a beer bottle in hand. It's a lot less *Dame*."

Ivy's breath catches, and her brows jump, surprised I remember the drama she went through with her mom, fighting not to become a Colonial Dame. But I remember everything, from how soft her lips felt against mine to how red her face gets when she's angry.

She's quick to mask her shock and instead gets a flicker of determination in her features. Leaning in closer, a teasing seduction wraps around her voice when she asks, "Do you envision me a lot, Paxton?"

I chuckle, ready to play whatever game this is. "Do you really want to know the answer to that one, Rebel? Because I'll call your bluff and give you a straight answer if that's what you're wanting."

"If you're insinuating that you think about me during your solo time, that's a little pathetic considering all the women at arm's reach, unless—" She lets out a fake gasp. "Did your endless supply of women run out now that you got canned from the NHL?"

I click my tongue. "That was a good one. Low blow, but a good one nonetheless."

"Thank you."

The waiter places our drinks down and takes our order: a chicken pesto flatbread for her and a BLT for me. Once he leaves, Ivy takes a hearty sip of wine, looking away from me.

"Why don't we start over before things get out of hand and one of us says something they regret?" I suggest.

She nods. "You're right. You wouldn't want to end up saying something ridiculous like 'I love you.'" Blades doused in venom shoot out of her eyes and pin me against my seat.

A vise squeezes around my chest.

I have an endless amount of regrets, enough to sell out my home stadium. I hurt Ivy in ways I didn't realize at the time, but I never once regretted telling her I loved her.

"Ivy—"

"Okay, I'm going to stop being a bitch now." She takes one more sip of wine and places her glass down. "Let's start over for real. Go."

A halfhearted smirk hits my lips, but doesn't meet my eyes. Pushing through the defeated feeling, I decide to take this as my opportunity. "How do you like Boston?" I ask, easing into conversation.

"I love it. I found my home here. It suits me well."

"What do you do for work?"

"I'm a curator at the Contemporary Art and Lifestyle Museum."

My brows raise. "That's awesome."

"It is." She smiles proudly. "I get to research and sort through all sorts of memorabilia from the fifties to the nineties."

"I bet you love that. Especially going through the pictures." A flood of memories of Ivy glued to her camera when she was a teenager pours into my brain.

"Yeah." She nervously fidgets with her hair. Staring at me, her face suddenly twists as she changes topics. "I heard you tore your ACL at the end of the season."

"Yeah. Fucking sucked."

"And probably hurt like hell."

"That's for sure."

"Some might call that karma," she teases with a smug expression on her face.

I laugh. "I thought you were done being a bitch, Rebel."

"I never clarified for how long."

The give-and-take with her is something I missed, my cheeks continuing to rise as I soak in her sharp features. It's always a little bit of a mindfuck when I see someone from when I was younger and note how time has affected them, reminding me that I'm not a kid either. Not that I'm old by any means, but seeing someone who I haven't seen since they were a teenager as an adult in their early thirties makes me realize how much I've grown in between those years.

I've had a love-hate relationship with time, but Ivy seems to shine even brighter.

The waiter breaks our stare, placing our food in front of us. We each take bites, waiting for the other to speak.

It's Ivy who breaks the tension after politely wiping her mouth with her napkin and setting it beside her plate. "We should lay some ground rules."

"Ground rules?" My features draw in. "For what?"

"Well, we're both in Trent and Lucille's wedding party and will be spending an extended weekend together for their joint bachelor-bachelorette party."

"You finally got caught up to speed on their whole winter getaway plan?" I smirk, knowing since November that I'd be in a lodge with Ivy. Meanwhile, she didn't even know it was a possibility that I'd be invited to her brother's wedding.

"Yeah. At least I think so."

"How did you not know I was in the wedding?"

She shrugs. "I didn't ask Trent, and he didn't tell me."

"What happened to you guys? You used to be close."

"Nothing happened. I just—" Ivy stops herself, glancing down at her food.

"You what?"

Tension pulls at her brows as I watch a sorrowful expression wash over her. She avoids eye contact at all costs as she speaks. "Nothing happened. There wasn't any big fight or blowout. I just needed to get away from my life in Maryland, and he was collateral damage. We went on living our lives and got used to the distance. That's all."

"I wish things were different for you guys."

Her gaze snaps up, landing directly on me when she says, "I wish a lot of things were different, Pax."

My gut twists. That vise around my chest compresses even harder.

"Me too," I whisper my admittance.

A sheen of glassiness covers her eyes, but she's quick to blink her emotions away. "Fuck," she says in annoyance, then downs the rest of her wine. "Ground rules." She slams the glass onto the table, swiftly changing the energy. "Rule one: no bringing up the past."

"That's going to be near impossible. It'll be me, you, and Trent. You don't think one of us is bound to bring up some ridiculous memory?"

"Fine, if some stupid shit gets brought up, then whatever, but no bringing up *our* past."

I swallow, hating that rule but agreeing to her terms by nodding.

"Rule two: our interaction won't extend beyond their wedding."

"Meaning?"

"Meaning, we're acquaintances, and once the wedding is over, then there won't be a need for us to talk again."

"No." I lean back, crossing my arms over my chest.

"Excuse me?"

"I'm not agreeing to that fucking rule. What if I need to inform you about Uncle Jeff? Or what if I'd like to visit a museum while I'm here and need your advice on where to go?"

"God, you're making this difficult." *That's the point, Rebel.* "Okay, we'll only be in contact with each other after the wedding if necessary. Better?"

"Better." I grin, fully aware that my version of what is necessary is far different from hers, and I'll have no issue bringing that to her attention later on.

"Rule three: no physical contact."

"I can't shake your hand? What if I accidentally bump into you? What if we're paired up at the wedding and you have to loop your arm around mine? Should I inform Lucille about your provisions?"

Her jaw tightens in frustration, giving me a bump of excitement from pushing her buttons like I once used to. "You know what I mean," she grits out.

"Nah, I'm not sure I do." I push my back off the seat, leaning my chest against the table to get close to her. I can get a whiff of a warm vanilla scent as she squares off with me. "Why don't you spell it out for me and tell me exactly what you mean by no physical contact? If I'm allowed to give you a high-five, then it's clearly not *all* physical contact."

Ivy moves in closer. If anyone glances at us, they'd assume we're about to kiss, and in thinking such, my attention drops down to her lips. I watch as they pull up into a smirk, then I bring my focus back to her sapphire daggers.

"It means I'm not fucking you, Paxton."

I don't think I've ever been so turned on by someone turning me down.

"Anyway," Ivy says, settling back into a comfortable position. "Those are my three rules. Do you have any?"

"Nope."

"Well, if you think of any, you can let me know. I'm sure we can survive the long weekend and the wedding. And then we'll continue to carry on and go our separate ways."

"Except for when you visit my uncle," I blurt out.

Her throat bobs. "Occasional visits."

"Every day. You go and visit him every day after work, Ivy."

"Didn't think Uncle Jeff would blow up my spot and tell you I've been there every day." She glances down at her half-eaten flatbread. "If you knew when I was visiting, why didn't you just show up?"

"I wanted to give you alone time with him," I say, and she nods. "Didn't think he'd have it in him to set us up, though."

She chuckles, the first time all night. When she glances up at me, her guard has lowered as she says, "When the hell did he become a matchmaker?"

I laugh along with her. "It must be all those pain meds getting to him."

Ivy's triviality leaves her expression, and she stares at me with somberness. Her mouth parts as if she wants to ask me something, but no words come out.

Feeling exposed by how she's looking at me, I reach for my water. I can take her sass, the up-and-down emotional roller coaster, even her fucking rules—but I can't bear her asking me how I'm doing when it comes to Uncle Jeff.

And I think she can sense it because she changes the subject, asking me how I like Boston.

The night moves on with the conversation feeling lighter and not as intense. Ivy still makes it clear that she resents me, but it's more in a playful way than how it was earlier in the night. I don't blame her for how she feels, but I would like to make it up to her somehow, if she'd ever let me.

"Where are you staying?" Ivy asks as we step into the glacial weather. Her muscles instantly tense up as she wraps her arms around herself.

"The Hilton right next to the hospital."

She nods. "All right. Well, I'm the other way, so I guess I'll see you—"

"Can I walk you back to your place?"

"I don't need anyone to walk me home."

"I know you don't, but I'd like to."

I stare at her as she contemplates what to do. Her nose turns red from the cold, and a blast of wind harshly hits our cheeks.

A shiver climbs down her body at the same time she sighs. "Fine. Let's go."

She turns, and within a millisecond, I'm by her side. We walk across a cobblestone street, her heels getting stuck between the spaces every now and again. Whenever I try to brace her, she shoos me away while murmuring curses to herself about her choice of shoes.

When we get to her apartment building, a doorman greets us. "Evening, Ms. Hartwick."

"Hey, Clint." Ivy gives a wave, quickly guiding me inside.

"You got another delivery while you were out," he informs her.

Her head falls back as she groans. "Thanks for letting me know."

I don't bother asking what their exchange is about because I doubt she'll tell me. Instead, I quietly follow her to the elevator, waiting for her to say I've reached my limit and can leave. However, she seems distracted by news of her delivery as she focuses on finding her keys in her purse.

When the elevator dings, I follow her out, only to come to a screeching halt when we spot dozens and dozens of boxes filling the hallway.

"Are you kidding me?" Anger colors Ivy's cheeks a scarlet red as she storms to her door.

"What the hell is this all about?" I take a peek at the return address on one of the packages and spot Meredith Hartwick's name on the label.

My curiosity has officially been piqued. I enter Ivy's apartment, but before I can even begin to check it out, I know that I have to figure out what's going on and help her because she's slamming her purse onto the couch and yanking off her heels, tossing them across the room, and nearly breaking a coffee mug.

"Whoa. Hang on." I settle my arms on her arms to stop her from doing any damage. "Fill me in. What's going on with your mom?"

Taking a deep breath, she regains her composure enough to explain. "She's pissed at me and decided to pack up all of my things without telling me, and is dumping everything here—again, without telling me. Essentially washing her hands clean of me, all because I didn't do what she wanted."

I nod, waiting for her to explain further about the thing Meredith wanted her to do, but she doesn't give me any more information. An idea forms in my head, and even though I know I'm straddling the line of defusing a bomb or detonating it, I do it anyway. Breaking contact, I move away from her and into the hallway.

"What are you doing?" Ivy asks.

"What does it look like I'm doing?" I pick up a stack of two boxes and carry them into her living room.

"I don't need you to carry any of it in. I can do it on

my own. I just needed a few seconds to be dramatic, but I'm fine now."

I glance over at her, another stack in my arms. "Only a few seconds? You sure about that?"

She fixes me with a scowl, putting her hands on her hips. "Very funny."

I pay no mind to her telling me she doesn't need my help and continue moving her stuff inside. She tries to take over, reaching for the first box she spots in the hallway. It's sizable with some weight to it, and I watch as she struggles to lift it.

Silently, I take it from her. She opens her mouth to protest, but I don't let her speak. "Don't start," I state. "Go back inside, pour yourself another glass of wine, and let me carry the rest of these in."

She huffs and puffs like the pain in the ass she's always been, but she eventually does what I say, and by the time the hallway is cleared, her hair is up in a bun, and she sips on her drink, staring at the boxes.

I tiptoe around the stacks, silence blanketing the length of her apartment. Her eyes stay trained on the blocks of cardboard in front of her, not paying any mind to me. Knowing that I don't belong in this space or this version of her world, I get the sense that I'm overstaying my welcome.

But she hasn't told me to leave.

She hasn't said anything.

I clear my throat, hoping to get her attention, but it doesn't work. So I use a different tactic. "Do you think that straightener you scarred me with is in one of these?"

She blinks herself out of her thoughts, amusement lighting up her face. "I did *not* scar you."

Lifting up my hand, I showcase a small, faded scar on my hand. Ivy's jaw drops. She places her glass of wine down and hurries over to me.

"You still have a mark!" she says in disbelief, examining it for herself.

"I carry you with me everywhere I go."

Her fingertips run over the slightly discolored line, causing every single one of my nerve endings to light on fire at her delicate touch. Yearning stirs in my heart, wanting her to continuously drag her fingers over me so I can endlessly feel her skin against mine, even if it's only in a featherlight connection.

Slowly breaking contact, Ivy draws in a breath as if bringing herself back into the present. Stepping away, she weaves in and out of her past. "I doubt that straightener made it into these boxes. I probably threw it out years ago."

"We could always open one and see," I suggest. I act casual, shrugging as if it would be nothing, but my fingers itch to see what type of treasures are buried inside. Half of what's in there are my memories too. Good ones. The types of memories I cling to whenever I feel disconnected.

"That would violate rule one: no bringing up the past."

"We agreed we can bring up stupid shit—you burning me with a straightener classifies as that."

She chuckles, her shoulders easing up as they slouch. "Fine. But only because I'm buzzed and curious if my iPod Nano made it in there."

Grinning, I open the box next to me, tearing the label right at where it says Hartwick. Ivy scurries closer, eager to see what's there.

"Oh god, I remember these." She pulls out several skinny, colorful scarves lying on top.

"And I remember this," I tease, taking out a neon purple bikini top. "The first time I realized you had boobs was when you were wearing this," I say as I laugh at the memory.

She swats my arm before yanking the bathing suit out of my hands. "Perv."

We go back to searching through her belongings, moving around low-rise jeans, Love Spell perfume bottles, and an unpeeled *Vote for Pedro* bumper sticker. The heavy dose of nostalgia makes both of our cheeks rise.

I spot two pairs of shutter sunglasses and put on the black ones. "Put these on," I say, passing her the white ones.

Ivy glances up at me, and the second she sees what I'm wearing, she bursts into laughter. "You look ridiculous," she says, taking the glasses from me and putting them on to look just as stupid as me.

"So do you."

"Why the fuck were these cool?"

"No idea."

The room fills with our laughter. My veins light up from her playfulness as she pretends to pose for a selfie, pressing her lips together in a way that makes her look like she's making a duck face. The sensation of her loosening up around me creates immense relief in the painful places my body holds on to.

"Ivy?" A man's voice comes from behind us, and when I check over my shoulder, I spot a guy in an expensive-looking suit poking his head through the door that I must not have shut all the way.

Both of us take the sunglasses off as he enters like he belongs here.

My spine automatically straightens, tightness setting in my jaw. "Who's this?" I ask Ivy as if I have the right to know.

He ignores me, looking directly at Ivy when he says,

"I see you moved on rather quickly after rejecting my proposal."

"Proposal?" My attention whips to Ivy.

"Warren, I—"

"Don't bother," he cuts her off. "I was just stopping over to see if we could work things out, but I can tell there's no point." He shifts his attention to me. "Good luck with her. She's a bolter, and not just with me."

My eyebrows raise as I watch him back out of her apartment until he disappears.

Ivy and I stand in silence, and all of this is beginning to click for me. "Your mom wanted you to marry him," I quietly state.

She nods, tossing her belongings back into the box and folding the flaps over.

The reality of another man getting the privilege of calling her *wife* spikes my envy in ways I forgot existed, making my heart beat rapidly out of pace. For years she's been an image in my head, never acknowledging the fact that she could belong to someone else.

Selfish, illogical, delusional—call me all of those things. But in my dreams, Ivy's always been mine.

"I need to go to bed." She dismisses me, walking away from the stacks of boxes.

"Okay," I whisper, even though I'm longing to know more of this situation and why the fuck Warren decided to *warn* me about her being a "bolter."

Ivy turns from me, and I war with myself, wanting to stay and learn more about who she is now.

But my sensibility wins, and I move toward her front door. "I'll see you soon."

"Yeah, the winter getaway thing." She makes a clear boundary, letting me know I'm not seeing her prior to that. I'll continue to give her space when she visits Uncle Jeff, and even if I wanted to take her out to dinner again, I don't have her number to ask her. I changed mine years ago, and the first call I made from my new number was to hers since I had it memorized. An old man answered each time I tried to reach her, so I'm assuming she's since changed her phone number too.

Reaching the doorway, I pause before glancing at her once more. "See you in a couple of weeks."

CHAPTER SEVENTEEN

2006

December

OH MY GOD.

My jaw hangs open, my eyes wide enough to fall right out and roll onto my keyboard as I stare at my computer screen.

Paxton added me to his Top 8 on MySpace. The hierarchy of friends, the people who are most important to you, the ones who you care about the most—and there's my profile picture set as number eight. Trent is number one, followed by his friends on their hockey team, and then *me*!

A flushed feeling washes over my body as my insides bounce around in excitement. A giddy squeal leaves my mouth.

We've gotten closer over the past few months since I dropped by to give Uncle Jeff pictures of the games he's missed. Sometimes Uncle Jeff is there, sometimes not, and Pax and I hang out. We've exchanged numbers, and even though we barely text, it still feels incredible to know he has the option if he wants to.

I'm not an idiot, though. I know he likes to hook up with girls, and I assume it happens quite often when he and Trent sneak off to parties.

But no girl has even been in his Top 8.

I'm his first.

"He's my best friend, Mom!" Trent's voice booms from down the hall. Knowing that he's talking about Pax, I immediately dash out of my room to see what Trent's yelling about.

Mom's standing in the doorway of Trent's bedroom with her hands on her hips and a sour look on her face—surprise, surprise.

"I understand that." Mom's tone is calm, as if she's trying to appease him. "But I don't believe he'll fit in with the crowd tonight. I'm sorry."

"It's a New Year's Eve party. We'll spend most of our time in the game room away," he rebuts.

"Trent, I'm sorry. He can't come over for this one."

"We can't just uninvite him," I state as I travel over to them.

Mom spins in surprise while Trent pops his head out of his room with a hopeful expression on his face.

"Trent didn't invite him yet," Mom says.

"I did," I lie. But I know Mom abides by her rules of etiquette, and since she's been priming me for a lifestyle filled with decorum and politeness, I know I have her between a rock and a hard place.

Her eyes narrow, angry that I put her in this position. "Next time, you need to ask me before you invite guests."

"You told me I could invite my friends."

"I was referring to the girls in your freshman class. Not juniors on Trent's hockey team."

I shrug. "Oops."

She purses her lips together and drags her attention back to Trent. "Tell him he must dress and behave appropriately, especially when he's in front of my guests."

Trent nods, and Mom spins on her heels, disappearing down the stairs.

Once she's out of earshot, Trent whispers, "Thanks."

My wheels get turning, and I don't let him off this easily. "You owe me."

"What do you want?"

"Me and my friends get to hang out with you and yours in the game room. We're not getting stuck in the boring party in the ballroom while you guys get to have all the fun in a separate room."

"Fine, but the second you do something annoying, you're out."

"You have yourself a deal." I give him a curt nod and head to my bedroom to get ready for the New Year's Eve party.

Anticipation runs through my bloodstream as I move back to my room and glance over at my computer. Butterflies fill my stomach as my mind fantasizes about the possibility of Paxton being my New Year's kiss.

Mom might have impossible standards and be difficult to get along with, but she can throw a party. She had her designers decorate every spot in our home where guests will be, including the game room.

It makes me despise her a little less when I enter the

game room and it's adorned floor to ceiling in New Year's decorations. Colorful balloon towers are on the perimeter, with huge red 2007 balloons secured to the back wall. The stereo is playing "SexyBack" by Justin Timberlake, and a new arcade game, *Dance Dance Revolution,* is set up off to the side.

Mine and Trent's friends fill the space, the room fully taken over by Windsor Prep students plus Paxton. Flashy dance lights flicker colors every now and then as people mingle, play pool and video games, or take pictures on their digital cameras.

We're far enough away from Mom and Dad's party that we won't bother them. Although no one will probably get wild, seeing that the majority of their parents are also guests.

I glance at my reflection in the TV, making sure I look okay. Smoothing over my metallic silver dress, I then adjust my thick, black belt around my waist to make sure it's centered and check that my matching leggings underneath aren't wrinkled.

"Hey." Pax's voice comes from behind me, and with a huge smile, I spin to greet him.

"Hey!"

"Like my new wardrobe?" He lifts up his arms to showcase a salmon-colored polo and khaki pants.

I chuckle. "Trent's clothes?"

"Yep. Apparently, the Hartwicks' parties come with a dress code. Uncle Jeff would have a field day if he saw me in this."

"He sure would." I hold up my digital camera dangling from the wrist strap and start to take a picture.

"Don't you dare!"

Pax invades my space, every single cell in my body getting zapped by tiny lightning bolts as he tries to get my camera from me, wrapping his arms around my waist. His fingers move to tickle me, and I fold over into his hold, both of us laughing as fireworks go off in my heart.

"Give me the camera, Ivy." Pax's breath fans across my cheeks.

"Never!" I wiggle against him.

As we continue to play-wrestle, the heat of someone's stare falls on us. Both sensing it, we look up and spot Trent from across the room with his features twisted. The moment it registers with Paxton that my brother's watching us, he immediately moves away from me.

"Paxton! We need you on our team!" someone calls from the pool table.

"You got it!" he responds a little too quickly and gets away from me as fast as possible.

Trent's interest shifts, and he's no longer looking at me or Pax as he goes to play a video game with his friends.

The music gets louder, and more people show up as the night moves on. I've pretty much stayed on one side of the room with my friends from school, while Pax stays on the opposite end.

Every once in a while, I glance over to see what he's doing, and my most recent check-in has made my hopeful heart plummet.

He's sitting on the couch with several junior girls surrounding him. They're all tuned in, clinging to every word he says while his face lights up as he speaks. The joy emanating from his smile shows just how much he loves the attention.

My heart falls lower and lower.

I'm not stupid. I'm aware of his growing reputation, and I know that he has girls over to his place whenever he's not expecting me.

But maybe I am stupid for thinking he'd consider me more than what I am—and more than whatever kind of relationship he has with those girls.

"Ms. Hartwick?" Stella, one of our housekeepers, taps me on my arm, getting me out of my head.

"Yes?"

Stella's face tugs in disappointment as she says, "Your mother would like you to make an appearance upstairs."

My shoulders slump, my entire body language whining with my voice. "Seriously?"

"I'm sorry, sweetie. She wants you to say hello to the Dames."

Nodding, I know I have no choice.

I follow Stella up the stairs, leaving my friends and the vivacious party behind. Frustration turns my mouth into a frown as I make my way to the ballroom, not to mention the building resentment that *I'm* being pulled away from the party. Just me. Not me *and* Trent.

By the time I enter the glamorous event Mom has put together, my arms are folded across my chest, and my face has a permanent scowl on it.

There's a jazz band playing upbeat music, and some couples dance, while others are mingling over glasses of wine at their tables. The chatter and laughter are loud, indicating that the alcohol has already hit their bloodstream.

"Ivy," Mom says, coming over to me with an extended arm. "You couldn't have freshened up before coming in here?" she whispers between her teeth with a forceful smile plastered on her face.

Before I can respond, a group of women is coming up to me and kissing me on the cheek. One of them, with so much hairspray in her hair that it doesn't move when her head does, tells me how she moved away ages ago and hasn't seen me since I was a toddler.

"You're blossoming into such a lovely young lady," the woman says.

"Thanks." I glance over at Mom, who's glaring at me. Clearing my throat, I correct myself. "I mean, thank you."

"Your mother tells us that you're looking forward to becoming a Dame in a few years. Let me tell you, the Maryland chapter is by far the best!"

"That's good." I shift from foot to foot, trying my best to be polite while wanting to run away.

"And who knows, maybe by the time you become a Dame, your mother will become co-chair!"

"Oh, you!" Mom hushes her, and the group falls into a fit of chuckles, and I feel like I'm missing out on some inside joke.

Once my conversation with those ladies is finished, Mom drags me around the room to say hello to the other guests. Dad is too preoccupied with his associates from work to say more than two words to me, while the parents of my friends in the game room pry for information on how the high school party is going.

By the time I've made the rounds, it's getting closer to midnight, and my cheeks hurt from faking a smile. Mom finally lets me be excused so I can carry on with the night, but when I enter into the quiet hallway, I become depleted.

My body feels heavy as I shuffle my feet along the floor. Instead of going back to my party, I decide to go to my bedroom to have some alone time.

When I get to the only spot in this house that feels like home, I stare at myself in my mirror. Disappointment fills the space between my bones, knowing that I'm not the daughter Mom wishes she had, and I'm not the girl Paxton wants.

I'm just me.

Wiping the smudged eyeliner from under my eyes, I try not to fixate on how differently I envisioned tonight going. But my mind can't help but imagine what it would be like getting my first kiss from Paxton as the clock struck midnight.

I check the time, and it's minutes away from 2007.

Maybe with a stroke of luck, this will be the year everything changes. I'll no longer feel small and uncomfortable in my own skin. I'll feel like *me,* and that will be enough.

"There you are." Pax's voice comes from nowhere. I twist to see him entering my room, and I hate the way my heart does a little dance as he steps closer to me. "I've been looking everywhere for you."

"Didn't seem like you missed me much when you had a crowd of girls around you earlier," I blurt out. His brows raise in surprise, and honestly, I'm just as shocked that flew out of my mouth. Blood rushes to my cheeks because this is the first time I've acknowledged my jealousy. I try to mask my flushed face by focusing my attention on the floor. "Sorry, I'm just annoyed because my mom made me schmooze with her guests—plus, tonight isn't ending like I'd hoped."

He moves closer until his shoes are in my direct line of vision. "What were you hoping for?" The tone of his voice rolls over my body, causing goose bumps to rise.

I shrug, trying to come off cool as my face nearly burns off.

Then, my entire insides light on fire as Pax hooks his finger under my chin, tilting it up to look at him. My pulse whirls in my ears as my heart thrashes against my ribcage. The sight of his mesmerizing hazel eyes this close makes me weak at the knees, and I understand why every other girl is drawn to him. There's mischief and temptation weaving through his multicolored irises, making it impossible to look anywhere else. I'm so transfixed by him, I almost miss it when he speaks again.

"What were you hoping for, Rebel?"

The sound of his nickname for me makes it harder to breathe.

"I…" I swallow, building up the courage to admit my desire. "I was hoping someone would kiss me at midnight."

He smirks, his attention dropping to my lips, then back to my eyes.

Nervousness blasts through my veins.

He removes his finger from my chin, and just as I'm about to back away in disappointment, he splays out the rest of his hand, cupping my cheek.

Oh my god. He's about to kiss me.

I'm going to be kissed by Paxton Rhodes.

Neither of us breaks the other's stare as the space between us gets smaller and smaller. An invisible string wraps around our bodies, drawing us closer, the heat between us intensifying.

He parts his lips, and my lashes flutter closed.

"Pax?" Trent's voice floats from down the hall, immediately destroying the moment.

In the blink of an eye, Paxton is on the other side of the room, rubbing the back of his neck as he sighs. He almost looks…angry? Like he's pissed at himself that he almost just kissed me.

I go to speak, but Trent beats me to the punch. "Pax, are you up here?"

"Yeah." Pax sticks his head out of my room. "I was just checking to see if your sister made it through socializing with the Dames."

"Oh." Trent appears and looks at me, asking, "You good?"

"Yeah. I'll be downstairs in a minute."

"Okay." He turns to Paxton. "Dude, come on, Poppy is looking for you, and she—" He stops himself, glancing at me, then goes to whisper something in Pax's ear.

Pax's cheeks lift as he excitedly chuckles. "All right, I'll be right there," he responds, and Trent starts his journey back to the party. Pax goes to follow him, but turns back to me. "Don't spend all your time up here, okay? I really want to hang out with my other Hartwick friend too."

As if he just threw billions of needles at all the party balloons downstairs, all my hope deflates. His words of seeing me as a friend puncture me straight in the chest, letting me know that what happened a few moments ago was a lapse in judgment and not something I should assume would happen again.

I nod, and he gives me a soft smile before leaving.

Pax disappears to be with Trent, and I realize that the two times tonight when we've gotten close, he immediately stopped it because of my brother. I'm his best friend's little sister, and I'm beginning to think he'll always keep that line drawn between us.

Emotion wells behind my eyes, and I bite down on my lip to keep myself in check.

I now know why it's called a crush.

Because wanting a person you can never have destroys you bit by bit. The weight of their presence feels thrilling at first, until it's too late to realize that you've been crushed by the false hope of someone you're not allowed to have.

I could never tell if Pax liked me back, and truthfully, I'm still not sure. But I know he doesn't hesitate to be with other girls, so that should be a sign that he most certainly doesn't think of me the way I think of him.

A fuse gets lit inside me. It's small but mighty, and

although I might always have a crush on Paxton, I don't want to be the girl who waits for him when he waits for no one.

2007 is the year I'm going to start building my confidence.

CHAPTER EIGHTEEN

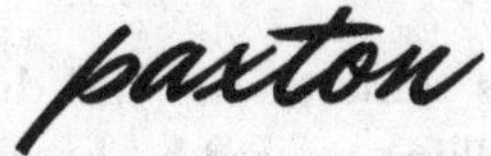

2007

June

TRENT'S PARENTS are away visiting their friend's new estate for the weekend, so it seemed like the perfect opportunity to take advantage of the end of junior year.

We got the guys from the team together to spend the day hanging out in Trent's backyard—and I use the term "backyard" very loosely. It's more of an entertainment complex, with a tennis and basketball court, an in-ground pool, a terrace with a fire pit and seating arrangements, and a large cabana area.

"You guys wanna hit the pool?" Trent asks as we finish off our basketball game.

"Fuck yeah," Harris, our teammate, responds, already taking off his sweat-stained T-shirt.

We all follow his lead, heading to the pool. Our team is on the offseason until the end of August, so we have time to fuck off and have a little more leeway to act like assholes. The twelve of us together, with all this free time during summer break, is a recipe for trouble, and all of us can't wait.

"I'll go grab us some towels and drinks," Trent calls out as he starts walking toward his house.

Reaching the pool, I immediately spot Ivy effortlessly moving through the crystal blue water. When she notices us approaching, a sparkling smile appears on her face.

"Hey, guys," Ivy says with a tickle of amusement in her voice.

"Hey," we all say in unison.

We congregate near the tables and chairs, dropping our belongings and waiting for something to drink before we dive into our next activity.

Ivy slowly steps out of the pool, water whooshing around her body as she gracefully ascends. She's wearing a neon purple bikini, and her hair is up in a loose bun. As she rounds the corner, making her way to us, I notice she looks…different.

With finals and all the end-of-the-school-year chaos, it's been a while since I've spent time with Ivy. She still came to my apartment to update Uncle Jeff on my plays after my asinine move on New Year's, but the season came to an end shortly after, and she hasn't dropped by as much. I saw her briefly on her fifteenth birthday back in March, but she was running out the door with some friends to go see a movie. Since then, I've hung out with her and Trent at scattered times, but she was always fully clothed.

This is the first time I'm seeing more of her.

I swallow, watching the way the droplets of water roll down the length of her body.

Suddenly, I realize I'm not the only one who's keen on

how mature she's gotten. The guys on my team are also staring and being really fucking obvious about it.

Possessiveness claws at my chest in a way I've never known before as I watch her talk with them.

"Your towel is over there," I interrupt her conversation and gesture with my chin to a stray towel on a chair, which I'm assuming is hers.

Ivy's brows knit together, puzzled, but then she flips back to her exchange with Harris and James, laughing at something they said.

I can't even hear their back and forth because of the pounding in my ears. Blood rushes to my face out of envy as I watch Ivy flirt. The others have their eyes glued to her, noticing her in ways that make my insides rage with red-hot jealousy.

"Get your towel on, Ivy." My voice comes out in a command, the deepened pitch forcing everyone to turn and stare at me. Some of the guys make faces, knowing why I snapped, but I don't pay them any mind. My direct line of sight is on Ivy, who's giving me a fiery death stare.

We're several feet away from each other, but the air is so thick, no one dares to walk in between our staring match. My heart pounds as tension wraps around my muscles.

Ivy doesn't move an inch.

Except for now, when her lips twitch as they curl up into a taunting smirk.

"No," she says.

My teammates erupt into a fit of varying sounds, most of them taking jabs or laughing at me.

"But," Ivy interrupts the noise. "I *was* just about to go inside and grab something to eat." She sashays over to her towel and wraps it around her wet body, making sure to lock eyes with me when she does. "Would anyone like something to eat?"

Sid, the horniest motherfucker on our team, opens his mouth to say something, and I pin him with a glare. If he even *thinks* about saying something remotely close to an innuendo, I'll make it so he can never play hockey again.

When he notices the wrathful glower on my face, he shuts his mouth.

"We're gonna order some pizzas," Harris says. "But thanks, Ivy."

She nods and goes toward her house. Once we watch her walk through the sliding glass doors, all madness breaks loose.

"You got a thing for Ivy!" James accuses me, and the others chime in.

"No, I fucking don't!"

"Then what the hell was that towel bullshit about?"

"Seriously," Sid complains. "We were all enjoying the view."

The second he says that, my jaw flexes, and Elias points his index finger at me. "There's that look on his face again!" He laughs while calling me out.

Panic rises in my chest, and my cheeks get even hotter. "Shut up!" I snap, the anger in my voice demanding them to listen. "What the fuck is wrong with all of you? Ivy is Trent's little sister—she's off-limits. None of you should've been gawking at her like she's your next hookup."

"What?" Trent appears with a stack of towels in one hand and a case of soda in the other.

Shit.

Everyone fidgets uncomfortably in their spot, me included, as he makes his way closer.

"Did I hear that correctly?" Trent addresses everyone except me. "Did Pax just say you were checking out my sister?" A jumbled noise of throats clearing and mumbled replies is the best answer Trent can get. "Well, that's the first and last time. I know she's getting older, but I also know all of you—*none* of you are allowed to touch her. Like Pax said, she's off-limits." My stomach sinks. "Got it?"

Once we all reply, agreeing to never let that happen, Trent allows the energy to shift back to how it was earlier. A bunch of people jump into the pool after downing their drinks.

I'm about to dive in next when Trent stops me.

"Thanks for speaking up, man," he says while the others are out of earshot. "I knew I could count on my best friend to help ward off dickheads when the time came." He laughs while he glances over his shoulder at our team.

Warring emotions slice my insides into tiny scraps.

"Any time, man," I manage to squeeze out of my throat that's slowly constricting.

Trent heads into the pool, and I watch as all of them have fun.

For my entire early childhood, people were always coming in and out. No one was constant, including my mom. It was impossible to be close with any of my friends because I knew I'd always get uprooted eventually.

I've waited *years* to have a friend like Trent.

But then there's Ivy. She's also an amazing friend, and I've denied any lingering feelings of wishing our friendship would shift into something else. I even told myself the New Year's Eve mishap was on the shot of vodka I had earlier in the night, despite being completely sober when I almost leaned in to kiss her.

But I'm not sure I can lie to myself much longer, considering how enraged I became at the prospect of another guy having her.

A pit in my gut burrows itself inside me and grows until there's an ache.

I can't like Ivy.

I can't *do* anything about liking Ivy.

Because it would destroy the only two friendships I've ever had. The only two people I've ever cared about aside from Uncle Jeff. And the two people who've cared about me in return.

My head gets cloudy from my overwhelming thoughts. I excuse myself, needing some space.

I slip through the sliding glass door, making my way through their mudroom and into the ornate kitchen. Going to get a water bottle, I try to catch my breath, even though I have no clue why I can't breathe to begin with.

"Can you grab me one?" Ivy says from the other side of the refrigerator door, causing me to jump.

Closing the fridge, I go to pass her the water and am met with a harsh scowl.

"What?" I ask, the thoughts of her being off-limits seeping from my brain the more I stare at her in a bikini top and cutoff shorts.

"Care to explain what that whole towel thing was about?" The sound of her snarky little attitude bleeding through her voice gets a forbidden fire crackling in my chest.

"Care to explain why you were flirting with my teammates?"

"Why can't I flirt?"

"Because you're…you—I don't know, you just can't."

"So you can get with whoever you want, but I'm not allowed to?"

"Not when it's someone on my team."

Ivy shrugs as if it's no big loss. "Guess I'll just keep talking to Kellen, then."

My spine straightens. "Who's Kellen?"

"A guy from school. So that shouldn't bother you. Or..." She tilts her head, assessing me in a sarcastic manner. "*Does* it bother you?"

I bite down on my bottom lip to stop myself from speaking the truth. "No," I manage to get out. "Why would it?"

"I don't know, Pax, why might it bother you?" The pleasure she gets from putting me in the hot seat is evident in the way her cheeks lift up.

"It doesn't. You're my friend, and I just want to make sure whoever you're going to talk to treats you right."

"Oh yes, you've made it very clear that we're friends."

There's a pinch at my heart, knowing she's talking about New Year's Eve and knowing neither of us has ever acknowledged it. "Ivy—"

"No, it's okay. I'm glad you're my friend." She pauses for a beat, her gaze fixed on me. "But you know what?"

"What?"

She tiptoes closer, every movement slowly calculated, until she's invading my personal space. "I think a hint of jealousy also looks cute on you."

My mouth drops open, fucking stunned that Ivy just called me out.

She giggles, pleased as hell with herself, and pivots on her heels. I'm frozen in shock as I watch her walk away as if she just won a game I wasn't aware we were playing.

When I'm finally able to think straight and get my feet moving, I peer out the back window and watch Ivy join the rest of the group. She drops her jeans shorts and carefully steps into the pool.

But for a brief moment, she looks over her shoulder, toward the kitchen window. Although she most likely can't see me, she smirks as if she's expecting me to be watching her.

My bloodstream whirls with enticement.

Ivy is off-limits.

She knows this.

I know this.

But I don't know if the two of us will be able to tame this temptation by playing whatever game has just started.

CHAPTER NINETEEN

July

MOM AND DAD took Trent to some special academic luncheon with Dad's associates so it'll look good on his college applications, which means I have this mammoth house to myself for the time being.

On this lazy summer day, I stretch out on my bed watching an episode of *Gilmore Girls* while occasionally glancing at my new Jack Sparrow poster that's hanging next to my TV. I tap on my laptop, setting up a Facebook page, which is kinda like MySpace, only boring in my opinion. You can't change the background or pick a song to play when someone visits your page, but a lot of people are switching over, so I figured I'd give it a try.

"What's up, Rebel?" Pax appears from thin air, making me yelp in surprise. "Whoa, didn't mean to scare you."

"How the hell did you get in here?"

He makes his way toward my bed. "Your workers

know me by now, so I asked them to let me in, and they did."

"Jeez, so much for security," I joke, sitting upright. I scoot over so Pax has some room, and he plops down next to me on my bed.

My nerve endings tingle with excitement.

He's been hanging out in my room more often, popping over to say hello whenever he's here to visit Trent. I guess he didn't get the memo that Trent isn't due back for a couple of hours, so this time around we'll be together in my room a lot longer than usual.

"What are you working on?" Pax peeks over my shoulder to check out my laptop.

"Just finishing up my Facebook page."

"Ah. I still have to make one of those."

I turn my computer to face him. "Go ahead. You can start your account now."

Taking it from me, he moves to lean his back against my headboard, and I follow suit, sitting right next to him. Our arms touch the teeniest amount, but it's enough to make my insides think that I'm going on a roller coaster. But even though my stomach twists and jumps as I watch him make his account, I try to act as neutral as possible.

When Pax gets to the "About Me" page, he speaks it out loud. "High school: East Valley." He types his answers, continuing to talk. "Hometown: It's complicated." I chuckle at his loaded joke. "Sex: Your place or mine?"

"You're such a perv." I roll my eyes.

"Would it be better if I put 'yes, please'?"

My attention falls off him. "No."

"I'm teasing, Rebel." Pax takes his arm and makes a space between my back and the headboard, wrapping around my waist.

Every single particle explodes, heart racing at the speed of light as he tugs me in closer to his side.

"I'll delete it," he says, paying no mind to the fact that he's holding me in a possessive embrace as if it's a natural occurrence.

"O-okay."

A smirk plays on his lips as he does what he says, leaving "sex" and "relationship status" blank on his Facebook page.

Heat swirls in my veins, a flurry of eagerness barreling through me, making it hard to breathe or think or fucking exist with his arm wrapped around me.

"I need a profile picture," he states.

I say nothing because I literally can't.

Pax takes it upon himself to break our contact for a brief moment, reaching for my digital camera on my nightstand. When he settles back next to me, he places his arm where it was, only this time his hand is slightly lower. His pinky finger touches the space where my tank top and shorts part.

A rush of electricity zaps my body.

Paxton's finger is touching my hip.

"Ready?" he asks, lifting the camera up.

"Wait, you want me in it?" I blink, surprised.

"Yeah."

Without any hesitation, I smile right into the camera as he takes a selfie of us. My breathing becomes erratic as I watch him upload it to my laptop and make the image his profile picture.

"You know that'll probably ruin your chances of hooking up with someone," I state, looking at how couple-y we appear.

"If that's the case, then maybe we should make it your profile picture too." He can barely get the words out before starting to laugh.

I give him a playful smack to the chest even though there's a prideful part of me that enjoys he's a little bit jealous. Seeing his reaction last month when I was being flirty with the team was something I never expected. I didn't purposefully do it to get a rise out of him, but I'd be lying if I didn't wish I could do it again.

It was also the day it clarified that he does, in fact, like me in some capacity. Although I'm not sure if I can lure him out of the friendship territory, the way his hand is clinging to me feels like we're straddling a *very* thin line.

"What else are you up to today?" Pax asks, putting my computer to the side.

"Just watching *Gilmore Girls*."

"Guess that means I have to watch it too while I wait for your brother." Pax stretches out his legs, getting more comfortable. "Where is he anyway?"

"Trent's at a lunch, meeting people who will make his college applications look good."

Pax nods. "Does he get a choice in that or no?"

"No. Our futures are pretty much planned out for us. Trent will go to Johns Hopkins University—which is only an hour away, so you don't have to worry about him vanishing," I clarify, and Pax smiles. "And he'll study finance, just like Dad, and join a fraternity, just like Dad, and then eventually work at a firm, just like Dad."

"That sounds awful."

"Yeah."

"What about you?" Pax asks, his gaze dancing all over my face as if he can't figure out where to focus. "Is your future planned out?"

"I will be inducted into the Dames after high school, and I can go to college if I want, but it won't matter where or what I study because I'll be married into a well-off family that's part of our inner circle and become a trophy wife."

"Fuck that!" He immediately sits upright, his arm letting go of me. "Ivy, you told me a while ago that you wanted to study art history. Do you still want to?"

"Yeah."

"All right, so do it. Go to a good school, one that you love, and make a life for yourself outside of this high-society bullshit." His cheeks become blotchy from getting pissed off. I've gotten so used to hearing that this was my future, I never thought fighting against it would be worth it. "Fuck the Dames. Fuck marrying a rich asshole you don't love. Fuck becoming a trophy wife."

I peer up at him, a smile parting my lips.

"What are you grinning about?" he asks, his shoulders relaxing.

"It's nice knowing that someone is angry on my behalf," I admit, sensing my own cheeks warm up.

"I just want what's best for you, and following that plan isn't it."

"Thank you," the words fall out softly.

"Of course. It's important to have someone remind you of your worth."

"When's the last time someone did that for you?"

Pax's gaze instantly drops, focusing off me. He's silent for too long of a stretch, and my heart starts to ache for him. Reaching out, I gently tug on his arm, gesturing for him to come back to sit next to me.

He moves to where he originally was, only this time his arm is by his side. I don't mind, though. I study him and the sorrowful expression that's etched on his face.

"I don't like talking about this kind of stuff," Pax says, clearing his throat.

"I get it." Somehow, both of us lowered ourselves a bit, and now our heads are resting on the headboard as we turn to look at each other. "But I want you to know, I want what's best for you too. That's what being a good friend is."

That time, the meaning of *friend* is sincere. No layered implication behind the word, only the purest definition.

The line between Pax's brows eases as he smiles in relief.

My chest stirs, wanting to understand more of him. The brokenness of his past, his dreams for his future, and everything in between. "You want to go to college?" I ask.

"Not really. My goal is to play professional hockey. Besides, I couldn't afford it."

"There's always community college, and you could take out a loan if need be."

"Nah, I'll save schooling for the straight-A kids." He gives me a playful nudge. "For now, I'll keep my sights set on hockey."

I nod, watching Paxton shift his attention to the TV. He doesn't want to talk anymore, and I'm not going to push him. So, instead, the two of us lie side by side in my bed watching *Gilmore Girls* for the next hour.

We don't touch. We don't talk much.

But the way he's gently breathing, relaxing into my mattress, lets me know that there's some sort of comfort he finds in this moment.

And I feel it just the same.

CHAPTER TWENTY

August

"REBEL? REBEL?"

The sound of Pax's voice makes me wonder if I was dreaming of him as my eyes flutter open. Checking the time, it's a little past midnight, so I put my head back on my pillow and attempt to fall back asleep.

My door slowly creaks open. "Rebel?"

"What the hell?" I spring awake, realizing I wasn't dreaming.

"I need Gatorade," Pax tries to whisper as he trips over something.

"What?" Popping out of bed, I turn on my lamp, letting the soft light brighten up the space. When I spot Pax, he has a lazy smile on his stupidly hot face, and his eyes are heavy and glassy. "Are you drunk?"

"I got everyone drunk," he slurs, trying to steady his footing.

"Who's everyone?"

"Harris, James, Sid." He holds up his hand as if trying to count. "And Trent. Plus, me."

I massage my temples, already anticipating the headache their hijinks are about to cause me. I didn't even know the guys on the team were over. Last I heard, Trent and Pax were going to watch a movie in the game room and were going to pass out down there.

"Did my mom know the rest of the guys were coming over?"

"No. But focus, Ivy. I need Gatorade." Pax forces a serious expression, and I bite back my laughter. "There's no Gatorade in your fridge, and I don't know where you people store your fucking Gatorade in your fancy house."

"Let's go," I say, shaking my head. Pax's gaze languidly dances over my body, the corners of his mouth gently lifting.

Suddenly aware that I'm in an old lace camisole and rolled-up Soffe shorts, a wave of heat hits my cheeks, but I try to ignore it, leading Pax out of my room and down the hall.

Somehow tripping over his feet, he crashes right into me. "Shit—" he starts to say, but I slam my hand over his mouth.

"Shh!"

The last thing he needs is my parents finding out that he's drunk and got Trent wasted too. He'd never be allowed back over.

We tiptoe downstairs, and I get Pax to hang tight while I go grab several Gatorades that he couldn't find.

When we miraculously make it to the game room without a peep, Pax stops before we open the door. "Wait." His hand carefully touches my arm.

I pause, my brows drawing in as he places the drinks in his hand on the floor, then takes the ones in my hand and does the same. "What are you doing?" I ask.

He doesn't answer, but instead tugs his Blink-182 shirt off.

My heart gallops as I admire him in a white tank top. Swallowing, I ask again, "What are you doing?"

"Put this on." He extends his shirt toward me.

"Why?"

Pax sighs as if he's already over having this conversation with me. "Because they're gonna stare at you, and I'm gonna hate it," he admits, making butterflies go haywire in my belly.

"A guy shouldn't tell a girl what she can and cannot wear." I cross my arms, even though I get a certain type of satisfaction seeing him envious.

"I know, but I'm drunk and too tired to have this argument with you. Put it on." He holds it closer to me. "Your brother is passed out, so we don't have to worry."

I blink as the pieces finally connect in my brain. Pax doesn't want to cross the line with me because of Trent. Not because of some other girl or because he doesn't like me as much as I like him—it's because of my *brother*.

That's fucking stupid.

"You don't want me to be your girlfriend because of Trent?" I rip the Band-Aid off, getting straight to the point instead of beating around the bush like we have been since New Year's.

"I don't do relationships."

"Okay, a hookup then. Whatever you wanna call it."

"I'm not gonna hook up with you."

The butterflies abruptly die as my stomach falls to the floor, becoming crushed by his statement. "Oh," I softly reply.

Pax lets out an exasperated sound, his head hanging as he leans his body weight against the wall. "I'm too shit-faced for this," he mumbles under his breath. Lifting his head back up, his eyes have difficulty focusing on my face as he begins to explain, his words slurring as the alcohol acts as his truth serum. "I moved around a lot when I was a kid. And not home to home—it was shelters, cars, motels. I never had a real friend until Trent and you. I don't wanna fuck up my friendship with the both of you over the fact that I think you're hot." He extends his hand out one more time. "Now please, put on my fucking shirt."

Reaching for the shirt, I take it from him while my clashing emotions ride a wild wave inside my chest. It's all out there in the open. He likes me, but he likes me too much that he won't do anything about it.

The dismay that's causing my heart to sink is suddenly met with a shot of hopefulness as I slip his T-shirt over my head, letting it fall down my body and hit my thighs. The intoxicating scent of mint and spice is like a warm hug around my curves, enough to put me in a hypnotic trance as I stare at Pax through rose-colored glasses.

"I like the way it looks on you." His voice gets raspy in a way I've never heard before. But before either of us let our hormones whisk us away, he stops it by picking up the Gatorades.

We silently open the door to the game room, the overwhelming smell of liquor quickly canceling out the lingering Paxton scent I got when putting on his shirt.

"Oh shit, Ivy's here!" James calls out the second he spots me, causing Harris and Sid to cheer.

I laugh at the sight before me: my brother passed out on the couch with a missing sock, Harris poorly attempting *Dance Dance Revolution,* with Sid and James off to his side, purposefully hitting the wrong parts of the platform to mess him up, and discarded bottles and cups everywhere.

"Hey, guys," I answer, placing down the Gatorade.

"Your brother's a fucking lightweight," Harris informs me, out of breath from erratically trying to dance.

I glance over at Trent, who's loudly snoring, and I'm tempted to run back upstairs to grab my camera.

No one says anything about me wearing Pax's shirt, which lets me know they're too drunk to notice or care.

"You wanna drink?" James asks me.

"Sure," I say, at the same time Pax says, "No."

Twisting my head to look at him, I fix him with an agitated scowl before answering again. "I'll have whatever you guys are having."

"You're not getting drunk, though," Pax declares. "I can only get one Hartwick shit-faced at a time. And your parents will have my head if they find out I got you drunk."

I watch as he takes it upon himself to pour several liquids into a plastic cup for me. His eyes lock with mine as he hands it over, paying attention to my every move as I bring the cup to my lips. As the alcohol hits my tongue, my face scrunches.

Pax chuckles. "Okay, good. I don't have anything to worry about."

"At least not for tonight," I say, handing the cup back to him. "I'm sure at some point in my life, I'm going to get as drunk as you guys. But for now, you can finish this."

He finds the exact spot I took a sip from and brings the drink to his lips. His gaze fixates on me as he gulps down the entire cup, and for whatever reason, heat rolls down my spine.

I've now come to realize that something is definitely wrong with me if I think the basic activity of *drinking* is in some way sexy when Paxton does it.

The moment breaks when Sid joins in, helping himself to another round of whatever alcohol they have.

Even though all of them are supposed to be calming down and nursing their bottles of Gatorade, they somehow got a second wind. The night moves on with Trent still passed out on the couch, while the rest of them get even more wasted while attempting to teach me a drinking game called Kings, sans alcohol for me.

My cheeks hurt from smiling and laughing at their ridiculousness. They couldn't keep up with their own game, all five of us now sitting down on the floor as I watch their heads get too heavy to hold up.

"Craziest place you guys hooked up?" Sid slurs, asking all of us the question after he asked numerous absurd ones.

"Parking lot of Taco Bell," James blurts out.

"Locker room." Harris leisurely smirks with pride. "Hers."

The guys try to give him high-fives while commending him, then their attention falls on Paxton.

He shakes his head, not wanting to answer the question. "I don't know."

"Probably because there are too many options," James jokes.

"What about you, Ivy?" Sid focuses on me, his eyes barely open, but I can sense the alertness in wanting to know my answer.

"What the fuck?" Pax interjects. "You can't ask her that shit." As much as he wishes his words had gusto behind them, I can tell he's slowly fading out.

"I said hook up. That could mean anything. It doesn't have to mean sex," Sid clarifies. "You've kissed someone before, right, Ivy?"

The warmth of Pax's stare on the side of my face has me fighting back a smile as I nod.

"Who?" Pax suddenly gets a rush of energy as he moves toward me, the scent of vodka filling my nostrils.

There's no point in trying to hold back my smirk as I witness the jealousy unfurl in his muscles. There's something so pleasing about watching cool-as-a-cucumber Paxton get riled up over me being a typical teenager and kissing another teenager.

Did he seriously think I would never kiss anyone?

Boys are idiots.

I chuckle. "Kellen."

"Isn't he on the football team?" James chimes in.

"The football team, Ivy!" Paxton reprimands me as if disappointed in my life choices, causing more laughter to fall from my lips.

"What can I say? I'm into athletes." Sass is wrapped around my statement, and it lands on Paxton. His cheeks get blotchy as the hypnotic hazel eyes flicker with another dose of possessiveness.

The speed of my fluttering heart picks up pace, hitting against my chest. Neither of us is capable of tearing our attention away from the other.

Luckily, Sid moves on to his next question.

Before I know it, the energy in the room quiets down. Harris lightly snores as he spreads out on the other couch, James dozes off on one recliner, while Sid passes out on the other.

Pax fights to stay awake as he sprawls out on an air mattress. I toss him one of our many spare blankets, and he's barely capable of getting it to cover his legs.

Chuckling, I crouch down to help him, neatly laying the blanket over him. He softly smiles as I spend a few seconds taking care of him.

"Good night, Pax," I whisper.

"Wait." He reaches out so I don't move away from him. "When was it?"

"When was what?"

"When did you kiss Kellen?"

My brows knit together. "A few months ago, why?"

"After New Year's?"

"Yeah."

Pax forces his eyes to open wider even though they're fighting against him. "Was he your first kiss?"

Unease stirs in my stomach. "Yes."

His face drops, and his eyelids suddenly shut. Silence drapes the room while I wait for him to say or do something. But he doesn't.

Assuming he fell asleep, I gradually rise and tiptoe away from him and the rest of the boys.

"It was supposed to be me," Pax mumbles.

Spinning around to make sure I heard him correctly, I spot him with his face smushed into the pillow, staring at me through tiny slits in his eyelids. "What?" I softly ask.

"I should've been your first kiss, Rebel."

Goose bumps scatter across my skin at his declaration. The void between us seems deeper, yet filled with an intense yearning of not wanting to miss any more opportunities. How someone can feel so close yet so far away causes my ribs to tightly squeeze around my heart.

Our connection is locked on each other until Pax can no longer hold it, and his eyelids gently close, drifting into sleep.

Quietly, I turn the light off and whisper into the dark room, "I wish it was you, Pax."

CHAPTER TWENTY-ONE

PRESENT

"YOU'RE HERE!" Lucille beams, wrapping me in a warm embrace before I can fully enter the lodge she and Trent rented out for their winter getaway.

"It's great to see you, Lucille," I reply, trying to survey the space to see who's next to greet me. I fought with myself the whole car ride here, wanting to turn around so I don't have to be under the same roof as Paxton until Monday morning. But I know how important this is to Lucille and Trent, so here I am.

I haven't seen Paxton since the night Warren barged into my apartment. A part of me wonders what would've happened if we weren't interrupted. Where would that night of teenage nostalgia have led us? Would we have been sucked into a moment of stupidity like we did once before? Would I have unleashed old secrets and let my grief spill out? Would I have kicked him out before it got to either of those options?

I think I'm better off not knowing the answer.

"Let me show you around and have you meet the rest of the gang." Lucille takes my wheelie suitcase out of my hand, being the perfect host as she gives me a tour.

I've seen my fair number of lavish estates during my lifetime, but nothing quite like this. It's as if a mansion and a log cabin had a baby and created a flawless vision of Lucille's winter getaway. The grain of the oak floors sparkles with the wood's natural charm, creating an inviting energy. A hint of pine needles and peppermint swirls around us, not in an overpowering way but in more of a cozy cottage feel. Considering how huge this house is, it's impressive that it can capture a snuggly essence. The first floor is spacious, with a large kitchen flowing into a living room with a fireplace. I make a mental note to make sure I spend some time reading there.

Leading me to the wooden staircase, Lucille gestures to the hallway off to the right. "The guys are staying there, while us ladies are upstairs." As we ascend, she keeps filling me in. "There's a loose itinerary for the weekend, but nothing's set in stone, so if you'd rather do something else, by all means, please do it and enjoy your time here. This isn't just a weekend for me and Trent. It's for all of us to squeeze a mini-vacation in."

We round a corner and enter what seems to be a master suite. There are three other women chatting with each other while they sip mimosas.

"Here she is!" Lucille introduces me to the rest of her bridesmaids. "This is Ivy, Trent's sister."

All three of them rush up to me with the same amount of enthusiasm, talking over one another.

"I'm Celeste," a woman with a gelled back, high bun says loud enough for me to hear and the others to quiet down. "I'm *so* excited to meet you."

"Likewise," I say to this complete stranger.

"Pia," says another woman, gracefully extending her hand out for me to shake. She's tall, with a model-like physique and brilliant emerald eyes. "We're beyond thrilled you could join us for the weekend. I know my Delta Gamma sister like the back of my hand, and it means the world that you're here."

"Oh, you all are sorority sisters?"

"Me, Celeste, and Pia are," Lucille explains. "And Felicity is my cousin, who might as well be my sister at this point."

"Hi!" Felicity singsongs the one word with a southern drawl before giving me a tight hug. It must be a family thing.

"Let's get this woman something to drink," Pia says, drifting to the dresser to pour me a mimosa.

I'm able to acclimate quickly, relaxing on the buttery-soft chenille couch, while Felicity sits next to me, and Lucille and Celeste lounge on the king-sized bed.

"Since Lucille and Trent went ahead and planned this event themselves," Pia says, throwing a playful glare at Lucille. "There wasn't much maid-of-honor duties I could do with pre-planning, but now that we're all here, I can finally give you ladies this!" She disappears and comes back with light pink present boxes wrapped with big, burlap bows on top.

Carefully handing out each gift, she gives me mine with my name beautifully written in calligraphy in the corner.

"Pia, you shouldn't have gotten us anything," Lucille states as she also gets handed a gift.

"Nonsense. This is your bachelorette weekend—whether your fiancé is here or not. Go ahead, open!"

We all follow her instructions, first taking out a light pink silk robe with our names embroidered on the front.

Felicity, Celeste, and I have *Bridesmaid* on the back, Pia showcases hers, which has *Maid of Honor,* and Lucille's white robe says *Bride.* Next to the robe is a smaller gift box, with an under-eye face mask, essential oils, lotion-infused gloves, and Tylenol.

We all thank her, and she gives us a round of hugs. "I figured I might as well include the Tylenol in case we get a little crazy with these mimosas." She chuckles.

"God willing!" Celeste lifts her nearly empty glass in celebration. "I'm kid-free for a couple of days and ready to get my drink on!" We laugh at her comment, then she turns her attention to me. "I know these three don't have any children yet, but what about you, Ivy? Are you a mom?"

"Uh, no." I politely smile, though it doesn't reach my eyes.

"Married? Boyfriend? Spill the tea. I already know all of their gossip, time to hear yours!"

"Oh my god, Ivy," Lucille interjects, shuffling off the bed. "We didn't even let you unpack yet—I'm sorry!" She shifts her attention to the other three. "I'm going to get her settled in her room, and then we'll reconvene."

Lucille leads me out of her master suite, and the second we're out of earshot, she whispers, "I'm sorry! I didn't tell them about Warren because I didn't want to air your dirty laundry, but maybe I should've given them a heads-up on what not to talk about."

"Don't worry about it. I swear it's no big deal," I assure her as she guides me into what I'm assuming will be my bedroom.

"I'll go talk with them—"

"Lucille, I appreciate it, but I truly mean it when I say I don't care. I'm not upset about breaking up with Warren, or any other guy I've been with over the past decade. I have no problem going back in there and telling

Celeste whatever gossip she wants to know about my plethora of douchebags."

Lucille finally lightens up, laughing. "Well, whenever you get your belongings put away, feel free to join us. Who knows, maybe one of the other women will be retelling their douchebag stories."

"You got it." I place my suitcase on my mattress, then glance over my shoulder. "Speaking of men, where are the guys? I haven't heard a sound from downstairs since I got here."

"They went to check out the main resort building. They should be back soon. Once they're here, we can officially start the festivities!"

Anticipation coiled in apprehension enters my bones. "Sounds good."

CHAPTER TWENTY-TWO

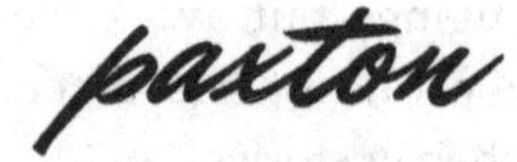

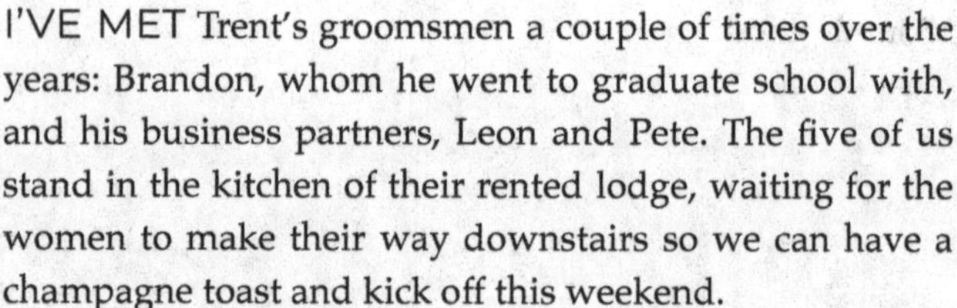

I'VE MET Trent's groomsmen a couple of times over the years: Brandon, whom he went to graduate school with, and his business partners, Leon and Pete. The five of us stand in the kitchen of their rented lodge, waiting for the women to make their way downstairs so we can have a champagne toast and kick off this weekend.

My heart officially lost its composure this morning. It's been beating erratically, thumping against my ribcage nonstop, waiting to see Ivy.

Lucille is the first to make an entrance, followed by three of her bridesmaids whose names didn't stick. One of them, who could very well be a model, fixates her attention on me, and I notice a flicker of desire in her eyes, but she's not the one I'm interested in spending my time with. Now or ever.

That person is reserved for the dark-haired beauty entering behind them, half of her body being swallowed by a knit sweater that she's tugging at the sleeves. Warmth fills my chest as she moves closer into my vicinity, just her mere presence setting me alight.

I watch as she and Trent greet each other with a stiff,

one-armed hug. He goes to introduce his groomsmen to her. "This is Brandon, Leon, and Pete."

"Nice to meet all of you," Ivy says as they each give her a hello.

Trent's attention lands on me. "And obviously you know Pax."

"I sure do." The sapphire shade of her eyes captivates me as something passes through them that is difficult for me to read, yet still makes my pulse whoosh through my veins.

"I heard the three of you were inseparable back in the day," Lucille says. "Trent was telling me some teenage stories. Sounds like you guys were quite the misfits."

Ivy's lips twist, not wanting to smile but unable to keep herself in check. "Yeah, we had some fun." My mind flashes to the ridiculous set of rules she came up with—the first one being that we can't bring up the past unless it's within the realm of some stupid teenage memory.

"We'll have plenty of time to hear the stories later," the model-looking bridesmaid interrupts, handing us each a flute of champagne. "For now, we're going to toast and get this party started!"

Once everyone has a glass, we raise it up as the bridesmaid leads the speech. "To Lucille and Trent, may you have an incredible bachelor-bachelorette party or winter weekend getaway—whatever the hell you two want to call it! And may the rest of us have one helluva time too!"

We cheer, our glasses clinking together. As I bring it up to my lips, I lock eyes with Ivy. Neither one of us breaks our connection as we tip the drink back. The heat in our stares hits me harder than the champagne ever will.

Ivy has been doing a phenomenal job at avoiding me all day. Granted, there were times our group broke off and did separate activities, but I can't help but notice how she's been at the opposite end of the room or grabs someone to talk with the moment I realize she's free.

After we spent some time on the snowmobiles while the women went to do something else, we all reconvened at the cabin.

"You guys want to hit up the bunny slopes before the evening?" Lucille asks all of us.

The group seems to be in agreement, myself included, until Ivy speaks up. "I'm not much of a skier, so I'm going to sit this one out."

Lucille's face drops. "You don't ski? Why didn't you tell me that?" Her attention whips to Trent. "Better yet, why didn't *you* tell me that when we were planning this?"

Trent shrugs. "I didn't know she doesn't ski."

"It's fine," Ivy assures Lucille. "I obviously knew you guys would want to ski at some point, so I brought a book with me. I plan on getting that fireplace going and drinking hot chocolate while curled up with a good story. Don't worry about me. You go have fun!"

"I feel awful you'll be alone."

"I'll hang back with her." The words tumble right out of my mouth to the point where my face looks just as shocked as Ivy's. Clearing my throat, I school my features. "I really shouldn't be doing too much physical activity anyway," I explain. "My ACL recently healed, and I don't want to risk fucking it up again."

"Didn't your doctor clear you?" Ivy asks, her jaw tensing as she tries to smile.

"It never hurts to be on the safe side." I give her a smirk, one that I know will get under her skin.

"It's settled then! Pax will keep Ivy company while we're out," Lucille confirms.

The group gets ready to head out while Ivy disappears upstairs. Once all of them leave, Ivy still doesn't emerge from her room.

"Stubborn pain in my ass," I mutter under my breath while I go to set up the space for her.

She said she wanted to get the fireplace going—well, I'm going to make it roaring.

She said she wanted hot chocolate—I'm going to make the most delicious mugful she's ever had.

I'll do whatever it takes to get Ivy to let me back into her life.

By the time the fireplace crackles, warming the large living area, I scour the kitchen for hot chocolate ingredients. Knowing Trent, he wouldn't have skimped on getting groceries delivered ahead of time.

I spend time whisking milk and cocoa powder in a small saucepan when I hear a slight creak coming from the staircase.

"About time you stopped hiding," I say, not looking over my shoulder but knowing she's there. I can feel it in the air—the shift of energy, the way my body reacts as if it's electrified whenever she's nearby.

"I wasn't hiding. I was changing my clothes and picking out which book to read," Ivy says, her voice getting closer as she speaks.

When I finally look her way, I quickly glance at the flare yoga pants she's wearing and sense my heart beating rapidly for an entirely different reason.

"You started the fire," she states.

"Yep, and I'm working on the hot chocolate now. Just

need to grab your chips from the pantry and you'll be all set."

"My chips?" Ivy approaches, peeking at the saucepan.

"Yeah. I made sure to pack a bag of Cool Ranch Doritos for you. Although they'll probably taste gross with hot chocolate, but I wouldn't put it past you."

"You remembered my favorite kind of chips?" The sound of her voice makes me pause. The words lose their edge as she breathes them out, incredulously.

Shifting my body toward her, she peers up at me as if she's taking me in for the first time. "Of course, I do," I state.

"What else do you remember?"

"I remember that you hate ketchup, you had an unhealthy obsession with *Pirates of the Caribbean*, crickets creep you out, you enjoyed documenting everything on your digital camera, you were Team Jacob, your favorite TV show is *Gilmore Girls*—should I go on?"

She blinks, as if not fully believing that she's awake and actually having this moment with me. So I step in closer, allowing the warmth from my body to fill the slim space between us.

"You remembered—"

"Everything, Ivy. I remember everything about you."

Her breathing gets unsteady, flowing from her parted lips. A flush color climbs up her neck and gradually paints her cheeks as I watch her in admiration. My ribcage rattles as I wait for a reply.

Realizing that I've rendered Ivy speechless, I decide to push my luck a little more. Taking my fingertips, I carefully swipe a stray hair away from her face. A slight hitch of her breath lights my bloodstream up with delight. I guess the "no physical contact" rule she made up doesn't include gentle touches.

"I knew you so well back then," I say, my volume softening. "Let me learn who you are now."

My hand trails down her shoulder and the length of her arm, stopping at her hand, which clutches a book. She still doesn't say anything, but I know my request isn't completely off the table because she would've told me to fuck off by now.

Conflicting emotions pull at her features. She goes to speak, but suddenly her nose wrinkles, and a look of disgust wipes away her initial thought. "Is something burning?" she asks.

"Shit." The realization has me twisting toward the stove where the milk settled in the saucepan.

"I'll make a new round."

"No, I'll do it," I say, moving to put the saucepan in the sink. "Go sit down by the fireplace and read your book like you planned. I'll bring your hot chocolate over in a few minutes." Her mouth opens to protest, but I immediately cut her off. "Don't fight me on something as little as hot chocolate, Ivy."

The little twist of her lips, holding back her smile, lets me know that I was correct—she was going to fight me on who was making her a drink. Instead of arguing, she nods and heads toward the couch next to the fireplace.

Neither of us speaks across the room as the time passes. When I finally walk over carrying our hot chocolate, I take a moment to notice how breathtaking she looks.

A beige wool blanket is wrapped around her lower half as she nestles into the corner of the couch. The glow of the fireplace casts an amber light over her face as she intently reads. Long, dark hair is pulled to one side, exposing her shoulder as the sleeve of her sweater hangs loosely on her.

"Here's your hot chocolate," I say, forcing Ivy's attention onto me as I offer her the drink.

"Didn't burn this one?"

"Can't make any promises. Drink at your own risk."

Sitting down next to her, she adjusts to face me. I watch as she brings the hot chocolate to her lips, the whipped cream on top hitting the tip of her nose, and she chuckles. She takes a sip, then quickly cleans off her nose before I have the opportunity to.

"How is it?" I ask, grinning.

"Not bad for a rookie."

Laughing, my attention drops down to her foot poking out of the blanket. She has on low-cut socks, and right above it, next to her ankle bone, is a very small inked image. "Do you have a tattoo?"

"Huh?" she responds, my question throwing her off. I gesture to her ankle as I lean in closer to see her tiny tattoo. It's extremely simple, as if someone took a black pen and drew a minimalist doodle of a flower. "Oh, yeah, just a little one," she says, slipping her foot back under the blanket.

"Can I see it again?" I ask, wanting the chance to memorize how it's delicately detailed into her skin.

"What? No. It's a tattoo, Pax. I'm sure this isn't your first time seeing one."

"It's my first time seeing *yours*."

Ivy readjusts herself, accidentally kicking the book she was reading into my line of sight.

My head cocks to the side when I notice the cover is a guy with his abs on full display, and now my priorities suddenly shift from tattoos to something entirely different. "I didn't know you were into smut, Rebel," I tease, gleefully waiting to get a rise out of her.

"What?" Ivy puts her mug on the coffee table, and I do the same.

"You're reading a book with a naked guy on the cover."

"He's not *naked*. He's shirtless."

"Same shit. Either way, I didn't know you enjoyed reading this." I pick the book up, watching the heat rise to her face. "This is one way to start learning who you are as an adult. Surely, you can't be a Dame if you have a tattoo *and* you're reading something like this—they'd have you ostracized."

Ivy smirks. "Thankfully, I never was inducted, so I have nothing to worry about."

"How did you escape that? Did Meredith Hartwick find you reading something like—" I flip open to a random page and start reading it out loud. *"My pussy gets so wet when he—"*

"Oh my god!"

Ivy lunges for me, like I knew she would, and I move back, holding the book up in the air as she struggles to reach for it, and I attempt to read more.

"His hard cock slams into—"

"Give me my fucking book!"

She leans across the length of my body, sending shockwaves through my core at the feel of her being this close to me. The two of us laugh as she climbs up my torso to try to reach my extended arm.

"His cum drips down my thigh—"

Ivy's hand covers my mouth, our chests rumbling together as more laughter builds between us. She finally yanks the book out of my grip and immediately goes to right herself, adjusting her posture.

"So immature," she says, catching her breath.

Sitting upright, I respond, "I just enjoy getting under your skin."

"Yeah, well, you succeeded." She smooths over her

hair. "And there's nothing wrong with reading smut—or romance."

"I one hundred percent agree."

The thought of her reading something like this makes me need to readjust my jeans, as my mind suddenly pictures her getting herself off. Hundreds of dirty scenarios flood my brain in an instant.

She glances at me as if she's unsure of what to make of my comment and pissed that there was a glint of enticement hitting her eyes. "I fought with my mom not to become a Dame," she says in response to my earlier comment, and I bring myself out of the lewd images I've conjured up of her and back into the present so I can pay attention. "Took an early summer program at Harvard, as I'm sure you remember—or maybe you don't because we were out of each other's lives by then."

You cut me out of your life, Ivy.

The words burn on the tip of my tongue, and my insides wring tight with remorse. I know the moment when everything blew up in our faces. It was the exact reason why I *didn't* want to act on my impulses, out of fear that we'd end up exactly like this.

But there was some part of me that always held on to the hope that she'd come back and involve herself in my life like she'd always done.

That never happened, though. I was left with no contact. Blocked on everything. She wasn't even living at home when I'd visit Trent. She was up in Boston.

She cut me out of her life. Even though it was an agonizing parting, shredding me to pieces and shattering my heart in more ways than I thought possible, I always assumed I hurt her even more if she had to act as if I never existed.

"Mom was always waiting for me to return once I finished college," Ivy continues. "But I made Boston my home, and she couldn't force me to get inducted into her chapter from several states away."

"At least you got out of it," I reply, even though I want to say so much more.

I want to apologize and have her believe it.

I want to throw her stupid rules out the window.

I want to make up for lost time.

I want to know everything I missed out on.

I want to make her mine.

"Heard you had a pretty wild time in college," I say, remembering the bits of information I'd get from Trent whenever Ivy would occasionally talk with him.

Ivy chuckles. "Yeah, I was living out the *Jersey Shore* lifestyle."

"No fucking way." I laugh.

"Oh yeah, I even wore leopard print dresses with a fake tan to the club." She hides her face in embarrassment.

"I can*not* picture you like that. Did you have a poof in your hair? Please tell me you didn't have a poof."

She nods, her laughter building along with mine. "It was a weird phase!"

"Apparently!"

"What about you? Didn't you have any cringe-worthy phases?"

"I'm sure I did, but I was mostly consumed by hockey."

Ivy leans her back against the couch, her gaze dancing over my face as she settles into a soft smile. From the window behind her, I can see that snow is starting to fall. "How was it making the NHL?"

"One of the best feelings in the world."

"Your dreams finally came true."

"Not all of my dreams, Ivy."

"It seemed like that was your only dream back then."

Rule One: No bringing up our past. Broken.

"I know." I inch closer to her. "But it wasn't."

"I can't go down this road, Pax. Not here, not now." She pleads with me to end this conversation before it truly begins, as if she wasn't the one to start it in the first place. But I'm holding onto hope that the words *not now* imply that there will be a someday. "We're on a mini-vacation," she continues. "We're supposed to be letting loose and enjoying ourselves, not rehashing the past."

"Fair enough." I nod, although I'm not giving up that easily. "So in the spirit of letting loose and enjoying ourselves, what do you say if we reenact one of those sex scenes from your book?"

Her jaw flies open, and I can't keep a serious expression on my face for the life of me.

"Only in your fantasies," Ivy states.

"We've never reenacted a scene in my fantasies, but I'll be sure to add that to the list now that I know what gets you going."

She squirms in her seat, an obvious blush coloring her cheeks.

"What's the matter, Rebel? Can't come up with a comeback?"

Ivy runs her fingers through her hair, adjusting her composure and slipping back into her self-assurance as if my comment had no effect on her. "Sorry, I got distracted imagining what it would be like if we reenacted the scene where he uses the showerhead on her," she says, toying with me as a little lift in her lips appears. Leaning toward the coffee table, she uses two hands to hold her mug and takes a sip of the hot chocolate. Her lashes close, and she lets out a soft "mmm" sound as the drink slides down her throat.

Blood rushes to my lower half, sparks shooting off inside me as I watch her taunt me.

She slowly opens her eyes, instantly locking with mine. "What's the matter, Pax? Can't come up with a comeback?"

A strangled chuckle comes from the back of my throat as I readjust myself. "You win."

"I knew I would."

"I'll win the next round."

"And who says they'll be more?"

"I'm sure this won't be the only time we bring up this topic, Ivy." I wink, and her pupils automatically dilate.

There's a flicker of desire in her eyes, but it becomes trapped by hesitation, so I don't push it. I'll find the right timing soon enough.

Reaching for the remote, I change up the energy between us. "Let's watch something."

"Okay." Ivy relaxes on the couch as I put on Netflix.

When I opt for *Gilmore Girls,* I hear her chuckle. The show starts, and Ivy is instantly immersed. I glance over at her, her head resting on the arm of the couch as she lies on her side, curled in a ball. Her toes brush my thigh, and the smallest connection makes me smile.

We stay this way for the rest of the time, Ivy watching her favorite show while I watch her enjoy it as the snow gently falls outside.

CHAPTER TWENTY-THREE

"THERE'S nothing better than a spa day," Celeste declares in her bridesmaid robe.

We just finished up a massage and facial, and now we're getting pedicures. We've been talking wedding prep, although my mind is finding it difficult to focus. My thoughts keep drifting to my time with Paxton yesterday.

"Let me learn who you are now."

His plea rings in my ears, and I'm still unsure of what to make of it. We never were and could never be, so what would be the point of reopening an old wound? Although the second he outwardly admitted he fantasizes about me, I wanted to pounce on him.

It wouldn't be the *worst* thing in the world if we broke the physical connection rule, would it? We're both adults and more mature than we used to be. Since we both agreed on remaining acquaintances, it would purely be to scratch an itch.

The ongoing debate in my mind doesn't quit until I hear my name being spoken.

"Ivy, when's your final fitting for your bridesmaid

dress?" Pia asks, zapping me out of my Paxton-induced haze.

"Beginning of April," I state. "I love the light pink color."

"Rose quartz," she corrects.

"Oh, yes, that's what my wedding planner is calling it," Lucille fills me in. "It's a rose quartz and champagne color palette. Your mom actually linked me up with the planner. She apparently did your sweet sixteen."

I snort. "Jeez, I tried to block those memories out. My mom made me wear a bejeweled dress and hideous tiara. Hopefully, she's not expecting the same for your wedding."

"No, your mom hasn't been that bad." I give her a knowing look, and she cracks under the pressure. "Okay, she's been a *bit* overbearing."

"If you need her off your back, just let me know and I'll create a scandal so she can fixate on something else."

Lucille chuckles. "Sounds like a plan."

"Speaking of plans," Felicity interjects. "Last night we had dinner with the guys. How about tonight we have ladies' night?"

"Yes!" Celeste exclaims.

"We can get dressed up and do cocktails at one of the bars in the main lodge." Pia starts to put the plan in motion.

"I'll make reservations for dinner," Felicity says.

"I think they have a jazz club on the lower level," Lucille suggests.

"Drinks, dinner, and dancing. Sounds perfect," Celeste states, and all of us agree.

An evening away from Pax could be just the remedy to push these lingering thoughts out of my head.

The bar is chic, with plush booths, flickering candles, and odd-shaped light fixtures overhead that are dimly lit. Long black cloths drape over the tables, hitting my calves as I sit down. The scent of bourbon, warm and oaky with a hint of sweetness, encompasses the room.

We're seated in a small, U-shaped booth across from where several people stand conversing at the bar while they wait for the bartender to assist them. Lucille, Pia, and I are the ones actually sitting in the booth, while Celeste and Felicity sit on the opposite side of the table in padded dining chairs.

A waiter greets us, and we place our drink order, which arrives promptly.

The five of us get a little too eager with the drinks, our laughter becoming louder and our topics of conversation becoming more off-color.

"It was the worst date of my life!" Pia says, all of us in hysterics as she recounts an awful hookup.

"I'll do you one better," Felicity shares. "I was on a first date with a guy, and it was interrupted…by his *wife*!"

"What!" I nearly sputter out my pinot noir as we all gasp in horror. "Men are such scum."

"*Some* men," Lucille says, letting me know that my brother isn't on that list.

"What about you, Ivy? Do you have any shitty dating stories to add to the mix?" Celeste asks, then downs the last of her margarita.

"How much time do you have? I can go on forever."

"Spill!" she encourages.

I chuckle to myself, replaying all the appalling moments. The alcohol flowing through my veins makes me find these stories humorous instead of causing a bitter taste in my mouth.

"I once met up with a guy from Tinder at a coffeehouse, and before I even sat down, he said, 'Before I pay for your drink, are you planning on coming back to my apartment after this?'"

"No!" Lucille gasps.

"Please tell me you didn't go home with him," Pia says.

"Hell no. I immediately left. And even if I did go home with him, I'm sure he would've been awful in bed. I have a losing streak with that too."

"Even with Warren?" Lucille asks. Whatever she's drinking must be getting to her head if she brought up Warren when she was so apologetic about the mention of a partner just yesterday.

"Who's Warren?" Celeste eagerly asks.

"Oh my god." Lucille slams her hand over her mouth, realizing she brought up the topic.

I give her a look to let her know it's completely fine. "He's my ex. And yes, even Warren didn't know how to make me come. I don't remember the last time a man successfully completed the task."

"I'm so glad vibrators exist," Pia announces. "If you're hooking up with someone, it makes it more fun, and if you're not, then you can have fun by yourself."

"To vibrators!" Celeste cheers, raising her glass.

The four of us laugh, joining our glasses with hers. "To vibrators!"

I take another swig of the red wine, letting it warm up my insides as my muscles start to loosen. Lowering my glass, my attention goes to a set of eyes that are staring back at me.

Blood rushes to my cheeks as I squirm under the heat of Pax's stare.

He's leaning his body weight against the bar with a drink in hand. The smirk on his face and the glimmer of satisfaction shining through his features let me know that he heard every single word that came out of my mouth.

My pulse speeds up the more I gaze at the alluring expression on his face. He looks all too pleased that the men I've been with are horrible in bed and looks way too eager to prove a point.

He's wearing a black button-up shirt with his sleeves rolled up, exposing his strong forearms, and matching dress slacks. I've never seen him like this before. He looks so…grown.

My body gets hotter, the alcohol allowing my lustful thoughts to be set free. Neither of us breaks our stare, his sexy smirk growing wider, making my legs clench.

"Our dinner reservation is in two minutes," Felicity says, making me realize I missed their entire conversation.

They start to gather their purses, but I remain still.

My eyes locked on Paxton.

Something crosses between us. The temptation of a challenge? The thrill of a game? The risk of breaking the rules, just this once?

I'm not sure what it is, but I sense the shift, and I know he feels it too.

"Hey! When did you get here?" Pia says when she spots Paxton as she and the rest of the women begin to leave the table.

"I came in for a beer while I waited for the rest of the guys," he explains. "Don't worry, we're not crashing your ladies' night."

"You better not be. We're just getting started!" Celeste says, then turns to look at me. "You coming, Ivy?"

Glued to my seat, goose bumps prickle on my skin as

Pax waits for my response. His brow arching in a dare, causing all sensibility to trickle out of my brain.

"I'll catch up with you. I just need to talk to Pax for a second," I respond on impulse.

"Don't be too long," Felicity says as they begin to part ways.

"She won't be," Pax assures them, his comment sending a tingle down my spine.

As they exit, I scoot myself into the center of the booth. Once Paxton can no longer see my group, he slides in next to me. We sit dangerously close, with our knees grazing one another's.

I try to keep my focus ahead of me, on the strangers at the bar instead of staring directly at him.

"That dress looks beautiful on you." The hoarseness in his words that I've only truly witnessed once prior strikes my core, creating an intense pining inside me.

"You've only seen the top half. The bottom could be covered in leopard print for all you know. Or worse, I could be wearing jeans under my dress."

He pushes away the tablecloth, admiring my jade-colored dress from where it hits my lower thighs all the way up to the skinny straps wrapped around my shoulder and crossing over my exposed back.

Desire ripples through me in a way I haven't felt in a very long time.

I reach for my wine.

"How much have you had to drink?" Pax asks.

"Not enough." I bring the glass up to my lips, and he chuckles.

"I overheard your conversation."

"How convenient."

"It wasn't on purpose. I thought you'd all be at dinner by now." He carefully places his hand on my thigh, and my hormones go haywire. It's such a simple touch, yet it stirs my body with more intensity than I've felt with the previous men I've slept with. "But now that I heard what I did, I'm definitely intrigued."

"Does the thought of incompetent men who are unable to get women off make you hot, Paxton?" I tease him, but he pays no mind.

"No. It pisses me off." His hand starts to slide its way under the hem of my dress. "And makes me want to make up for their lack."

My eyebrows shoot up. Our eyes lock as I stare at him in disbelief. His fingertips threaten to inch further up my leg. "*Here*?"

"Why not?"

"First off, we're in public." My voice gets lower as I realize what we're discussing.

"Which will make you come faster."

"No, it won't."

"Wanna bet?" His lips tug into a smirk, and my head spins from how flustered he's making me. "I'm sure you've read a public sex scene in one of your smut books, and the woman comes in an instant."

"Second." I skip over his comment and push through the indecent thoughts that have just entered my brain. "We made rules."

"Fuck the rules, Ivy."

"We made them for a reason." Mainly so my heart doesn't explode into billions of jagged little pieces again.

Paxton leans in closer, wetting his lips before speaking. "When I said I wanted to learn who you are now, I wasn't just talking about your favorite TV show." My pulse races. "I want to know everything. What you love, what you hate." He drags his fingers leisurely up and down my thigh. "I want to befriend the broken shadows you hide from the world. I want to know what lies beneath your anger. I want to memorize the way your chest rises and falls quickly when you're turned on—like it's doing right now."

"Paxton..." I whisper as a rush of quarreling emotions erupts inside me—the majority of them I'd rather avoid for the rest of my life. "I'm not going to let you in that much," I admit the truth, bluntly letting him know that there's zero chance his goals will be reached.

Pax nods in understanding. A flash of disappointment pulls at his features, but it's quickly replaced by a look of determination. "Then if you won't let me learn who you are in those ways, will you let me learn how you like to be touched?" His voice comes out thick, causing my mind to go hazy.

Lust takes over the emotions I'd been avoiding, successfully covering them up with risqué images the moment Pax's free hand grazes the space between my shoulder blades.

"At the very least, let me prove you wrong and get you to come in public." He baits me, and I sense myself risking taking the lure. "It'll only be for tonight, then you can go on with your ladies' night as if I didn't just give you a mind-blowing orgasm. And we can go back to your stupid rules tomorrow." He gets closer, his deep pitch brushing against the shell of my ear when he says, "I call you rebel for a reason."

Desire pools between my legs at his comment, my body temperature rising to a dangerous heat. My gaze flickers over the room to make sure no one's attention is on us.

The voice of logic encouraging me to protest is getting smaller and smaller until it disappears and is replaced by my yearning to feel Pax's touch.

The clamoring in my chest makes it hard to hear my own words as I say, "I'm wearing tights."

Dropping both of his hands to my legs, he doesn't

hesitate to slip under my dress, ripping a hole in my tights with one quick motion.

I gasp, staring at him as cool air hits my skin.

"Problem solved," Pax states.

"I have to go to dinner after this."

"Guess you'll have to go with a run in your stockings."

"Asshole," I mutter, scowling at him.

Not allowing my annoyance to linger any longer, I gradually part my legs open, widening for him.

Pride swirls around Paxton's hazel eyes. "Atta girl, Rebel."

My lashes flutter closed as I attempt to get control over my breathing. I feel him shifting his posture next to me as I wait for his touch. Expecting him to make a beeline for my panties, I jolt in surprise when I feel his hand clutch the back of my neck in a possessive, yet somehow gentle hold.

"Open your eyes."

Pax's command makes my insides do somersaults, and I do what he says, making direct contact with him. He turned his body to face me completely, and he's slightly leaned over as if we're engaged in some type of important conversation.

His calloused thumb massages the base of my neck, relaxing me.

A shaky breath flows from my lips when he tenderly begins to run his other hand along the inside of my inner thigh.

"Have you ever been touched in public?" he asks, making me squirm as his finger runs over the lace fabric covering my clit.

"No," I whisper, glancing around to see if any of the strangers are catching on.

"Good." Satisfaction swims through Paxton's

response, and he automatically claims this moment as ours, forcing my panties out of the way and pushing one finger inside me.

I suck in a sharp breath, dizziness filling my head.

Impulsively grabbing my wineglass, I down the rest of it, letting every single drop hit my tongue as Paxton continues to work me.

"You need another drink," he states, sliding a second finger through my wetness.

Heat courses through my veins as my hips naturally move with his rhythm. My dress slides up and down, brushing against my legs.

"Excuse me," Pax calls out to a passing waiter. I whip my attention to Paxton, staring at him like he's fucking insane as my heart pounds wildly. The waiter stops in front of us, and Pax changes his tempo, moving his fingers faster. "Could we get her another drink?"

"Of course," the waiter responds.

Blood rushes to my cheeks, and I struggle to remain as calm as possible.

"What were you having again, Ivy?" Pax teases me, grinning as he speaks. "Sauvignon blanc?"

Fucking asshole.

He knows I wasn't drinking white wine. He watched me drink red.

Shaking my head, I rest my hands on the table, forcing myself to keep my composure.

"I must've forgotten what you were drinking. Why don't you tell him?" Pax winks.

I hate that I love this so much.

"Pinot n—" I jolt, Pax's thumb instantly rubbing against my clit as I begin speaking. "Pinot noir." The waiter nods, hurrying off to get my drink, and the second he's gone, I whisper, "I hate you."

"Hate me all you want, Rebel. I'm still going to make you come all over my fingers in public."

My stomach constricts, tension building between my thighs.

Pax softly presses his lips on the side of my neck, causing my skin to prickle. He slowly moves his mouth toward my ear. "I always dreamed of being able to touch you again." His words make my breath hitch. "Tell me you thought about it too." Pax rapidly moves his finger against my clit, adding and taking away pressure. Flames ignite in my core. My teeth sink into my bottom lip, knowing that I'm getting closer and I'll need to be quiet. "Tell me that despite your fucking rules, you thought about me making you come."

His touch sends me into a hunger-filled delusion, unable to think or reason clearly. A fog of desire makes it difficult to get out any other word aside from "Pax," the hushed tone of his name coming out as a stifled moan.

Paxton's free hand reaches for my chin, drawing my attention to look directly at him. Those gorgeous hazel eyes suck me in like they have for decades prior. My chest moves quickly, my composure slipping through the cracks.

"Tell me you thought about us, Ivy."

Too vulnerable to shy away from him, I begin to nod. But the second I reveal my answer, a firestorm of desire bursts through my veins as his fingers drive me over the edge. I gasp, realizing what's about to happen, but before I can scream out his name in the bar for all to hear, Pax's lips are on mine.

It's been years since our lips touched, and somehow, it feels even better than it did the first time.

He claims me wholly.

His tongue laced with a hint of liquor tangles with mine as his touch scorches me with passion. My sensuality becomes unearthed as he continues to kiss me into oblivion—kissing me as if he's making up for lost time.

My moans disappear into his mouth as I tremble in his hold. His fingers continue to run through my wetness in an electrifying way, despite my thighs clenching around his hand.

Sparks race up and down my spine at the same speed as my pulse.

Pleasure rattles through me, and I move my hips against his hand, not caring how obvious we look. I fist his nicely ironed shirt, twisting it into a wrinkled mess, letting my orgasm reach its peak.

Paxton's hold on me strengthens, not willing to let me out of his grip. He continues to possessively kiss me, declaring each swallowed moan as his.

I melt into him, my body finally starting to relax.

A light, relaxing sensation trickles into my bloodstream, causing my muscles to go slack.

Pax breaks our kiss very slightly. Our labored breaths panting against each other's swollen lips. Carefully, he drags his hand out from under my dress, and there's a sudden ache, already missing him.

We slowly create space between us, though not really wanting to. Our gazes are locked, neither of us sure of what to say to the other. Light chatter of the other patrons comes back into focus, and the reality of where we are and what just happened sinks in. Heat rushes to my cheeks, and I'd bet anything that my face is bright pink. My focus goes off Pax as I fix my hair and readjust my dress.

Pax slides a glass of pinot noir across the black tablecloth, putting it right in front of me. "Guess the waiter dropped it off at some point."

I grab it from him, gulping down the glass as quickly as I can while I regain my sanity. After chugging it, I place the wineglass back on the table. "I should go meet up with the girls." I start shifting out of the booth, and Pax begins to do the same.

"Yeah, your brother will be here any minute."

Both of us lock eyes, a mortified look on both of our faces as we realize that Trent could've shown up at any point. Pax glances around the room to make sure Trent or any of the groomsmen aren't in the bar with us. His shoulders relax, letting me know we're in the clear.

And with that, I grab my purse and leave the table.

CHAPTER TWENTY-FOUR

ALL THE WOMEN are drunk off liquor while I'm still riding the high of Paxton getting me off earlier in the evening. The rest of the night, I couldn't keep my focus on anything else, but I played it off well.

We're sprawled out in the living room, lounging on the comfy couches, laughing as we recount the evening that just happened. The four of them have heavy eyes, their dresses disheveled and hair unkempt. I join in on their drunken conversation even though I haven't had anything to drink since my pinot noir with Pax.

"Don't laugh at my dance moves!" Celeste says as she herself laughs. "I'm planning on using my skills at your wedding, Lucille!"

"We're going to need to get you some dance lessons before then," Felicity teases.

Celeste waves her hand. "I already have a husband who loves my killer moves. I don't need any lessons."

Pia sighs. "I hope one day I have a husband who loves my embarrassing quirks."

"There are going to be single men at the wedding!" Lucille pops up with a second wind of energy.

"Did you find out if Paxton is single yet?"

A rock lands in my gut. I shift in my seat, feeling the run in my stockings, my bare thigh brushing against my dress. Jealousy curls around my bones in a way I haven't experienced in years.

A loud thump at the front door has us turning our attention to the shit-faced men barreling into the cabin. Trent's wearing a dopey, boyish smile as the other three groomsmen, Leon, Brandon, and Pete, hoot and howl as they enter. Paxton is at the back of the group, laughing at the sight.

"My beautiful bride!" Trent shouts when he spots Lucille on the couch. He rushes to her, wedging his way in between her and Felicity.

"Looks like guys' night was as fun as ladies' night," Celeste states as the rest of them find spots in the living room.

"It sure was," Paxton says, sitting down on the arm of the couch, directly across from me. "What have you ladies been up to?"

"We were just chatting." Pia twirls a strand of hair around her finger, giving Paxton her best bedroom eyes as she speaks.

"Actually, Pax, you were the subject of the conversation," Celeste says.

"Celeste!" Pia plays it off as if she's embarrassed.

"I was?" Pax's attention floats around the room, glancing over at me.

My heart moves quicker than I'd like it to. I readjust my legs, crossing one over the other, and I catch Pax's eyes land on the ripped fibers of my tights, which now reach down to my ankle.

"Well, now that Celeste brought it up…" Pia playfully glares at her. "We were curious if you're single." Her head tilts to the side as a flirtatious grin appears on her picture-perfect face.

Anxiety shoots through my bloodstream as I brace myself for the *yes*. Envy fills my body as I picture the two of them fucking in one of the bedrooms here by the end of the night. I intensely watch Paxton as his lips lift upward. He doesn't look at me, but I know he can feel my stare because his grin continues to grow.

"Technically, yes. But I recently started pursuing someone."

Holy shit.

"Holy shit!" Trent's spine straightens. "*You* want to be in a relationship with someone? The guy who can't even remember how many threesomes he's had and never wanted to commit to someone? Never gonna happen."

Pax scratches the back of his neck, growing uncomfortable. "We'll see where it goes."

A surge of mixed emotions—but mainly panic—ripples from my head to my toes. *We'll see where it goes.* It's not going anywhere. We said we'd only connect with each other for the duration of the wedding festivities. It was one of my rules.

"The only thing you had that was remotely close to a relationship was that on-again-off-again drama with that girl when you were like eighteen," Trent slurs. "What was her name?"

"Courtney." Her name pops right out of my mouth, leaving a sour taste. Both of them shift their attention to me, but mine lands directly on Paxton as my heart clatters.

"That's right." Trent snaps his fingers.

"My neighbor's cat is named Courtney," Felicity drunkenly chimes in, and I've never been more thankful for a change in conversation.

Everyone continues to talk, hopping from one topic to

the next, each becoming more ridiculous and brash than the previous. But the sound of my pulse whooshing in my ears makes it difficult to hear, let alone focus on their incoherent exchanges.

Quietly, I excuse myself, my heels softly padding up the stairs and into my room.

When I shut the door behind me, the sounds from the boisterous living room dampen. Sitting on the bed, I screw my eyes closed, taking a deep inhale and slowly releasing an exhale. Before I can attempt to clear my thoughts, there's a knock at my door.

"It's me, Rebel." Pax's deep voice has the tiny hairs on my arms rising.

"Yes?"

He takes that as an invitation to enter my room, carefully closing the door behind him. Our gazes connect, the space between us growing tense, half yearning and half aggravation.

"I might've broken the no physical contact rule, but I was serious when I set the boundary of us not talking once the wedding is over," I state, loathing the immediate ache in my chest as soon as I utter those words.

He inches closer, hovering over me. "Did you get spooked when I said I was pursuing you?"

"Yes."

"Should I go back downstairs and let Pia know she's got a shot?" Pax taunts, chuckling as soon as he notices my jaw clenching.

"You're a free man. You can do what you want." My heart riots against my statement.

"I'm not interested in her, Ivy." Pax's voice gets thick. He crouches down in front of me, and air gets caught in my chest. "I know you don't want things to extend beyond the wedding." His fingers delicately wrap around my calf as he lifts it up, then gradually peels my high heel off my foot. "And I plan on respecting that." He places my foot on the floor, moving to my other leg. "But if you change your mind, I'll be waiting for you." He discards my other heel, then lets his hand linger on my calf. His calloused fingertips skim over the rip in my tights, lightly touching my skin.

I wet my lips, desire brewing in my core. My battling emotions interlace, wrapping around my mind, making it challenging to settle on how to react.

Pax leans forward, placing a chaste kiss on my forehead.

Tingles waterfall down my body as I wait for him to lower his head slightly, sealing our evening with an intense kiss.

But instead, he stands up, looking over me with a soft smile. "Get some rest. I'll see you in the morning."

I nod, watching him slowly move toward the door and out of the room. Every single place he touched me lights up, yearning for more.

Including my beaten-down, barricaded heart.

CHAPTER TWENTY-FIVE

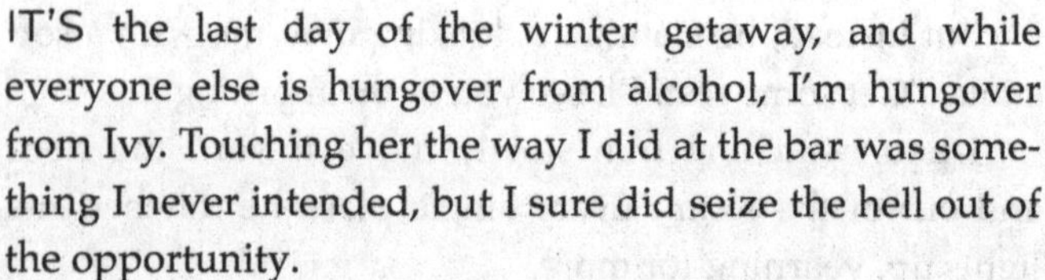

IT'S the last day of the winter getaway, and while everyone else is hungover from alcohol, I'm hungover from Ivy. Touching her the way I did at the bar was something I never intended, but I sure did seize the hell out of the opportunity.

"I heard you're pretty good on the ice," Pia says, sitting down next to me on the bench, lacing up her skates.

"Some might say that," I respond.

"Guess I'll have to check you out and make my own judgment then."

She flashes a smile, and I chuckle, knowing that she doesn't have the slightest chance of making anything between us happen. Now that Ivy is back in my life, *no one* stands a chance.

"Everyone ready?" Lucille bursts with enthusiasm as she asks the group. This is our last big activity of the weekend, and even though we're all pretty tired, no one wanted to turn down the bride-to-be's final request.

We follow her onto the rink, and the moment my blades hit the ice, I'm ignited with passion. But it's quickly shrouded by a heavy sadness, still coming to terms with the fact that I was forced to say goodbye to what was the epicenter of my life. It wasn't on my terms. In fact, every time I had to say goodbye, it was never on my terms.

The group inevitably splits off, going at different speeds around the rink as loud pop music chimes from the overhead speaker. My body glides, but not as effortlessly as it once did. I note how I'm weaker on my right side, and frustration begins to simmer.

Before I can get lost in my emotions and regrets, I glance around the rink, watching Trent and Lucille hold hands. My attention bounces around to the others when I realize Ivy isn't in sight.

Looking behind me, Ivy cautiously skates, glued to the railing. Her eyes land on me, and without thinking, I skate over to her.

"I'm fine," she insists before I can even begin to speak. "I just haven't skated in a while."

"Need a steady hand?" I extend myself as an offer.

Ivy shakes her head. "No. I'm fine."

"Do you always turn people down when they try to help you out, or is it only me?"

"Everyone. You're no exception."

"Well..." I smirk, biting my tongue.

"Well, what?"

"Yesterday, there was *one* thing you allowed me to help you out with."

Her eyes dart around the rink, making sure no one heard me. As she opens her mouth to say something, Pia glides right up to me, trying to steal the spotlight.

"I don't know, Paxton. I have yet to see these massive skills you're known for," Pia teases, vying for my attention.

"Being with Ivy is more important."

The shock on Ivy's face is evident, and as if on cue, she loses her footing, slipping on the ice. Quick to react, I reach out and grab hold of her. The shape of her body was perfectly molded for my hands.

"Do you need assistance, Ivy?" Pia genuinely asks. "I can see if someone—"

"I'm fine," Ivy states, trying really fucking hard to be polite.

"Are you ready for that hand I offered earlier?" I ask, adjusting myself beside Ivy.

"Whatever," she mutters, threading her gloved fingers between mine. I latch onto her, knowing the closeness will be fleeting despite the yearning need to never let her go.

One of the other bridesmaids calls for Pia, and she skates over to them, leaving me to be alone with Ivy once more.

"You've been favoring your left side," Ivy says.

"You checking me out, Rebel?"

She glares at me, making it impossible not to laugh. "Don't flatter yourself, Paxton."

"Any time you glance my way, I'm honored."

Ivy rolls her eyes but stays silent. The others continue to skate around us as we take our time, her relying on me to keep her steady. Letting me do something like this, as minimal as it might seem, lights my soul up in a way that has only happened with her.

I felt it the moment she barged her way into my apartment at fourteen years old, showing Uncle Jeff pictures of my games. I just didn't know what to do with it back then.

"We wanted to take a moment to thank all of you for joining us this weekend," Lucille says as we sit around the table in the cabin. She wanted to cook us dinner as a way to thank us for coming. "We know you all have busy lives and schedules, so we appreciate you carving the time out to celebrate our upcoming nuptials. Anything you'd like to add, Trent?"

"We're looking forward to partying with you all in May," Trent says.

"To the soon-to-be Mr. and Mrs. Hartwick," Pia exclaims, raising her glass.

Everyone clinks our glasses together, then dives into the dinner that Lucille prepared. Conversation floats around the table, but every time I try to engage, I notice Ivy's stare from the other end. The moment my eyes connect with her sapphire blues, she looks away.

I can't figure out what she's thinking, but I know her wheels are turning.

As the evening folds into night, Ivy continues to keep her distance but glances over at me every so often. The expression that flickers on her face gives me a strum of hope that she's considering my words from last night in her room. Anticipation swirls around my rib cage, needing to know if she changed her mind and wants to give me a fair shot.

Give *us* a fair shot.

We never had one, and it's about fucking time we did.

People announce they're headed for bed, Ivy included, and I follow their lead, going to my room.

The cabin settles down, becoming quiet. I debate with myself on whether or not to stroll up to Ivy's room and ask her to tell me what's been on her mind this evening.

But I don't want to suffocate her, and she could just as easily come downstairs to talk to me if she wanted to, so I decide to attempt to sleep instead.

With a T-shirt and gray sweatpants on, I slip under the covers and force myself to close my eyes.

Tossing and turning for what feels like hours, a gentle knock on my door has my body stilling.

"Pax?" Ivy's whisper floats its way over to me, the soft sound quelling any lingering tension around my bones.

"Come on in, Rebel," I rasp.

The door peels open, and silhouetted Ivy remains in the threshold. Pushing up on my elbows, I study her. The slit in the curtain lets the moonlight pour onto her. She's wearing a black pajama set with white trim around the edges and white buttons along the front of her shirt. Her eyes sparkle with mischief as she closes the door behind her and tiptoes over to me, hovering next to the mattress.

"What's up?" I ask, and the magnetic pull between us intensifies.

"I've been doing some thinking, and I'd like to make an amendment to our rules."

My lips twitch, but I school my features, not wanting to get my hopes up. "Oh?"

"I still think we shouldn't talk about old history, and we should only remain in contact after the wedding if necessary. But..." Her legs brush up against my bed as anxiety nips at my fingertips, waiting to see where she's going with this. "I think we can break the no physical contact rule for the time being."

"Meaning?"

"Friends with benefits until the wedding."

"Friends with benefits," I repeat, unsure of how I feel about that proposal. "The orgasm I gave you yesterday must've been phenomenal if it got you thinking like this," I tease.

She rolls her eyes, and her torso begins to twist away

from me. "On second thought, maybe this was a stupid idea."

"Wait." I stop her, and, surprisingly, she listens. "That's not exactly what I meant when I said I was trying to pursue you."

"Well, this is all I can agree to, and I think it's a pretty fair compromise. It'll be simple. We'll have a clear ending—once the wedding is over, so are our hookups. We'll both get our needs met, and there's no commitment, no strings attached." Ivy places her palms down on the bed, arching her back as she invades my space. "Isn't that the Paxton Rhodes way?"

I let out a halfhearted chuckle. Little does Ivy know, I want all the strings. As tangled, complicated, and dramatic as the strings might be, I want every single one wrapped around us, tying us to each other so that neither one of us is able to run away again.

"That's the Paxton Rhodes way for everyone except you," I state.

Ivy swallows as she hesitates before answering. "It's all I can offer you."

My pulse thrums loudly, wishing I could get more of her but not wanting to let her slip away from me again. My gaze drops down to her hands, and I reach out mine, my fingers filling the spaces in between.

Gently guiding Ivy over to me, my heart becomes whole as she molds into my arms. Tucking her hair behind her ear, I can feel her shaky breath brushing against my face.

"Are you sure this is what you want?" I ask.

"More than sure."

My hand cups her delicate cheek, my thumb slowly grazing her skin. I take a moment to study her in the glowing moonlight, her sapphire eyes spellbinding me in a way only she knows how. Her guard is dropped as she looks at me like she once did many years ago.

My heart beats in a way it's only ever done when Ivy gazes at me.

Although adrenaline rushes through my bloodstream, lust urging me to claim every inch of her stunning body, all I truly want to do is kiss her like we've never had this time apart.

I run the pad of my thumb over her plump bottom lip, wanting to memorize how soft it feels before I lean in to capture it with mine. The instant we connect, flames ignite between us. Unfiltered longing takes over, our breath becoming heady, our tongues roaming wild, our hands gripping onto the other for dear life.

No matter how much I try to force myself to move slowly, take time to worship her, my feral body has other plans. Blood immediately rushes to my cock as my thoughts twist from sensual to dirty as hell.

Lacing my fingers through Ivy's silky hair, I curl them into a fist at the base of her neck, breaking our contact. Her eyelids spring open as her chest quickly rises and falls.

"I need to taste you." My desire comes out in a husky demand.

Ivy stills for a brief moment, as if surprised that I'm yearning to lick her pussy. But as I stare at her with hunger pouring out of me, a flicker of a smirk appears on her face. She hooks her fingers into her pajama pants, leisurely pulling them down.

Urgency lights up my nerves, and I help her drag the last of the fabric off her legs. Heat courses through me when I notice she doesn't have any panties on. "Were you planning on getting lucky tonight?" I tease.

"It's just a coincidence." Ivy's words float over her exhale. She leans in for another kiss, only this time it's even more needy. Her hands sneak under my shirt, running her nails over my abs.

Lust swirling through every part of me. I break us apart for a brief moment to yank my shirt off. Then, as I lie down, I hook my hands around her thighs and position her right where I want her.

Ivy's legs are parted on either side of my head, her gorgeous pussy hovering over my mouth. The pads of my fingers glide along her skin, goose bumps following in their wake. I can hear Ivy's uneven breathing, filled with eagerness and a slight hint of nervousness.

We've never done this.

I've never had the honor of burying my tongue inside her, letting her sweetness satiate me. The anticipation is killing me, but I need to see all of her first. Even if it's just under the radiance of the moonlight, I need to see Ivy's body.

Gliding my fingers upward, I meet the fabric of her pajama shirt. I have no patience for fucking buttons, so I grab hold of the bottom of her shirt and yank it in opposite directions. Buttons fly everywhere, clinking on the floor as the fabric is ripped open. Annoyed, Ivy gasps in disbelief. I pay no mind, peeling her sleeves down her arms.

"If you keep destroying my clothes—"

"You'll probably keep begging me for more orgasms." With that, I force her hips down to my mouth, and she's immediately gratified as my tongue grazes over her clit.

Reaching up, I grip onto her tits, letting them overflow in my palms as I roughly pinch her nipples. Her head tilts back as she arches her back, looking absolutely exquisite as she fucks my face.

She tastes so intoxicating, I can't get enough.

My body lights on fire. My cock rams against my sweatpants, desperately wanting to be set free.

Ivy rolls her hips over my mouth, adding more friction for herself as my tongue feverishly strokes her clit.

I could live in this moment forever, but as I hear her sighs get louder, I'm suddenly aware of our surroundings.

Lifting her slightly up, I whisper, "Your brother's in the next room. You need to be quiet."

She nods, then drops her hips back down, and I can't help but smirk, knowing she's enjoying this as much as I am.

The moment I draw her clit into my mouth and suck, her legs begin shaking. Her gasps climb louder the closer she is to coming. Even though she's attempting to keep quiet, it's not working at all.

I lift her up once again, this time higher. "Turn around."

"What?" Ivy blinks rapidly as if I just woke her up from a dream.

"You need something in your mouth to keep you quiet," I state, shuffling to get my sweatpants and boxers down. "Turn around."

She smiles, now understanding my instructions, and repositions herself so that her mouth is aligned with my cock while her pussy faces me on full display.

Before I go back to devouring her, I push my fingers in and out of her wetness and watch the way her muscles react to my touch. She starts to moan but uses me to stifle her sounds, opening her mouth and dragging it down the length of my cock.

I'm seeing stars the instant she moves her head up and down, forcing herself to get every inch in her mouth as she sucks harder and harder.

We've never done this in the past, either, but I have fantasized about it more times than I can count. But my fantasies were nothing in comparison to the real thing.

Ivy fucking Hartwick is deep throating my cock.

And she's incredible at it.

I moan, getting lost in the sensations, but as soon as I make the sound, Ivy stops.

"Guess I'm not the only one who needs to keep quiet," she quips.

"I never knew you were this good at sucking dick."

"There are a lot of things you don't know about me, Pax."

With that, she goes back to getting me off, and I follow her lead, doing the same for her. Kneading her ass with my palms, I open her up wider and bury my face between her soft skin.

My pulse soars as I focus on pleasuring her. I lick, bite, and suck until she's a quivering, panting mess, right on the edge.

She focuses on me just as hard, causing my stomach muscles to constrict and my legs to stiffen. Both of us have staccato movements, trying to get the other off while on the brink of our own orgasm.

Our sweaty skin glides against one another as she circles her hips around my mouth, and I lift mine so my cock hits the back of her throat.

We get rougher as we sixty-nine, as if years of pent-up sexual frustration are finally letting loose. I force her pussy closer and closer to me, willfully ready to drown in her arousal.

As I continue to feast on her, her body becomes rigid for a brief second, and then she detonates with lust. Her muscles erratically flutter, and her entire body trembles on top of mine as she struggles to stifle her sounds despite having me in her mouth.

Ivy's wetness drips down my chin as I continue to lick her. I try to fend off my own orgasm so I can fully bask in Ivy, but it's no use. Her head moves at a hasty pace, and as she still trembles through her aftershocks, I can no longer keep my composure.

Heat coils at the base of my spine, every fiber of my being tense with desire, and with one more suck from Ivy, I'm exploding.

Sparks rush through my bloodstream as I come into Ivy's mouth and engulf myself between her legs to make sure my moans for her can't be heard by others.

Pure bliss unravels throughout my body.

My heart pounds inside me as the both of us begin to come down from our high. Ivy pulls her mouth away, and I can feel the mix of cum and saliva dripping down my length. She carefully peels her body off mine and turns to face me.

We try to catch our breath as we stare at one another. Admiring her glistening lips and messy hair, I smile. She does the same but is quick to end the moment, searching for her pajamas.

"Good night," Ivy says, getting her clothes back on. With a buttonless shirt, she crosses it over her chest and moves to the door.

"You're sleeping in your room?"

"Yeah, I told you we're keeping this simple. No strings." She winks.

I've been the king of simple. This is always how I've done things in the past with other women—and Ivy can pretend all she wants that this arrangement is straightforward.

But with me and Ivy, things have never been simple.

CHAPTER TWENTY-SIX

2007

October

"HARRIS, I got an awesome shot of you making the last goal," I say, checking out the pictures on my digital camera.

"Ivy, we're in the middle of a *game,*" Trent snaps.

"You're in the middle of a time-out because some guy on the other team got injured, which is why I came down to the bench to say hi to everyone."

After the night the boys got drunk at my house over the summer, the energy shifted a bit. They invite me to hang around, and a few of them ask me to take pictures of them at games. Coach doesn't mind when I pop over to say hello, as long as I'm not distracting them.

"Leave her alone, Trent," Pax interjects. "She's an honorary member of the team."

"Little Hartwick for the win!" Sid exclaims, making us laugh.

Coach starts talking to them, and I know that's my cue to leave. Climbing up the bleachers, I find my seat next to Dad.

"You've been spending a lot of time with Trent's team," he states, looking out on the ice as the game begins to pick up again.

"They're all really nice."

Of course, there's one teammate in particular I enjoy spending time with more than the others, but Dad doesn't need to know that. Just like he doesn't need to know that I still take pictures of the games Uncle Jeff misses and stop by the apartment to show him them... and to squeeze in some extra time with Pax.

Nothing has happened between us, and now that school and hockey have picked up, our attention has been pulled elsewhere. But we both know we have feelings for each other, and every small gesture, slip of the hand, sly smirk, and locked gaze has my emotions on overdrive.

"I'd like you to start spending more time with people in your grade," Dad continues, still not looking at me.

"I do."

We fall into silence as we watch Trent and Pax dominate the rink. After several minutes, Dad finally speaks again.

"Your mother had a meeting with the event planner for your sweet sixteen. She's getting several dresses sent to the house this weekend for you to try on."

"Okay," I mumble, knowing my sweet sixteen is just another event for Mom to show off. I didn't even get to pick the color scheme, and I doubt I'll have a say in anything else. It's not until March, several months away, yet she acts like it's tomorrow.

"Your mother and I both agree that you should have an escort for your sweet sixteen."

"An escort?" My voice rises in pitch from excitement.

For the first time since I sat back down, Dad turns his head to look at me. His face is filled with apprehension, but I'm too giddy to care.

If my parents are *requiring* I have a date, and *I* get to choose who that person is, maybe, just maybe, all the stars are aligning. I'll get to ask Pax, my parents will obviously approve because they know him and he's over the house all the time, and Trent will see it as his best friend helping his little sister, so there won't be any weird bro-code violation. It's all going to be so perfect and so easy.

My cheeks lift as I begin to beam over my seamless plan. I can sense Dad's eyes on me, but I turn my attention forward, looking directly at Paxton.

Four days have passed, and every time I go to bring up the sweet sixteen topic to Pax, I freeze. It's probably too early to ask him anyway. A guy like him doesn't plan a date that far in advance. And what would it mean if he did? Would he have to stop going out with other girls in the meantime? As much as I'd love that, agreeing to be my date wouldn't mean we're in a relationship.

My head spins from all the fake scenarios I've woven around my brain.

Sitting at my kitchen table, I push my science textbook off to the side and place my head in my palms. I usually do my homework in my bedroom, but this self-inflicted pounding between my temples called for a change of scenery.

"Hey," Pax says in my ear, coming up from behind me.

I shriek in surprise, my hands flying to my heart. "You scared the crap out of me!"

He bellows out a laugh. "Sorry. Couldn't pass up the opportunity."

"Yeah, you seem *real* sorry."

He continues to chuckle as he goes to get himself a drink. I didn't even realize he and Trent were home. I thought they went out hours ago.

My anxiety kicks into overdrive, debating whether or not to get it over with and ask him to be my sweet sixteen date since he's standing right in front of me.

"What are you working on?" Pax casually claims the chair next to me, his intoxicating scent making it difficult to focus on his question. He swivels my textbook to face him, and his features twist as he answers himself. "Oh, chemistry. I'm pretty sure I fell asleep during that class my entire sophomore year."

"I had to fight to keep my eyes open in first period today."

"I'm sure even if you did fall asleep, you'd still get an A." Pax gives me a smile so sweet, my insides tingle from the sugar rush.

My nerves become frayed, and I pick at my cuticles. "Um, so, there's something I wanted to ask you."

"I wanted to ask you something too."

"You did?"

"Yeah, but you go first."

"No, that's okay. Mine's not important."

I choked. So much for getting it over with.

"If you end up having a daughter one day, would you name her Ivy?" Pax asks.

My face scrunches in confusion at the same time I chuckle at the random question. "What?"

"I was watching an old episode of *Gilmore Girls* last week—"

"You were?"

"There was nothing else on. Don't make a thing out of it," Pax states, and I bite back my grin. "*Anyway*, as I was watching an episode, I got to wondering if you'd ever name your daughter the same as you, like Lorelai did. Although I still don't get how Rory is a nickname for Lorelai. If you ever end up naming your kid Ivy, don't give her a nickname that might as well have been the name written on the birth certificate."

Infatuation pours out of my bloodstream as I blissfully listen to him ramble about my favorite show. Sparks go off in my chest as I become unable to hide my smile.

"So…would you?" Pax asks, looping back to his point of the conversation.

"Definitely not."

"How come?"

"People hate ivy. Sure, it's pretty to look at when it's in someone else's yard, but the second people find it overgrowing in theirs, they complain that it's there and want nothing to do with it."

"I don't hate Ivy," he states, making my stomach jump.

"You must be the only one," I joke. "Also, there's poison ivy—I don't want my daughter associated with anything poisonous. If anything, I'd name her the opposite."

"What's the opposite of ivy?"

My head tilts to the side as I become deep in thought. When I finally figure it out, I can sense my face lighting up. "Daisy."

"Daisy?"

"Yep! They're delicate and cheerful, and I can picture

a little girl picking one from the ground and putting it in her hair in the summertime."

He nods, intently listening to me. "Way better than Rory."

I chuckle. "I think so too."

"So what was it you were going to ask me before, now that we got my question out of the way?"

"Oh, um…" Nervousness instantly crashes over me, wiping away the silly conversation we just had. "Well…" I clear my throat. "My mom's planning my sweet sixteen, which isn't until March, but she's already going crazy with everything. But I was wondering if…" My heart clamors against my rib cage. My tongue swells from the stupid amount of anxiety I'm getting over this. "I wanted to know if you…"

"Are you trying to invite me to your party? Of course, I'd go. I know I don't fit in with your family and other Windsor Prep kids, but that wouldn't stop me from going." He places his hand on my arm in an attempt to soothe me, but all it does is make me more tense. "Relax, Rebel. You don't have to freak out about inviting me. I wouldn't dare miss seeing you in a ballgown your mother picked out."

I squeeze out a laugh when in reality all I want to do is shrivel up into nothing and pretend like this conversation never happened.

"Ivy, could you—" Dad's voice echoes off the walls as he enters the kitchen. He pauses, noting Paxton's hand on me, and Pax nonchalantly removes it.

"Hi, Mr. Hartwick."

"Paxton." Dad gives him a curt dip of his chin as a form of hello.

"I'm going to head back to Trent." Pax rises and begins walking away. "Catch you guys later."

Dad's attention is fixated on him until he can no longer see him.

"What did you need me to do, Dad?"

He swings his focus back to me. "Never mind. I can have our housekeeper do it." Distracted by his thoughts, he exits the kitchen the same way Paxton did, without another word.

I'm left alone with only my science textbook and my feelings about Pax to keep me company.

CHAPTER TWENTY-SEVEN

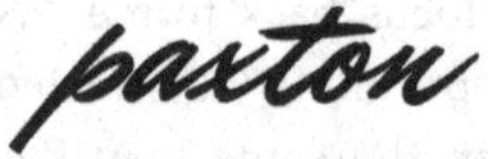

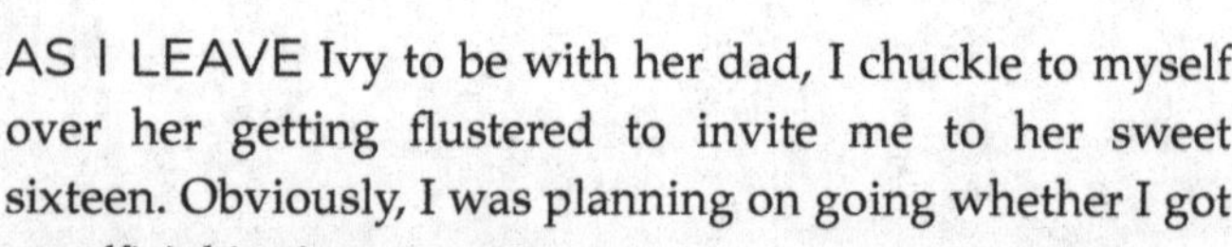

AS I LEAVE Ivy to be with her dad, I chuckle to myself over her getting flustered to invite me to her sweet sixteen. Obviously, I was planning on going whether I got an official invite or not.

Walking up the grand staircase, moving toward Trent's bedroom, the sound of leather-soled shoes pattering against the floor comes from behind me.

"Paxton." Mr. Hartwick's voice stops me dead in my tracks.

Glancing over my shoulder, I note his sour expression. The lines between his brows deepen in discord as he stands taller than usual. "Yeah?"

"I'd like to see you in my office."

With that, he pivots on his heels and walks off. Confused, my foot hovers over the step, unsure if I should continue going up toward Trent's room or back down the stairs and follow Mr. Hartwick.

After several moments of debating, I decide to find wherever his office is. Their home is filled with rooms that are barely touched but impeccably designed. It's a shame they don't fully enjoy these lonely corners.

When I move past an open door and get a whiff of old books and cigars, I peer in and spot Mr. Hartwick sitting at his large mahogany desk with Mrs. Hartwick standing beside him. Both of their focuses are laser sharp on me, causing my stomach to drop.

"Please come in," he states. "And shut the door behind you."

I do as he says, my internal alarm on high alert as he gestures at an empty chair across from him for me to sit in. My muscles move with caution as I lower myself into a stiff, oversized chair.

They stare at me in silence, watching my every move.

"Uh…hey?"

"Paxton, we'd like to go over a few things with you." His tone causes a prickling of unease to run under my skin. "We've witnessed you grow over the past several years, not only as a hockey player but also as a young man. We're aware of your hardships and watched you progress despite them."

My body relaxes, feeling instantly better knowing he called me in here to compliment me. "Thank you."

"We know that you are a good friend to our son, and he values your friendship above everyone else's, which is why we've welcomed you into our home."

"And I'm very grateful for that—"

"But that is where your role in our family ends," Mr. Hartwick's voice becomes stern, giving me whiplash.

"I'm not sure I follow."

The quietness becomes deafening as I wait for a response. Mrs. Hartwick continues to stand proudly next to her husband, not giving me a hint of what he might be referring to.

He lets me sweat it out for another moment until he finally speaks again, "As we noticed your friendship with

Trent grow, we've also noticed you've developed a fondness for our daughter."

My pulse stops.

I'm a deer in fucking headlights.

I struggle to remain unaffected by his comment.

"I-I'm sorry?" I sputter out.

"I know Ivy likes to insert herself and join in with Trent and his friends, and you are part of that group, which is fine. But anything beyond that will not be tolerated." He clears his throat. "Ivy's path is laid out for her. She will marry into a family with similar standards that we approve of."

My blood boils, liquid rage scorching my insides. I'm not sure if I'm more angry that he passively insulted me or if it's because he's not giving Ivy a choice on her future. "Shouldn't Ivy get a say in any of this?" I spit out.

Guess I'm more upset about Ivy.

Mr. Hartwick stares me down, his features turning to stone. I make sure not to flinch, glaring right back at him.

"Ivy has been made well aware of her future," he announces. "So your efforts in pursuing her will be deemed unnecessary in her eyes and unacceptable in ours."

I wasn't even *trying* to pursue her.

Was I?

I don't fucking know. I feel like I'm in some twisted mind game. All I know is that I don't want her in anyone's arms but *mine*.

"Is Ivy aware you're having this conversation with me?"

"No. And she won't be made aware." He pins me to the chair with his glare. "You won't speak of this to her or Trent. And you won't be making any advances toward Ivy."

I scoff. "And what happens if I choose not to follow these ridiculous rules?"

"You've been working diligently at your chance for a hockey career. We'd hate to see you leave the team."

The boiling sensation triples, becoming ignited with wrath. My jaw clenches hard enough to snap my bones. "Are you threatening me?"

"I'm advising you to make a wise decision. Who do you think donates to your hockey scholarship in order to keep you on the team?" He leans back in his chair. "Courting our daughter will be fruitless in the long run. I suggest you agree to our terms, and that way you can work on having a legitimate career and continue your friendship with Trent."

"And my friendship with Ivy?"

"Will remain platonic and distanced."

My head spins, millions of thoughts racing at the speed of light. There's a tightness in my chest that I can't shake off. It constricts more and more at the thought of keeping Ivy at arm's length.

But my hand is forced.

What else can I do?

If we magically ended up together, they'd never approve and do anything they could to separate us. They'd probably still hate me if I ever got a large cash flow and achieved my dream of going pro. And I'd lose my chances at being scouted for hockey if I'm kicked off the fucking team.

The whirling sound of my pulse gets louder.

And I'd also lose Trent. My first real friend.

Bile shoots up my throat.

Staying silent, I nod, the muscles in my neck grating against my joints as I resentfully agree. Mr. Hartwick gives me a shit-eating grin, as if we just made a business deal of a lifetime. My gaze flickers up at Mrs. Hartwick, who also looks pleased but is a lot less arrogant about it.

No other words are uttered, so I rise.

I jet out of the office and find the nearest bathroom to puke in.

CHAPTER TWENTY-EIGHT

2008

February

UNCLE JEFF HANDS me a bag of Cool Ranch Doritos and sits down across from me at his kitchen table.

"Pax was on fire during the game," I say, pointing to another picture I printed out as I crunch down on my chips.

"He just keeps getting better and better." Uncle Jeff beams.

My belly twists as I witness him admire the photographs. Things between me and Pax have been strained over the last few months, and I'm not sure why. Regardless, I still show up here for Uncle Jeff, despite Pax barely keeping a basic-level conversation with me.

What was really the nail in the coffin was when Pax started making out with some girl at the New Year's Eve party *directly* in front of me.

I don't know what the hell happened, but Pax suddenly became too busy to spend time with me or was always preoccupied when he was around. I guess his feelings for me were only fleeting, which I should've assumed by his track record, but I always clung to the hope that he saw me differently. To say I'm hurt is an understatement.

I guess this is why he never wanted us to venture down this road to begin with. The repercussions would've been way worse if either of us actually did act on our feelings.

The sound of the front door to their apartment sparks anxiety in my veins. My heart nervously flutters as I watch Pax enter in a worn hoodie with his backpack slung over one shoulder as he carries in a stack of mail.

"Hey, Uncle Jeff," he says before his eyes land on me. "Oh."

My brows raise, unimpressed by his greeting.

Pax slowly walks over to us. "I wasn't expecting you here."

"Well, you should've," I say with maybe a little too much bite to my tone. "Uncle Jeff wasn't at your last game."

Paxton's gaze shifts off me and doesn't land on Uncle Jeff either when he places the mail down in front of him. As I wait for some type of response, my attention gravitates to the stack of envelopes, noting the midnight blue one tucked in the middle. My stomach clenches knowing the invitation to my sweet sixteen is right there.

"I think I'll head into the shower and leave you two to catch up," Uncle Jeff announces, pushing his chair away from the table. "As always, thank you for the pictures, Ivy. You're welcome here anytime." His eyes bore into Pax for a brief second, then he trails down the hallway and into the bathroom.

There's a long beat of silence as a rosy color creeps up Pax's neck and blots his cheeks. He forces a casual smile as he says, "What've you been up to, Little Hartwick?"

Little Hartwick.

The name splashes me with acid, burning a hole through my skin. That's what everyone else calls me, not Pax. I'm his Rebel.

"Did I do something to you?" I snap.

"What?" He looks at me, dumbfounded.

"You've never called me Little Hartwick before. And it really feels like you're avoiding me and don't want to be around me. So I want to know if I did something to you to make you feel that way."

His posture rounds as he sits in the chair Uncle Jeff just got up from. "No. I'm sorry, Ivy. I've just been—"

"Busy."

"Yeah."

We lock eyes. Tension rises in the space between us. I try to get a read on what's happening behind those hazel irises, hoping he'll give me some inkling into what's really going on. His lips part as if he's about to say whatever words are on the tip of his tongue. But he stays quiet, his fingers fidgeting on the table. He nervously plays with the mail, and when there's a flicker of blue in the white envelope stack, he breaks eye contact and glances down.

In sparkly silver, Paxton Rhodes is written in calligraphy.

I hold my breath as I watch Pax's brows crinkle together. He peels it open and slides out the invitation. A sudden wave of shock hits his face as his attention jumps back to me.

"I'm still invited?"

"I told you that you were months ago." I cross my

arms over my chest. "But if you keep acting like a jerk, I might have to revoke the invite."

His features soften, warming my insides. "I'll be there," he proclaims. "Whether I'm allowed to be or not."

Despite his acting weird and distant recently, I would never tell him he's not allowed. I had planned on him being at my party from the beginning, although it was a little bit of a fight for me to get my parents' approval. But Trent pleaded with them as well, claiming he doesn't want to be stuck with my "annoying friends" all night, and since we already told Paxton about it, it would be in poor taste not to invite him.

Since it was a struggle just to agree to have Pax as a guest, I didn't bring up him being my escort, and considering how he's been acting lately, I'm not sure he'd be interested.

My BlackBerry phone chimes, letting me know my driver, Henry, will be here to pick me up.

"Henry's on his way?" Pax asks, already knowing the answer.

"Yeah," I say, gathering my things.

"Does he ever tell your parents that he's picking you up here?"

"Nope. As long as I show up for the things I'm supposed to—like this stupid dinner tonight—then they don't even notice I'm gone. And Henry would only tell them if he thought I wasn't safe. But he knows I'm safe with you."

Pax's features light up at the comment, but he doesn't say anything back.

We give each other a stiff goodbye, and before I know it, I'm in Henry's car on my way home.

As soon as I enter, our housekeeper, Stella, quietly rushes me to my room and tells me that Mom is expecting me to be dressed in the outfit she picked out, which is lying on my bed, and downstairs in the sitting room next to our dining hall in ten minutes.

Taking my damn time, I change out of my school uniform and into a plain, ivory dress that stops at the knee and a cropped knit sweater. Grimacing, I place a pearl necklace around my neck, hating how it looks. I don't bother running a brush through my hair or fixing my makeup. Whoever she's having over for dinner is going to have to deal with it.

As I make my way downstairs, toward the sitting room, I hear soft classical music playing from a speaker, followed by some chatter and polite laughter.

"There she is!" Mom is dressed to the nines, her smile wide with glee when she notices me entering. Gliding over to me, her hand gently rests on my back as she escorts me closer to her guests.

Dad is perched on his armchair, holding a crystal glass with a splash of alcohol in it. Next to him on the couch is a couple around my parents' age, and directly across from them is a boy who's around mine. Trent is at the other end of the room, giving me an expression to let me know he hates this as much as I do.

"These are the Coldwells. They're visiting from out of state. Your father and Mr. Coldwell are fraternity brothers," Mom explains as I shake their hands and introduce myself. They go on to tell me the generic comment of hearing wonderful things about me from my parents and then explain how they put in a good word for Trent's application to Johns Hopkins.

"And this is their son, Calvin." Mom redirects me over to the boy.

Before I can say hello, Calvin rises to greet me. He's tall and no doubt attractive. But his eyes are pale blue and not swirling in complexity like familiar hazel ones. His hair is trimmed perfectly at his shirt collar and doesn't sit like a messy mop on the top of his head. The way he smiles is nice, but there's no hint of mischief.

"Hi, Ivy," Calvin says, extending his hand. As I take it, I give him a polite hello back.

Mom gives my arm a light squeeze as if she's overcome with excitement. "Ivy, Calvin will be your escort for your sweet sixteen."

Air gets lodged in my chest.

My cheeks fall in disappointment, but I force them back up as Calvin beams at me with utmost delight.

Conversation about parties, guest lists, and floral arrangements swirls around the room. But the only thing I can focus on is the sound of the patter of my heart slowly sinking.

And sinking.

And sinking.

CHAPTER TWENTY-NINE

PRESENT

I STAND off to the side as everyone says their goodbyes at the cabin, feeling as if everyone knows that Pax and I sixty-nined last night, even though they don't. The itch to leave as soon as possible becomes unbearable the longer everyone hugs.

I give everyone a quick farewell, making sure to thank Trent and Lucille for this winter weekend getaway that surely messed with my head and hormones.

As I walk to my car, I hear snow crunching behind me.

"Hold on," Pax calls out.

Stopping, I wait for him to appear next to me. "What's up?" I ask.

"Makes more sense for us to drive back together instead of having a car service pick me up, don't you think?"

"You didn't plan a way back to Boston? Have you been assuming that I'd drive you back this entire time?"

"Not assuming, hoping. And I'd be more than happy to drive us back." He opens up his palm, waiting for me to drop my car keys in it.

I clutch onto the small piece of metal as I get a glimpse of everyone else getting ready for their car service to pick them up and bring them to the airport, because no one else lives within driving distance aside from me...and technically Pax.

Rolling my eyes, I respond, "You're not driving. I am. Get in." I don't wait to see if he has any type of reply, getting into my car as swiftly as I can.

We drive for several miles in silence, his presence making it challenging to concentrate on the road ahead of me.

Out of the corner of my eye, I watch Paxton adjust the heat vents and his chair as he stretches his legs. He then goes to touch the radio.

"Don't mess with my music," I state.

"I hate this song."

"*I* like it." A complete and total lie, as I have never heard this song in my entire life and couldn't even name who the singer is.

He sighs and resigns himself to leaning back against the passenger seat. We go back to silence, the friction between us escalating. It's just us, our veiled thoughts, and this unfamiliar song.

"So about last night," Pax says, cutting a knife through the air.

My heart flip-flops. "What about it?"

"You're still on board with everything you suggested? The whole friends-with-benefits thing?"

"I'm the one who suggested it, aren't I?"

"Yes, but I wanted to make sure it still felt right now that we're out of the moment."

"It still works for me as long as it does for you."

Pax hesitates before saying, "Yeah." He clears his throat, then changes the subject. "You looking forward to Trent and Lucille's wedding?"

"I'm happy for both of them, and I'm sure the wedding will be lovely."

"But…" Pax picks up on my unspoken words.

I sigh, hating how much he knows me. "I'm not looking forward to family members asking if I'm next. Or worse, asking me why I'm not already married with kids."

"Why aren't you?" he boldly inquires, making my eyebrows shoot up.

For the first time during this ride, I take my attention off the road and place it onto him. "Why aren't *you*?" After a beat, I shift my gaze back toward the windshield.

Pax's voice comes out low, encased in humble regret. "Because I'm an idiot and missed what was right in front of me."

Burning hot tears immediately prick at my eyes, but I'll be damned if I let him see one roll down my face. I'll cry in the comfort of my own home. Alone.

Gripping onto the steering wheel, my knuckles turn as white as the snow surrounding us as I fight to keep my composure. Clearing my throat and lingering emotions, I ask, "Are you taking a date to the wedding?"

"Wasn't planning on it." His energy shifts along with mine, releasing the seriousness of this prior statement. "What about you? Has Meredith given you hell about bringing an *escort*?"

I chuckle, remembering a distant memory of my sweet sixteen. "Of course she has. I'm sure she'll have some poor man primed and ready to be on standby when I show up with no one on my arm."

"I feel bad for him already. He has to deal with Meredith *and* your stubborn ass all in one night."

"Hey!" I whack his chest the best I can while driving, making Pax laugh. "I'm not stubborn. I'm independent."

"You know, we could save this poor nameless guy and just go as each other's dates."

I try my hardest to ignore the way my pulse picks up speed and my body suddenly gets flushed. "That would go against the whole friends-with-benefits thing, don't you think? We're supposed to be hanging out and hooking up. No dates."

"You're right." He inches closer, invading the minimal space I have in this car. "No dates." His pitch deepens as his fingers delicately sweep my hair off my shoulder. "Just friends." Ever so softly, he presses his lips to my neck, causing me to shudder.

The road in front of me becomes out of focus as Paxton continues to trail soft kisses up and down my skin. Lust hazing over my thoughts, I tilt my head, giving him more access. His lips curl up into a smirk against me just before he begins nibbling on my earlobe. Goose bumps scatter across my body as an ache between my thighs builds.

In a sudden snap of logic, I nudge him off me. "Get back on your side," I say, unable to conceal my grin. "If you keep doing that, I'll end up driving us into a snowbank."

"If you weren't a stubborn pain in the ass and let me drive us back, I would be concentrating on the road. But since I'm not, I get to concentrate on you." Paxton leans back over, sucking hard on my neck.

"You're so annoying." I laugh, shouldering him away.

Pax rests back in his seat, laughing along with me. He

doesn't try to make a pass at me for the rest of the trip, but sure as hell continues to complain about me not letting him drive. We banter back and forth for the duration, keeping things between us light and easy.

When I eventually pull up to the Hilton Hotel he's staying at, both of us procrastinate saying goodbye. We had a weekend with zero obligations and expectations, and now that the winter getaway is over, we're back to our regular life. The one where Uncle Jeff is in the hospital, Paxton is retired, and I push everyone away. It'll be a miracle if our friends-with-benefits plan plays out as seamlessly as I'd suggested.

Sensing myself deflate, I press the back of my head into the headrest, waiting for Pax to leave the car.

"I'm in room 418," he states.

"Okay?" I blink, waiting for him to say more, but he doesn't. "And you're telling me this, why?"

The familiar tug at the corners of his mouth makes my veins buzz. "In case you're having one of those nights where you're looking to get your needs met. I know where you live. Now you know where I'm staying."

"I'm not going to knock on your door in the middle of the night and say, *'Hey, I'm horny, let's bang.'*"

"Then what do you suggest?"

"Take my number like a normal person."

We take out our phones, exchanging numbers. As Pax gives me a little wink when he goes to say goodbye, I know that he proposed it that way on purpose. So he can finally have my number, and we can finally talk again.

CHAPTER THIRTY

MY PHONE LIGHTS up my pitch-black bedroom, waking me up. Lifting it up to see who in the world is bothering my sleep, I can't deny the little dance my heart makes when I see who it is.

PAX

Rebel

ME

Yes?

PAX

I'm horny, let's bang

I snort, then quickly type a response.

ME

It's 2 a.m. and I have work tomorrow.

PAX

Your point?

ME

I need to sleep, asshole

PAX

You can sleep when you're dead

ME

Sorry, it's just you and your hand tonight

Three chat bubbles pop up, then disappear. A smile widens on my face as it happens a few more times as he debates how to respond. My pulse races when he finally sends me a message.

PAX

Send me a picture

My eyes widen, knowing he's serious. Our hookup this past weekend wasn't just a fluke. It was the start of our friends-with-benefits relationship, and this is how Paxton wants to keep the ball rolling.

I bite down on my bottom lip. I'm not good at taking sexy pictures, and honestly can't remember when the last time I sent one to a guy was.

Nervously reaching over to my nightstand, I turn on my lamp and let light spill into my bedroom. I unbutton my pajama shirt, letting one sleeve hang off my shoulder. Most of my breasts are exposed, but there's a sliver of fabric covering them as I hold up my phone and squeeze my arm to my side to create more cleavage. I take the picture, making sure not to get my tired face in the image, and send it over to him.

PAX

Goddamn, Ivy

Laughing, I button myself back up and turn off the light.

PAX

I didn't think you'd actually send me one

ME

I'm full of surprises

PAX

Got any more surprises you'd like to send my way?

ME

I'll send you more tomorrow. That one will have to suffice for tonight

PAX

It sure will

ME

Enjoy. Goodnight

I place my phone down and roll over on my pillow, hoping to fall back asleep and get my mind off Paxton.

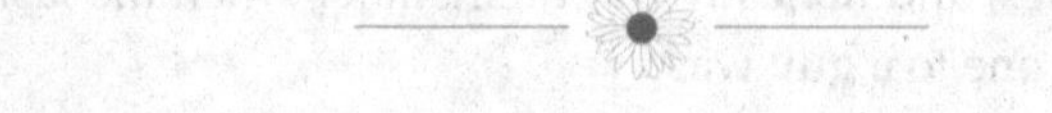

Stepping into the storage room of the museum, I stroll past decades of preserved fashion statements, vintage decor, and laminated pieces of paper conserving someone's past.

It's no wonder why my life path landed me in a museum. For most of my existence, I treasured preserving sacred moments, no matter how small. And in my adulthood, I became wistful, missing a place and time that I can never revisit and never fully replicate in the present. So this is a way of not only honoring my stories but also the stories of all the artists I discover, wondering if their nostalgia has ever kept them up at night.

Reaching Zaina, who's taking note of what we have left to work on for our new *Journey of Love Through the*

Ages exhibit, I spot her speaking with the librarian, Mrs. Esposito.

Zaina's eyes light up when she sees me. "How was your brother's winter getaway thing?"

"It was…interesting." I fight back a smile, but she can see it forming.

"Was Paxton there?"

"Oh, who's Paxton?" Mrs. Esposito asks. She's a charming woman in her seventies who enjoys all the tea we spill every time she's around the both of us.

"He's my brother's best friend."

"And the guy she used to be in love with," Zaina adds.

Mrs. Esposito gasps. "Are you two falling back in love?"

"She and Paxton are just friends," Zaina says with a dramatic flair.

"Oh, sure." Mrs. Esposito chuckles. "I know how that goes."

I shake my head, laughing along with her. Playfully, I glare at Zaina, who grins at me, waiting to get all the dirty details once we're able to talk in private.

The day flies by, and when my break rolls around, I head to the back office to get some downtime. My phone buzzes in the pocket of my pants, and when I take it out, I immediately smile at Pax's name on the screen.

PAX

It's tomorrow

ME

Can you keep it in your pants for 24 hours?

Zaina walks through the door, timing her break perfectly with mine.

"I need your help with something," I say. Before she can respond, I grab her wrist and rush her into the employee bathroom with me.

"Is everything okay? What's going on?" She stares at me with her eyebrows drawing together in concern.

After locking the door, I hand her my phone. "I need you to help me take nudes."

"What!"

"Not like *nude* nudes—just tasteful, slutty pictures of my ass or something," I explain, causing Zaina to explode with laughter. "I'm not good at taking pictures of myself. I can't get a decent angle, and I need them to look hot."

"And the man who you're so concerned about looking hot for wouldn't happen to be your ex, would it?" she teases.

"He's not my ex, but yeah. He probably gets a hundred nudes a day. I need mine to stand out."

"You're ridiculous, but fine. Turn around." She positions me against the wall so that my back is facing her. I press my forearms to the cool tile and arch my back. "We're about to take this friendship to a whole new level," she says, shimmying my pants down. They rest at the bottom of my ass, giving almost an entire view but not quite.

As Zaina fixes my thong, I say, "I love you. You're the best."

"Yeah, yeah," she playfully replies while setting her shot up. "Push off from the wall a little and fist your hair."

I do as she says and hear her shuffling behind me to take different angles. After a few seconds, she passes me my phone to look at, and when I deem that one of the pictures is passable, I hike my pants back up and send it to Pax.

"He better fuck you good after this," Zaina says as we exit the bathroom.

Before I can reply, I glance down at my phone and see texts come in at rapid-fire speed.

PAX

Holy fuck.

I need to see more of you

Send me another

Who took the picture?

Grinning, I type out a response to his last text.

ME

My friend Zaina

PAX

Thank her for me

"Pax thanks you," I whisper to her, unable to stop smiling.

"And soon *you'll* be thanking me too." Zaina winks.

A rush of heat cascades down my body as dirty Paxton fantasies filter through my mind.

Slipping my phone into my pocket, I attempt to shift my focus back to work.

But it's no use.

Paxton Rhodes has completely invaded my thoughts. Once again.

CHAPTER THIRTY-ONE

I'M SO INCREDIBLY HORNY, I could combust.

It's been two full days of sending nudes and dirty texts back and forth to each other. Two days of nonstop foreplay.

Neither of us has taken the plunge and invited the other over. I don't know what's wrong with us, but torturous, drawn-out foreplay seems to be our thing. We've had *years* of practice.

But today, I can't take it for much longer. My insides are wound so tight, I might snap in half before my workday is over.

Picking at my cuticles, I watch Zaina instruct her team on where to adjust the exhibit pieces that I chose. I attempt to focus on the numerous items that are being reworked, but a chorus of *aww*s coming from behind has me turning my attention to the mail clerk headed my way.

"Special delivery, Ivy," he states, holding a vase filled with colorful flowers. Mrs. Esposito and a few of my other coworkers are behind him, glancing over him to see my reaction.

My features draw in as I go toward him. "What do you mean?"

"These are for you."

He extends the flowers to me, and I cautiously take them, spying a note card in between pink and red rose petals. I spot Zaina and Mrs. Esposito grinning from ear to ear, along with others, while they wait for me to open the card.

Fumbling to open it up with my free hand, I say, "Who the hell got me flowers? And why?"

"It's Valentine's Day, dear," Mrs. Esposito reminds me at the same exact time I see what's written on the card.

Happy Valentine's Day, Rebel.

I must be wound a little too tight, because an angry flush stains my cheeks, immediately stealing my lustful desires and replacing them with bitterness.

We agreed on sex.

Sending me flowers on Valentine's Day is crossing the line. It implies strings, and I cannot have any strings attached when it comes to Paxton.

"I need to take care of something," I state to the entire room, whose eyes are on me. Holding the vase in a death grip, I rush to grab my coat.

"You okay, babe?" Zaina asks, worry laced around her question.

"Yeah. I just need to iron something out." I shuffle to get my arm through the sleeve of my jacket. "I'm taking my break early. Be back soon."

Irritation boils in my bloodstream. I don't even notice the cold when I step outside. My eyes zero in on the roof of the Hilton Hotel across the way, and I can hear Pax's voice telling me which room he's staying in—418.

My fingers curl around the vase, water sloshing around as I march toward the hotel.

In the blink of an eye, my anger leads me in front of Pax's room, and my fist ferociously bangs on the door.

"What the hell—" Pax's voice echoes from behind the door. When he opens it, his face automatically shifts from annoyance to concern when he notices me. "Ivy? Is something wrong?"

"Yeah, something's wrong! This!" I violently lift up the bouquet, water spilling out and splashing onto my hand.

Pax's head tilts back as he laughs, then he spins around and walks back into his hotel room.

"What the fuck are you laughing at? This isn't funny, Paxton." My jaw sets tight when he doesn't answer me, but continues to act like I just made the best joke in the world. Stomping into his room, I slam the door behind me, which only elicits another chuckle from him.

As I approach him, my brain finally registers what he looks like. Hovering over his dresser, he stands completely naked except for a white towel wrapped around his waist. His muscles are glistening from the shower, making me lose my train of thought for a second.

But *only* for a second.

"Sending me flowers is against the rules." The vase makes a loud thumping noise as I drop it down onto the dresser.

"You never said anything about flowers in your bullshit rules."

"Having a bouquet delivered to my place of work on fucking *Valentine's Day* isn't what friends with benefits do."

"Should I have had them delivered to your apartment instead?" he quips.

My fists ball up as a frustrating sneer comes from behind my pursed lips. "You shouldn't have sent me roses."

"Roses not your thing? I don't know a lot about flowers, but next time I can see if they have lilies, or carnations, or dais—"

"Shut up. You know what I mean."

Pax pauses, his gaze drifting down my body and slowly coming back up to meet my eyes. "I forgot how hot you look when you're pissed."

"Oh, don't try to charm your way out of this," I snap, although the sensation swirling around my veins would like to say a different response.

"I'm being completely serious." He takes a step closer. "The way you look is so sexy."

"What, do you have a business attire fetish?" I push open my jacket, placing my hands on my hips so he can get the full image of what I wore to work: a white button-up tucked into my navy blue slacks.

"I have a *you* fetish," Pax states, his voice thickening with need. "Everything you do." He closes the small gap between us. "Everything you say." Placing his hands on the arms of my jacket, he slides it off me, letting it drop to the ground. "And everything you wear turns me on."

Pax's attention drops down to my chest, which is moving at a hurried speed. My body betrays me, giving in to his lustful gaze. Carefully, he brings his fingers up to my shirt and starts to carefully unfasten the buttons.

"Not planning on making a mess of my clothing today?" I quip.

"Your clothes are safe. But I can't promise I won't make a mess of you."

Instantly, his hands wrap around my torso, and his lips claim mine in a frenzied kiss. Before I can think twice, I allow my shirt and bra to fall to the floor. Pax's hard cock pushes against his towel, begging to be uncaged. Our hands rake down each other's bodies, not sure of where we want to spend our focus on first, as our kisses become more desperate.

Fumbling to get to his bed, I struggle to get out of my pants. Attempting to step out of them, I trip, causing both of us to fall to the floor.

"Shit," I say out of breath. "Sorry." Wiggling out of my other pant leg, I begin to stand, but Pax pulls me back down.

"You're not going anywhere, Rebel." He flips me onto my back, pinning me to the carpet with his body. My insides light up with fire, feeling his weight against me, impatiently waiting for him to make the next move.

His captivating hazel eyes darken in a way I've only witnessed a few times. Holding himself up with one hand, he uses the other to yank his towel off him. Reaching down, he rubs the head of his cock over my thong. Hitting right against my clit, I gasp.

"You told me if I thought of any ground rules to let you know," he says, letting his fingers sneak under the thin fabric of my panties.

"I did." I try to speak the words in a firm voice, but it's no use as he begins to circle my clit. Applying the right amount of pressure, I writhe under him, aching to have him inside me.

"Rule one." Pax slides through my wetness. "If we're going to do this for the next couple of months, then you're mine. No hooking up with anyone else, no talking to anyone else, no looking at anyone else."

"Same rule applies to you?"

"Yes."

"Deal."

"Say it." He pushes two fingers inside me. My back arches off the carpet. "Say you're mine."

My lashes flutter shut as he curls his fingers, pumping

in and out of me, the sound of my arousal becoming increasingly obvious. "I'm yours."

"Look at me when you say it," he demands, eliciting goose bumps to scatter across my vulnerable skin.

Peeling my eyelids open, our gazes lock. The way he's hovering over me is too reminiscent of a past experience. My heart pounds out of fear of getting too close and getting hurt again.

But then Pax brings the heel of his palm up to meet my clit, and I lose all rationale. His hips impatiently rock, his length moving against my thigh for added friction.

"Rebel…" Desire flames in Pax's eyes, casting a spell over me.

"I'm yours." I moan at the sensations flowing through me. "For the next few months," I'm quick to add before getting too wrapped up in the magical way he's making me feel.

Pax smirks. "Still a pain in my ass, even when I'm about to make you come." He leans down to kiss me, so I'm not able to make a remark.

My head gets foggy, getting lost in the gentle swipes of his tongue. I push up to meet the movements of his hand, tension coiling tighter and tighter around my veins.

He pulls his lips away slightly. "Second rule." His breath tickles my mouth. "If you're going to let me treat you like my whore in the bedroom, then you let me treat you like my queen outside of it. And if I want to buy you fucking flowers, I'm going to."

My legs tremble. "I hate that rule."

"I'm not gonna do this friends-with-benefits bullshit unless you agree to it."

Heat builds in my core as he changes tempo. I know I'm losing this battle, so I'm fast to give in to his request. "F-fine."

Pax's lips curl into a sexy smile. "Good girl."

The moan that falls from my mouth is branded with so much need, I'd be embarrassed if I were with anyone else aside from Pax.

"Oh, you like being called that, Ivy?" he taunts in a voice that makes me move my hips at a quicker pace against his hand. "I thought you liked being a little rebel. Were you saving being a good girl for when I fucked you?" He baits me, and I gladly take it, nodding my head.

My lungs desperately search for more air the closer I get to falling over the edge.

But he doesn't allow me to finish, slowly withdrawing his fingers from me. I whimper from the loss of contact, and it makes the cocky motherfucker smirk wider. "You got so wet for me."

Pax delicately brings his index finger up to my mouth, leisurely tracing my lips. I taste my arousal on the tip of my tongue as my heady breaths brush against his calloused skin. Once he makes sure to cover me in my wetness, he brings his fingers to his mouth, sucking them clean. His eyes close shut as if he's savoring every last drop of me.

Fireworks go off inside me from watching him. Needy and aching, I spread my legs further apart, hoping he'll soon settle between them.

As I adjust myself, his eyes open up, and he brings his hand to either side of me, trapping me under him. Our chests connect with every swift breath we take. Our gazes are fixated on one another. The tension between us crackles with every drawn-out second that goes by.

"How do you want me to fuck you?" he rasps, the vein that's protruding from his throat hastily fluttering.

"Do whatever you want to me. Just don't come inside me."

Pax reaches between our bodies, lining up his cock with my entrance. "Whatever I want?" His eyebrow quirks. "You sure about that?"

Nodding, I sense my hair knotting against the carpet. "I'm yours, Pax."

"That's right, Ivy." He begins pushing into me. My mouth hangs open in a silent scream as he stretches me. "You're all mine."

My entire body trembles as he fully enters me. Sparks flare all throughout my bloodstream. I sink my nails into his arms, bracing myself for what's about to come.

Pax lets out the most delicious-sounding groan. "I missed how fucking perfect your pussy feels." He rocks his hips, gradually picking up speed.

"I missed how you feel inside me." I'll yell at myself later for letting that slip, but for now, I work with his pace, feeling the carpet scratch my back with a delightful sting.

He grabs my legs one by one, hooking them over his shoulder as he positions me to get a deeper angle. He expertly moves his body in a way that hits just the right spot.

Pax's focus is glued to me, unwilling to look anywhere else. With each thrust he makes, a flicker of satisfaction appears on his face at the sight of my reaction. It's so hot witnessing him get off to getting me off.

I've never been with a man who cared this much about my pleasure, or who got this turned on at the way they make my insides spiral with white-hot lust.

Reaching in between our slick bodies, I sneak my hand to where we're connected and circle my clit.

Pax's eyes follow my hand, and he creates more space between us. "Fuck yes, Rebel. Touch your gorgeous pussy for me," he pants, causing me to moan. He kisses my knee, his attention still on my fingers as he continues to pound into me.

My body gets flushed, the sensations overtaking me. My eyes clamp closed as my veins light up in ecstasy. Lust winds inside me, and my legs start to shake.

"That's right, Ivy," Pax coaxes. "Be a good girl and come for me."

My last shred of control gets ripped away at the sound of his voice, and my orgasm fiercely runs through me. I scream out in pure intoxication, trembling and shaking beneath Pax as the fibers of the carpet scrape against my skin and knot my hair.

Heat courses through my bloodstream over and over again, endlessly supplying me with passion as Pax continues to roll his hips. He lets out a string of curses, gripping onto my body in a bruising way, forcing himself to keep his composure until I'm finished.

Gasping for air, I flutter my lashes open and see Pax staring at me with the most depraved and hungry expression. The millisecond I begin to settle down, he pulls out of me and fists his cock.

His chest is reddened and moving up and down at a fast pace as he moves up my body. His breath comes out labored, a throaty moan pulling at his vocal cords as he spills onto me. Warm spurts of cum cover my breasts, chest, and neck, coating me with his desire.

The image and sensation of his lust dripping down my nipples instantly make me want more of this.

More of him.

More of feeling like I'm his and he's mine.

Pax carefully moves off me as we catch our breath. Silently, he walks over to where his discarded towel lies on the floor as I begin to sit up.

Coming back over to me, his gaze dances all over my body as he adorns a wide, prideful smile. "You look fucking gorgeous with rug burns on your back and my cum all over your tits."

Warmth rushes to my cheeks, beginning to burn my skin. He extends his hand, helping me stand, and gently uses the towel to wipe me.

"I-I need to get back to work," I say.

Pax nods. "You can use the bathroom to freshen up."

Scooping up my clothes, I walk into the bathroom to examine myself. My chest is still sticky, my hair is wild, my lips are swollen, and delicate red marks paint my skin.

Clearing my throat, I screw my head back on as I take another towel, adding water and soap to it in order to get rid of the pasty feeling.

"What time do you work until?" Pax asks from the other room.

"Late. I have an unveiling tonight."

"Unveiling?"

"Yeah, every time we have a new exhibit, we do an unveiling. Nothing major, I just give a little speech in front of the board, some donors, and whichever museum members want to attend, and then it officially opens. But I certainly can't present looking like this. I'll have to run home and change before it starts." Staring in the mirror, I move on to fixing my makeup the best way possible.

"What kind of exhibit is it?"

"A *Journey of Love Through the Ages,*" I announce, wiping the mascara smudge from under my eyes. "It's cute. We had to make it immersive so that it does well with social media influencers since it's running through the summer. Hopefully, we'll draw in a bigger crowd if people start making reels about it."

"Sounds interesting."

Moving on to my clothes, I get dressed. "It is. Each decade from the fifties to the nineties has its own setup, and people can get a glimpse of what romance and dating were like at different points." Running my fingers through my hair, I make sure I look decent enough to return back to work, then step out of the bathroom.

Pax is fully dressed, sitting at the foot of the bed. It's the first time since coming in here that I realized he's in a regular hotel room. He's got enough money to pay for a suite on the top floor of the Hilton, and yet he chooses the standard option.

"Why are you smiling at me like that?" he asks, calling me out.

"I'm glad you stayed down-to-earth."

His head tilts to the side. "What do you mean?"

I chuckle to myself, grabbing my jacket. "I'll see you later, Pax."

"I'll be sure to send more roses your way so we can reenact what just occurred."

I toss him a playful glare, then glance back at the flowers on the dresser, choosing to leave them there. And with that, I exit.

CHAPTER THIRTY-TWO

paxton

SHINY TILED floors and bright lights greet me as soon as I enter the Contemporary Art and Lifestyle Museum. It smells clean in here, not like the disinfectant smell from Uncle Jeff's hospital, but fresh and inviting. To the left and right are separate exhibits that wind their way around multiple hallways, and in the far back is a large staircase leading to more displays for people to view upstairs.

In the center of the wide space, there's a woman in her early twenties working the informational desk, cordially grinning at me. "Hello, are you here for the unveiling?"

"Yes, I am."

"Can I please have your name to look up in our system?"

"Oh, I'm not a member."

Her shoulders drop. "I'm sorry, this is a members-only event. You're welcome to join if you're interested. There's a onetime annual fee, or we can break it up into monthly payments—"

"Here you go." My credit card and ID are already fished out of my wallet and sliding across the counter.

"I'll pay the full amount. I just want to make sure I get there in time." I checked the time of the event online, and I know I'm pushing it close.

The woman types my info into her computer and charges my card, then instructs me toward the second floor, where the unveiling is.

I move past other displays, quickly passing by artwork and glass-encased memorabilia in order to get to the staircase. When I arrive at the top of the stairs, I hear Ivy's voice floating through the space.

This is no tiny event, as there are upward of at least seventy people in suits and dresses, listening to Ivy speak into a microphone. A photographer stands off to the side, capturing the moment as I hang in the back of the crowd.

"As you move throughout the exhibit, please take your time to fully immerse yourself in the experience," Ivy speaks with authority and pride. Joy races through my bloodstream as I admire her. "Travel back to the fifties and sit in our Thunderbird replica, where you can catch scenes from various romance movies as if you're at a drive-in movie. Dance in our disco-themed room during the seventies. And be sure to snap a Polaroid with you and your friends when you make your way from the eighties and into the nineties." She glances around the room, and her attention lands on me. She falters for a millisecond, not long enough for anyone else to notice, and continues. "This-this exhibit contains iconic fashions from celebrities, well-known photographs, artwork, TV shows, and sacred mementos from our recent history. For me and my team, this exhibit has been a labor of love—no pun intended." People softly chuckle. "And we are proud to introduce *Journey of Love Through the Ages*."

Everyone claps, myself included, and chatter starts up as people disperse. The crowd parts down the middle, as if purposefully creating space for us. My heartbeat echoes as I stand at the opposite end, marveling at Ivy.

Several people come up to her, shaking her hand and asking questions. I can't make out what they talk about, but I notice her glance my way every few seconds.

Anxiety builds in my feet, yearning to dash over to her, pick her up in my arms, and tell her how proud I am of her. But instead, I hang back and lean against a wall as I watch her full effect.

This is what I want.

I want to know who Ivy is *now*.

I want to witness her growth, see her in her element, and take note of how much she has evolved into an incredible woman over the years.

Minutes go by. I'm not sure how many because I've been lost in watching Ivy interact with everyone. But I know a good amount of time has passed because people have finally given Ivy space and are roaming through the exhibit.

She slowly drifts over to me. "You're bordering on stalker status again," she quietly teases.

"I don't think you should be name-calling museum members."

Laughing, Ivy asks, "You're a member?"

"Yep. It was the only way I was allowed to see you in action."

"There's not much to see. That was it."

I watch as her attention floats over the room, a slight lift in her lips as she watches people enjoy her accomplishment. Warmth grows in my chest, a never-ending surge of awe flowing through me.

"Well, well, well." A woman appears next to Ivy. "Who do we have here?"

Ivy narrows her eyes at the woman, giving her a joking glare, then shifts her focus to me. "Pax, this is my best friend, Zaina. She's the exhibit designer and did a flawless job. Zaina, this is Pax."

Zaina extends her hand for me to shake. "Pleasure meeting you, Pax."

"Same to you."

"Thanks for making my friend smile when she got back from her 'lunch break,'" she says in air quotes.

"Thanks for being her photographer the other day."

"Okay, that's enough from you two!" Ivy interjects.

"You're lucky I just popped over quick before checking in with Roy," Zaina says to Ivy and then shifts over to me. "Roy is our director, and if I didn't have to go talk to him, I would've gladly stayed here all night chatting about Ivy with you."

"We'll have to take a rain check," I state.

"Most definitely." She gives Ivy a wink and parts ways.

I smirk. "She seems awesome."

"She definitely is." Someone catches Ivy's eye, and she holds up her index finger, indicating that she needs a few seconds. "I'm sorry, Pax, I have to go back to schmoozing."

"I get it. Go do your thing, Rebel."

Her lips twitch. "Thanks for coming."

"Of course."

Ivy hesitates as if she's struggling to break apart from me, but she eventually does.

Standing on the sidelines, I watch as she bounces from person to person, sophisticatedly moving through the space in a delicate, maroon-colored dress, which she must've changed into before the event started.

I casually stroll around, but I'd rather wait to see everything until Ivy shows me herself. My attention gravitates toward the disco area where a handful of others laugh while doing cringe-worthy dance moves. A man slightly older than me reaches for Ivy, and the two join the group, dancing horribly together.

It's innocent and playful, but it ignites a dormant jealousy in my bones.

I've had to watch her dance with others before. And I swear, this will be the last time.

CHAPTER THIRTY-THREE

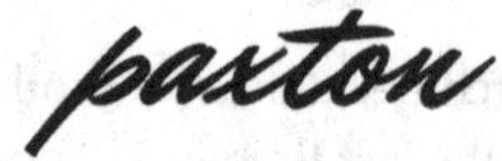

2008

March

ANXIETY SPINS a web inside my abdomen. It takes a lot for me to get nervous. In fact, Ivy's sweet sixteen party might be my worst experience with anxiety to date.

"You clean up well," Uncle Jeff says by our front door. He chuckles to himself as he witnesses me in a suit. I had to borrow one from Trent, but I bought myself a new white button-up shirt since I grew out of my other one. I didn't know what to do with my hair now that it's getting longer, so I'm sure the contrast between formal attire and skater hair is a comical sight.

"Thanks," I respond.

"Be careful driving." He hands me the keys to his car. "And have fun—but not too much fun."

Biting back a grin, I say, "I will."

Tapping my pants pocket, I make sure I have Ivy's

gift, then head to the car, grateful Uncle Jeff is letting me have it for the night.

Ivy's gift isn't anything extravagant, but I figured it would mean a little bit more to her than the endless amount of generic jewelry she'll probably end up getting.

Her parents could've hosted the event in their ballroom, where they have all their other fancy parties, but instead they're having it at a swanky venue overlooking the water.

Uncle Jeff's car hums loudly as I pull into the lot. A slight rattle comes from under the hood, which we've yet to address, as I pass by rows of luxury cars. As I park, I will my anxiety to subside, still not completely sure why I'm even feeling it to begin with.

The large vestibule is filled with flowers I don't know the name of, and a giant "Ivy's Sweet Sixteen" banner stretches from one wall to the other. Laughter consumes the space as a group of girls wearing brightly colored dresses rush past me to get to the ballroom, the wide-open doors leading them straight in.

As I slowly follow their lead, hoping to run into Ivy before entering the massive party, I hear the DJ playing "Low" by Flo Rida. Imagining Meredith Hartwick's face when she listens to the crude song while teenagers awkwardly grind on the dance floor causes me to laugh to myself.

But the humorous moment is automatically smothered by the reality of entering a Hartwick event. I stand in the doorway, scoping out the venue. Flashy neon lights, a grand balloon arch, and over-the-top centerpieces make it difficult to land my focus, but I still scope out who's in attendance as if I'm looking into a fishbowl.

Mr. and Mrs. Hartwick are dressed formally, paying no mind to the song as they converse with other adults who look just like them. I don't spot Ivy or Trent anywhere, but there are other Windsor Prep kids crowding the dance floor, some of them looking familiar from the parties I've been to with Trent, but no one I know well enough to hang out with. Everyone is graced in designer brands, mingling in their cliques.

The longer I stand on the edge of the room, the more distance I feel between me and the rest of them.

I know I don't belong here.

Mr. and Mrs. Hartwick don't want me here, and for the first time since entering Trent and Ivy's lives, I'm starting to understand why. I don't fit in with this world.

Feeling exiled, my feet retreat backward, not ready to enter. Instead, I pace the vestibule, watching guests excitedly arrive and scamper into the party.

I aimlessly stroll down a hallway, passing the restrooms, then stumble upon what looks like a private lounge room. Poking my head inside, it's quiet with no one in sight. There's an empty couch and chair, a full-length mirror, and a closed door off to the side connecting to some other place in the venue.

Using this time for a quick moment of respite, I sneak inside and flop down onto the couch. Ivy's gift pokes my leg, and as I carefully draw it out of my pocket, a defeated sigh releases from my lips.

I hold the clear CD case, looking at my chicken scratch written on the mixed CD. *For my Rebel*. It's just a compilation of songs that remind me of her or us.

Nothing special.

The door off to the side swings open, and my head whips around to a startled Ivy.

"Pax?"

She glides over to me, and all I can do is gawk at her. "S-sorry, I know I'm not supposed to be in here." I rise, getting a better look at her.

My heart pounds with amazement. She's in a

sapphire blue ballgown with the neckline making a heart shape. The top half is bedazzled with rhinestones and slowly tapers into smaller gems until the bottom half, which is like a shimmery night sky. Her hair is half up and half down in tight curls sprayed down by a pound of hairspray, and each of her ears has a dangling silver jewel hanging from it.

"It's okay. You can chill in here if you want," Ivy says, snapping me out of my trance.

"I was just looking for you."

"Well, here I am." She lifts up her arms, showcasing her dress as if I hadn't just been admiring her. "What do you think?"

I swallow. "You're perfect."

The blue in her eyes deepens, the spellbinding color intensifying from the similar shade of her dress.

"Really? You don't think all of this is a bit…much?" Ivy swishes around the fabric.

"I think you look perfect in anything." Warmth creeps up my neck, inching its way to my cheeks. I curse myself for having this stupid reaction and hope she doesn't notice.

"Don't say that too soon. My mom is forcing me to wear a tiara."

I chuckle. "I would expect nothing less from her."

A knock on the door that I had come in through draws our attention away from each other. I notice a guy around our age with a fresh haircut and a newly pressed suit staring at Ivy.

"Hey, babe, your family is looking for you," he says.

My brows shoot up. "*Babe?*" I ask, my line of sight directly on Ivy as she scurries to his side. They look like they could be on the cover of a teen magazine, posing as the epitome of a flawless couple.

My bloodstream drowns in green envy. Shock rattles

my core the more they gel together. Clearly, I missed out on some *vital* fucking information.

"Pax, this is Calvin," Ivy begins to introduce us. "Calvin, this is my brother's best friend, Pax."

"Nice to meet you." He extends his hand, but I ignore it.

"You have a boyfriend?"

"Um…" Both of them shift uncomfortably. "We've only been on three dates so far," she states.

"But who knows, maybe after tonight…" Calvin's voice trails off. His eyes rake over her in a way that makes her innocently blush, but I *know* the intentions behind that look.

Staking claim, I step in closer to him, letting the few inches I have over him be enough to intimidate him. Jealousy bites down into every word as I speak. "After the party tonight, you'll be going back to your house, and Ivy will be going back to hers. Unless you have some perverted plan you'd like to make her privy to."

"Paxton!" Ivy snaps, and if looks could kill, I'd be bleeding out on the floor right about now judging by the expression on her face. She's quick to plaster on a smile and shifts her focus over to Calvin. "You'll have to forgive him. Pax and Trent can be stupidly overprotective at times."

"I get it." He nods, unfazed. "But you guys have nothing to worry about." He gives me a smile, slipping his arm around her waist. My eyes burn a hole in the spot where he has his fingers splayed on her hip, and I think Ivy can sense it.

"Can you let my mom know that I'm just touching up my makeup and I'll be right there?"

"Sure." Calvin gives her a peck on the top of her head and thankfully leaves.

Once he's gone, Ivy's face twists with annoyance. "What the hell was that?"

"I could ask you the same thing! You come to my home how many times to drop off pictures for Uncle Jeff, and you've failed to mention that you're dating some preppy kid?"

"First off, you're rarely around anymore. Second, you don't tell me about all the girls you hook up with, so why should I tell you about Calvin?"

I open my mouth to respond, but I've got nothing.

She's one hundred percent right, and I hate that she is.

Ivy crosses her arms over her chest, waiting for me to say something. The light above us refracts off one of the rhinestones, bringing awareness back into my body. I don't want to cause any issues on her big night. I want her to have fun, even if she doesn't like how overboard her mom has gone with all of this.

"Sorry," I say, forcing myself to calm down. "I was just caught off guard. That's all."

She takes a beat, then slowly drops her hands. "Okay."

"I'll let you finish getting ready and see you out there." Taking a step toward the exit, I realize I'm still clutching onto her gift. "Oh, here, this is for you."

I pass her the CD and notice a smile appear when she reads the little message I wrote on it. "Thank you."

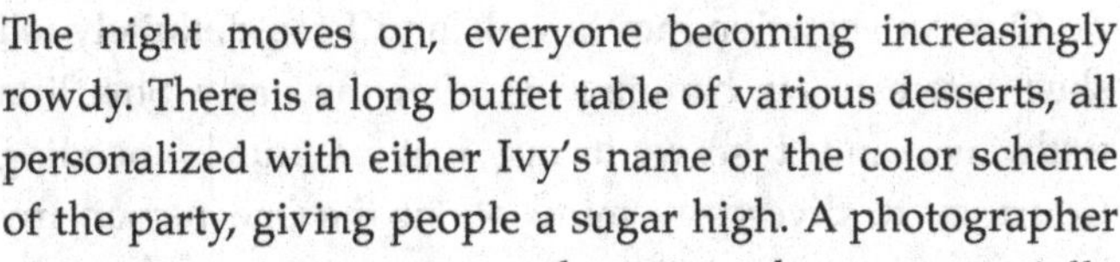

The night moves on, everyone becoming increasingly rowdy. There is a long buffet table of various desserts, all personalized with either Ivy's name or the color scheme of the party, giving people a sugar high. A photographer walks around, capturing each moment he can, especially when guests start trying on items from the prop table, like shutter shades or feather boas.

I sip on my soda, wishing I had some alcohol to mix into it, when Trent nudges my shoulder. "Secured a girl for each of us tonight," he says with a proud smirk.

"I taught you well." We both chuckle at how my charm has rubbed off on him. "Which ones?" I ask, desperately needing a distraction from the thought of Ivy and Calvin together.

"Those two." Trent gestures with his chin to two girls whispering to each other a few tables away from us. "No clue who they are. The one in the pink dress has a mom who's a Dame, so that's why she's invited. And she asked to bring her friend, the blond. They're seniors like us, but they go to some boarding school."

"Boarding school." My interest is piqued. A sly look passes between us, and we chuckle once more before heading over to them.

"Hey, ladies," Trent says, sitting down next to one in a hot pink dress. "This is Pax."

I place myself next to a blonde girl wearing a big chunky necklace. "Nice to meet you."

"You as well. I'm Courtney." She smiles, but it doesn't light me up like it would to see Ivy smile.

Courtney is pretty, but her eyes don't captivate me with a dark gemstone blue hue. She's sweet, but there's no feisty energy about her. She laughs at everything I say, but it doesn't feel fulfilling like it would to bring joy to Ivy or press her buttons until she snaps.

Our conversation moves well, and I can definitely tell she's interested in hanging out after the party. She flirts with me, and I serve it out just as much, needing Courtney to divert my mind off of the one person my brain goes back to.

The DJ suddenly shifts the energy of the room,

announcing that he's going to slow it down for all the couples. A light strum of an acoustic guitar plays over the speakers.

Trent rises and extends his hand out to the girl he's been talking to. "Care to dance?" he asks, and she blushes, taking his hand.

I follow his lead. "Would you like to dance?" I ask Courtney, and she places her palm in mine.

"Of course."

We make our way to the dance floor, a sea of couples swaying back and forth. Courtney falls into place, pressing her body against mine and resting her head on my shoulder. I hold on to her, one of my hands clasping hers while the other lays on the small of her back. We slowly shuffle around, getting lost in the song "You and Me" by Lifehouse as it flows over the crowd.

My attention lands on the couple at the center of the floor. Ivy and Calvin.

His back is turned to me, and her head peeks over his shoulder.

She looks up, and her line of sight falls directly on me.

Our eyes lock, neither of us willing to break the connection.

She holds on to Calvin tighter, and I do the same with Courtney, as if, in some way, our squeezing them will somehow transfer over to each other.

I hate this.

I hate that I'm so close to Ivy but can't touch her.

I hate that she's being pushed into this world while I get forced out of hers.

An ache in my heart builds, causing an endless pang of hurt against my ribcage the longer we dance with each other through other people.

The volume of the song increases as the chorus picks up. The lyrics hit both of us like a slap in the face.

And it's you and me
And all of the people
And I don't know why
I can't keep my eyes off of you.

Gutted by those lines, an unfamiliar burning sensation fills my eyes. Glancing down, I break our connection and spin Courtney around.

By the time the song is over, Ivy is further away on the floor, smiling up at Calvin.

And I'm left with a gigantic hole in my chest.

CHAPTER THIRTY-FOUR

May

"THANKS FOR TAKING ME MINI GOLFING," I say to Calvin. The uplighting around the columns near my front door brightens his features under the night sky.

"Of course." He brushes an errant strand of hair off my cheek, then carefully presses his lips against mine. "I'll text you tomorrow. Have a good night."

"Good night."

We part ways, Calvin stepping toward his car and me going inside my house. Closing the door behind me, the silence bouncing off the cathedral ceiling becomes blaring. Mom and Dad took a vacation somewhere, and all of our houseworkers have been excused for the night.

I could've invited Calvin inside, but we've been taking things slow.

I'm not even sure if he's my boyfriend. I mean, we text almost every day, he takes me out on dates, and we like to make out, so I guess that means he's my boyfriend.

But he hasn't officially asked me to be his girlfriend. Is that even the protocol? I don't know how this sort of stuff works.

My thoughts follow me upstairs and down the hallway toward my bedroom. Passing Trent's room, I hear muffled sounds coming from his TV. The door is open, so I decide to pop in to get advice on this boyfriend-girlfriend stuff—not that he'd be keen on the idea or ever had a girlfriend of his own, but he can at least let me know what the formalities are.

Peeking my head in, his flat-screen TV plays a scene from *300*, a movie that he and Paxton became obsessed with. The low rumble of snoring catches my attention, and my eyes drift over to Trent, passed out on his bed.

Chuckling to myself, I leave him alone and decide on bringing up the topic another time.

When I get into my room, I move to my pajama drawer to find something comfy to change into. My fingers drift over the endless pile of cotton until they reach the very bottom of the drawer, where Paxton's Blink-182 T-shirt from a few years ago is bunched up. My mind jumps to the mixed CD he gave me for my birthday. I played it as soon as I got home from my sweet sixteen, the very first song catching me off guard. I knew his favorite band would be on the CD, but I didn't expect "I Miss You," nor did I expect it to be the opening song.

As my thoughts become more tangled up in boy dilemmas, I change into Pax's shirt and a pair of sleep shorts. I go to put on my birthday CD, but as I start to hit play on my stereo system, something out my window grabs my attention.

The lights from the terrace cast a glow on the figure sitting on one of the benches in the courtyard. Long legs are outstretched, and familiar messy hair gently blows in the breeze. I watch as he brings something up to his lips, and a few seconds later, a plume of smoke clouds the space around him.

Without thinking, my impulses guide me from my room and outside to join Pax.

He doesn't hear me as I tiptoe into the beckoning summer air, a slight mask of humidity coating my skin, letting me know that hotter days are within reach. Jitters run down my spine as I get closer to him, smelling the faint scent of skunk near the wooden bench.

"Hey," I whisper so I don't startle him too much.

Pax immediately spins around, a small smile playing on his mouth when he realizes it's me. "Hey," he responds with a low rasp.

Carefully joining him on the bench, I notice that his eyes are bloodshot, and there's a joint between his two fingers. I've seen him drunk a handful of times, but never high. The unknown territory excites me, washing a wave of thrill over my body.

"You just getting home?" he asks.

"Yeah, I went out with..." My voice trails off, and I clear my throat, switching the subject. "I didn't know you and Trent had plans to hang out tonight. I haven't seen you in a while."

"Yeah, we've both been busy with our own stuff. He told me your parents would be away this weekend, so we had planned to chill and smoke, but your lame brother fell asleep early."

I chuckle. "Well, lucky for you, the better of the Hartwick siblings has arrived," I say with a hint of flirtation woven in between my words.

Pax's gaze rakes over me. "Nice shirt." He smirks, looking directly at the band logo. Or my chest. It's hard to tell what he's zooming in on.

"Thanks, an old friend gave it to me. I used to

consider him one of my best friends, but he's barely been around lately," I dig at him.

"It's the end of the school year. We've both been busy getting ready for finals and shit."

"Yeah, I guess." It still seems like he's been distancing himself from me even more ever since he found out Calvin exists. "Are you excited to graduate?"

Pax lets out a humorous laugh and brings the joint up to his lips. I watch as his cheeks draw in as he takes a long drag. The joint leaves his mouth, but he waits several seconds before blowing out smoke, turning his head away from me as he does so none of it covers me. He's silent, choosing not to answer my question, and I realize I might've stumbled upon a sensitive topic.

"Is that why you're out here smoking? Because you're concerned about graduating?" I ask.

He shrugs. "Trent's headed off to Johns Hopkins in August, and a bunch of my friends on the team got scholarships to different universities, but my grades aren't good enough to get a scholarship anywhere." His attention drifts down to his shoes. "Can I tell you something that no one knows?"

Sparks fly around my ribcage. "Of course."

"The East Coast Hockey League is a step down from the American Hockey League, which is basically the minors. Lots of guys have worked their way up to the majors from there," he states.

I wait for him to say more, but he doesn't. My head tilts to the side, wondering if this was just a weed-induced comment that he thinks is earth-shattering. "Okay…"

"The East Coast Hockey League is considering me."

"What!" I burst out of my skin with glee. "Pax! This is huge!" Elated, I stare at him, expecting him to be jumping for joy just like I am, but he remains stoic. "Have you smoked too much? Why are you not excited about this?" I shake him, hoping to elicit an ecstatic response from him.

"I don't want to get my hopes up. Things like this can easily fall through, so until everything is signed and I'm standing in a new uniform with my hockey stick in my hand, I'm not going to get excited."

"Well, I am," I proclaim. "Paxton Rhodes, you're going to know exactly what you'll be doing after graduation because you'll be signing with an East Coast League team," I beam, a wide smile stretching across my face.

His attention moves over to me, and his expression softens. "Thank you for believing in me, Ivy. I want you to know that I believe in you too. Anything you want to do, you'll be able to accomplish it because you're a badass. Don't let anyone take that away from you. You want to go to get a degree, do it. You want to leave this life and travel the world? I'll be waiting for you."

Heat swirls around my cheeks as my pulse speeds up. "You'll be waiting for me?"

"Hell yeah. I have no roots. I never did. I want to travel and see what else is out there, and the second you want to join me, you'll have the space next to me."

I smile even though an ache burrows in my chest for him not having a solid foundation. "Exploring the globe together sounds fun."

Pax presses his back against the bench. "I'm lucky to have you as a friend, Rebel."

Friend. I hate that word. But if I can't have him in a romantic sense, then I'd rather have him as a friend than a stranger. "I'm lucky to have you," I state, neglecting the "friend" part. A teeny tiny sliver of guilt crawls up my spine as the image of Calvin pops into my head. I probably shouldn't be wishing for Paxton to be my boyfriend when Calvin has pretty much claimed that role.

"Let's go back inside and see if we can wake Trent up so we can finish watching the end of our movie," Pax says. He goes to take another hit, this time shorter than the last, and while he blows out a cloud of smoke, he goes to put the joint out.

"Wait." My hands fly to his, stopping him. "Can I try smoking before you put it out?"

"No way."

"Come on, Pax."

"I'm not going to corrupt a future Dame," he teases.

"Fine. If you don't want to corrupt me, then I'm sure I can find another boy who will."

His jaw tics, his own joke coming back to bite him as a flicker of possessiveness passes through his eyes. The joint wiggles between his long fingers as he debates on what to do. Finally, he gives in. "This is the first and only time, got it?"

"Okay." I nod, sitting up straighter. "Teach me what to do."

"What do you mean, teach you? You just smoke it." He lifts the joint toward me. "You just put it between your lips, and you…you…"

"Suck?"

"Goddammit, Ivy," Pax mutters in frustration as he adjusts in his seat. My face reddens, realizing my innocent question came across suggestively. "Here." He closely holds the joint up to my face.

With our eyes locked, I inch forward and let it hit my mouth. Parting my lips, I take a deep inhale.

"Fuck, Rebel," Pax says in a tone I've never heard before. It's dark and deep and makes my insides light up in a way that's foreign to me—making me immediately cough out whatever I attempted to draw in. I've instantly squashed whatever the hell was just blossoming between us. "Oh, shit." Pax chuckles. "You okay?"

"I'm fine," I somehow manage to get out in between wheezing. He pats my back as I continue to cough. When I'm finally able to breathe like a normal human, I sit upright. "Let me try again."

"I think you smoked enough."

"Pax, it didn't even count! Let me do it again." This time, I take the joint from him, pinching it between my fingertips. I try once more, taking a smaller drag that burns the back of my throat.

"Hold it in for a few seconds so it hits your lungs," Pax instructs.

I do as he says, then slowly exhale. I repeat the act again, and before he can take it away from me, I do it a third time.

"That's enough." He grabs the joint from me. "You're gonna get fucked up if you take more hits."

"I don't feel anything yet."

"Give it a few minutes." He rises and extends his hand out. "Come on. Let's get you inside."

"Ivy. Ivy." A deep whisper tickles my ear. "Rebel."

"Huh?" My heavy eyelids open into tiny slits, spotting Paxton leaning over me with a grin on his face.

He laughs. "Oh my god, you're so fucking stoned."

"Don't tell my mom." If my muscles weren't so relaxed and feeling like they're weighed down by lead, I'm sure I'd feel some sense of fear.

"Don't worry, Rebel." Pax slides one of his arms under my knees and the other under my upper back, crinkling a chip bag as he moves. "It'll be our dirty little secret."

I cling to those words, making sure to tattoo them to

my brain so I can be sure to play them on repeat when I'm sober.

My eyelids close over as he carries me somewhere. I try to put the pieces together from the events of our evening. We couldn't wake Trent up, so instead we raided my pantry and made a mess—all the while we were hysterically laughing to the point of tears in our eyes and sharp pains in our sides. Then we went to the game room to watch music videos, and I guess I fell asleep sometime after staring at Gwen Stefani's platinum blond hair for what felt like five hours but was probably thirty seconds.

My back rests against something soft, and Pax slips his hands out from under me. Confusion clouds my mind until plush fabric covers the length of me, and I realize I'm on my bed.

"Let me know if you need anything," Pax quietly says.

"You're leaving?"

"I'm gonna crash in the other room."

"Don't leave."

He sighs, and after a few moments of stillness, he carefully sits down at the foot of my bed as if he's forcing himself to keep some distance. "I'll hang out for a couple of minutes."

"Thank you," I mumble into the pillow.

My eyelids close once more, and my body relaxes tenfold knowing that Paxton's looking after me.

CHAPTER THIRTY-FIVE

PRESENT

THE MUSEUM IS QUIET.

I asked to be the one to lock up after the unveiling so I can have a few minutes of calmness, looking at it all. Most of the lights are off, aside from a few of the pin spots. The soles of my shoes softly tap against the floor as I slowly wander around, my maroon-colored dress gently brushing against my thighs.

"You hang out in empty museums a lot?" Paxton's voice comes from the other end of the exhibit, causing me to jolt in place.

My hand springs to my heart. "I had no idea you were still here!"

"I wouldn't have left without saying goodbye." He strolls over to me, the dim light shadowing his face, adding another level of mischief to his features. My pulse jumps, remembering what we did in his hotel room mere hours ago, and as he continues to capture my attention, moving closer to me, I desperately want a repeat of events.

"I didn't expect you to stay the whole time. I'm sure it was boring."

"Not in the slightest." Pax approaches me, and his hand reaches out to hold mine. "I loved watching you light up, making the rounds, talking to everyone, letting them congratulate you. I could've stayed here forever just to witness how happy you were."

I swallow, unsure of how to respond. His thumb gently massages the top of my hand, the peaceful caress coaxing me to let my guard down.

"I was wondering if you could give me a private tour," he says after a long stretch of silence.

"Sorry, no private tours after hours."

"I'd be more than willing to pay an extra fee." Pax wraps his hands around my waist, pulling me toward him.

Giggling in his arms, I glance up at him. "Well, if that's the case, then I'm sure I can arrange something for you." I break his hold, threading my fingers between his.

I guide him through the exhibits, explaining every last piece on display. Pax asks endless questions, genuinely interested in my work. I'm pretty sure Roy, the director of the museum, had less inquiries about everything than Pax does.

When we move into the nineties, Paxton makes a beeline for the Polaroid camera. He angles it upward in a similar way we'd take our selfies in the past. A comforting nostalgia creeps its way into my chest as he snaps a picture like he would on one of my old digital cameras.

"Damn, I feel old knowing that pop culture from the

nineties is now being displayed in a museum," Pax says, chuckling. He shakes the Polaroid picture while we wait for the image to show up.

"Tell me about it. They even floated around the idea of having me create a Y2K display." My mind flips to the pile of boxes sent from Mom, which are *still* shoved to one side of my living room. They probably hold enough relics to create a multitude of two thousand-themed exhibits if I ever dare to go through them.

Reconnecting with Paxton is enough for my fragile heart. I'm not ready to dive headfirst into agonizing memories, and I don't know if I ever will be.

"Let's see the picture," I say.

Pax holds it up so we can both see it, and a smile forms on both of our faces as we admire our picture. "You wanna keep it? You can add it to your stack of photographs."

I shake my head. "I don't have a stack of pictures anymore. I don't remember the last time I printed one out now that everything's on my phone. You keep it."

He slips the Polaroid into his back pocket, and the two of us casually move toward the hallway, knowing that we've seen everything in the exhibit. We take gradual steps closer to the staircase, slowly passing each decade.

"I can't get over how incredible you are, Ivy," Pax's voice rasps in a soft timbre.

I shrug. "I'm good at my job, just like you are."

"Were."

Halting, I turn to look directly at him. "Just because you're retired doesn't mean you're still not insanely talented, Pax." My eyes bounce back and forth between his, unable to figure out where to focus. "This is taking a toll on you, isn't it?" I whisper the question.

"Everything is."

"Retirement and Uncle Jeff?"

"And you." Pax's words land in the center of my chest, striking me.

"Me?"

Pax delicately loops a strand of my hair behind my ear. Splaying out his hand, he cups my face, and I lean into him. "You were the one I let get away. And I never forgave myself for it. As much as I pretended to over the years, my life was always missing something." He lets out a shaky breath. "I was always missing you." His words are encased in deep sincerity.

"Pax…" I warn him through a whisper.

"I know, I know. The rule is we're only doing this until Trent's wedding. But just for right now, let's pretend we're not."

With that, his lips are on mine. My brain can't process his comment because my senses are overflowing with all things Paxton. Each swipe of his tongue and caress of his lips draws me more into a haze.

But he suddenly breaks the kiss, leaning his forehead against mine. "Let's go back in time," he whispers.

Hesitancy creeps its way center stage as a flurry of memories from our past flashes before me. "What?"

Pax intertwines his fingers with mine and carefully pulls me toward one of my displays. "Let's go back in time," he repeats. "You think we would've hooked up in the fifties?" he asks, leading me to a Thunderbird replica at the drive-in experience for the fifties exhibit.

Relief washes away my worry when I realize he's not suggesting we go back to *our* time. "I think my parents would've forbidden you to enter our house, and I would've never met you."

He laughs. "True. Your parents hating me in every era seems the most plausible." He lingers next to the entrance of the car. There are no doors, so patrons can easily move in and out of either side. There's a projector screen across from the car, still playing clips from movies since I've yet to shut it off. A scene from *An Affair to Remember* plays as Pax guides both of us into the car.

We slide in, settling onto the leather bench seat. The roof of the car darkens the space, making it more intimate. Butterflies fill my stomach, and I glance around, making sure we're out of the line of sight from the security cameras.

"But let's say by chance you did meet me," Pax continues, his voice getting thick. "Do you think you would've been with me?"

"Do I think I would've defied my parents and snuck around their backs just to see you?" I play into this fantasy world, getting lost in a past we've never lived through. "Probably." I smile.

"You'd sneak out of your house and meet me in my car that I parked down the block."

"And you'd take me on a date to get milkshakes at one of your favorite spots."

Pax carefully brushes my hair away from my face. "Followed by a drive-in movie." His hand slides down the side of my neck, down the length of my torso, and settles onto my hip. "But instead of watching the film, we'd be doing something like this." His other hand grips onto me, and in one swift motion, he swings my body to straddle on top of his.

Letting out a girlish laugh as my legs spread apart to be on the outside of his, I wrap my hands around the back of his neck. "I'm not sure," I joke. "This would be pretty scandalous for the fifties."

His fingertips graze my inner thigh, pushing away the hem of my dress until he makes contact with my panties. "Guess you're a rebel in every era." Clutching the back of my head, he brings me in for a powerful kiss at the same time his other hand begins to tease my clit.

I sigh into his mouth, passion igniting in my veins. The bulge in his pants has me rocking my body over his, yearning for more.

Our tongues tangle as our hands get greedy. Hushed moans come from the back of Pax's throat the longer we continue to draw out this moment.

Never could I have imagined myself doing something like this in my place of work—with Paxton, no less.

I should be cautious.

I should double-check that no one else is here.

I should quadruple-check we're not in view of the security cameras.

But my logic flies out the window the more Pax wants me. He reaches for his pants, undoing the button and zipper. Lust consumes me at the sight of his cock, eagerly ready for me. I wrap my hand around it, slowly moving up and down. Pax tips his head back, leaning it on the top of the leather seat. His teeth sink into his bottom lip, fighting the urge to loudly groan as if this were the best hand job of his life. Taking my thumb, I swipe the tip of his cock, letting his pre-cum paint the pad of my finger.

His breath gets heavier, like he can't handle not being inside me any longer. "Ride me." His demand blends into a needy plea.

Enjoying how much I can control his pleasure, I smirk and align my body with his. Our gazes are glued to each other as I push the lace fabric of my panties out of the way and sink onto him. A moan that is much too loud falls from my lips at the sensation of him stretching me out and hitting me at this angle.

He trails kisses on my collarbone and drags his mouth down to a small space of exposed skin from my slight V-neck in my dress. I roll my hips over his, shuddering every time his cock slams against that glorious spot inside me.

My hands move in a frenzy, trying to tug at his short hair and grip onto his shoulders and scratch the back of his neck. The intensity in my heart overflows with each pounding beat. Pax clutches my hips so hard, I'm sure I'll have bruises in the shape of his fingers. He changes up the tempo, and I allow him to take control, moving our bodies in a way that neither of us can keep quiet.

With my senses on complete overload, desire igniting flames into each fiber of my being, I clamp my eyes shut. Heat courses through me, my skin becoming slick with lust.

"Would you have let me fuck you like this at the end of our date?" Pax asks with his voice so deep that I get goose bumps.

"Yes," I cry out.

"Good," he says through labored breaths. "Because I'd want you just as much then as I do now." He moves at a quicker pace, every single vein in my body getting electrified. "In every decade, every era, every lifetime—I'd want you, Ivy."

An explosion of euphoria ripples from the top of my head, bursting all the way down to the tips of my toes. My moans pour out of me in bliss, and Pax lands his lips on mine, swallowing each sound I make.

Trembling in his arms, I can feel the strong beat of his heart against my body. His movement becomes sharper, and I know he's about to come.

Before I can bask in the aftershocks, I hop off him and get on my knees. Without hesitation, I wrap my mouth around his cock, tasting both of our pleasure as I suck.

"Fuck," he murmurs, knotting my hair into his fist. He lets out a sexy groan and fills my mouth with his cum.

I keep sucking until he's got nothing left to give, then slowly pull away.

Glancing up at him, his hazel eyes look mesmerized as he stares at me with a sleepy grin. Taking his thumb, he wipes my chin, which has drips of his remanence.

I move to sit next to him as he fixes his pants. "I guess you're right," I state. "I am a rebel in every era."

Pax smiles and leans over for a soft, delicate kiss.

CHAPTER THIRTY-SIX

TRENT

How's Jeff doing?

"TRENT WANTS to know how you're doing," I say to Uncle Jeff from across the room.

"I'd be fine if my nephew didn't decide to waste his money on some swanky hotel room," he responds, sitting on a couch.

Uncle Jeff was moved out of the ICU and will be receiving treatments on an outpatient basis as of now. I got him the best suite this Hilton has to offer, while I'll continue staying in my room a few floors below him. His immune system is shot, so he's not allowed out aside from going to the hospital for treatments, so I wanted to get him a room that was big enough for him to move and not go completely stir crazy.

So here we are, hanging out and watching a hockey game on his hotel TV. Uncle Jeff claims he hates having a big suite, but I know he appreciates it.

He was the same way when I bought him a house back in Maryland. As soon as I got my first fat check, I made sure he had some place to live that was bigger than our apartment. It was the least I could do considering everything he's done for me. I wanted to buy him a huge house, but he fought me on it and opted for something average and simple.

ME

He's a pain in my ass

TRENT

Haha, I guess that means things are looking up

My attention drifts over to Uncle Jeff, and a knot of uncertainty twists all of my veins. It's obviously a good thing he's out of the ICU, but I'm still not completely convinced everything will be fine. He still looks frail, and his energy level is low. He's definitely not back to his usual self.

ME

I hope so

TRENT

Have you been able to get out and get your mind off things?

ME

Yeah, here and there

TRENT

I bet there are plenty of women who'd offer to be your distraction

ME

Haha, I don't know if even that will help this time around

TRENT

Oh right—you're "pursuing someone." I almost keeled over when I heard you say that. That was a lie to get those bridesmaids off your back, right?

Guilt burrows its way under my skin. Sure, we're adults now, and we've all grown, but I still don't know if Trent would be cool with me fucking with his little sister.

Gnawing at my bottom lip, I decide to put my feelers out there to get a sense of how Trent would take the news.

ME

Not a lie

TRENT

No fucking way

Not to be a dick, but I can't picture you settling down with anyone

Heat circles around the collar of my shirt. I shift in my seat, second-guessing my choice to tread into this conversation.

ME

We'll see what happens

TRENT

Who is it? If it's that Playboy model you hooked up with a few years ago, then I fully support.

ME

I'll let you know who if it pans out

TRENT

Deal

A frustrated sigh exits my mouth, pissed at myself for

chickening out. Putting my phone to the side, Uncle Jeff glances over at me.

"Everything all right?" he asks.

"Yeah. How are they doing?" I gesture my chin toward the TV in regard to the hockey games. It's my team, the Cobras, versus the Islanders. Lately, I've had a difficult time watching the games all the way through, so I tend to watch the highlights afterward and text my team members in support.

"Eh, not their best. Probably because they lost their star player."

I humbly smile to myself. Before I can respond, another incoming text draws my attention away.

TRENT

Have you seen Ivy at all?

Anxiety pricks the ends of my fingers as they hover over the screen, debating how to respond. Definitely can't tell him the truth, that I've been banging his sister and we have a sex agreement up until his wedding. However, this could be a good time to dance around the idea of me and Ivy being a couple. Even though she has it in her mind that this thing between us has an expiration date, there's no way in hell I'm letting her go that easily.

ME

A little bit

A knock at the door stops me from typing out my next text. "Expecting someone?" I ask Uncle Jeff as I walk over to the door.

Uncle Jeff's eyes are glued to the TV, ignoring me. Opening the door, I spot Ivy on the other side with a tote bag filled with stuff. As if I time-traveled back to our teenage years, I blink several times to bring myself back into the present.

"Oh, I didn't know you'd be here," Ivy states. "Sucks for you, I only brought a bag of Cool Ranch Doritos with me."

She pushes past me as if she owns the place, and I follow in tow. Uncle Jeff's face brightens in a way I haven't seen it light up all day.

"How the hell are you, Ivy?" he asks, perking up.

"I'm great. And soon, you will be too once you see the snacks I brought for you." She places her bag down on the small kitchenette table and begins taking items out of it: chips, M&M's, and cookies.

"He shouldn't be eating that kind of food," I make sure to whisper to her politely.

"Relax, I already spoke with Uncle Jeff's doctor, and she cleared it. As long as he only has junk food in moderation, it's fine. Besides, it'll hopefully put some weight back on him."

Ivy traipses over to Uncle Jeff, showcasing everything she brought with her. He chooses Oreos, and she dives into a blue bag of Doritos. The two settle next to each other, watching the game.

Tingles radiate down my body, loving how Ivy made her way back into my world without missing a single beat.

This feels like how it's always been.

This feels *right*.

CHAPTER THIRTY-SEVEN

2008

August

OUR HOUSE HAS BEEN PULSATING with stress the closer Trent gets to leaving for college. You'd think he's moving to an entirely different country by how everyone has been so frantic lately. Thankfully, he has everything packed and ready to go, so Mom and Dad finally started to calm down. Dad is currently golfing with his business buddies, and Mom is at a Dame gathering, while Trent, Pax, and I hang out at home.

I'm perched on my mattress while Pax makes himself comfortable in my desk chair. Both of us watch Trent as he aimlessly paces around my room.

A lingering sadness hangs in the air, which none of us has been addressing for hours. So I decide to bring it up. "So is this the last time the three of us are going to be together for…a while?"

Neither of them looks at me or says anything in response, and I know they're letting the reality of my question sink in.

For the past several years, the three of us became our own little unit. Yes, our closeness has ebbed and flowed depending on what's going on in our lives, but in the back of our heads, we've always known that the three of us are there for each other. Now with Trent going to Johns Hopkins and Pax leaving to be a part of the Knights—a team that's part of the East Coast Hockey League—who knows when we'll all be in the same room again.

"I guess we'll see each other around the holidays," Pax says, tugging at his shirt collar. "Which sucks."

My gaze drifts down to my comforter, my nails tracing the outline of the white thread. "Yeah."

"Okay, I just need to say something," Trent blurts out, snapping our attention toward him as he continues to pace. "It's really awkward, but I just need to get it out there." Pax and I glance at each other, then back at Trent. "Ivy, I know you're still going out with that Calvin kid, right?"

"Um, yes."

"He seems nice, but I know you're getting older and..." My brother looks at me with an expression that lets me know he's *really* uncomfortable. "He's being good to you?"

My face gets hot. "Yes."

"He's not like...pressuring you to do stuff?"

"Oh my god, Trent!"

"Is he?"

"No!"

"Because Pax and I will take care of him right now if he is."

I shield my face with my hands in embarrassment so I

don't have to see their sets of eyes on me. "Trent, stop. He's not pressuring me."

"We're not going to be around as much, but if Calvin or any other guy does some shit you don't like, tell us."

"Jesus," I mutter under my breath.

"Ivy." Pax's voice commands my attention, and I slowly peel my hands away from my face. "If some guy tries some shit, you need to tell one of us. I don't care what time it is or how busy you think we are."

"Okay, god, can we finish this conversation already?"

"Fine," Trent says. "I just needed you to know that we're still here for you."

"Noted." I grab my laptop to offer myself some type of distraction, making it known that I'm no longer interested in talking to them about this.

Thankfully, Pax changes the topic. "What time do you have to leave for move-in day tomorrow?" he asks Trent.

"Around ten. What time is your flight to South Carolina?"

"Gotta be at the airport at seven." Pax has been training with his new team for several weeks, but got some time off to be home for a little bit. Now he leaves again to officially prep for the upcoming season in the fall.

"You need to post a shit ton of pictures on Facebook so I can see what you're up to," Trent says.

"I guess I should also change my info to say I graduated high school and I'm officially on the Knights."

Lifting my laptop off my lap, I hold it out for him. "Here. Sign in to your Facebook and update it."

Pax takes it from me, and I watch as he logs in. His head tilts to the side, brows drawn in as he looks at something on the screen. "Who's Courtney?" he asks Trent. "She sent me a friend request and a message saying, 'I keep thinking about the night we danced. Hope this isn't too forward, but I'd love to reconnect.'"

My brother goes over to him, glancing at my computer. "Click on her picture." Pax does as he says, and a flash of realization appears on his face. "Boarding school girl."

A similar awareness brightens Pax's features. "Oh, yeah!"

My stomach twists in jealousy, but I do my best to ignore it as I witness him accept the friend request and talk with Trent on how best to reply back.

Once they're done, I suggest going out for ice cream since I don't want to sit in here any longer talking about Calvin or Courtney or whoever else.

The three of us hop in Trent's car and drive off for our simple adventure for the day. It's nothing exceptional, but laughing with both of them under the blazing summer sun and forgetting all that's lingering in the near future feels like the perfect way to bookmark our friendship, with the promise of picking back up during the chill of winter.

CHAPTER THIRTY-EIGHT

ivy

December

NERVOUSNESS MAKES my fingers tremble as I zip my boots up over my bright blue tights.

"Are you ready yet? We're not going to some five-star restaurant. You don't need to spend this much time getting ready." Trent barges into my room for the hundredth time. His university isn't too far of a drive, so he occasionally stopped by during the semester, but now that he's officially home for winter break, he's been a massive thorn in my side. To think I was concerned I'd miss him when he went off to college.

"Shut up." I stand up, smoothing out my black dress. I glance at myself in the mirror before Trent has a meltdown and nod my head. "I'm good."

"Finally."

We bundle up in our winter coats, and he drives us to a nearby pizza place where we're meeting Pax for the first time since the summer. He got in earlier today and spent the afternoon with Uncle Jeff, and promised us that he'll spend the rest of the evening with us. He's only in Maryland for a short visit, then he goes back to his team in South Carolina.

The scent of garlic and fresh bread makes my stomach growl as we enter. I grab a table while Trent orders a pizza pie and a pitcher of soda. The door opens behind me, a gust of cold air combating with the heat from the brick ovens.

"Hey, Rebel." Pax's voice beckons me, and I spin around, ready to jump up and leap into his arms to give my best friend the biggest hug.

But as I stand up, I freeze.

There's a girl beside him, their fingers interlocked in a way that couples do. In a way that Paxton has never done because he doesn't do relationships.

"Hi-hey!" I shake off my initial reaction, grinning.

Pax breaks his connection with the girl and embraces me. I hold him close, knowing that he'll be slipping out of my grasp within milliseconds.

"Ivy, this is Courtney," he says, releasing me and turning our focus to the girl next to him.

"It's *so* nice to meet you." She beams, her pearly whites sparkling.

"Yeah, you too." The envy coiling around my joints lets me know how much of a lie that statement is.

"What's up, man?" Trent comes over, and he and Pax do a one-armed hug. Pax introduces Trent to Courtney, and the four of us sit down.

Even though it's supposed to be the three of us.

Trent and Pax dive into conversation, catching each other up on everything. The pizza arrives, and everyone grabs a slice and begins eating.

"How's it feel to be back?" Trent asks.

"It's surreal. My life has turned into a roller coaster

these past few months, but it's great to finally see you guys and, of course, Uncle Jeff."

"Oh my god, Uncle Jeff is the sweetest," Courtney says with her hand on her heart. "I'm so glad you invited me over."

"You know, Uncle Jeff really misses you, Pax. You should probably spend time one-on-one with him while you're home," I blurt out.

My comment catches Pax off guard. He pauses, holding the slice in the air. "I will."

"Good. Because when I went over to watch your game with him last week, he kept talking about how excited he was to see you." I glance over at Courtney. "I go over and visit Uncle Jeff whenever I have the chance."

"That's so sweet," she says, oblivious to the point I'm trying to get across. "Do you go to college locally?"

"Oh, I'm a junior in high school."

"Aw, that's cute."

My bloodstream ignites with annoyance. "You hear that, Pax? Being a junior is *cute*." I do a little squeaky voice dipped in sugar to emphasize the word. "You guys must've missed the memo when you were in high school." Trent kicks my leg under the table, and I take that as my signal to stop being rude.

"So, Courtney, what about you? Do you go to college?" Trent politely asks, and I hide my eye roll.

"Actually, I'm taking a gap year to travel. Which is really convenient because I get to visit Paxton when he's on the road." They turn to look at each other, both of them smiling and starry-eyed.

"Europe's a cool place to travel," I say in between bites of my pizza. "Much better than the East Coast. Trent and I have vacationed in a couple of different countries with our parents, so if you want any tips on where to go, I can help."

"I did a few weeks over there in October."

"Then you should do Australia next. I always wanted to go there."

"I think I just want to stay put for the time being, but Australia is definitely on my list someday." She gives me a fake smile, then turns to Pax. "Maybe we can take a trip during your offseason."

He nods, taking a huge bite so he doesn't have to speak.

Trent brings up more topics, easing the tension as we continue to eat dinner. We had originally planned on going back to our house afterward, which I've been looking forward to, but now that there's another guest tagging along, bitterness prickles beneath my skin.

When we're finished eating, we head to our separate cars.

"What the fuck was that all about?" Trent asks me from the driver's seat.

"I don't know what you're talking about."

"You were a bitch to Courtney for no reason."

"She's annoying."

"She literally said four sentences before you started giving her an attitude."

"Four *annoying* sentences." I stand firm in my argument.

"Well, you better remove that stick from your ass before we get home, otherwise you're going to ruin Pax's first night back."

I slouch in the passenger seat. "Fine."

When we arrive home, I slip on my polite mask, just like I do when I'm meeting one of Mom's friends or when I have to attend a Dame function.

We chill in the game room, which has basically become my own hangout spot since Trent moved into his dorm. I let our housekeeper, Stella, know that I want to be responsible for this space, so I clean it up and keep it orderly. Except for today, because a stack of my DVDs is laid out on the floor and my *Twilight* book rests open on one of the couches.

"Have you seen the movie yet?" Courtney asks, pointing toward my worn book.

Trent snorts. "She went to the midnight premiere."

My eyes narrow, shooting daggers at him, and Pax laughs. The two of them make themselves comfortable, taking up space on the other couch. I shift my attention back to Courtney and do what Trent asked—play nice. "Twice. How about you?"

"Oh, I'm not a really big reader, so I didn't go see the movie. But a few of my friends are and chew my ears off about the books and now the movie."

"That's sad."

She tilts her head to the side. "What is?"

"That you don't like reading."

Pax coughs and springs to his feet. "Ivy, can you help me grab some drinks from the kitchen?" He gives me a look that tells me he's not really asking.

Silently, we leave Trent and Courtney to talk, while the two of us make our way into the kitchen. Stopping in front of my refrigerator, he turns to face me.

"What's going on?"

"I'm coming to get drinks like you asked me to forty-five seconds ago," I snap.

"No. I mean, what's going on with you and Courtney?"

"Nothing." My arms fold over my chest. "Who even is she?"

"I met her at *your* sweet sixteen."

"Well, she must've crashed it because I've never seen her a day in my life."

"She was there with a friend, whose mother is a Dame," he explains.

I glance down at my feet. "We've been texting whenever you can, and you never once mentioned her."

"Are you still with Calvin?"

My face scrunches. "I'm not sure what that has to do with anything."

"Are you?"

Slowly, my gaze comes up to meet his. "Yeah."

"Okay. You haven't mentioned Calvin either when we've been texting."

"So, I have Calvin and you have Courtney, and that's it."

"No." He places his hand on my arm, his calloused hand searing a hole through the fabric of my shirt. "We still have each other."

But not in the way I wish we did.

It'll always be like this. We'll always have each other. Close, but just out of reach.

CHAPTER THIRTY-NINE

PRESENT

TIME SEEMS to move quickly and slowly all at once. My days are consumed with the museum, my evenings are reserved for Uncle Jeff, and my nights I spend tangled in bedsheets with Paxton.

Except for tonight.

Zaina has been begging me to join her at a new karaoke bar she discovered, so I gladly obliged. She's wearing a sleek little black dress, while I chose a silver dress with a plunging neckline.

Laughter fills the bar, strangers supporting and cheering for one another when they get enough liquid courage to perform on the stage with strobing neon lights.

"Excuse me, ladies." The bartender interrupts my conversation with Zaina to hand us each a drink.

"Oh, we didn't order these," I state.

"These are from the two gentlemen at the end of the

bar," he clarifies, pointing to them.

They're in their early thirties, like us, and judging by the hungry expression on their faces, they're definitely on the prowl.

"They're hot as hell," Zaina whispers to me. She raises her glass in a grateful acknowledgment, and they do the same.

"I don't drink cosmos," I say to her through a forced smile at the men staring back at us.

"You do tonight, girl."

Chuckling, I pick up my glass and tip it toward them as a thank you. Leisurely sipping on the drink, disappointment starts tugging at me as I start to wish this exchange happened with Pax.

"Whoa, what just happened?" Zaina asks me.

"What are you talking about?"

"You just went from grinning to frowning in zero point two seconds."

"I didn't even realize. I must've got caught up in my thoughts for a moment." I take another sip. "But I'm good now," I add, with a smile.

Her dark eyes narrow, studying me. "You're full of shit. Take another gulp of your cosmo and then start telling me what's the matter."

"I swear nothing's wrong. My mind just wandered, thinking about P—" My phone vibrates on the bar, lighting up with a text.

PAX

Are you free tonight?

"Thinking about Pax?" Zaina continues my sentence, staring at my phone with me.

"Maybe."

"Hand over your phone."

"What? Why?"

"I want to talk to him. Hand it over."

Wishing this cosmo had already hit me, I unlock my phone and slide it over to her. Zaina smirks, typing something to Pax. Once she's finished, she gives it back to me.

"Drink up, Ivy! It's time to let loose!" Zaina beams.

My mouth hangs open when I read what she texted.

ME

Hey Pax, this is Zaina. We're at a bar called Lyric Lounge, and these insanely hot men are buying me and Ivy drinks, but my best friend won't stop pouting because she misses you. Bring your sexy hockey ass down here and claim her. Otherwise, someone here will.

"You can't send him that!" I shriek.

Zaina gives me an extra-wide smile. "Too late!"

"Ivy and Zaina, you guys are up," the person handling the karaoke announces into the microphone, snapping our attention away from my phone.

"What song did you sign us up for?" she asks me.

"You'll just have to go up there with me and find out."

CHAPTER FORTY

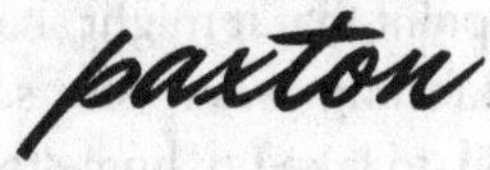

TWENTY MINUTES after receiving Zaina's text, I'm entering Lyric Lounge. The unmistakable sound of two women laughing through their rendition of "Wannabe" by the Spice Girls draws my attention to the stage. Lo and behold, a tipsy Ivy and Zaina attempt to sing through their performance.

Grinning, I take a seat at the lengthy bar and order a beer, enjoying the show.

They end the song giggling off the stage, and the host takes the mic from them. "Once more, let's give it up for Ivy and Zaina!" he says, and then introduces the next karaoke performer.

The crowd cheers, and I clap along with them, waiting for Ivy to spot me. To my disappointment, she doesn't notice me as she and Zaina wobble off to the side. Two men are seated at a small table, pulling out chairs for both of them and handing them drinks.

The blood in my veins mutates into vengeful green envy as I witness the interaction. Ivy tilts her head back with laughter at whatever the guy with a gold chain around his neck says to her. His focus goes to her exposed neck, then dips down further in hopes of getting more of a peek of her silky skin.

My jaw clenches as my grip around my beer bottle strengthens to the point that it might shatter.

Zaina wasn't kidding when she sent me that text. There are men ready to take Ivy home tonight.

I thought I made the rule about us only engaging with each other crystal clear. But obviously, I'm going to have to remind her of our deal.

Rising to approach them, the gold chain guy gets up at the same time and excuses himself from their table. My eyes ping-pong from him and back to Ivy, debating who to address first. My feet choose for me, heading straight for my woman.

Getting closer to Ivy, she lifts her line of sight, and her bloodshot, sapphire eyes land on me. For a millisecond, a look of surprise hits her face, then suddenly shifts. A sparkle of wickedness dances over her features, her lips curling up in a tantalizing smirk.

Ivy knows I'm pissed, and she likes it.

"Well, well, well. Look who decided to show," Ivy says, crossing her leg over the other.

I sit down where the gold chain guy was sitting, and Ivy goes to pick up the drink he bought for her. Intercepting, grabbing the glass before she can bring it to her lips, I let my possessiveness seep out into my words, "Well, well, well. Look who forgot the rules." Taking her drink, I down it in one quick gulp.

"Damn, Pax, you sure know how to make an entrance," Zaina exclaims. I had forgotten she was sitting across from Ivy with the other man, and when I glance over at her, she gives me a look of approval.

"After the text you sent me, it seemed like the only option," I say, smiling, knowing she's team Ivy and Pax.

Before Zaina can respond, the drunk guy she's with

whispers something in her ear, pulling her attention off us. I shift my focus back to Ivy, who continues to seem quite entertained by my presence.

"I forgot how sexy you look when you get like this." Her voice soothes my riotous heart.

"Get like what?"

"Jealous." Ivy reaches for my shirt collar, her manicured nails dance around the hem, grazing my skin. She toys with me, a yearning building inside me with every breath I take.

"Were you flirting with that guy?"

She bites down on her bottom lip, studying my face. "Maybe. What are you gonna do about it?"

Fireworks go off in my chest. Lustful tension floods my body as I crave to answer her question right here in the middle of this bar for everyone to watch. I inch closer, ready to whisper the most obscene response I can conjure up, but as I open my mouth, someone else beats me to the punch.

"Next on the list is Ivy! Let's welcome her back to the stage!" the karaoke host says into the microphone.

My gaze goes to the stage and back to Ivy, who's perking up and excited to sing again. Chuckling, I say to her, "I never knew you were a karaoke queen."

"There's a lot you don't know about me." She rises and presses a kiss to my cheek.

Zaina begins to cheer, and so does everyone else. Grinning ear to ear, I watch Ivy make her way to the stage. But before she hits the first stair, the douche with the gold chain appears from thin air and steals her attention for a split second. My spine goes rigid when I watch him put his hand on her lower back and whisper something to her. Laughing off whatever he said, Ivy goes toward the karaoke host to pick her song.

"All right, everyone," the host says into the mic. "Ivy

is all about the blasts from the past! She's bringing us right back to the early two-thousands with 'crushcrushcrush' by Paramore!"

Zaina goes wild, shouting for Ivy, and I find myself doing the same. The song starts, drums building as Ivy takes center stage. The light frames her body perfectly, making her radiate with confidence and sensuality.

Exhilaration swells in my chest as she sings the first line of the song.

"I got a lot to say to you. Yeah, I got a lot to say. I noticed your eyes are always glued to me." Ivy works the crowd while her focus is aimed directly at me.

In all the time I've known her, I never realized she could carry a tune and own a fucking stage. I feel idiotic for not knowing and regretful for not finding out sooner. But more than that, I feel truly mesmerized by her presence. Fully consumed by the way the glowing light illuminates her skin, the way she twirls her hips, and the way her voice sinks its claws into my veins as she sings, *"If you wanna play it like a game, well, come on, come on, let's play."* Ivy winks, indulging me in a public round of foreplay.

Heat courses through me, my temperature increasing more and more as she continues. And I know with complete certainty that once she's off that stage, I'm acting on my desires.

As I continue to stare at her, my view suddenly becomes obstructed by some man whistling at Ivy. Tension clamps down on my jaw when I realize it's the gold chain guy. He places drinks down on the table and sits in the empty seat next to me.

"Got you guys another round." The gold chain guy points to the drinks as he speaks to his friend and Zaina. Glancing over at me, his face immediately morphs into shock. "Holy shit. You're Paxton Rhodes."

"I am." Disdain leaks into my voice. "And you know the woman in the silver dress who you've been hoping to fuck?" I point to Ivy on stage.

"She's so sexy."

"She's *mine*."

Flustered, he steps over his words in a stuttering apology as he puts his hands up in innocence. He continues to go on about being sorry, but I tune him out, focusing on the only person I care about.

Ivy circles her hips in a taunting way, the entire room becoming enamored by her. Everyone claps to the beat of the bridge as she continues, "*Rock and roll, hey. Don't you know, baby, we're all alone now. I need something to sing about.*" Her eyes are locked on me, her body continuing to move in a teasing dance. "*Rock and roll, hey. Don't you know, baby, we're all alone now? Give me something to sing about!*"

Desperation hits my core, yearning to reach out and touch her. My heart hammers in my chest faster than the beat of the song. Everyone else in the room disappears, and it's just me and her as she toys with me from afar. There are only a few seconds left of her performance, but I don't know if I'm capable of waiting that long.

"*Let's be more than, more than this.*" She sings out the final line of the song. Logically, I know it's the lyrics, but the way Ivy strikes the lines directly at me gives me a sliver of hope, wondering if there's some truth hidden behind them.

Ivy gets a round of applause as she goes offstage, making a beeline for me. A flirty grin pulls at her lips as she approaches our table.

"You were so awesome!" Zaina exclaims.

"Thanks!" Ivy responds. Her focus goes back to me, but when she opens her mouth to speak, her attention falls on the gold chain guy next to me. "So, Josh, what did you think of the song?"

"No fucking way, Rebel," I blurt out. Ivy slowly turns back to look at me, her eyebrow arching. A tickle of amusement hits those gorgeous sapphire eyes, and it's all over for me. "Let's go." My large hand encircles her delicate wrist, and I whisk her through the crowd.

She lets out a mischievous giggle as I push my way through people. Someone else starts doing karaoke, so everyone's attention is on them and not on what I'm about to do to Ivy.

I pull her into the nearest bathroom and lock the door behind us. It's dim, but I can still see the twinkle of roguishness dancing over her features.

"Finally deciding to act on those jealous feelings?" she provokes.

Inching closer, I invade her space, making her chin lift to look up at me. "I thought I made it clear that you're mine."

"Not clear enough."

Before I can think, my lips are on hers. The taste of citrus and alcohol stains my tongue as Ivy becomes less inhibited, pushing her body against mine. Blood rushes to my cock at the feel of her. I weave my fingers through her brunette strands until I'm at the nape of her neck. Balling my hand into a fist, I tug at her hair harder than I ever have, and she instantly moans into my mouth.

"Oh, you like that, Rebel?" I taunt, breaking our kiss.

Ivy nods in response, thrusting her hips toward me in a silent plea. Strengthening my hold on her hair, I tug once more, only this time I move her head to the side, giving me access to her throat. Dipping down, I trail my lips along her sensitive skin. Kissing, licking, and sucking until Ivy becomes a jittery mess, panting while struggling to grind against me. I sneak my other hand under her dress, and I barely brush my finger on the outside of her panties before she moans again.

"Fuck, that feels so good," Ivy croons, her body melting into my grasp. Sneaking my way under the small scrap of fabric, I push two fingers inside her pussy, and she sucks in a breath.

"And who's making you feel so good?"

An impish smirk spreads across her face. "Hmm…I'm not sure. What's your name again?"

My muscles tense, coiled tight from Ivy's playful teasing. Withdrawing my fingers from inside her, I spin her around to face the sink. A long mirror, clouded with drops of water staining the bottom, is directly in front of us. Our eyes lock in the reflection, and I note how fast Ivy's chest is moving up and down.

I undo my pants zipper as I speak to her. "Guess you'll have to watch me fuck you so you never forget." My cock springs free the moment I bend her over. Flipping up her sexy dress, I take my time admiring the view. I can feel her watching me in the mirror as I graze my hand over her ass. My palm crashes against her silky skin, the spank eliciting a raspy moan from her.

My attention floats over to our reflection, her expression lighting up with anticipation as she braces herself on the porcelain sink. Lining up my cock, I make sure to keep my eyes on her as I move her thong out of the way and slowly stretch her out, inch by inch. She looks at me with pure pleasure and trust, turning me on even more.

Her warm pussy envelops me, and I nearly get lost in the sensation, but I don't let myself lose control. Not yet, at least.

"Eyes on me," I say to Ivy through the mirror. "The whole fucking time, Rebel." The second she nods, I slam into her and witness every muscle in her face burst with desire.

I keep it slow at first, pulling completely out and then thrusting into her. Reaching forward, I yank on the low neckline of her dress, exposing her tits, and Ivy watches me pinch and squeeze her nipples.

"More," she whines, pushing her ass against me.

I can't help the smile that shows up on my face. "Keep begging."

"Pax," she pleads. I stand perfectly still as she moves her body back and forth against the sink, getting herself off on my cock. Small whimpers escape from her mouth, but it's nothing like the sound I hear when I'm crashing into her. "Pax, please?" She keeps moving, attempting to get what she needs. "I need more. Please, Pax."

Heat pours down my body, not realizing how hot it would be to hear her beg. "You want me to fuck you hard?" My voice grows deeper and darker. Ivy nods in response. "Then tell me who you belong to."

"You."

Fulfillment bursts through my bloodstream. Even if it's just for now, Ivy is mine. And she knows it.

Tightly clasping her hip with one hand, my other hand fists her hair hard enough to make her scalp sting. When her attention is focused on my eyes, I fuck her hard and fast.

Ivy's wetness coats me, dripping onto my skin as I continue to go rough with her. Her tits bounce forward and back, almost hitting the faucet as her fingers curl onto the edge of the sink. A glow of lust shines on both of our faces as we struggle not to break eye contact.

Tension coils around the base of my spine as I become hypnotized with how fucking sexy she looks. Her hair is a wild mess as her mouth hangs open, letting out loud sounds of pleasure.

I clench my jaw, forcing myself not to come.

I need to keep watching her.

I need to keep admiring how incredible she looks giving into her desires.

"Fuck," she moans. "This feels amazing." Her eyes start to get watery, overwhelmed by the sensations, and mascara lightly smudges under her eyes.

I don't even recognize myself in the mirror—this primal, possessive part of me coming to life the more I bury my cock inside her.

Releasing my hand from her hair, I move it down her dress and travel around to the front of her body. Shoving the fabric of her dress out of the way, I circle my fingers around her clit. Her body trembles in my hold, succumbing to the sensations.

I watch in the mirror, both of our muscles tightening, our sounds and movements getting sharper. My thrusts get more feral as my hunger for her is unleashed.

Ivy sucks in a shallow breath and, on the exhale, is consumed by her orgasm. Her pussy spasms, tightening around me, begging me to follow her lead.

"That's my Rebel. Come all over my cock."

Ivy can't control her moans as she rides her high. My body gets flushed, adrenaline rushing through my bloodstream. I indulge in one final squeeze of her pussy and pull out, instantly coming all over her ass and legs.

We can barely catch our breath as we stare at each other's reflections. Sweat glistens on our skin, both of us looking like a complete and utter mess.

As I gasp for air, I grab a paper towel and clean her off before tucking myself back in my pants.

Ivy straightens her spine, adjusting her dress. She glances up at me, thoroughly satiated. "What'd you say your name was again?"

I can't help but chuckle at her teasing me. "Let's go back to your place and I'll remind you."

Ivy smiles. "Works for me!"

CHAPTER FORTY-ONE

A REPETITIVE BUZZING sound wakes me up from my sleep. As I flutter my eyes open, the first thing to come into view is Pax's giant arm wrapped around my torso. I smile to myself as flashes of last night's events come trickling into my memory. How we made it from the bar to my apartment without stripping each other down along the way, I'll never know, but once we got here, we couldn't get our hands off one another. There's a soreness between my legs, but all it does is widen my grin.

That is, until the buzzing starts again.

I blink myself awake a little bit more and realize the sound is coming from my phone. When I see "Mom" on the screen, a loud groan involuntarily gets let out.

"Definitely not the sound I was hoping to hear from you when you realized I slept over," Pax says, his voice layered in drowsiness.

"Sorry. It's not you. It's my mom."

"Meredith is cockblocking me before I'm even awake," he mumbles into my hair.

Chuckling, I shift away from my phone and focus on

Paxton. "Who said you were going to get lucky again today?"

"I'm already lucky since I got to wake up next to you."

I want to roll my eyes, but I don't. There wasn't any hidden agenda in his statement, trying to butter me up so we could have sex again. He was being sincere, and that scares the hell out of me.

I stretch, creating some space between us, then get out of bed. Wrapping my powder blue robe around me, I ask, "You want some coffee?"

"Yeah." Pax gets up, and I try my best not to stare at every toned muscle, but I'm failing miserably. "I'll make it," he says, walking past me and out into my kitchen as if he owns the place.

I grab my phone, then trail behind, watching him comfortably move around my space.

"What do you have going on today?" Pax asks.

I lean my weight against the counter. "I have a few errands to run, but aside from that, nothing. You?"

"I'm free all day." He searches my cabinets for mugs, but I don't let him know that they're in the one right behind him. When he finally finds them, he places two down on the counter right next to me and says, "I was thinking we could spend the day continuing what we started last night." I try to hide my smile, but he catches it right away. "You like that idea," he states.

"I could possibly, *maybe* get on board with that idea."

Pax grins, and in one swift movement, he puts his hands on my hips, lifts me up, and places me down on the countertop. A yelp of surprise comes from my mouth, followed by a round of giggles. My legs dangle off the counter, and he widens them, stepping in between.

"We could spend the entire day naked." His lips softly brush against mine, then he continues to speak lowly, leaving little kisses across my jaw. "I could fuck you all over your apartment. I could—"

My phone buzzes next to me, jolting me out of my moment with Pax. At the same time, our eyes drift down to look at the screen.

"Answer it," he says.

"No."

"She's going to keep calling." He picks up my phone and hands it to me. "Get her five minutes of nagging out of the way so she doesn't interrupt us all day with phone calls. I'll cook us some breakfast so we can refuel, and then I'm fucking you in the shower."

My lips twitch. "Fine." I take my phone from him and hit the answer button. "Morning, Mom."

"Ivy, I've been trying to get a hold of you since eight." Mom's shrill voice rings in my ear as I watch Pax scour my fridge for some breakfast ingredients.

"Normal adults sleep in during the weekends."

"Only the childless ones do."

My heart drops to my stomach, but I'm quick to put it back in place. My hurt immediately shifts to anger as tension builds in my body. "Was there a purpose to this phone call, Mom?"

"Yes, I wanted to check in about Lucille's bridal shower."

I hop down from the counter and decide to help out Pax since he's looking all over the place for a spatula and skillet. Putting my phone down, I push the speakerphone button and continue talking. "What about it?"

"You're still planning on attending, right?" she asks.

"Of course, I am. Why wouldn't I go?"

"Well, I never know with you. You don't have the best track record on attending events."

"I'll be there." I crack a few eggs into a bowl, even

though I have no idea what Pax is making or how many eggs he needs.

"Good. Now, for the wedding, have you found yourself an escort yet?"

Pax immediately shifts his attention over to me, and I know exactly what he's thinking, but I'm quick to shut it down. "I—no," I say to Mom while I glance at Pax.

She lets out a disappointing sigh. "Ivy, we need to get you a date for the wedding. You can't show up alone."

Pax points to himself and mouths the word *me*. I shake my head while he nods his. We go back and forth, and his face looks so dopey and hopeful that I start to laugh.

"Are you even listening to me?" Mom gets shrill, and I realize that I wasn't paying attention to what she has been going on about.

"Sorry, Mom, I'm cooking breakfast and am a little distracted."

My reply elicits another sigh from her. "Joseph Baker, do you remember him? He's a very successful lawyer in Manhattan. Anyway, his parents are friends of your father's and are attending the wedding and recently mentioned that Joseph is divorced—"

"Mom, please do not set me up with any men. I promise that I'll figure this one out on my own."

"Fine." She says the one-syllable word as clipped as possible. "But if you can't find anyone, Joseph will be available."

"Wonderful." I make no attempt to disguise my sarcasm. "I'll see you at Lucille's shower."

"See you then. Remember not to wear white."

"I will. Bye." I quickly press the end call button, then look over at Pax.

"Lovely conversation with Mrs. Hartwick, as always," he states.

"Yeah." I go to the sink to rinse my hands. "Can't wait to hear it from her when I show up to the wedding solo."

"She'll get over it and then be on your case about something else. Sounds like not having kids will be the next thing to harass you about, judging by her comment."

I let out a halfhearted chuckle. "You heard that part?"

"Her voice is hard to miss, even when she's not on speakerphone."

"That's for sure."

Silence stretches between us while he cooks, and I force myself not to get lost in my thoughts. I rarely allow my mind to wander into a web of hypotheticals. What if I followed the path my parents set out for me? What if I ended up with one of the men they handpicked for me? What if I ran off with Pax? What if my life turned out very differently when I was eighteen? It's been years since I opened Pandora's box. I worked very hard to chain those thoughts away and throw away the key. There's no way I'm about to unlock them now.

"Are you ever going to go through the boxes your mom sent you, or are they now a part of your living room?" Pax teases, thankfully pulling me away from my thoughts.

Spinning around, I glance over at the pile of taped-up memories pushed against my back wall. "I don't know. I feel like the cardboard gives the room a shabby rustic look."

"It's definitely a unique design concept." He places an omelet on a plate and begins making another. "Although I'm sure those boxes have enough in them to fill up a Y2K exhibit at your museum."

I snort. "I've had the same thought."

"I can help you go through them. We got interrupted last time by that guy, Walter."

"Warren," I correct.

"Ah, yes, that was his name. Warren. The man who *warned* me about you being a bolter." Pax's attention is laser-focused on me, waiting to disclose why.

I shrug. "What can I say? I've made quite the reputation for myself." Feeling the itch to end this topic, I tug on my robe. "I'm gonna go get dressed."

Pax tilts his head back in laughter. "Bolting away from this conversation?"

"Possibly," I say, pivoting toward my bedroom.

"You're a piece of work, Ivy."

"Glad you find my antics amusing." My voice carries as I step into my room.

"You can avoid the conversation and get dressed, but I'm still fucking you after breakfast."

Smiling to myself, I respond, "Deal."

CHAPTER FORTY-TWO

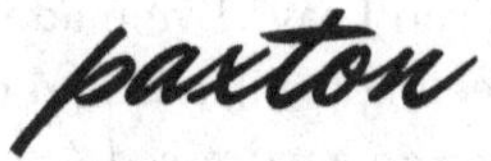

2009

April

THE PAST FEW months have been a whirlwind. It's nearing the end of my first season with the Knights, and I just caught wind that I'm being drafted to the AHL. I'm fucking ecstatic and want nothing more than to share my good news, but the one person I want to talk to the most hasn't answered me in what feels like forever.

I texted Ivy a few weeks ago to see how she's been and have heard nothing back.

I've been checking her Facebook for updates, seeing her post pictures of a new group of friends I don't know, wondering why the hell she's been ignoring me.

"Are you even paying attention?" Courtney snaps me into the present moment, both of us in a hotel room in between my games. We're shirtless as she straddles my hips with a scowl on her face, pissed that I wasn't into the line of kisses she was leaving from my chest down to my abs. At least, I think that's what she was doing.

"Yeah—sorry."

"I can't believe you're not even focused on me, considering everything you did."

My eyes narrow. "After everything I did?"

"You cheated on me, Pax—"

"Whoa, whoa, whoa." I push up on my palms, getting eye level with her. "I did *not* cheat on you, Court."

"I told you I needed space."

"Exactly."

"That doesn't mean we're broken up and you can go off and screw whoever slides into your inbox."

I scrub my hand over my face. I'm not having this fucking conversation again. It was a miscommunication, and I thought we were done.

I don't know how Courtney and I ended up in this spot. Things got strained after the holidays, her trust in me wavered, and we started getting into stupid, little fights on a daily basis. She got angry when I told her my career is my number one priority and not our relationship. Honestly, that should've been the red flag she needed to walk away, but we somehow got increasingly complicated and tangled in a dysfunctional relationship.

I've tried pulling the plug, but then she somehow guilts me with waterworks. My head spins from trying to keep up our status.

The more I've been gaining traction in my hockey career, the more I've been getting random girls messaging me on Facebook. I never took the bait until I thought Court officially ended things. I thought I was single, so I acted like I was. If I were in college like Trent, I'd be doing the same exact thing. In fact, the way he's been updating me on his college life, I'm pretty sure he's scoring more in his first year at school than I am in my first year on the Knights.

My phone rings on my nightstand, showing Uncle Jeff's name. As I go to reach for it, Courtney scoffs.

"You're seriously going to answer that?"

"You mean, am I going to answer the phone call from the guy who I owe my life to? Yeah."

Continuing to grab my phone, Courtney huffs, jumping off me. She tosses on her shirt and fluffs up her blond hair. "I'm going out. I'll be back later. Maybe."

"Okay," I say, unaffected by her supposed threat. She rolls her eyes right before slamming the hotel door behind her. Clicking the answer button on my phone, my mood instantly lifts. "Hey, Uncle Jeff."

"That was some fucking play tonight," he says, pride flowing through the earpiece.

A grin spread across my face. "You watched the game?"

"Of course, we did. We started screaming when you got a hat trick."

"We?" I cling to the word he let slip.

"Yep, Ivy came over. She left a little while ago. Don't worry, I made sure to stock up on Cool Ranch Doritos."

"She, um, she watched my game?" I pace the room, staring at the hideous pattern on the carpet. Nerves spike in my stomach in a way that only happens when Ivy is brought up.

"I don't think that girl has missed a single game of yours since the two of you crossed paths."

"She got the flu last year and couldn't go to—" I stop myself from going off topic on a random Ivy fact that is stored in my brain. "I was just surprised that she still watches even though I haven't been around since the winter."

"Something happen between you two?"

Fuck if I know. "No. We just haven't caught up recently. I've been hyper-focused on playing—which leads me to my next topic." I take a deep breath, gearing up to tell him the news. "There's talk of me getting drafted to the AHL."

A shaky breath comes from the other side of the phone. Uncle Jeff clears his throat, and his words come out with the utmost sincerity when he says, "I'm so proud of you, Pax."

My eyes sting, hearing him struggle to keep his emotions in check. "Thank you. I couldn't have gotten this far without you."

We're both quick to gloss over the tender moment and go on to talk logistics of the draft. The teams, contract, and sports manager—the business end of the deal. By the time the conversation ends, I've completely forgotten about the Courtney drama and am left with a smile on my face.

Grabbing my clunky Dell laptop off the hotel desk, I plop down on the bed with the intention of Googling the myriad of questions Uncle Jeff asked, but out of habit, I drift over to the Facebook tab, noticing that Ivy is online.

No longer willing to wait for her to text me back, I message her.

ME

Hey Rebel

IVY

Hey!

ME

Heard you watched my game tonight

IVY

I might've

ME

Why haven't you texted me back?

IVY

What are you talking about?

My eyebrows crinkle together, and as I get ready to type a reply, she messages me back.

IVY

Oops, sorry. I somehow missed it

I thought her response would offer me some relief, but it doesn't. Instead of the unease of assuming she'd been ignoring me, I get a prick of loneliness being second string in her world. Yeah, she might still watch my games, but maybe that's just because she likes watching hockey.

ME

How's life?

IVY

Crazy! I'm sooo busy!! Can't wait for junior year to be over so I can do nothing but sunbathe by the pool

ME

Can I crash one of your sunbathing sessions?

IVY

Only if you wear a bikini

I laugh, imagining how ridiculous I'd look in one of her bathing suits.

ME

If you get to pick my outfit, then I get to pick yours

The tips of my ears burn, realizing how my comment might come across.

IVY

What would you pick?

A warm flush washes over me. It's impossible to tell if she's flirting through messages, but it feels like we're bordering that line. Not like we haven't in the past, but it's been a while.

IVY

I have a plethora of bathing suits—one piece, tankini, bikini, swim dress

ME

Bikini

IVY

To match you?

Smiling at my computer screen, I type out my response

ME

Something like that

She goes quiet for a few seconds as I impatiently wait for her to say something back.

IVY

I have to get ready. Calvin is picking me up in a few mins. But I'll text you tomorrow. Congrats on your win tonight!

I bite on my cuticles, knowing that I should just type a goodbye, but I don't.

ME

Is he treating you right?

IVY

Yes.

ME

Good.

There are a few moments of quietness between us, and just as I hear Courtney on the other side of my hotel room door, getting ready to enter, Ivy messages me back.

IVY

I miss you

ME

I miss you too

CHAPTER FORTY-THREE

July

I'VE SEEN Mom angry with me plenty of times.

But I've never witnessed her appear like she's about to combust at the news I just dropped.

As we stand in the vestibule of Oak Ridge Mansion, where I'm about to be forced to start taking my very first course to become a Colonial Dame come this time next year, Mom's eyes go wide. Her hand wraps around my wrist in a vise grip, and she somehow effortlessly guides me into the ladies' room without it looking like I'm moving against my will so we can talk in private.

"What did you just say to me?" Her tone is pressed, as if she's highly suggesting I change my answer.

"I broke up with Calvin."

Very dramatically, she pinches the bridge of her nose and paces the length of the bathroom, her heels clicking against the polished floor. "Why on *earth* would you do that?"

I shrug. "It just fizzled out."

Truthfully, we both felt like we hit our expiration date. The breakup happened last week. It wasn't anything gut-wrenching. We both knew that the minute spark we had was gone.

We tried to regain it last month when we had sex. I knew my first time wouldn't be a life-changing night filled with passion, but I was still expecting to feel something. We tried a few more times after that, and it was... okay? I guess?

Aside from the whole sex thing, our time together got boring. We didn't have anything new to talk about, and we'd do the same thing over and over again. We don't have a lot in common, and while that has the potential to add some excitement to a relationship, it fell flat for us.

"You're about to be a senior. This is your most important year," Mom says.

"Actually, junior year was my most important for grades. Senior year is when I find out which colleges I've been accepted to."

"No." Mom draws out the one-syllable word nice and slow as if I'm an idiot. "Your senior year is when you turn eighteen, making you eligible to become a Dame right after you graduate. You can't get inducted without an escort. That is unheard of!"

I blankly stare at her, the two of us living in two different centuries.

She aggressively points a finger at me. "You better fix this."

"Fix what?"

"Whatever you did to Calvin, apologize to him and make it right."

My hands land on my hips, hitting against the fabric of this bland, cream-colored dress she made me wear. "I didn't do anything to him. I'm not getting back with him to save face. There's no point. There's no future for us. I want to be with someone who—"

"God, you are so naïve," Mom mutters, glancing up at the ceiling as if she's pissed with the universe that she was given me as a daughter.

"What are you talking about?"

Her gaze lands back on me, her intense blue eyes making it impossible to glance away. "I thought I raised you better than to be one of those girls."

"What type of girl?"

"The stupid ones who ruin their lives over the false promise of love." She steps in closer, and my body goes rigid. "Men lie. Do not be one of those girls who bend over backward and loses herself over pretty words. You need to have the upper hand."

"Okay," I say, not really knowing what she means.

"At the end of the day, the words mean nothing, love is fleeting, and beauty fades. But your reputation and status will continue to grow if you allow it."

Blinking, I take in the information she threw at me. A knot intricately weaves its way tighter and tighter around my chest, forcing me to take shallow breaths. She just dropped that she didn't marry Dad for love but for money. "Okay," I repeat, only this time it comes out much weaker.

"Calvin comes from a family with a similar status to ours—in fact, their status is better than ours. Don't do some stupid act of rebellion to try to stick it to me and potentially ruin your entire future."

"I'm not reb—"

Her hand goes up. "I don't want to hear it. Now, let's go. I'm co-chair. We can't be late."

As she nudges me out of the bathroom, she cements her signature, dignified smile on her face. Moving into the dining hall, fellow and incoming Dames greet us. We part ways, Mom sitting at the table toward the front of the room while I sit at a table toward the back with other girls who will be starting this course with me.

I've seen them before, and we politely exchange hellos. Sitting down, I wonder if my smile is properly in place like Mom's or if they can tell I'm holding back tears.

Mom and the other Dames start their introductions, but I can't focus, my mind going a mile a minute.

Does Dad know she married him for money? Did the other women here do the same? Is that what's supposed to happen? Is this an unspoken agreement between upper-class families?

I always knew my parents wanted me to marry within their circle, but I always assumed they wanted me to *love* the guy.

Glancing around at the girls at my table, I worry if they share the same fate as me. If everything in their world is deemed secondary to who they'll end up marrying.

Nothing is more important to my parents than the weight of my future last name.

What a sad existence. To be surrounded by a room filled with women sitting on their own talent and passions and knowledge because it's not viewed as worthy as the man standing next to them.

My skin itches.

My leg bounces up and down in a very ill-mannered way.

The pounding of my heart reverberates inside me.

I hate it here.

Mom and the others continue to speak, training us to be the epitome of a picture-perfect woman. As they drone on, my phone vibrates in my purse. I sneak it out, and the girl next to me catches a glimpse. Judging by the expression on her face, you'd think I just pulled out a bag of cocaine.

Ignoring her, I glance at the message on my screen.

PAX

Heading home for the weekend, you around?

ME

YES.

I'm at a Dame meeting with my mom. Get me out of here

PAX

When and where?

I text him the info, letting him know to meet me at the front gates and not to go into the facility. Mom is bound to stay and gossip after this, so I'll just tell her I have plans with a friend from school and be on my merry way.

Since Pax got drafted to the American Hockey League, there have been pros and cons that have gone along with it. The pro being that his team is only a four-hour drive away, so when he's practicing, he can come visit during his downtime. The con is that he hasn't had a lot of downtime, as his coach is working him extra hard to prep for the fall season. He visits some weekends, so we've only seen each other a few times since I finished out the school year.

And seeing him immediately after this shit show of an afternoon seems like the perfect remedy.

"Hey, Rebel," Pax says as I hop into his car that he recently bought himself.

"Hey." Twisting my head, I make sure no one saw me get in by the front entrance, then I shift my attention over to Pax. My veins light up when I have a moment to take him in. He's wearing a loosely fitted tank top, and the muscles in his biceps are more pronounced than ever before. His dark hair gently blows in the breeze filtering in from his window. His sunglasses mask his hazel eyes, but I know they're staring back at me by the way he's smiling. I have to force myself to keep my composure so my mouth doesn't hang open and begin to water at how hot he's looking right now.

"Nice dress," he teases.

"My mother's pick."

Hitting the gas, we head onto the road. "Are we going back to your house?"

"No. Let's go somewhere else."

"If I recall correctly, you promised me a day of sunbathing by the pool."

My lips tug, thinking back to our brief conversation over the spring. Wanting to keep true to our plans and feeling the desperate urge to let loose, I come up with the next best option. "Let's head to the beach."

He nods in agreement, and I lead him to a private beach my family is a part of. You have to pay to be a member, and because of that, there aren't flocks of people crowding every inch of the sand. It's remote and isolated.

As he parks, I search his car for some things we can utilize. A small bottle of sunscreen rests in one of the cup holders, and I spot an old jersey and a few other T-shirts in the back that we can use to lie on. He has an open water bottle that is probably too hot to enjoy, but will suffice if we need to hydrate.

"I can't imagine a dress is very comfortable for the beach," he says as we step out and into the summer heat.

"You're right." Reaching behind me, I tug at the zipper.

"Ivy—what the hell are you doing!" He frantically

looks around to make sure no one saw me drop the straps to my dress.

"Getting out of my dress," I state the obvious, getting down to my blush-colored bra and panties.

Pax glances over at me and then quickly turns away. "I can't—I can't see you like that."

"A bra and underwear are pretty much the same thing as a bikini, and you've seen me in a bathing suit countless times. In fact, I'm pretty sure my underwear covers more of my ass than any of my bikinis do." I toss my dress and shoes into his car.

He still has his head turned the other way, but I can note the way his cheeks turn red, and I'm pretty sure it's not only because it's hot outside. I chuckle, enjoying how flustered he is. It's been a very long time since the two of us have been alone, and I almost forgot what it felt like to be teetering on the edge of flirting when no one else is around. A boost of confidence juts through my bloodstream, knowing that Paxton can get so rattled when he's around me. It's a fun little game that we haven't played in a while—and after today, I'm more than willing to partake in some fun.

"Never thought of you as a prude, Pax," I tease. "Has your reputation been nothing but a lie?"

"I'm not a prude, Ivy. And my reputation is none of your concern."

Getting up on my tippy toes, I poke his cheek. "So serious."

He cracks a smile, finally looking at me. "You're a pain in my ass."

With that, he moves away from his car, and we walk onto the scalding hot sand. We're quick to lay down his shirts to get some relief, planting ourselves on them. As I rub sunscreen over the places I can reach, Pax takes off his shirt. My gaze connects with his abs, which have never been pronounced before, and a flushed feeling rushes to my face.

"You mind getting my back?" I ask, extending the bottle of sunscreen.

Pax wordlessly takes it, and I spin around. Air gets trapped in my throat the instant his fingertips brush over my skin. Calloused and rough, his hands smooth the lotion over my back. My body becomes electrified. He carefully lifts my bra strap, getting the small sliver of skin underneath. His hands slowly drift downward, covering the rest of me.

My heart can't remain calm.

I'm losing at my own game.

Putting on sunscreen should be harmless, but this seems like we're inching closer to dangerous territory.

"All good," Pax says as if he's unaffected. He doesn't ask me to do the same for him, so we lie down and let the sun bask over us.

We chat, catching each other up on the little things that've been going on in our worlds. My pulse finally settles down as we fall back into our usual dynamic.

"How was your Dame meeting?" Pax asks.

"About as wonderful as you'd imagine." I flip over onto my belly, crossing my arms so my cheek can rest on them while I look over at Pax as he gazes at the ocean. The conversation with Mom from earlier today plays over in my head, and my mind wanders, weaving down paths it's only ever tiptoed through before. "Do you ever wonder about your parents?"

Pax whips his attention to me. His features are pulled in tight, but more from confusion than anger. "Why do you ask?"

"I'm curious about what goes through your head."

He softly smiles, then flips over onto his stomach and mirrors my position so that our faces are in direct line. "I don't really think about them much anymore," he shares. "Maybe, here and there, I'll wonder how my mom's doing. But Uncle Jeff is my parent, and I wouldn't be here without him, so I'm glad he took over."

I admire his sun-kissed cheeks and pillowy lips. "I'm glad he did too. Otherwise, we never would've met."

Pax inches his head a little closer to me, causing my insides to buzz. "What goes on inside your head, Ivy?"

"Lots."

"What've you been caught up on today?"

You. My parents. My future. I nibble on my bottom lip, debating what to share with him. "Do you believe in love?"

His forehead crinkles. "I…yeah, I guess so? Why?"

"Do you believe love is enough?

"Enough for what?"

"To live and have a sustainable future."

"Why wouldn't it be?"

I shake my head, wishing these thoughts would fall right out of my ears. "I don't know. I had this talk with my mom before, and it's been messing with me."

"What did Meredith do this time?"

I smirk, enjoying the fact that he refers to her by her first name, going out of his way to be impolite and not call her Mrs. Hartwick. "She's upset I broke up with Calvin," I state.

Pax's eyebrows shoot up. The two of us rarely mention the two C words: Calvin and Courtney. "You broke up with him?" His voice rises in surprise. "Why?"

"Things got boring. We didn't have a spark anymore."

"You gotta have that spark." His leg brushes against mine, on purpose or by accident, I'm not sure, but oh my god, did my veins just fill with millions of sparks.

"How are things with Courtney?" I ask, needing to know before we potentially cross a line.

Pax lets out an exasperated sigh. "Things with Courtney are complicated."

"Complicated? Paxton Rhodes does not do complicated."

"You're right. So whenever we're on our stupid breaks, she does whatever she wants, and I do whatever I want."

"Whatever you want, meaning..." I wait for him to say more. Instead, his lips curl upward, and I need no further explanation. "That sounds like a shitty relationship."

"It's whatever." He shrugs. "We have fun when the drama subsides."

"Are you in love with her?"

"Damn, Ivy, what's with these tough questions today?" He laughs in a desperate attempt to lighten the mood.

"Sorry," I say, not knowing how to feel about the information he disclosed. I wish I hadn't asked and assumed they were a happy couple instead of picturing him hooking up with other women in between their mini-breakups, knowing full well that they'll end up back together.

"Let's go for a dip." Pax quickly shifts the energy as he speaks. He nudges my arm, and the two of us venture away from our spot and walk toward the shoreline.

Neither of us brings up Calvin or Courtney again, enjoying our blissful ignorance for the afternoon. Pretending like we actually have a shot with one another as we flirt and laugh.

But at the end of the day, it'll never be more than this.

CHAPTER FORTY-FOUR

PRESENT

AS PAX KISSES his way down from my neck to my shoulder, I try to ignore the same thought that's been getting louder and louder over these past several weeks. *This all seems too good to be true.*

Even my birthday a couple of weeks ago was perfect. I didn't want to do anything, so he planned a *Pirates of the Caribbean* movie marathon, and he cooked me dinner. It was so simple, yet just what I wanted.

"God, you're clingy," I joke while reminding myself that all of this is going to end soon.

Attempting to shove the rest of my makeup in my toiletries bag as I stand at my bathroom vanity, Pax lifts his head from my shoulder, and his strong arms come from behind and wrap around my waist.

"I'm not going to see you for a couple of days. I need to get in a few extra kisses."

Smiling, I gaze up at the mirror. Warmth pours from

my heart, admiring how perfect we look together in the reflection.

I rest the back of my head against his hard chest, easing more into his hold. "Is that your way of telling me you'll miss me?"

"You have no idea how much I missed you, Ivy." His deep resonance coaxes butterflies to take flight in my stomach.

Our gazes connect in the mirror as he holds me, both of us looking blissfully peaceful. I wish I could take a picture of this moment and frame it. Have it as a keepsake and bury it underneath relics of my past, only pulling it out when I can't quell my masochistic heart.

Sorrow suddenly strikes through me, killing off the hopeful flutters that were just dancing around my insides mere seconds ago. Grieving something that never was, my eyes begin to prick.

Noting the sensation, I immediately straighten my spine and keep my emotions in check, stuffed deep down. "I guess I'll miss you too," I say, getting back to packing my makeup. "Unless that man, Joseph, my mom wants to set me up with is there, and he sweeps me off my feet."

Pax playfully glares at me. "Not funny."

"I'm kidding." Spinning around so we're face-to-face, I continue, "It's a bridal shower. No men are invited. So you only have to worry about a random man at the airport sweeping me off my feet."

"Too late. That already happened."

Before I can come up with a response, his lips are on mine, stealing my breath and the rest of my remaining sanity.

By the time we make it out of the bathroom, I'm running close on time to catch my flight. "Oh, here," I say, passing him my spare key before I forget.

"Is this your way of inviting me to live with you?"

"No, I figured you might want a break from your hotel room, so you can hang out here while I'm away."

Pax smiles, slipping my spare into his pocket. Since he insists on driving me to the airport, he takes my belongings from me as we head out the door. Just as I'm about to leave, I get a glimpse of the stacked cardboard boxes in my living room, reminding me that my single sanctuary in my parents' home is now barren.

Polite laughter and the sound of teacups clinking against porcelain saucers fill the rooftop terrace of a posh restaurant where Lucille's bridal shower is being held. It's half covered by a canopy, while the other half is open to the elements. With the early spring air, it feels nice to let the sun hit my arms while I mingle with the rest of the bridesmaids. Thankfully, I'm at a table with Pia, Celeste, and Felicity instead of Mom.

"Pia, you did an incredible job at picking out this place. It's beautiful!" I tell her, and I glance around the space. The rooftop is trendy yet elegant, with an infusion of greenery around the brick walls. Every table has a tall crystal vase with a medley of white flowers, and every so often, when a breeze hits, I get a whiff of a sweet, clean scent, reminding me of the change in season.

"Thank you." Pia beams. "I hope Luc loves it as much as I do."

"I'm certain she does," I say, and Celeste and Felicity agree.

Lucille is glowing with joy as people come up to her. The excitement of marrying my brother in a month is bubbling over. She grins so much *my* cheeks just hurt from watching her.

"We should mingle with the guests," Pia softly instructs the three of us. We nod and disperse, stepping into our bridesmaid duties. Between all of us, we should be able to hit all eighty-seven guests.

It was supposed to be a much smaller, intimate event, but rumor has it Mom kept adding women to the guest list. If she went this overboard with invites to the shower, I can only imagine how many people are expected to show up at the wedding.

I respectfully say hello to extended family members, some of whom were at my parents' holiday party and witnessed me turning down Warren.

"How are you holding up, dear?" my Aunt Florence asks, clasping her hand to her heart with pity.

"I'm wonderful," I state. "I'm so glad to be here celebrating Lucille."

"Your time will come soon enough."

She pats my arm as if consoling a child, and I force a well-mannered smile, then find an excuse to talk to someone else.

After dipping in and out of different groups and making small talk, I find myself with one of Mom's friends and fellow Dame, Ruth. Out of all the Dames, I remember Ruth to be the most down-to-earth. She's since moved, and I haven't seen her in ages, but judging by her slingback sandals and lack of gems around her neck, I'm sure she's still pleasant to be around.

"My goodness, Ivy, you look more beautiful each time I see you!" Ruth greets me with a warm hug, and I thank her for the compliment. "Tell me all about life. What are you up to these days?"

As we begin to chat, a familiar scent of floral perfume

hits my nose, and out of the corner of my eye, I spot Mom making her way into our conversation.

"Oh, I'm so glad you ladies are catching up," Mom says, politely hugging Ruth.

"Me too," Ruth states. "I was just about to ask Ivy what she's doing for work."

I open my mouth to speak, but Mom starts before I can.

"She finds nice pictures to hang up."

Ruth tilts her head to the side, then looks over at me, asking, "Interior design?"

"No." I give Mom a sharp glance before turning my attention back to Ruth. "I'm a museum curator. I graduated from Harvard, and now I work at an art museum in Boston."

Ruth's eyes go wide. "That's sensational!" She beams. "You must be so proud, Meredith."

"I am," Mom says. "I couldn't get Ivy to join a sorority at Harvard, though," she jokes, letting out a little laugh. The comment causes my spine to stiffen, reminding me of how she used to brag to others that I got into Harvard—when she barely even wanted me to attend in the first place. And how the bragging soon stopped once she realized I wasn't going to be following through with being a Dame, or at the very least, a sorority member. "But that's our Ivy," Mom continues. "Always doing things to the beat of her own drum and surprising us. Although I always thought she'd be married with kids by now."

"Not on the horizon for you?" Ruth asks me.

"Um, I'm not sure."

"I think she scares men away with her independence," Mom whispers as if she's telling a crude joke.

"There's nothing wrong with being a strong woman, Mom."

"Indeed," Ruth agrees. "But if you're considering

having children one day, you might want to freeze your eggs."

"What?

"I know it sounds absurd, but my husband is an obstetrician, and he always recommends that women in their early thirties freeze their eggs if they may want children later down the line. It gets tougher to conceive as you approach forty. And the fact that doctors refer to it as a geriatric pregnancy is blasphemy! I tell my husband he's not allowed to use that phrase."

Ruth and Mom chuckle while my throat dries up.

"If late thirties are geriatric, I don't even want to know what we're considered," Mom adds, and the two continue laughing.

I force a smile as a wave of uneasiness crashes into my belly. A simmer of panic trembles right beneath the surface, and I'm not even sure why.

Excusing myself, I go to my table to grab my glass of water. Tiny ice chips slide down my throat in an attempt to cool down my insides. I rarely let myself think about these topics, but now that it's been forced in front of my face, my mind spirals with concern. This strange feeling of a ticking clock intensifies, which is beyond stupid. Anxiety and annoyance battle it out in my head, and by the time everyone gathers back to their tables and the bridal shower toasts begin, my head settles on neither emotion and opts for a third option.

Immense sadness weighs down my bones.

I move through the event with a grin on my face, eating brunch, playing outdated bridal games, and supporting Lucille as she radiates graciousness. All the while, a hole in my heart grows.

The ache follows me the rest of the day, and by the time I'm ready to call it a night, the pain has quadrupled in size and has turned into a gaping pit carving out my chest.

Mom and Dad are out with our extended family, and I'm all alone in their house. Lingering in the doorway of my childhood bedroom, I realize I didn't have time to process how much of it had changed when I was getting ready for the bridal shower earlier in the day.

It's void of all the life that once lived in it.

Nothing hanging on the walls, all the shelves cleared out, dead space taking up the majority of the room aside from my bed and empty dresser.

Tiptoeing around the place I once called mine, I glide my fingertips over the top of my dresser, making a steady line until I hit a small divot in the wood. Pressing into the tiny sunken space, my lips pull upward, remembering how it got there. The very first time I met Pax and managed to burn my dresser *and* him.

An anchor filled with nostalgia soars down into my gut the more I think about life back then.

Becoming overloaded by the past, I slump down onto my bed. My eyes prick with emotions I don't let to the surface until a singular tear rolls down my cheek. My lashes become cloudy with the impending tears to follow as I struggle to take my shoes off.

For the first time in a very long time, I glance down at the tattoo on my ankle. Folding my knee up so I can see it closer, I examine the simple, tiny flower.

Of course, Pax immediately noticed it when we were at the winter getaway. But thankfully, he hasn't brought it up since and isn't aware of the meaning behind it.

Pax doesn't know that I got this tattoo for us.

My fingers run over the small daisy.

I got it for the three of us.

CHAPTER FORTY-FIVE

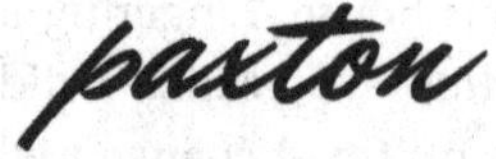

2010

March

ME

Surprise, fucker. I'm in town

TRENT

wtf what are you doing home?

ME

I'm playing a game a few hours away tomorrow, so I figured I'd drive over and hang out instead of going crazy in another hotel room

AS A RED TRAFFIC light gleams overhead, I shift around in the seat of my car, sending over the text, conveniently leaving out the part that Courtney is also in my hotel room and is a big reason why I want to drive several hours away from it. I know exactly how things will go down with her: She's pissed at me for some reason, we fight, and both of us act like assholes to each other, we go on a "break" and fuck around with strangers, then she begs and pleads and cries to let her back into my life—and I stupidly do. I'm not cut out for this on-again, off-again shit. But I have no idea how to end it for good, especially when she travels with me to all of my games.

When Trent was messaging me yesterday about coming home from college for the weekend to visit people in town, I wasn't planning on being one of those people, but the arguing with Courtney got to be too much, and I had to get the fuck away. Even if it's only for a little bit.

TRENT

I'm heading to a party in a little bit. I'll get you the address. Meet me there

While I wait for him to send me the details, I debate texting the other Hartwick. It was Ivy's eighteenth birthday two weeks ago, and I tried to Skype her, but the video chat only lasted a few minutes because she had plans with friends. The distance between us is becoming more apparent—literally, because being part of the AHL has me traveling a shit ton, but also as friends.

TRENT

8053 Hubert Ave. I'll be there in a half

I do a mental recollection of the street names near Trent and Ivy's house and begin heading toward the party. Sure, I could've spent the night with Uncle Jeff, but he'd ask too many questions about Courtney that I'd rather avoid. So partying with my best friend is the option I'm going with tonight.

The street is lined with high-end cars on either side of

Hubert Avenue as I round the corner. The moment I find a spot to park and shut off my car, I can hear the muffled bass of dance music coming from the large estate with iron gates that are slightly ajar so people can make their way inside.

Trent won't be here for another twenty minutes, but I'd rather crash a random party than sit in my car alone with my thoughts. Making my way to the gates, I make eye contact with a cute redhead who whispers something in her friend's ear. Her friend glances over her shoulder to look at me, and a familiar stir of enticement runs through my bones. They wait for me to get closer before flirting.

"Are you one of Ben's friends?" the redhead asks, showcasing ample cleavage.

"Who?" I respond.

She laughs. "Guess not. Ben is the guy who lives here. His parents are on vacation."

"Oh. Nope, never met Ben before. I'm meeting my friend here in a little bit."

"So there are two of you!" The redhead beams, turning to her hot friend, and both of them giggle. She then loops her arm around mine, and they both guide me into the front yard. "Stick with us and we'll show you around. And maybe if you're lucky, we'll also give you and your friend a tour of the bedrooms."

Walking up the stone pathway, a wide smile parts my lips. "Sounds good to me."

We pass by shrubbery that probably costs as much as my car, and finally get closer to the mansion. Groups of college kids drink, smoke, and gossip, and one of them calls over to the redhead. While she and her friend go say hello, I stare at the colossal house in front of me. Huge panels of glass windows make it easy to look into the party. The opening notes of "Bad Romance" by Lady

Gaga start playing, and exciting shrieks come from everywhere as girls rush to where the speakers are to start dancing. In no time, guys are following their lead, attempting to get their hands anywhere they can as they poorly dance with them.

I chuckle, watching the sight before me as lights flash over them. Everyone's gripping onto red Solo cups and chanting the words to the song.

As the lights quickly shift from green to pink, someone in the center of the room catches my attention. Squinting, I make sure what I'm seeing is accurate.

It's Ivy.

And she looks fucking *hot*.

She's always gorgeous, but this time…it's different. The red dress she's wearing is extremely tight, very low-cut, and extra short, showing off her long legs all the way down to the highest pair of heels I've ever seen her in.

Temptation bursts through my veins, heating my insides to the point of boiling. I swallow, watching in awe at how she moves her body to the music. I've seen her dance a bunch of times. But not like this.

She's confident and sexy on the dance floor as her friends surround her, attracted to her rousing energy.

But as I continue to stand frozen, gazing at Ivy, I suddenly feel further and further away from her. A bunch of strangers crowd around her, cheering her on, and I'm reminded of how separated our lives are.

I'll always be on the other side of the glass, looking in.

All of this—the mansions, luxury cars, lavish parties—this is her life. It always has been and always will be. And I'll always be the bastard kid whose uncle took him in, wishing I could fit perfectly into Ivy's life like her missing puzzle piece, but knowing that'll never be an option.

Just as a lump in my throat grows, the ache is

suddenly stifled by the sight of some douche weaseling his way to Ivy. The instant his hands grip onto her hips and they start dancing, my despair is melted by my scorching rage.

"Oh, fuck no," I forcefully blurt out, my hands balling into fists.

Heads whip around to stare at me, and the redhead starts talking. "Everything okay?"

Ignoring her, I march into the house, body-checking anyone who happens to be standing in my way.

"Ivy!" my voice bellows over the music. Everyone turns in my direction, and the crowd parts like the Red Sea, stopping right at Ivy, who's standing in the middle of the room. The guy she was dancing with still holds on to her, and if I witness it for a second longer, I'm going to lose my shit completely. "Hands off of her," I command, and he listens, cowardly slinking back into the shadows of the crowd.

Caught off guard, it takes Ivy a few seconds to register that I crashed the party until I stalk over to her. She clenches her jaw in annoyance. "What are you doing here?"

"What are *you* doing here? This is a college party," I snap.

Ivy rolls her eyes. "I'm graduating high school in a couple of months. A bunch of us are here. And technically, *you're* not in college either."

"You can whine and bitch all you want on the way home. Come on, let's go."

"No."

The people around us tighten the circle, awaiting my response. But instead of giving them more shit to gossip about, I tilt my head to the side and let my defenses slip for a millisecond as I lock eyes with the sapphire daggers in front of me. "Ivy…"

"Why should I go back with you?" She crosses her arms, accentuating her chest. Distracted by how she looks, my gaze drops downward for a beat, but by the time I glance back up at her, she's already smirking. She fucking caught me and knows she threw me off.

Regaining my sanity, tension builds back up in my muscles. "You can either leave with me now or wait fifteen minutes until your brother gets here and deal with both of us bringing you home."

I get my second eye roll of the night, but she doesn't put up more of a fight, knowing that leaving now is the better option. "Whatever," she says, with a hair toss.

The moment we go to leave, the party sparks to life once again, and people talk and dance as if we didn't just press the pause button on their fun. As Ivy struts out of the house with me tailing behind, I force myself not to pay attention to how the red fabric of her dress hugs her body.

Ivy's heels patter on the pavement, and I go to catch up to her but get intercepted.

"Hey, where are you going?" the redhead rushes over to me. She places her hand over my torso as a way of letting everyone know that she's claimed me for the night.

Ivy looks over at us and scoffs.

"Someone heard this crazy rumor that you might be going to the NHL. Is that true? You're Paxton Rhodes, right?" the redhead persists.

Ivy walks further away from me, quickening her pace with angry stomps.

Brushing the redhead's hand off me, I respond, "I gotta go." Then I jog over to Ivy, who's already passing the iron gates.

"Since I'm not allowed in the party, do you want me to sit in your car while you get your dick sucked?" Ivy snaps, causing me to do a double-take. Never have I heard such a crass comment come out of her mouth, and for whatever reason, it's making me chuckle. "It's not funny, Pax!" She whips around to face me. "That was embarrassing. I've been to plenty of parties before. I don't need you acting like I'm doing something heinous and escorting me back home."

"I know."

"So what the fuck was that for then?"

"I..." My gaze wanders, staring at the dark road with a line of cars parked as far as I can see. Heat suddenly fills my cheeks as Ivy waits for me to answer. The truth dances on the tip of my tongue, wanting me to blurt out that my jealousy got the best of me. And I hate being away from her for so long. And I hate that we don't talk as much anymore. And I *really* fucking hate the thought of another man gripping her hips.

"Earth to Pax." She waves a hand in front of my face.

"I just wanted you to be safe," I say. Not a lie, just not the full truth. Ivy dramatically drops her shoulders and groans, but before she can start complaining, I interject, "I know, I know. I did it in a shitty way. I'm sorry. Let me make it up to you."

"How?"

"We can wait until Trent gets here, and the three of us can go hang out somewhere."

"He's gonna give me crap about this dress."

I allow my attention to drop down to assess it for myself, and she's right. Trent would totally flip if he saw her wearing the skimpy outfit. My eyes linger a little longer than they should, my thoughts drifting to places they shouldn't. Temptation nips at my fingertips, and it fucking hurts to tame it.

"I could take you home instead." Panic zaps me, realizing how that might've come across. "And we could watch a movie or something," I add. "I never saw the third *Pirates of the Caribbean*."

"It sucked. The first two are better."

"Movie marathon of the first two, then?"

"Fine. But you still owe me a wild night of partying."

"I'll make it happen one day."

As we head toward my car, I send Trent a quick text.

ME

Ivy was at the party. I'm driving her back home. She's pissed, so I promised I'd hang out with her for a little to chill her out. I'll catch up with you later

It's a quick drive to Ivy's home, but the silence coming from her makes it seem like hours. Pulling into the familiar, long driveway up to her mansion, reminiscence punctures my heart. I came here once over the holidays, but Ivy was out, and aside from that, I haven't been here since a short visit in the summer.

I follow her inside, noting how quiet it is. "Where are your parents?" I ask as we walk upstairs to her bedroom.

"An event for one of Dad's business partners."

Ivy opens the door to her room, and I instantly smile, feeling invited by her teal-painted walls with an array of posters hanging on them. There are new pictures of her and some friends pinned on her corkboard, and her collection of concert tickets and movie stubs has gotten bigger, but it still feels like Ivy.

Being nosy, I poke around her stuff to see what I've missed out on. Moving around a bottle of Love Spell perfume, my eyes bulge, noting a stack of thick envelopes. "Holy shit," I say, picking them up. Shuffling through a pile of college acceptance letters, pride bursts through my bloodstream when I spot Harvard University written in crimson red on the envelope. "You got into Harvard!"

Ivy bites down on her bottom lip, attempting to hold back a smile as she nods.

"Why didn't you tell me?" I can't contain my joy, my voice getting louder with excitement.

"I don't know. I didn't tell anyone yet."

"Why not?"

"It just doesn't seem real, I guess."

"It's fucking real, Rebel." My cheeks burn from grinning. "You got into all of these schools—including Harvard. That's your dream school!"

She loosens up, allowing herself to smile along with me. "They offered me an opportunity to do a special art history program over the summer too."

"I'm so damn proud of you, Ivy."

Yearning builds inside me, needing to pick her up in my arms and spin her around, celebrating how amazing she is. But I can still sense her guard is up, probably still annoyed I spoiled her fun for the night.

"I'm proud of you too," Ivy says.

My brows draw in. "For what?" I ask, placing the acceptance letters back on her desk.

"Is it true what the girl with the red hair said? Are you getting drafted to the NHL?"

"Nothing's set in stone. But..." I draw in a deep breath, unable to fathom the words that are about to come out of my mouth. "If I keep up this winning streak, yeah, I'm headed to the NHL at the end of the season."

"Oh my god!"

"I'm not getting excited yet. Not until the papers are signed. I'm just focusing on one game at a time."

Ivy nods, understanding my stance and taming her reaction. "Okay." She moves toward her dresser, searching for something in one of her drawers. I go back to checking out her things when she throws me off guard with a question. "Were you going to hook up with her?" Ivy asks.

"What? Who?"

"The girl with the red hair."

"I—where is this coming from?"

She digs out my old Blink-182 shirt from her drawer and tosses it on her mattress. "Just curious why you'd give up a chance to hook up in order to bring me home. Unless things with you and Courtney are going well."

The name of my sort of girlfriend makes my stomach twist. She was completely wiped from my brain the second I saw Ivy at the party. "Things with her are—" I immediately stop when Ivy reaches behind her back, and the sound of her dress unzipping echoes in the room. "What are you doing?"

"I'm changing into my PJs." She gestures to my old shirt on her bed.

"Yeah, but you—you can't..." I watch as the straps slide off her shoulder. The moment her dress drops to the floor, a wave of heat crashes over my body.

"We've had this talk before. A bra and panties are the same thing as a bikini, Pax. Chill."

Rubbing my hand over the back of my neck, I try my fucking hardest not to glance over at her. I stare at her bookshelf across the room, forcing myself to read the titles: *The Summer I Turned Pretty, Paper Towns, Nick & Nora's Infinite Playlist*. It's not working. My heart picks up its pace, fluttering way faster than I'd like it to, as I answer, "It's different."

"I bet the guy I was dancing with wouldn't have minded."

My gaze swings back over to her. "Don't fucking start that, Ivy."

Her head cocks to the side, assessing me with a smirk

on her face. "Why? Does the thought of someone seeing me with my dress off bother you?"

My jaw flexes. The veil concealing my desires is becoming thinner and thinner. I can't fucking help it. I sweep my eyes over her body, noting the way she squirms under the heat of my stare. "No," I lie through my teeth.

"Then why don't we go back to the party and you can hook up with that girl and I'll hook up with the guy I was dancing with."

I laugh at her fucking delusion. "There's no way you're losing your virginity to that douche."

"I'm not a virgin, Pax."

"What?" A fury of emotions takes over my insides, causing me to tremble with envy, misery, and regret.

"You can't be serious. You'll sleep with anyone who looks your way, but *I'm* not allowed to sleep with someone? I didn't think you'd have that type of double standard."

"I don't with other girls."

"Then why with me?"

Because you should be mine.

An inferno rages inside me, years of pent-up tension pounding my bones. And she senses it.

Her eyebrow quirks as she pads closer to me. "Does it bother you that other guys get to kiss me?" She inches nearer, and my spine gets rigid, forcing myself to keep it together. "Does it bother you that someone else gets to see me naked? Does it bother you that someone else knows what I taste like—"

"Ivy, stop."

"Why?" She takes one final step closer, leaving a breath between us. Her barely covered-up body makes my heart skip beats. My composure snaps when her voice taunts me, asking, "Are you jealous?"

"Yeah, I am." My heart strikes hard enough to break my ribs as I finally speak the goddamn truth. "And I know I don't have the right to be, but I don't give a fuck. *I* was supposed to be your first kiss." I close the gap between us, our chests touching as my years of regrets come pouring out of my mouth. "*I* was supposed to be your first date. *I* was supposed to be the first guy who ever touched you." She takes a step back, and I move forward until the back of her knees hit the mattress, and she sits down. My arms press into her bed, caging her in as I hover over her. "*I* was supposed to be your first fuck."

Ivy's dark-blue eyes widen with shock at my admission. Her rapid breaths fall from her parted lips, hitting mine. A rosy color forms on her cheeks as she gazes at me. "You never made a move, Pax," she whispers, emulating my regret.

"I'm changing that right now."

CHAPTER FORTY-SIX

PAXTON'S LIPS crash onto mine.

A lifetime of constrained yearning overflowing into a singular kiss.

Fireworks that have been waiting *years* to explode set off in my heart, bursting into my veins.

He's kissing me.

Paxton Rhodes is actually kissing me.

His arms wrap around my bare torso as if they belong there. I thread my fingers through his dark, messy hair like I've wanted to do for so long. There's a brawl in my mind between logic and lust as he climbs up on the bed, causing me to lie down under him.

"Pax." The sound of my voice grates against my throat.

As if hearing me speak his name gives him a double dose of reality, his muscles go tense. "Fuck," he says, pulling away in a panic.

I grip onto his shirt so he can't get away. I'm not going to lose him before I have the chance to fully have him.

His heart pounds against my fist that's clinging to the fabric. Longing swims in his hazel eyes as they drift down my body and then back up to my face. My breath shakes as I witness warring emotions flicker over his features.

"I shouldn't have done that," Pax rasps.

"I wanted you to."

"Ivy, this would never work." His shoulders begin to soften slightly, and I tug him closer.

"I know." My body buzzes with desire so powerful, I can no longer brush it off.

"I don't want to fuck things up between us." His mouth inches closer.

"You won't."

I let go of his shirt and cautiously loop my hand around the back of his neck. He adjusts himself slightly, pressing his hips against mine. My pulse whirls, causing my heart to race at the speed of light.

"Your brother's my best friend." Pax brings his attention to my lips, and they part, anxiously waiting for him to kiss them again. "Your parents will never approve of me. You're supposed to be with someone different." He continues to list all the reasons why we shouldn't break this boundary any further. "You're going to Harvard. I'm going to be traveling for hockey."

"I know," I softly say, tilting my chin up so our mouths are perfectly aligned. "I know this would never work." Despite the tiny part of me that believes it could. We'd just need to work through the obstacles, but we could figure it out. It's mostly untangling things on my side except for—"You have Courtney," I say as the thought pops into my head.

Pax clamps his eyes shut, his jaw tensing in frustration that I brought her up. "Don't talk about her."

"Are you still with her?"

"It's complicated, Ivy." He opens his eyes, locking his focus on mine.

"It's another reason why we wouldn't work."

"Yeah." He barely gets out the strangled word.

Taking my hand, I carefully trail my fingertips along his jawline. His stubble is prickly against my skin, and as I get closer to his lips, I'm met with his trembling breath. Our chests are glued to each other, panting in quick succession. I'm unable to think clearly, instantly forgetting all the reasons why we shouldn't do this as I lift up the smallest amount, joining our lips.

Pax kisses me back, this time with more fervor than before. His tongue teases mine as his hand runs along the side of my waist, leaving goose bumps in its wake. When he hits the hem of my panties, he freezes.

"Tell me to stop," Pax says into my mouth. The sound of his deep resonance makes my insides shudder with need.

"No."

As if turned on by my defiance, his kisses become more passionate. He drags his lips to my neck, delicately drawing in my skin and releasing it. A soft moan escapes me, causing him to do the same.

Pax breaks contact for a brief moment, yanking his shirt off as fast as possible. Pushing myself up, my hand reaches out to touch him. His stomach contracts as I graze over the muscles I dreamed of feeling for so long. Trailing my fingertips over the dusting of hair that starts from his lower stomach and travels downward, the instant I hit his belt, he rushes to unbuckle it.

Before I can blink, Pax is down to his boxers and readjusting both of us on my bed. The heat from his body sets mine on fire the more our skin touches and our legs tangle.

We kiss and caress, taking advantage of this moment as if it's the only one we'll have.

As if we're running out of time.

Pax's calloused fingers skim over my bra, and I push into his hold. Sneaking his other hand around my back, he's quick to unclasp it. Both of us struggle to catch our breath, and he sits up to carefully drag the straps down my arm and dispose of my bra.

His hungry gaze travels all over my body, leaving me with a twinge of nervousness. My bravado from earlier is gone. There's no escaping my vulnerability as I lie almost completely naked before Pax. My cheeks get hot as my inexperience peeks through. The four times I did it with Calvin were in no way enough to prepare me for Pax's expertise. I haven't been with anyone since, and I wasn't planning on hooking up with that guy at the party. I just said that to get under Paxton's skin, and it clearly worked.

"Are you okay?" Pax asks, studying the emotions on my face. "We don't have to do this."

"No, I want to!" I implore. "I-I'm just not really sure what I'm doing."

"I thought you said you weren't a virgin."

"I'm not. But I only did it a few times. I'm not as experienced as you."

Pax delicately places his hand on my hips, rubbing his thumb over my skin in a soothing way. "I don't care about any of that." He bends forward, placing a chaste kiss on my lips. "I only want to do this if you want to," he whispers.

"I do. I *really* do." My hands run along the length of his back, drawing him closer. My heart crashes in my ribcage as a deep-seated thought falls out. "But I also don't want to be just another girl you sleep with."

His eyes widen as if shocked that I would even have that idea. "Ivy, you're not. I *swear* you're not." He kisses me with urgency. "You have no idea how much you mean to me—how much you've meant to me all these years." His hands grip onto me tighter. "God, Ivy, please never think you're just another girl to me. You're not. I love you."

Both of our bodies still.

Holding our breath at the admission.

Was he just swept away by the moment? Or was it real?

I part my lips. "What—"

Pax's mouth crashes against mine once more, stifling my question. Passion radiates from every inch of him as he hazes my senses with the way he kisses me. Hormones race through my bloodstream as I try not to read into his words.

But he holds me like he loves me.

And teases my body like he loves me.

A burst of lust rushes through me, and I shuffle to get my panties off. Pax helps me, sitting up and pulling the fabric down my legs.

My hands tremble when I realize I'm lying completely bare for him. He swallows as his hazel eyes drink me in.

His voice comes out raspy and deep when he asks, "Has anyone ever made you come before?"

"I think so?"

Pax smirks in a way that makes me need to clench my thighs together. "That's a no," he states.

Carefully parting my legs back open, he runs his fingertips along my inner thighs, ramping up my heart rate. Our eyes are glued as he eases upward. He studies my face, witnessing me gasp the moment he grazes my clit.

My body squirms against my bedsheets as Paxton touches me. His fingers move in and out of me, causing a continuous waterfall of heat to pour throughout me. He's gentle and attentive, but the expression on his face is painstakingly sexy. He's enjoying this just as much as I am.

His other hand roams my body, making contact with the parts of me he never has before. My attention drifts down to see a damp spot on his boxers, and it causes my insides to tingle.

Suddenly, my veins wring tight with a sensation I've never felt before. "Pax," I call out. He moves his fingers faster, tension building until it becomes almost too much to bear. "Pax!"

"Trust me, Rebel. Just let yourself go. I got you."

His words make me melt, and I do exactly what he says, giving in to the overwhelming feeling. Instantly, an explosion of pleasure ruptures inside me. My legs shake in a way they never had before. The sounds coming from me are ones I've never made. I fight to keep my eyes open to watch Pax stare at me in a sensual trance, but the sensations are too strong.

My back arches off my bed as I bunch up my sheets, moaning in ecstasy.

"Fuck, Ivy," Pax says, truly captivated. "You're doing so good, baby." He brings his mouth to mine, capturing each of my moans.

I lose myself in his arms, finally coming back down. Relaxing my muscles, I try to catch my sprinting breath. Pax tenderly brushes stray hairs off my cheek, smiling at me.

"I was wrong," I pant. "No one's ever made me come before."

He chuckles. "I'm glad I could be your first."

"I wish I could be your first for something." My admittance comes out hushed. As our bare chests connect, I feel his heart rate pick up while he stares at me. His lips open to speak, but then he closes them. There's something he wants to say but won't. "What is it?" I ask, halfway reading his mind.

"I never..." Pax shifts, his hard length brushing up

against me. "I've only ever used a condom. I never had sex without one."

"I'd be your first?"

He nods. "But we don't have to—"

"No." I tug him closer to me and dip my thumbs into the waistband of his boxers, starting to pull them off. "I want you to feel all of me."

Paxton wastes no time taking off the only article of clothing that separates us.

My eyes broaden when I finally see all of him, and I hear him let out another chuckle. Buzzing with anticipation, I wait for him to hover over me once more, but instead, he takes my hand and has me sit upright with him.

"Come here," he croons, outstretching his legs.

"What am I doing?"

"You're going to be as if you're sitting on my lap, but face me."

I climb over his legs, kneeling one of my calves on either side of him as my hips linger over his. My gaze latches onto his as one of his hands grips my hip while his other aligns his length with my opening. Slowly, he guides my body downward, sinking onto him. I wrap my arms around his neck, my fingernails digging into his skin as I feel all of him.

Paxton lets out a deep moan, his eyes shutting for a brief moment when he's completely inside me. "Oh my god," he groans in pleasure. But he doesn't get too lost in his desire, quickly focusing back on me. "You okay?"

"Yeah," I barely get out the word.

Delicately, he moves each of my legs to wrap around his body, having me sink further. My mouth hangs open in a silent scream, the angle I'm at causing an overload of bliss to flicker throughout me. There's barely any space between us, our heavy breaths crashing against each other's skin as he takes my hips and starts rocking me.

I hold on to him, yanking at his dark roots as he continues to guide us closer to the edge of euphoria. Curse words get strangled by his groans while my body naturally syncs up with the pace.

This is by far the closest I've ever felt to someone.

Sweat glosses our skin as we grind against each other. Our lips and tongues make contact with any area we can find. My moans get louder. Pax's grip gets tighter. Our hearts pound against the other's chests.

We're messy and wild and vulnerable.

And it's fucking beautiful.

"Ivy," Pax grits. "I'm gonna come." His eyes search mine for a response, but instead, I place my palms against his cheeks and kiss him as hard as I can.

We swallow each other's moans, my body lighting up in ecstasy once more as pleasure rips through my veins.

Our movements get choppy, unable to keep up our tempo. Pax lets out the hottest sound I've ever heard him make. And finally, our bodies still.

We don't want to let the other go, staying frozen in time as we breathe in each other's air.

We stay like this for several minutes until we decide to readjust by the headboard. Pax's boxers are back on, and I opt for his old Blink-182 shirt that I pulled out of my drawer just before this transpired. We've settled under my comforter, cuddling and talking.

"This was way better than watching *Pirates of the Caribbean,*" I joke.

Pax chuckles in agreement. "Let's commemorate the moment," he says, reaching toward my nightstand. When I notice he's grabbing my digital camera, I give him a wary look. "Not like that," he assures me with a laugh.

He turns it on and goes to look at the photos. "There's only one picture saved."

"Yeah, I deleted the rest once I downloaded them to my computer," I state, sensing my face becoming rosy.

"But you chose not to delete this one?" Pax turns the camera so I can see it, even though I know exactly what it is. The picture of us from a few years ago, when we were sitting on my bed making his Facebook profile. His picture has since changed to an image of him playing hockey, but the one of us is still lingering on his profile.

I nod in response.

Pax flips the camera around, angling it upward to capture another picture of us. "Now you'll have this one forever too." He presses his lips to my cheek at the same time he presses the button, and I just know I have the dopiest smile on my face.

The second we're done taking the picture, his phone pings with a text. Then another one comes in. Followed by a few more.

"What the hell?" Pax pats my bed, searching for his phone.

I lift up the blanket to help him look, and when neither of us can find it, he gets up and looks through his jeans pockets. I follow his lead, getting out of bed, and hear his phone go off once more.

Moving our articles of clothing off the floor, the moment I pick my bra up, I see his phone glowing. A few arbitrary texts from Trent pop up, and just as I'm about to tell Pax I found it, an incoming call flashing Courtney's name signals his attention.

"Shit," Pax mutters as he reaches for his phone. He's quick to cover his screen in hopes that I didn't see her name, but he wasn't fast enough.

A weight drops in my belly at the same time reality slams into my brain. *This will never work.* Our words from earlier ring loudly throughout my body. All the reasons we stated ping-pong back and forth. College, his career, my brother, Courtney—Oh god, I just cheated with him. I think? Maybe not because he said things were complicated?

I run my hand over my stomach. Pax gets dressed before I can fully process that this is over.

Our unfiltered moment, where we let ourselves indulge in our true desires, has ended.

Nausea rolls around my insides as Pax adjusts his belt. My throat gets thick, emotions becoming lodged inside.

"I gotta head back," he says, fishing for his car keys. He keeps his attention off me as he continues to speak. "My hotel is a few hours away, and I have a game tomorrow. I just came for a short visit to clear my head."

"Okay." My voice comes out soft as I will it not to crack.

"I, um…" Pax finally brings his focus back to me, and his hazel eyes flicker with sadness. "I'll be playing at this stadium again in the beginning of May. Maybe you and Trent can take the ride, and we can hang out for a little bit. And once I'm done with all the press interviews and I figure out which team I'm playing for next season, I'll be around during the summer."

"Okay," I repeat.

"I-I'll see you soon." Pax tiptoes over to me and very delicately brushes his lips on my forehead. It's so light, it feels as if it's a phantom kiss.

I watch him leave and sink back down onto my bed.

My lashes bristle with tears as the ache in my chest intensifies.

My bedsheets, which were filled with passion and bliss mere minutes ago, are now empty and cold.

Minutes tick by, but I don't. I know full well that I'll forever be stuck here. Right where he left me.

CHAPTER FORTY-SEVEN

PRESENT

"HOW WAS LUCILLE'S BRIDAL SHOWER?" Zaina asks while we go through several paintings the museum recently received.

"It was nice. She was ecstatic, and my mom and I were able to make it through the weekend without clashing too hard, so all in all, it was a good time," I state.

We continue to look at the artwork, and my attention lingers on one specific painting. It's a silhouette of a couple holding hands, a warm glow from a streetlight surrounding them.

"I overheard chatter that they want to extend your *Journey of Love Through the Ages* exhibit," Zaina says, drawing my focus away from the image of the strangers.

"Really?"

"Yep! It's gaining a lot of traction on social media. I eavesdropped on Roy talking, and he's considering extending it at least another six months."

"Oh my god," I say, smiling as a sense of accomplishment swims through me.

"You hit the nail on the head with your concept. People connect with the idea of love and time coming together."

I smile, but it doesn't reach my eyes. "Yeah. I guess you're right."

Uncle Jeff and I sit on his small terrace attached to his hotel room. We're overlooking the bustling city streets, with a combination of modern buildings and classical structures surrounding us.

"What's the latest on your treatment?" I ask.

Uncle Jeff's attention drifts over to a car on the adjacent street, honking their horn at a jaywalker, followed by a stream of curses that they yell out the window as they drive off. "They started another new trial medication last week. If I knew I'd be here this long, I would've found an apartment." He chuckles to himself.

"Any inkling on when you're finishing up?"

Keeping his focus off me, he shakes his head. "How are things with you and my nephew?"

"Nice change of subject."

"Thanks." Uncle Jeff turns back to look at me, smiling as he awaits my answer to his question.

"It's been good reconnecting with Pax," I say, noticing how the muscles in my chest clench. Time is closing in. Trent and Lucille's wedding will be here in a couple of weeks, and Pax and I will finally put an end to things. "Getting to know each other as adults is quite different than when we were teenagers. But, I know once you're done with your treatment, he'll head back to Maryland with you, so I don't imagine the two of us becoming that close again."

Uncle Jeff is quiet.

An unsettling feeling floats through the air, circling the space between us.

"That's what you're planning on doing after your treatment, right?" The need for confirmation that there will be an *after* pulls at my words as I speak. "You're going back to Maryland when you're all finished, right?"

He smiles at me, but not the kind that's full of humor and joy like I've known from him. This smile makes a lump form in my throat as I force my reaction to stay in check.

"I'd like that," he answers.

"Is…" My mouth suddenly gets dry, my voice coming out as a whisper as I struggle to speak. "Is there a possibility that won't be an option?"

"Nothing's certain, kid."

My vision blurs as my eyes begin to water. "I thought —I thought this treatment was pretty damn certain."

"We'll see."

"We'll see?" Panic seizes my chest. "How are you so calm about this?"

Uncle Jeff leans over, planting his hand on my shoulder. "It is not the length of life, but the depth of it." There's mist rising in his eyes, but he remains grounded. "You know who wrote that quote?"

I do a mental recall of one of my literature classes from Harvard and finally land on a name. "Ralph Waldo Emerson."

"Yep. I knew you'd get that one." He slowly drops his hand and looks away as he continues to speak. "I came across that quote a little while back, and it seemed quite fitting. I've found the true value of my life comes from my impact on others—not my title or the thickness of my wallet or the years I've spent taking up space on this planet."

I can't hide my anguish, tears teetering over the edge and spilling down my face. "You've made an incredible impact on others," I say, my voice barely above a whisper.

"Raising Paxton and watching him grow into the man he is today was by far the greatest experience of my life."

"Did you tell him?"

"No. Not yet. I'll tell him when the time is right."

I nod, understanding why Uncle Jeff is wavering on when to tell Pax. There will never be a good time to deliver that news to someone.

The two of us sit in stillness as I let this new knowledge sink in.

Uncle Jeff's voice slices through the silence. "Did you ever tell him?"

Glancing back at him, I study his face, trying to comprehend his question. The lines around his eyes soften as he stares back at me. There's a sharp twist in my lower belly, letting me know that he's referring to my repressed secret. Uncle Jeff is the single soul who knows, and we only spoke about it once.

"No," I state, and Uncle Jeff nods his head. "But I never told you it was his."

"You didn't, but I had a strong feeling it was."

A light smile appears on my lips. "I assumed you always knew too."

CHAPTER FORTY-EIGHT

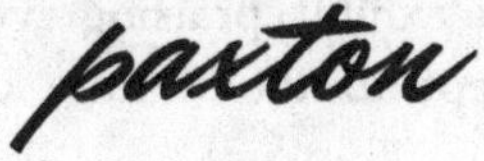

MY HEART SKIPS a beat sitting next to Ivy on her couch, admiring her post-sex glow as she reads something on her laptop. Her nipples poke through my shirt that's wrapped around her soft skin, and her swollen, glistening pussy is on display as she folds her leg. If Zaina hadn't texted her immediately after we finished telling her to check her computer, we'd be on round two right now.

Ivy nibbles on her cuticles, her eyes scanning the screen as she reads whatever Zaina messaged her about. Her hair is piled on top of her head in a messy, loose bun, several strands framing her perfect face.

Time has been my enemy, the days rapidly blending together, which has led us to Trent and Lucille's wedding this weekend. Our agreement to end our arrangement looms overhead, paining the center of my chest.

But I'm not letting her go that easily.

This time, I'll fight for her.

"Wow," Ivy whispers to herself.

"What is it?" I ask.

"*The Boston Globe* wrote an article about my exhibit."

She turns her laptop so I can read it. My lips automatically split into a smile as the words "innovative," "transformational," and "brilliant" pop out. The journalist gushes about Ivy's exhibit, praising everything from the overarching concept to the minute details that were displayed.

"This is incredible." I beam. "I'm so proud of you."

Her cheeks get rosy as she takes her laptop back, closing it. "Thank you."

My gaze flutters all over her, taking her in, enamored by the woman she's evolved into. Yet, I can't help but feel a sense of regret for all the years and experiences I've missed out on. And a double dose of regret for not making the most of the moments I did have with her when we were younger. "I never asked you what made you get into this career," I state. "Why art history?"

She shrugs. "I guess it's sort of like you and hockey. It just clicked with me. There's really no rhyme or reason to it."

"Yeah, but why did you want to work in a museum? You could've been a professor or…I don't know what else you can do with that degree," I admit, chuckling. "But I want to know why you had your heart set on working at a museum."

"It was the most fitting for me."

"How so?"

There's a certain glow about her as she bares more to me, letting more of her vulnerability shine through. "I feel like, if there was something tangible to represent my soul, it would be a museum. A safekeeping of everything and everyone I ever loved, preserved and sanctified. I could walk through different exhibits of different parts of my life, and I'd cherish all the minuscule details that really put the whole museum together."

Blown away by her depth, I melt, listening to her

exquisite analogy. "That's truly so beautiful. And it makes perfect sense for you."

"Plus, I enjoy learning about history, and those who don't learn from their past are doomed to repeat it." Ivy's focus lands on me, and the room freezes for a moment, tension lingering in the air from her comment.

"Ivy." My voice softens, noting a flash of hurt appear on her face. She's quick to hide it, masking with a guise of indifference. Inching my hand closer to hers, I try to continue. "I—"

"I need to get dressed," she announces, cutting me off. She springs off the couch faster than I can blink and disappears into her bedroom.

My gaze follows the flicker of her swift movements, my tongue burning with the desire to tell her that I've learned from my past. *Our* past. And we're not doomed to repeat any of it.

Things are different this time.

I'm different.

"Ivy," I call out, my body launching me from my seat as I trace her footsteps to her bedroom. My pulse jumps even though she closes her door.

"I'm getting dressed," Ivy responds.

"I want to talk."

"We're not doing this, Pax."

"Doing what?"

"Rehashing the past." The pitch of her voice is getting higher behind the closed door. "It was one of my rules that I made *months* ago."

"Who the fuck cares about the rules, Rebel?"

"I care." The door swings open to a fully dressed Ivy, glaring up at me. "We leave for Trent and Lucille's rehearsal dinner tomorrow. And the day after that is their wedding. You remember what that means, right?"

My stomach churns so violently, it causes a

resounding ache throughout my body. My insides brutally riot against her question and my impending answer. The pounding in my heart is enough to shatter my ribcage, getting sliced by the jagged edges of my broken bones.

The sapphire eyes I fell in love with decades ago pierce right through me.

"Yeah," I grit out. "I know what it means."

As if the reality of my answer hits her, both of us fully acknowledging that whatever this is will be over in a couple of days, she blinks, processing the actuality.

"Good." Her voice isn't as strong as it was mere seconds ago. "Just making sure we're still on the same page." Scooting past me, she reenters the living room and starts mindlessly tidying up.

I watch as she folds, then refolds one of her blankets. Then she moves to the stack of boxes filled with the past, which she has *yet* to go through and might as well make them a part of her decor, and tries to push them together in a neater pile to take up less space. They've been here for months, and she won't let me—or herself—open them except for the first night they arrived.

Ivy's desperate to suppress her buried thoughts and emotions, containing her history and attempting to keep it locked away.

But I'm right here.

CHAPTER FORTY-NINE

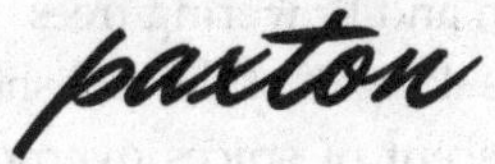

I'VE BEEN to my fair share of elaborate events over the course of my life. Of course, they first started when I became friends with Trent and Ivy, but ever since making it pro, I found myself being invited to more and more galas that I could've never imagined attending as a kid living in a small apartment with Uncle Jeff. However, Trent's wedding is taking the cake with the most lavish event I've been to, and I haven't even attended it yet.

They bought out an estate known for its extravagant gardens for the entire weekend. And while I don't know Lucille that well, she doesn't strike me as the type to go this extremely over the top with her wedding. This has Meredith Hartwick's prints all over it.

The estate has three buildings: the main manor and two villas. The wedding party is staying in one of the villas, and the rehearsal dinner is being held in the main manor. The entire estate looks as if it's inspired by a luxurious European palace, each building having an air of grandeur with steep roofs and intricate stone carvings on the columns. The gardens themselves stretch over endless land, dark green rolling hills out in the distance. There's a pergola with pink and white flowers woven around every inch, which will act as the altar for tomorrow, and the reception will be held in an enormous tent in between a majestic fountain and flowering trees.

My shoes squeak against the polished flooring of the main manor, the scent of spices overpowering the floral smell for a quick second as a waitstaff walks by with another round of hors d'oeuvres.

Ivy has successfully kept her distance from me today —aside from when we rehearsed walking down the aisle arm in arm earlier. We traveled here in the morning, avoiding talking about any topics of depth on the plane. It's clear that she already has one foot out the door, eagerly anticipating shutting me off after tomorrow's final song.

Everyone mingles, the sense of celebratory energy swirling around the room. I pretend to be engaged in a conversation with the other groomsmen while I watch Ivy from across the room, laughing at whatever Lucille just said. Her face lights up, seemingly unaffected by the fact that we have a countdown to when we're over. She looks stunning in a blue dress, which showcases her eyes and her hair in elegant waves draping down her shoulder blades.

Before I can stop myself, I break free of the conversation I was half listening to and make my way to the other side of the crowd with tunnel vision, fixated only on Ivy.

"Paxton." A voice summons me, pulling me out of my trance. There's a slight tap on the back of my suit jacket, and when I turn around to see who it is, I have to force myself not to scoff in her face. "I've been so busy with the wedding preparations, I haven't gotten a chance to say hello," Meredith says as if she has always adored me. She leans in for a hug, and we do an awkward embrace. "It's been a while since I've seen you. How are you?"

"I'm doing pretty good," I state.

"Jody," Meredith calls over to another woman around her age. "This is the groomsman I was telling you about, Paxton. He's an NHL player."

I couldn't hide my scoff that time, but neither of them noticed. Of course, now that I have a title and money attached to my name, she finds me worthy of speaking to.

"He and Trent grew up together," she continues. "Although he lived on the outskirts of our community with his uncle. How is Jeffery doing, by the way?"

"Jeffery?" I try my hardest to conceal how much the question rubs me the wrong way and the fact that she referred to him by his full name as if they go way back. I don't even know if she had more than one conversation with Uncle Jeff.

"Mom," Trent interrupts, appearing from thin air. "The photographer was looking for you."

"How come?" she asks, her spine straightening with annoyance.

"I don't know. She has a question about something," he states. Meredith huffs, and before I can hear her excuse herself, Trent pulls me away. "Sorry," he says in a hushed voice. "I hope I got to her before she said anything too offensive."

"I've been dealing with your mom's bitchiness for years. Don't worry about me. Go get yourself a drink and enjoy your rehearsal dinner."

He nods but doesn't move. I watch as he surveys the space, his eyes landing on his soon-to-be bride. The tension on his face eases as he breaks into a soft smile. I wonder if I look so obviously in love when I stare at his sister.

"I didn't get to say thank you," Trent says, forcing his attention back to me.

"For what?"

"Always pulling through for me. I know shit has changed over the years, but I'm glad we're still best friends."

"Of course, man."

My conscience causes my gut to twist. If he knew Ivy and I were hooking up, would he still have the same sentiment? If he knew how I treated her in the past, he *definitely* wouldn't.

The night moves on, and once the guests have left, the wedding party regroups in the villa. The building is quite large, with vaulted ceilings and terra-cotta-colored walls that split off into two separate wings: one side for the women and the other for us men.

"Okay, lovebirds, get in one last kiss for the night because you won't see each other until you're at the altar tomorrow!" Pia calls out to Trent and Lucille.

We obnoxiously cheer as they give each other a kiss, and once they part ways, so do the rest of the groomsmen and bridesmaids. As the women begin talking about what time hair and makeup start, I sneak up to Ivy.

"Can I talk to you for a sec?" I attempt to squeeze in some one-on-one time.

Her brows draw in as if confused that I would want to speak with her. "Sure," she says and then glances behind her to the other women. "I'll be right back." The voices disappear into the distance, and we're alone in the hallway. Ivy peers up at me, her face twisting in concern as she waits for me to say something. "Everything okay?" she asks.

"Yeah. I just wanted to know if you wanted to join me in my room." I flash her my signature killer smile.

"Sorry, but the girls have the rest of the night planned with prepping Lucille for tomorrow."

"Okay." My insides rattle, feeling her slip away and

being desperate to cling to her. "We're spending tomorrow together, though."

"What if I'm busy with bridesmaid duties?"

"You can slip away for a little bit. They'll be fine."

Her lips curl upward ever so slightly, and she begins to pivot on her heels toward where the rest of the women went. "I'll see you tomorrow, Pax."

"I'm looking forward to it."

CHAPTER FIFTY

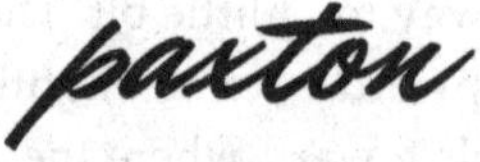

ALL THE GROOMSMEN and bridesmaids congregate in the foyer of the main manor, excited jitters racing through us. Lucille is hidden in one of the rooms in here, so none of the guests can peek through the glass panes to catch a glimpse of her dress.

The wedding planner rushes to line us up, and Ivy makes her way over to me, giving me the opportunity to admire her beauty. Her hair is curled and pinned up in a low bun, and she wears a light pink, form-fitting gown. Her dazzling smile is infectious, and my mind suddenly jumps to the last time I saw her in a gown—her sweet sixteen.

Who would've thought all these years later I'd have her on my arm and in my bed, but she's still not mine?

"You look very dapper," Ivy states, her eyes flickering over my gray tux. She loops her arm around mine, and my veins immediately light up.

"You look stunning."

"Thank you."

"Ivy, here you go," the wedding planner says, handing her a bouquet of various flowers. I don't know a lot about flowers, but I can only imagine whatever Ivy is holding is an exorbitant amount of money. "Okay, everyone," the planner calls for our attention, and we stop chattering. She speaks into her headset for a brief moment and goes back to talking to us. "The twelve-piece string band is about to start the processional song. The videographers and photographers will be trying their best to be on the sidelines, but make sure you flash the camera your beautiful smiles as you walk down!"

The planner talks into her headset once more and then nods her head at the workers on either side of the atrium doors. They pull at the handles, opening up to the outdoor gardens in synchrony. Ivy and I wait for the cue from the planner to exit the manor and begin walking down the long aisle. Once she gives us the go-ahead, we slowly enter into the sunlight with hundreds of guests twisting in their chairs to watch us walk toward the altar.

A long, off-white carpet is rolled out for the entirety of the walk to the altar. It's lined with flowers, encasing us in a never-ending floral scent. Rows and rows of guests turn to look at us as we make our way to a beaming Trent standing under the ornate pergola.

Ivy's grip on my arm tightens. "Oh my god, there are so many people staring at us," Ivy whispers through a smile.

"Staring at *you*," I whisper back. "Light pink looks beautiful on you."

"It's rose quartz," she cheekily corrects me as we start to pass some of the guests.

"Whatever color it is, it's gorgeous. I can't wait to get it off of you."

"Shh!" She tries to dig her nails into my skin through my suit jacket. "We're not supposed to be talking."

"You started it."

With grins glued to our faces, we proceed forward arm in arm until we get to the altar and part ways.

The ceremony starts, and I watch as Ivy becomes teary-eyed, witnessing her brother say his vows to Lucille. An image of me stealing the limelight and saying my own vows to Ivy plays in my head. My pulse yearningly whirls through my body. I've never envisioned myself getting married, but I suddenly can't get the thought of Ivy as my bride out of my mind.

We'd have a much smaller wedding. Her dress would be whimsical but not over the top. The flowers she'd pick would be simple, sort of like the tiny tattoo on her ankle, and they would be perfectly beautiful.

I get so wrapped up in future planning, I almost miss when Trent and Lucille kiss for the first time as husband and wife. All the guests clap, and the string band starts up again as the two of them walk down the aisle, with the wedding party following. Ivy links her arm with mine once more, and I notice the happy tears in the corner of her eyes.

"I can't believe Trent is married," she says as we drift down the aisle.

When we get back inside the manor, an explosion of cheering comes from all of us as we embrace the newlyweds. Trent and Lucille glow in a way I've only ever heard people refer to, but seeing both of them light up with pure love for each other makes the desire to have that with Ivy beckon me more than before.

The wedding planner congratulates them, but then quickly shuffles us along to take numerous pictures during cocktail hour.

By the time we're finished, we enter the ceremony, which is held in a tent, but no one would ever know it by how opulently it's decorated. String lights hang overhead, joining together in the center to create a massive hanging light fixture that glows over the temporarily installed hardwood dance floor. Each table is draped in long, off-white linens with candles and towering, overflowing vases as the centerpiece.

All the groomsmen and bridesmaids sit at a long, oval table together, accompanied by their significant others. My place card is right next to Ivy's, but on the other side of her seat is a place card that reads *Ms. Hartwick's Guest* in dark-colored calligraphy.

"What is this?" Ivy spots it at the same time I do, picking up the place card.

"Ivy?" A man pops up next to her, extending his hand. "I'm Joseph Baker. Our mothers are good friends."

Ivy clicks her tongue but forces herself to be cordial, shaking his hand. "Nice to meet you."

We take our seats, along with the others, and Ivy glances at me, the annoyance tensing her features, becoming very obvious.

Leaning over, I whisper, "Should we tell your mom we're fucking so you can avoid being set up?"

Ivy nudges me with her elbow, chuckling softly. Joseph steals her attention by making small talk, and I'm sure he's a decent person, but every time he speaks, it's like nails on a chalkboard grating against my eardrums.

Once the formalities of the champagne toast and dinner orders are out of the way, the party finally picks up. The band plays upbeat music, summoning all the guests to the dance floor.

I indulge in a couple of cocktails, letting whiskey warm my veins, while Ivy separates herself from me and Joseph. She floats around the space mingling with guests while I do the same, sensing the alcohol loosening me up.

But before the guests get too carried away with the endless supply of drinks, the energy in the room shifts once more. "All right, everyone," the singer says into the microphone. "We're going to slow it down for just a few minutes and invite all the lovely couples to take the dance floor with our bride and groom."

Taking a step back, I watch people call out to their partners and link hands. The guitarist plays an enchanting melody as the couples gaze at each other lovingly. My attention drifts around the guests until it lands on Ivy. There's a swelling in my chest as I watch her admire the other couples from across the room.

Probably sensing someone staring at her, Ivy's focus flickers off the people dancing and onto me. The moment our eyes fixate on each other, a sense of hesitancy builds between us, wanting to meet the other on the dance floor but unsure if we should.

Our connection pricks at my memory, a faintly similar feeling to when we were younger and our eyes locked at her sweet sixteen begins to crawl its way to my forefront.

Just as I'm about to start walking, Joseph intercepts my line of vision, talking to Ivy. A sudden strike of madness erupts in my core as Joseph takes her hand in his and guides her toward the dance floor.

Absolutely not.

My feet rush me toward the two of them, and just before Joseph can place his hand on her waist, I interrupt. "I'm cutting in."

"We haven't had a chance to dance yet." Joseph stares, mystified that I blocked his chance.

"You'll get over it." I steal Ivy from him, grasping her hand and waist. I can hear Joseph scoff, but I glide us away from him.

"Paxton!" Ivy reprimands, even though her body follows my lead and starts swaying to the music.

"Ivy, there's no way in hell I'm sitting on the sidelines again, watching someone else dance with you."

Her hypnotic blues dilate as she peers up at me. My

heart flutters when she pushes her body against mine, conforming more to my hold.

Everyone else is too busy in their own worlds to be paying attention to ours.

So for a brief moment in time, we get lost in the sea of couples, gently moving to the love song. My grip becomes a bit stronger, never wanting her to leave me. Her breath comes out uneven, as if she knows what's going through my mind.

I can sense her getting the itch to make a run for it.

"Tonight's our last night," she whispers, confirming my suspicion.

"Then we better make it count," I rasp, watching the goose bumps form on her arms. My hand begins to slowly roam, caressing her lower back.

Ivy's attention suddenly darts around the room, checking to make sure no one is observing us getting close.

But before I can touch anywhere else on her body, the song ends. The second the last note is played, Ivy instantly severs from my grasp, creating too much space for my liking between us.

As the music picks back up, Ivy appears flustered, her cheeks getting flushed as she searches for someone to talk to as a distraction. I step closer, and her body jolts as if she became electrified. "Want to go for a little walk?" I ask, a smirk stretching across my face.

Her lips twitch, letting me know she's willing to give in to her desires at least one more time despite her efforts to back away from me. "Yeah."

We casually leave the bustling dance floor. My hand tingles, wanting to reach out and hold hers, but instead I shove it in my pants pocket. I lead the way out of the ceremony tent and into the main manor, cordially saying hello to guests as we pass them.

"Where are we going?" Ivy asks in a hushed voice, her heels clinking against the white marble floor.

I scan the manor, noticing a few loiterers at the far end of the room. My attention drifts over to the staircase, which leads to the bridal suite. I gesture with my chin toward the stairs to answer Ivy's question.

My heart thuds in my chest with every step upward we take.

Ivy checks to see if anyone is watching us. They aren't, so she continues to let me guide her. When we get to the landing, I spot a private bathroom at the end of the hallway.

"Come on," I say, placing my hand along her lower back.

Giddiness overtakes us as we rush to the door with stifled laughter bubbling between us. Flinging the door to the bathroom open, I hurry her inside, and a second after I turn the lock on the knob, Ivy's pouncing on me.

Her arms wrap around my neck, her soft lips convincing me to do whatever she wants as they press into mine.

An ornate chaise lounge encased in a dark, velvety fabric is pushed against one of the stone walls, and I walk Ivy backward as her mouth attacks me, eventually getting the back of her legs to hit the lounge. She drops down to sit, perfectly aligned with the zipper of my pants as I stand over her. She reaches out to unfasten my belt, but I shake my head.

"Lay down," I instruct.

Ivy listens, and I position her body so that I have some space at the very end of the lounge. Ripping my tux jacket off, followed by my tie, Ivy parts her legs for me. Impatience radiates off her, and I know she wants me to move swiftly, satisfying her as quickly as I can, but that's not what I want.

I want to savor every inch of her.

Memorize the way each muscle reacts to my touch.

Linger in her taste.

I encircle my hands around her ankles and leisurely glide upward, forcing the light pink gown out of my way until I reach her flesh-colored thong. I push the small scrap of fabric to the side and admire her glistening pussy. "You're wet for me already?"

Her breath trembles as she nods.

"Good girl," I rasp, smirking at the way the two words make her wiggle under me.

My body heats up as I take my time touching her. Sliding through her wetness, teasing her clit, curling my fingers inside her, and then withdrawing them to hear her whine with need.

Hooking her legs over my shoulders, I lift her hips up so that her body is perfectly angled toward my mouth. Her gown bunches up right under her breasts, and if I knew it wouldn't cause problems, I'd tear the dress off her so I could see every part of her.

Dipping my head down, our gazes latch as my tongue sweeps over her clit. I do it over and over again, witnessing the tension sparking in her muscles as she lets out soft moans.

My cock aches, pressing against my zipper as I take my time to indulge in Ivy.

"Pax," Ivy cries my name out, causing my heart to strike harder. Her thighs tighten on either side of my cheeks as I become coated by her arousal.

There's nothing I love more than having Ivy's complete trust—surrendering her pleasure to me, allowing me to worship her, and handing me the control.

Her panting becomes sharper. Her legs shake. Her back writhes against the velvet.

As I devour her, she comes on my face, crying out in

sensual gratification. I get lost in her luscious taste and goddess-like sounds, allowing myself to be greedy and draw out this moment so I can commit it to memory.

Ivy reaches out for me, her fingers tugging at my shirt collar, and when I lift my head, she yanks me toward her.

"I need you inside me," she pants as I adjust our position. Her hands move down my body, fiddling with my belt buckle. I help her out, setting my hard cock free and aligning it with her entrance.

As I gradually push into her, we stare into each other's eyes with a deep connection. Neither one of us dares to look away or blink as I fill her with my desire. Our bodies slowly move in perfect synchronicity, both of us igniting with lust.

But as she gazes back at me with those sapphire eyes that I have loved for years, there's something else hidden behind them.

Goodbye.

My rib cage cracks open, and I interlace my fingers between hers, holding her hands as we continue to roll our hips. "Ivy—"

"No." She shakes her head, knowing exactly what I'm going to say. Knowing that I'm going to tell her this can't be it. This can't be the last day we're together. There has to be more for us.

We have a silent conversation as we continue to fuck. Desperation to grasp onto her forever overtakes my every move. Our breaths get labored, moans coming from both of us. If anyone were to overhear, they'd assume we were having the most delightful sex. But instead, a piercing pain in my heart intensifies with every thrust of my hips.

I cradle her face between my hands, kissing her with all my might. She kisses me back, her arms holding my torso in a hug that feels like it'll last for eternity.

We get swept away in each other's hold, kissing and

fucking each other into the chaise lounge. Letting ourselves meld into the other. Fusing our passion together.

I breathe her air, becoming immersed in Ivy.

I become so consumed, I nearly miss the scorching passion running through my veins, signaling that I'm about to come. My movements get out of sync as my legs stiffen. Quickly pulling out, I make it just in time, my cum exploding all over her pussy lips and clit.

We stare at each other as my muscles go lax. My gaze dances all over Ivy, adoring how disheveled and sexy she looks.

She smiles at me, as if she's not in the midst of shattering my heart into pieces. "We should get back before someone realizes we're missing," she states.

I nod and fix my pants while going to get her some paper towels to clean off my cum. Both of us adjust our clothes, making sure we don't look like we just fucked in the bathroom.

"We should go out separately," I say.

"Good idea. You go first. I'm going to fix my hair."

"Okay." Right before I leave, I lean over and give her forehead a tender kiss. She might think I've resigned to the belief that things are over for us after today, but I'm not going down without a fight.

Fixing my tie, I move out of the bathroom and into the hallway.

Just as I'm about to take another step, my body freezes when I spot a set of eyes looking back at me.

"Wouldn't be a party without Pax screwing someone in the bathroom," Trent says, chuckling.

I let out a forced laugh. "Who says I was screwing someone?"

"Well, if you weren't hooking up with someone, then you did a horrible job applying your lipstick." He points to my neck, and I instantly attempt to wipe my skin clean. "So who was the lucky girl this time? Pia?"

"Uh…" I attempt to move, hoping this conversation will end if we walk downstairs, but Trent doesn't budge.

"One of Lucille's sorority sisters? Or was it—"

The sound of the bathroom door opening behind me causes all the air to get sucked out of the main manor. My pulse stops, my breath getting caught in my lungs as I watch Trent's entire demeanor shift.

"*Ivy*?" Every single muscle in Trent's body tenses. Every feature in his face turns to stone except for his eyes, which are shooting me with lasers as he asks me the question.

"What?" Ivy asks, taking up space next to me. She tries to play it off cool, but the pitch in her voice and the expanding redness on her cheeks give her away.

"You *fucked* my little sister?"

"Oh my god, Trent." Ivy starts speaking because my mouth has suddenly dried up. "We're all adults. We all know sex is a part of life. It's no big deal."

"It's a big deal when it's you and *him*." Trent juts out his finger, pointing at me as if it were a blade. "You *know* he's a piece of shit when it comes to women. You've *seen* it. The one girlfriend he ever had, he couldn't stop cheating on—and he hasn't had another girlfriend since."

Every cell in my being shrinks as he reads me for filth. And I can't even deny his words.

"Yes, and even with that knowledge, I still made a choice. It's no big deal." Ivy stands tall. "Plus, we're a little too old for you to be doing this whole big-brother-protector thing."

"He's going to hurt you."

Ivy scoffs. "He won't. Trust me."

"Yes, he fucking will!"

I'm transported back in time as I watch them bicker

back and forth. I'm not capable of speaking or moving or breathing. My feet are nailed to the floor as I stand immobile, caught in my own demise. Hysteria shakes my bloodstream, realizing I might lose both of them at the same time. Urgency fills every crevice in my body, but no words come out of my mouth.

"I'm fine," Ivy says with finality, stamping her statement. "I was fine after he fucked me when I was eighteen, and I'm fine now."

Air is forced out of my lungs, a strangled noise coming out of my throat as all the blood drains from my face. Trent's body ices over as we let the words hang in the space between us, watching Ivy make her way down the staircase.

I watch Trent's features morph, the puzzle pieces connecting in his brain. Once he can no longer see Ivy as she leaves the manor, disappearing back into the party, his gaze shifts onto me.

Lead weighs down my bones from the look he's giving me. "Trent, I—"

"That's why everything changed," he states.

"What?"

"That's why she immediately left for Boston. That's why the three of us stopped spending time together. That's why things were never the same. God, I'm so fucking stupid. I thought it was because we grew up and got busy doing our own things. But everything changed because you couldn't keep it in your goddamn pants." He stalks closer to me, fury shooting out of his blue eyes as he invades my space, ready to hit me. And I hope he does. "You hurt her, didn't you?"

I swallow around the block of regret and guilt wedged in my throat. "Yes. I did." The amount of agony ripping through my veins as I speak the admittance aloud causes me to wince. My arms stay at my side, willing to accept Trent's assault. *Punch me. Please fucking punch me.* I brace myself for a hit, fully deserving of it. But instead, Trent stills. A wave of disappointment washes over him, like he was hoping his assumption was wrong. And that hurts me more than any punch to the face ever will.

"How could you do that?" Trent asks, staring at me as if he doesn't know me.

"Because I was an asshole twenty-year-old," I admit.

"And you're expecting me to believe you're not an asshole now that you're in your thirties?" His anger reignites. "After all the stories you tell me, you expect me to believe you're going to treat my sister differently now?"

"I—no." A sudden rush of anxiety hits me. Ivy ran away back then, and she's going to do it again now. *She's going to bolt.* "I promise I'll answer whatever questions you have. I swear I will prove to you that I've grown, but I need to go find Ivy." I move around him with urgency overtaking each step I take. "Please don't let this get in your head and mess with your big day—"

"Kind of fucking hard not to."

"Trent, I fucking promise I'll make this right by you and her. I'll explain everything, but right now I need to find her before she runs off." I take steps closer to the staircase. "Go enjoy your wedding day. Please."

CHAPTER FIFTY-ONE

2010

April

THE SOUND of forks scraping against our china makes me wince as I sit at our dining room table, looking back and forth between Mom and Dad while they eat their roasted chicken.

Mom glances up at me. "What's the matter, Ivy? Why aren't you eating?"

"I'm not very hungry," I say, rubbing my hand across my stomach. "I've felt queasy on and off all day."

"Are you coming down with something?" Dad asks.

"I don't know."

"Well, if you are, then you should go to your room and rest," Mom says, delicately placing her fork to the side as she speaks to me. "We have too many important events coming up. None of us can afford to get sick. Especially me, I'm chairing a fundraiser this weekend—"

"I'm not sick," I cut her off. "I just have a stomachache, that's all."

"Oh. Perhaps it's a feminine issue? I can have Stella bring you a Midol."

My heart stops.

Oh my god.

A hard knot constricts my throat, making it difficult to breathe.

My period is late.

Tremors build in my hands as a sense of dread shrouds me.

"Um, yeah, that's probably it." My attention shoots off her, dropping my line of sight to the floor as I push my chair away from the table. "I'm going to lay down."

I don't bother asking them if I can be excused, rushing out of the dining room. By the time I make it to my bedroom, I've broken out in a cold sweat.

Waves of nausea angrily crash into my belly as an overwhelming sensation of anxiety causes pandemonium inside my body. I run to my phone, immediately texting Pax.

ME

Hey.

I feverishly pace the length of my room, doing the math in my head while I wait for Pax to reply. *I'm four days late.* Tears burn my eyes. *This can't be happening.*

I call Pax, but it goes to voicemail.

I check his Facebook to see if he's logged on, but he's not. He's barely been active on his page over the past month. And we have hardly spoken at all since we had sex. I knew he'd be hyper-focused on finishing out his hockey season—especially with the high probability of him going to the NHL—but it still *really* fucking hurts that he's made next to no effort to talk to me.

I quickly scan through his recent posts and don't see any sign of Courtney, which gives me a speck of relief because that's one less issue we need to tackle if I'm... pregnant.

Warm acid shoots up my throat, and I run to my garbage can, almost not making it in time. My muscles ache as I heave into the trash.

Once I'm done, I slump on my carpet, adrenaline and exhaustion battling it out in my body. While my mind races at the speed of light, my focus falls onto my phone.

And I know for the rest of the night, I'll be sitting here, waiting for Pax to answer me.

CHAPTER FIFTY-TWO

May

IT'S BEEN three weeks with no period and approximately ten pregnancy tests, but I was semi-delusional, still holding out hope that maybe I was reading the tests incorrectly, and maybe I didn't get my period from all the stress I've been under with graduation coming up.

But as I hold on to the delicate image of my sonogram between my fingertips, another dose of reality caves in. My vision blurs over as I talk to the doctor. I found an obstetrician out of my hometown, about fifteen minutes away, hoping that she'd tell me something different.

As she speaks, I nod as if I'm paying attention, but I can't hear a damn thing. It's as if my head is shoved underwater, my pulse pounding against my eardrums as I hear her muffled words. My throat constricts as I make out the words "options" and "only a couple of weeks left to make a choice." I'm desperate for air, trying to take deep breaths as I attempt to remain as composed as possible.

It's as if I'm out of my body, watching myself take various pamphlets from the doctor and letting her know I'll contact her soon. I witness myself numbly drift out of the office and into the hallway of the medical building. I stand frozen outside of the OB-GYN office door, not really knowing why I haven't moved across the way to catch the elevator.

My body is made of bricks, impossible to gather the strength to move.

I stare at the elevator, then at the other medical office doors: neurologist, cardiologist, and hematologist.

I wonder if there are patients in there receiving life-altering news like I did.

The elevator dings, and I know I should walk to the door once it opens up and lets out a new round of patients, but I can't.

A few people file out of the elevator, crossing their paths as they go to their doctors' offices. The final person steps out, and the moment we make eye contact, my breath catches.

"Ivy?" Uncle Jeff is surprised to see me. "What are you doing in my neck of the woods? You got all the best doctors by you." His attention shifts to the OB-GYN sign, then over to the pamphlets and sonogram clutched in my hands. "Oh," he says in a gentle whisper, his entire demeanor shifting, and when he looks back up at me with concern, I burst into tears.

My bones clatter in my body as inconsolable sobs claw out of the back of my throat, bouncing off the walls. Uncle Jeff's arms wrap around me just in time, my legs going limp. A never-ending stream of tears pours out of me as he lets me cry.

He doesn't say much, but through my gasps of air, I

occasionally hear him say, "Everything's gonna be okay, kid."

It feels as if an eternity passes by the time my crying finally slows down. My face and hair are drenched in my regret, my muscles weakened by the weight of this reality. Eventually, looking up at Uncle Jeff, he gives me a soft smile, and I'm thankful fate put him here today so I don't feel as alone.

"Come on," he says. "Let's get out of here."

I nod, dragging my body toward the elevator while wiping mascara off my cheeks. He pushes the down button, and while we wait, my focus floats over the space. "Wait, don't you have a doctor's appointment?" I point to the array of medical doors. "That's why you're here, right?"

"I can reschedule. This is more important."

Gratitude swims around my heart as I allow myself to become calmer.

When we walk into the parking lot, I get a bubble of amusement witnessing him get flustered and not knowing how to handle this situation. "Uh, I'm not really sure what to do," he admits with a chuckle.

"Me neither."

Empathy swells in his eyes, knowing that my response holds a lot more weight than his current dilemma. He glances around as if searching for a clue on what to say next. "Want to grab some ice cream, and we can sit and talk?" He points over my shoulder to a small place across the way called Scoops.

I sense my lips tilting up in the tiniest smile known to man. "Sure."

By the time we're sitting at a table, I feel a bit more collected. I gather a spoonful of vanilla ice cream covered in rainbow sprinkles and let the sweetness fill my mouth as Uncle Jeff shifts in his seat. He carefully dances around the topic at hand, asking me how my ice cream is and making small talk about the weather.

A few customers filter in and out, but our table is tucked in a corner, so we have privacy. The sonogram is placed next to my cup of overflowing sugar, and both of us wait for the other to bring it up. My attention goes down to the black, white, and gray image, and I stare at the tiny blob. There's no shape to it yet, just a cluster of me and Pax mixed together.

"So…" Uncle Jeff has barely taken a bite of his ice cream as he fidgets with his spoon. "I take it your parents don't know."

I shake my head. "No one knows."

"Not even the father?"

"No."

Silence passes between us before Uncle Jeff speaks again. "Well, your secret is safe with me."

"Thank you."

"And I'll be here for whatever you need. Whatever you decide to do."

"I don't…" My chin quivers, and I bite the inside of my cheek, willing myself not to cry again. "I don't know what to do."

"Do you think your parents will be supportive if you keep it?"

I let out a humorless chuckle. "No. I'll be a stain on the family name." I can already picture my mother dramatically fainting at the news. The uproar it would cause among the community and the gossip circling around the Dames would be enough for her to exile me.

"Do you think they'd support you if you chose to get an abortion?"

My stomach clenches into a tight ball. "No." Tears swell behind my eyes, but I force them down. "I've gone through the scenarios in my head, and I think…I think I should tell the father first. Maybe we can figure out what to do together—I don't know."

He nods. "That's a good idea."

I get trapped in my own thoughts while finishing my ice cream, and once my spoon scrapes the bottom of the cup, I glance up at Uncle Jeff and notice he hasn't touched his. "Why aren't you eating?"

"My mind drifted for a few minutes," he responds. Droplets of chocolate puddle around his cup, but he takes a spoonful of the melted ice cream and forces himself to enjoy it.

A sting of remorse weaves its way into my chest as I watch him eat. In the past, I'd go to his apartment all the time to watch Pax's games with him, but it's been months since I dropped by. Partially because senior year got hectic and partly because every time I walk into Uncle Jeff's apartment, I can feel Paxton's energy lingering in the empty spaces, and it got too difficult to endure.

"I'm sorry I haven't stopped by in a while," I state.

He cracks a smile. "The last thing you should be doing is apologizing to me. You have a lot going on, and as much as I enjoy our game nights, I'm happier to hear you're out there living your life."

I twirl my spoon in my empty cup. "Pax's last game of the season is on Sunday."

"Yep." Pride flows through his words as he says, "If they win this, they'll be the champions, and Pax will head to the NHL."

"I can't believe he did it—I mean, I *can*. It just all feels so surreal."

"It sure does." He studies me for a brief moment, then he shifts back into conversation. "Will I see you at the game? I spoke with Trent yesterday, and Pax emailed him tickets for the both of you."

"Um, I'm not sure yet. I have a lot to do with school

stuff, and my mom's annoying me with Dame classes, so I don't know. I'll see."

Shockwaves of anxiety burst through my bloodstream. He texted me only once over the past few weeks. It was a lengthy message, but I reread it so many times, I have it memorized.

> Hey, sorry I haven't gotten back to you. I've been so zeroed in on winning the championships, I can't focus on anything else. But I'm almost at the end—I'm so close, I can taste it. I don't want to get ahead of myself, but I'm getting a good feeling about how things are going to unfold. You and Trent should come to the finals. The stadium is only a few hours from home. I'll email him tickets for you guys. My agent told me if we end up winning, then it's a done deal—I'll be a draft pick for the NHL—holy fucking shit!!! I'll have to move, train, and do press shit. It's gonna be a crazy summer. I don't know when I'll be able to hang out with you guys, but we'll find time to see each other because we gotta celebrate you graduating too! Hope you told Harvard that you're going so I can brag to everyone about my friend getting in. Proud of you, Rebel. We'll talk about stuff before you go off to college, okay?

I didn't respond.

And he didn't follow up with another message.

"Ivy?" Uncle Jeff pulls me from my thoughts. "You feeling okay? You look pale. Want me to drive you home?"

"No, it's okay." I stand up, gathering my things. "I'm just tired. But I should head back. I have a lot to think over."

He rises, cleaning up our trash. "You let me know if you need anything, okay?"

"Yeah."

"I mean it, Ivy. Anything at all. You know where to find me."

Nodding, I attempt to muster up a convincing smile even though I can sense my eyes starting to burn. I want to say goodbye, but I think if I try to speak, I'll unravel into hysterics, and I already hit my quota for the day. So, instead, I give him a wave and rush out of the ice cream parlor, my sonogram pressed firmly into my hand.

I spent most of the weekend in bed, comforted by my blankets and old *Gilmore Girls* episodes on repeat. Trent finished his school year before me, so he moved back home from college yesterday, but I only spoke to him briefly, staying as secluded as I can in my room.

I put the sonogram in an envelope so I don't stare at it for hours on end, but it's sitting on my nightstand, and I've ended up staring at the blank envelope instead, controlling myself not to open it up and look at what's inside.

I still don't know what to do.

But I know once I talk to Paxton, he'll stand by my side with whatever I decide to do.

I just don't know when to talk to him. Tonight is his last game of the season—the game that he's putting his entire future on—so I definitely don't want to tell him beforehand. But if I tell him immediately after, would it completely steal the joy of the moment he's worked so hard for out from under him?

As I toss and turn in bed, I also toss around the idea of Pax wanting to be in a relationship with me. We'd keep the baby, I'd follow him around during the NHL season, and we'd make it work.

We can make it work, right?

"Ivy," Trent says, tapping his knuckles against my door.

"Yeah?"

"Can I come in?"

I wipe any residual tears that might be staining my cheeks and sit up. "Yeah."

When Trent walks in, I notice that he appears taller than when I saw him last. He's looking more like an adult with scruff around his jawline. Little does he know, I'm the one who's playing the role of adult now.

"You okay?" he asks, his head tilting to the side when he spots me.

"I'm fine. Just waking up from a nap." I stretch and let out a fake yawn.

"Well, you better wake up. I'm leaving for Pax's game in twenty."

"I don't know if I'm gonna go."

"What?" Trent freezes as if my words acted as a wound. Behind him, I notice my corkboard, filled with an array of pictures. Newer ones with my friends bury the images from my earlier years in high school. But there's a special corner reserved for pictures of me, Trent, and Pax. No other pictures would dare replace those. But now I have this sorrowful ache in the middle of my chest, concerned that we won't take more pictures to add to the collection.

If I keep this baby, I'd like to believe that I'll have a fairy-tale ending where everything aligns perfectly. However, my ever-expanding fears are making me expect the opposite to be true. All of my relationships will explode, and nothing will ever be the same.

"What do you mean you're not coming?" Trent's voice pulls me out of my head. "This is Pax's big game. This is *it*, Ivy."

"I know. I have a headache, so I might go late and miss the first period."

"That's half the game."

"I don't feel good, Trent!" I snap. "I'll get there when I get there. Yes, I'm aware it's several hours away. Yes, I know it would be a better idea if I just drove with you. Yes, I know a good friend would be there for the full game. But it is what it is!"

Trent's brow rises in a surprised arc. "Whoa. Chill. I'll email you your ticket, and we'll go separately. I didn't mean to get caught in your PMS warpath."

"Get out!" My face gets hot with anger.

Trent listens, leaving me alone. By the time I lay my head back down on my pillow, my phone pings with an email from him, forwarding me my ticket.

I spend the next few hours arguing with myself on what to do.

After endless debating, I decided to take the drive to watch the end of the game. I didn't bother taking time to look nice. In fact, I'm confident that I look like crap with my eyes puffy and my hair unkempt. I also didn't bother wearing his team colors because I know they'll change after this. So I stand in the stadium concourse in my cutoff jean shorts and a plain white tee, listening to the raucous cheering coming from the stands.

A hard, fast pulse flutters in my throat as my heart stumbles over its own rhythm. Anxiety knots my chest so tightly, it's a struggle to breathe evenly.

I can't pinpoint what's causing my nerves to become

frayed the most: seeing Pax for the first time since we slept together, possibly delivering him the news at some point tonight, or if he's going to win the game.

I hover in the entryway of section 102, probably the best section in the arena. Shockwaves of nervousness shoot through my heels and up my spine with every step closer I take. The cheering fans get louder, everyone at the edge of their seats. The scoreboard is tied, three to three, and the entire arena is pulsating with exhilarating energy so powerful that it even causes the corners of my mouth to lift up.

I spot Trent and Uncle Jeff a few rows down, but I stand at the opening of the section, leaning against the cool cement wall as I watch the last few minutes of the game.

Each player aggressively fights for the puck, with the opponent's team ending up in possession of it. I hold my breath as they attempt a shot, but it's blocked. Pax gets the puck and works his way to the opposite end of the rink.

At the very last millisecond, Pax wraps around the goal and scores with a backhand shot.

An electric current rips through the stadium as everyone cheers.

"Oh my god," I say to myself, tears immediately pricking my eyes as I watch the awareness unfold on Pax's face. He looks awestruck, as if he's one of us watching from the stands. His teammates skate over to him, roistering and celebrating. Pax grins but still appears to be in disbelief, because he knows what this win means for him.

Pride spills out of my heart into every inch of my soul. Tears of joy are set free, streaming down my cheeks. I don't think I've ever been so happy for someone in my entire life. Pax has worked so hard for this moment, and it's here.

A sudden urge for connection runs through my bloodstream, and for the very first time, I place my palms on my lower belly to join with the half of Pax that's inside me. "Your dad's going to the NHL," I whisper. My hands shake, my heart nearly bursting out of my body at the acknowledgment.

The mayhem carries on around me as my breathing becomes strained. A myriad of emotions overwhelms me. Hope, panic, excitement, fear—I can't distinguish which one has taken over my body. But as people start to stand up to leave, I know I need to see Pax before I cross paths with Trent or Uncle Jeff.

I rush back to the stadium concourse in search of the locker room. I don't care if security gives me a hard time getting past—I need to see Pax.

"Mr. Brightside" by The Killers plays on the speakers overhead, and my pace quickens with the beat of the song. I scurry past the concession stands, my pulse ricocheting throughout every part of me.

I need to see Pax.

We're going to be okay. Everything is going to be okay.

My feet land me in front of the alcove to the locker room. Just as I'm about to enter, a hand stops me.

"We can't let you through, miss," a security guard says, glancing over at his coworker. Over his shoulder, I can see Pax's teammates making their way from the rink to the door of the locker room.

"Please—I need to see my boyfriend." I flinch in surprise when the word flies out of my mouth.

"Sorry, you'll have to wait," he states.

"It's fine, let her through," the other security guard says to him. "We let someone else's girlfriend go through."

The man who's standing in my way lets out an agitated sigh as he steps aside.

"Thank you!" I practically squeal.

I go to move forward, but the display in front of me stops me dead in my tracks.

My heart stops.

Time stops.

Everything stops except for the two people in my field of vision.

Just as Pax exits the rink, stepping into the small tunnel that leads him to the locker room, Courtney pounces on him.

They're smiling and kissing and holding onto each other for dear life.

Blood drains from my body as I watch their celebratory make out, the two of them oblivious to the world around them.

That was supposed to be me.

I always assumed the term heartbreak was a metaphor for sadness, but I now know that's not true because I can feel every inch of my heart becoming shattered. Each crack causes more and more of a searing pain in my chest as my hope gets demolished right before my eyes.

My ribcage aches so bad, it's enough to make me hunch over. My hands fly up to comfort myself, but to my surprise, they don't cling to my chest. Instead, they clutch onto my stomach.

Tears instantly flood my vision, and before I can witness one more second, I leave.

It's quiet.

I trudge up the stairs toward my bedroom. My phone goes off in my back pocket, probably another text from Trent asking if I'm going out with them to celebrate.

When I reach the hallway, it feels as if my legs are made out of cement, the weight of the predicament I'm in crushing my bones with more and more pressure.

I don't even remember driving home. One minute I'm racing out of the stadium, and the next I'm sitting in my car outside of my house with my cheeks drenched in sadness.

Pax said things with Courtney were complicated. He stopped posting pictures of her. He didn't mention her in the text he sent me.

But there they were, happier than ever, not a care in the world. And why should he have a care in the world? His biggest dream just came true, and he doesn't have any inclination that I'm carrying his child. He's blinded by ambition and cluelessness, all the while this secret is growing inside me.

The burden of keeping this to myself has eaten away at me. I thought I'd have more clarity after discussing this with Pax, but now I'm more lost than I was before.

My eyes burn, but I notice the light on in my parents' bedroom.

An anxious tremor rattles my body.

But I need someone to talk to.

I need some direction.

I need someone to tell me everything is going to be okay.

Without thinking, I enter my parents' bedroom. Mom is the only one in the room, seated at her vanity as she applies anti-aging serum to the fine lines on her forehead. Her eyes connect with mine through the mirror, and the second she sees me upset, she spins around to face me.

"Ivy?" Her voice holds more concern than I've ever

heard before, giving me a flourish of hope that she'll help me.

My chin quivers. "Mom..."

"Are you okay?"

An acidic, vomit-like taste coats my throat. My heart races, making me sweaty and clammy. I can't take a full breath, panting in nervous waves. "Mom, I—" A distressing sob comes out of me, unable to finish the sentence: *Mom, I'm pregnant.*

"What happened?" She walks over to me.

I can't stop crying. I wish I could tell her everything. I wish I could tell *him* everything. "He...he..." are the only words I can get out.

I can almost feel the chill in the air as the worry leaves her body, and she turns back to her normal self—cold. "Are you crying over a boy?" she asks.

My gaze falls to the floor as I nod, even though it's way more than that, and Pax is way more than just a boy.

"Is this boy someone your father and I would like you to have a future with?"

I shake my head.

"Then there's no point in crying." Mom puts her finger under my chin to get me to look back up. "And even if it were a boy we'd potentially want for your future, only stupid girls cry over boys. Don't be stupid, Ivy."

I stare at her eyes, the same color as mine but lacking any tenderness. What had gotten her to this point? Was she always this detached, or did her mother have the same talk with her when she was younger? Or did she realize she made a mistake marrying Dad, but became locked in by having me and Trent?

Her stoic features make it very clear that I will not be telling her my secret.

She steps away from me, going back to her vanity.

"Get some sleep. We have your dress fitting tomorrow morning, and I need you to be on time."

"Dress fitting?"

"For the Dame Induction," Mom struggles not to sound annoyed as she reminds me that I'm getting inducted into the Dames in July. "This is what I'm talking about. You're so exhausted over a boy that you can't even think straight. Go to bed and wake up feeling better."

"Okay." My voice comes out weak. "Good night."

I disappear from her and make it into my room. On instinct, I change into Pax's Blink-182 shirt and put on a random episode of *Gilmore Girls* before crawling under my covers. I've never wished more for a TV mom in my entire life than I have now.

I wish I could go to Mom for anything. I wish I could tell her what's going on. I wish she'd hold me as I cried in her arms.

I could never imagine being so callous toward my daughter.

I'd be the person she'd run to in a heartbeat if she ever needed help. I'd be her biggest supporter and stand by her side through any and everything.

For a third time tonight, my palm connects with my stomach.

"Are you a little girl?" I whisper while the sound of Lorelai and Rory's dialogue flows through my television speaker. "That would be really cool if you were." A tear drips down my face. "We'd be best friends. We'd be the new Lorelai and Rory, only we'd be Ivy and..." My mind flashes back to a couple of years ago. "Daisy."

Wiping my cheeks, I prop myself up, reaching to my nightstand. I take the envelope and glance at the ultrasound. The tiny blob gives me a sense of faith, and I let optimism eclipse my doubts, envisioning my path if I decide to keep it.

Maybe it doesn't have to be horrible, even if Pax isn't in the picture and my parents disown me. Maybe I'll be able to figure out this new life for the both of us.

I put the ultrasound back in, then, taking my ballpoint pen, I write *Daisy* in my prettiest handwriting across the front of the envelope. I prop it up next to my lamp that's on my nightstand and then grab another envelope. Only this one has Harvard printed on it.

Taking the pages out, I glance over the early art history program I was accepted into. It starts in June, a few days after I graduate high school.

The wheels in my mind swiftly turn as I conjure up a plan for myself.

If I accept the program, I can leave as soon as possible without anyone finding out my secret. I'll miss being inducted into the Dames, but I'll use my education as an excuse—even though Mom will end up having a meltdown about it.

But I don't plan on coming back here for a while.

I'll live up in Boston and go to school until I can't anymore. Then I'll take some time off and re-enroll once I feel ready. I won't tell my family until one day when I show up with a baby in my arms—that way, they won't have to deal with the embarrassment of a pregnant teenage daughter, and I won't have to feel burdened by their shame. And if I show up at their doorstep with their granddaughter and they want nothing to do with us, then that's their choice. We'll still have a great life, no matter who wants to be in it or not.

Picking my pen up, I begin filling out the form for the summer program. A rush of happiness moves through me as I feel more confident in my decisions.

Thankfully, I don't have to worry about my finances. I have a hefty savings, and I know I'll get more for graduation. But I might pick up a part-time job when I'm at school, just in case.

The clearer my vision becomes, the better I feel.

We'll be just fine.

The two of us.

Ivy and Daisy.

CHAPTER FIFTY-THREE

ivy

June

I STARE at two dresses in my walk-in closet. One is an elegant gold gown that a seamstress tailored to my exact size so that it'll fit me like a glove in a few weeks during my Dame induction. I feel bad the woman worked so diligently on it, considering I won't be wearing it. But no one knows that yet. I still haven't decided how I'd let my family know that I'll be leaving in five days to attend the summer program at Harvard.

I'll wing it.

The other dress is a simple lavender cotton dress that I'll be wearing under my graduation gown tomorrow morning. My parents asked Trent and me if we wanted to join them on their trip to Antigua, as if it were some sort of graduation celebration for me, even though they didn't realize their trip was the day after I graduated until I brought it up to them. Trent took them up on their offer, and I lied and said a bunch of my friends are having graduation parties that I want to go to. So while they're away, I'll pack up my belongings and head to Boston for my new life.

There's a knock on my bedroom door, and before I can answer, Trent walks in. He's already sporting a summer tan. "You ready for your big day tomorrow?" he asks.

"I guess."

He focuses on his phone for a moment, sending a text to someone. "You sure you don't want to go out after the graduation dinner with Mom and Dad?"

"Yeah. It's not really a big deal."

"I mean, you're going to Harvard in the fall. That's a pretty big deal."

Guilt swarms my insides. I don't want to lie to Trent, but I don't know how he'll handle the truth. "I'm just not in the mood to party. I'll be doing that nonstop for the next month with my friends." My face heats up from continuing to fabricate an excuse.

"Well, if you change your mind, Pax will be back from looking at apartments in Illinois, and we'll be going out."

"Okay."

Trent gets distracted by his phone again and steps out of my room to make a call.

My thoughts drift over to the one person I've been trying to avoid thinking about. But it's hard not to while Daisy grows inside me. Pax and I had a quick text exchange the day after he won the championship. I sent him a congratulations message and told him that I'm proud of him—because I am. After he thanked me, he asked when I would be free. Once again, I made up a story about how I have a million things to do before senior year ends, my finals are stressing me out, and my mom is suffocating me with Dame classes—the latter not being a lie. Pax kept the conversation weirdly cordial, letting me know he'll be looking at apartments in whichever city he's drafted to, and he won't be around much, but to reach out to him when my schedule opens up.

We haven't talked since.

He hasn't attempted to text me, and I haven't messaged him either.

The silence between us creates a harsh ache between the gaps of my wrecked heart. But I try my best to ignore it.

Trent, our parents, and I sit in an upscale restaurant for my graduation dinner. I received a special honors award, which I wish I were more excited about, but all I can think about is leaving. I have to force myself to be present during conversation, but the longer I sit here, the more my desire to escape pulses through me.

My gaze flickers around the room. Waiters in neatly pressed button-downs and black dress pants put on their best fake smiles as they hurry around the restaurant to serve a bunch of annoying patrons. Ambient lighting looks complementary on everyone, and the scattered candles add to the sophisticated glow. A pianist plays soft music in the corner, making it feel extra refined.

I hate it.

Crystal champagne flutes are placed next to our dinner plates, and Dad raises his in a toast. "Here's to Ivy," he states. "We know how hard you worked in school, and we're very proud of you. We're looking forward to seeing where your life leads you post-high school."

"Yes," Mom adds. "And we can't wait for you to become a Dame!"

The four of us clink glasses, and I pretend to take a sip.

"I'm meeting up with Pax in a few hours. You sure you don't want to come?" Trent asks me, but before I can answer, Mom speaks.

"You can't go out tonight! We have to meet the McAllisters for brunch," Mom says about another semi-casual business meetup that she and Dad are forcing Trent to go to, priming him for the future. "And then we leave for Antigua in the evening."

"Relax. I'll be fine to go to brunch."

"He'll probably just be coming home," I mutter under my breath, and Trent shoots me a look that tells me to shut up.

Mom ignores my comment and goes back to conversing with Dad about their travel plans. Their voices fade into white noise as my focus goes back on bolting to Boston. Nervousness stings the tips of my fingers, eager to get out of here so I can turn the page on the next chapter of my life.

When we get back home, everyone goes their separate ways. Trent gets ready to go out, Mom goes to check her luggage for Antigua, Dad heads to his office, and I get my PJs on and lie in my bed.

I glance around my room, thinking of all the things I should pack and what I should leave behind for at least six months. My attention goes to my corkboard, a giant collage of my years spent being a kid. It feels sacred, like it should be hanging up in a gallery as a way to memorialize my teenage years.

A wave of nausea casts over me. I've been lucky enough not to deal with much sickness, and I really hope that doesn't change.

"Hey," I say to my belly, my hands cradling that part of my body. "Chill out in there," I joke with Daisy.

Listening to me, the nausea subsides. A dull twinge emerges, and I shift onto my side, relieving the sensation. As my head turns on my pillow, my phone lights up with a text.

PAX

Congrats, Rebel

My body betrays me, smiling at the message. I lied to myself, saying I wasn't disappointed that I hadn't heard from him today, but I can't ignore the way my veins light up when I see him call me Rebel.

I type out a message telling Pax that we need to talk, but then delete it.

I do this several more times until I finally settle on leaving the text box blank and toss my phone onto my nightstand.

My eyes get heavy, and I drift in and out of sleep, visions of Pax, Boston, and a baby filtering through my brain until I eventually wander into dreamland.

A sharp, piercing pain radiates out of my lower stomach, jolting me awake.

My hand immediately goes to hug the area as I try to breathe through the intense cramping.

Thoughts race through my mind as I struggle to push myself up. The erratic beating in my chest causes me to tremble as I reach for my lamp, gently lighting up my bed in a soft glow.

Another round of cramps forces me to wince, quietly whimpering, "Ow, ow, ow," to myself.

A faint sensation of moisture on my thigh instantly ignites panic in my veins.

Chaotically thrashing the blankets off me, I lurch to the other side of the bed in order to inspect the space where I was lying down.

A small puddle of blood stains my white sheets.

A sickening wave of terror wells up inside me, tears streaming down my face as if my body was made aware of what is happening before my mind has.

"No." I brush my fingers between my thighs, hoping that the source of blood is coming from literally anywhere else in my body. When I draw my hand back up, bright red covers my fingers.

"No," I repeat to myself through more harsh cramping. "Daisy, *no*."

The weight of a million bricks comes crashing down on me when I finally acknowledge what's happening. My vision blurs with anguish as I clench my sheets, my knuckles losing color.

Falling over onto the fabric, I cry into it, forcing my sobs to get stifled.

There's no one I can run to for help, and even if I did, there's nothing they can do.

My body shakes with grief.

We had a plan, Daisy. It was supposed to be you and me.

A gaping hole in my chest emerges, and I don't know if it'll ever be mended.

Guilt stabs me, wondering if I caused this by not being sure if I should follow through with the pregnancy just a couple of weeks ago. *Is this my fault? Did I will this to happen?*

I curl into a fetal position, agonizing physical and emotional pain torturing every cell in my body.

I never realized how badly I wanted her now that I can't keep her.

Continuing to fade into my mattress, I cry alone.

For hours.

Until the sun rises.

Until I sense movement in the house, welcoming a new day.

CHAPTER FIFTY-FOUR

THE SOUND of my family and our workers starting their day springs me off my bed.

I wipe my tear-stained cheeks and change into clean clothes. Grief is forever sewn into my every cell, but my ability to compartmentalize comes through, forcing me to face the morning.

I have never in my life wanted to get the hell out of here as much as I do right now. My skin itches to leave. Bolts of energy strike through me, begging me to start over—*now*.

Leave everything behind.

Leave behind this suffocating life.

Leave behind the memories that make my heart throb with joy and loss.

Leave behind Pax.

It's time to start over.

As I begin to move, it's almost as if I can feel the armor coming over me, shielding me from any more pain. My muscles gain strength as my emotions shift gears. A surge of independence and coarseness beckons me to start my next chapter.

I glance around my room, taking in the posters, pictures, books, and cherished memorabilia. No longer am I the Ivy who lets this room be her only safe haven.

It's time for me to turn the page, step outside my comfort zone, and see what else is out there aside from high-society life, Trent, and Pax.

My gaze lands on the time, noting that my family will be leaving for brunch in about an hour. A rush of adrenaline floods me as I realize I have to escape while they're out, and that doesn't leave me much time to pack.

I rush to my walk-in closet, pulling out bins that I have been storing with the intention of using when it came time to pack for Harvard. Scrambling, my hands shake as I stuff as much as I can into each bin.

My summer program doesn't start until next week, so I'll stay at a hotel in the area in the meantime. I'd rather stay anywhere else than here, where my pain will haunt me. Some might say that I'm avoiding—I like to see it as taking care of myself. For years, I've wanted out, and now that the opportunity has approached even sooner than I anticipated, I'm taking it.

Once I have an array of clothing and shoes packed, I move to my dresser, quickly tossing my necessities into another bin. My attention catches on the small divot in the wood, and I almost get lost in a bittersweet memory, but I roll my shoulders back and brush it off.

I make sure to pack my books, DVDs, and iPod, but leave the items on my corkboard untouched. It's time for me to make new memories and friends. I can start a new board in my dorm.

Taking a peek out my window, I spot my family getting into the car and driving off to their meeting. I blow out a puff of air, feeling relieved that I don't have to keep hiding in here.

When my bins are full, I begin moving them from my

room to my car. I could ask one of our workers to help me, but I don't want to. This crisp independence ignites my strength, and I even allow myself to get a bit excited.

Once my car is ready to go, I go to my bedroom for the last time before embarking on my adventure. I take my backpack and put some last-minute small items in it, then sit down on my bed. Looking around, a sadness sweeps through me, already missing bits of my adolescence. My eyes drift down to my nightstand, where the envelope with Daisy's name is written on it.

Without thinking, I pick it up and stuff it in my nightstand drawer.

Emotions begin to clog my throat, but I force them down. I've done enough crying.

I have two things left to do before I can finally leave. The first is writing my parents a note, explaining that I left.

It's not the most eloquently written letter, but I explained about my summer program and shared that I felt like I would be letting them down by not being inducted as a Dame, so I felt it was easier to avoid their disappointment by leaving while they were out. I apologized for leaving without saying a real goodbye, and I apologized for not being the daughter they wished for the family. I also told them not to come up to Boston to try to convince me to come home. It would be a fruitless attempt as I am determined to move on and start fresh.

I place the letter on my mattress, then do the very last thing I need to do.

Opening up my laptop, I go to Facebook and block Pax, as well as block his email, so he can't contact me that way either. I stuff my computer into my backpack and zip it up. Then, taking my phone, I type out a long-winded message to Pax and block his number.

Lifting my chin, I allow myself to stand in the stillness of my room one more time. I draw in a breath, letting the air swirl around my lungs.

Then, I leave.

CHAPTER FIFTY-FIVE

THE FAMILIAR CHIME of my phone's ringtone continuously goes off, waking me up. I should've been up several hours ago, but Trent and I went out last night, and I might've drunk a little too much, and I might be a little hungover.

My phone keeps going off, so I reach for it, seeing Trent's name on the screen. "What's up?" I mumble, slumber still encasing my voice.

"Has Ivy reached out to you at all today?"

I spring upright, instantly awake. "No, why?"

"She left."

"What do you mean she left?"

"I went out to brunch with my parents, and apparently, while we were away, she packed half her shit and left a note to my parents apologizing."

"Wait. What?" I rub my temple. None of this is making sense. I must be too hungover and misunderstanding what he's saying.

"Yeah, I don't really know what's going on, but my mom is *pissed*. I've been trying to get a hold of Ivy and just wanted to see if she happened to call or text you."

"No, I didn't get any..." My voice trails as I pull my phone away from my cheek to check it. Lo and behold, a novel-sized text from Ivy sits unread on my screen. Anxiety bubbles in my gut.

"All right, keep me posted if you hear from her, and I'll do the same. Gotta go." Trent hangs up before I can process it.

Trepidation swarms my bloodstream, my heart thrashing against my bones as I begin to read Ivy's text.

IVY

> Thank you for sending me the congratulations text last night. Graduating is weird, but I'm ready for a fresh start. And with that, I need to move on from you too. It feels pathetic that for the past few months—years, actually—I've been stuck on you, even though you've made it clear time and time again that I shouldn't be. I'm headed up to Boston and starting an early summer program at Harvard. You're technically the first person I'm telling, and I know you'll be proud of me for following my passions, just as I'm proud of you for following yours. In another life, maybe we could've been celebrating together, but in this one, I think it's time for us to part ways for good. I hope the NHL is bigger than your wildest dreams, and know that I'll always be rooting for you on the sidelines.

I break out into a cold sweat, scrambling to call Ivy, but when I do, I get an automated message, and it immediately drops the call.

"Fuck." Rushing to throw on whatever gym shorts are closest to me, I try calling again and again.

Then I try texting her, and the message goes undelivered.

"She blocked me," I say in utter disbelief to myself, reaching for my car keys.

My whirling pulse dashes me out of Uncle Jeff's apartment and into my car. My mind races along with the engine, hoping Ivy didn't leave.

Maybe she's somewhere else in her ginormous house, packing her things. Maybe she's planning on leaving later today and is just giving me a heads-up.

I try her phone endlessly, an anchor of guilt collapsing onto me, crushing my bones into dust each time I get disconnected. A nagging voice in my head tells me that she's blocking me and running off because of how I've been acting. For months, I've been thinking about the night we spent together and feeling like shit for leaving her as soon as I could.

I told her I loved her.

And I didn't know how to handle that. I had never admitted it to myself. I don't even know how it slipped out.

It scared the shit out of me. I didn't want to fuck things up and lose both Trent and Ivy. I didn't know how that would've changed things for our future. I didn't want her to feel like she had to follow me while I was pursuing my dreams, and she wouldn't be following hers.

So instead of facing all of those things head-on, I avoided it.

And now it's come back around to bite me.

Pulling up to the Hartwicks' house, their iron gates open for me, and I drive up to their home. My clammy hands tremble, and I'm breathing as if I just ran a marathon as I get out of the car and leap onto her front steps.

But before I can reach the front door, it swings open, and Meredith Hartwick marches forward, claiming the space.

"Is Ivy—"

"She left," Meredith states, glaring at me.

"She left," I repeat, not wanting those words to be true.

"Trent got ahold of her and is on the phone with her now."

"Oh, good!" I go to move toward the door so I can crash the phone call, but she sidesteps me, blocking the entrance.

"You're not allowed in."

"What—why?"

Her features harden more than I thought they could as her dark-blue eyes puncture me. "I don't know what you did, but I know you're behind some of this."

"Excuse me?"

"I have never known my daughter to get distressed over a boy, but in April, she came to me crying about a boy breaking her heart. The only person she's ever cared about to that degree is you. She didn't even bat an eye when she informed me she broke up with Calvin, and I know she wasn't interested in any of the dates I had set her up with afterward. So I know you must've done something to push her over the edge and leave and change the whole trajectory of her future."

"The whole trajectory of what *you* want for her future," I snap.

"What?"

"Have you considered that maybe *you* pushed her over the edge, and she left because she wanted to start her own life, out from under your pretentious thumb where she'd be inducted into the Dames and her dreams would come secondary to whatever bullshit milestones you have for her?"

Meredith's jaw drops, appalled. "I highly suggest you rethink the way you're speaking to me, young man. I will not stand here and let you push the blame back on me when I know you're the one responsible for this disaster."

"No, I'm not—"

"Oh, really?" She marches forward, owning the space to the point of her intruding on my personal bubble, forcing me to step backward and place one of my feet on the slate step. "Then look me in the eyes and tell me you weren't the reason Ivy was crying. Tell me you didn't hurt her. Prove to me you're innocent."

I open my mouth to defend myself, but nothing comes out.

A knife twists in my chest, making it more difficult to breathe. Regret, blame, and contrition magnify to the point of my being unable to conceal the remorse tugging at my features.

Meredith stares at me, a sense of satisfaction in my pain lacing around the arrows of contempt that are shooting out of her. "That's what I thought."

"I-I need to talk to her." The desperation rises in my voice as I speak. I try to move to the door, but she blocks me once again.

"I think you've done enough."

"Please—"

"No—"

"Please. I can't get ahold of her. She blocked me—and I *need* to talk to her and find out what's going on and—"

"I think it's very clear what's going on. You caused her to run away from everything and completely upend her life. She wants nothing to do with you, or me, or anyone."

"Mrs. Hartwick, I'm in love with your daughter," I

blurt out. "And I leave for training in a few weeks, and I don't want to leave with her angry and not speaking to me. So if you don't allow me to talk to her on the phone, I'll drive up to Boston and bang on every single door until I find hers."

She stoically stares at me as I catch my breath from rushing my words out. My pulse thuds in my ears as I wait for her to speak.

"You're in love with her?" she asks.

I nod. "Yeah."

"Then let her go."

"What?"

"She's been enamored by you since the day you walked through my front door. I watched how she was so charmed by you for years. She's stopped herself from taking opportunities in the past, hoping you'd come around eventually. And now, she's finally gone ahead and moved forward. Give her the chance to experience life without you."

Pure misery comes crashing down on my shoulders, nearly toppling me over.

Had I been stopping her from taking opportunities all these years? Has she really just been waiting around for me this whole time? Did I absolutely destroy her and any chance of a future together by bitching out and avoiding her after we slept together?

Meredith watches me as if she's witnessing all of these questions appear across my forehead. She appears pleased that she's won this war and got me to surrender.

Well, fuck that. I'm not letting her get the last laugh.

"Then you need to give her a chance too," I state.

"Excuse me?"

"If you're *so* concerned about Ivy not taking opportunities, then you need to give her a chance to experience life without you stuffing her into a box, priming her to be a prototypical Dame and one day someone's vapid wife," I strike back, enjoying the look of distaste stamped across her face. "If you *truly* meant what you said about giving her a chance to move forward, I'll do it. As long as you do it too."

"I believe our conversation is finished."

"So you lied. You don't actually give a shit about her taking a great opportunity—"

"Yes, I do."

"Prove it." I throw her words back in her face.

Meredith's jaw sets tight, scowling at me. "As I just stated, our conversation is finished." She resigns our fight, neither of us feeling like we won.

As I watch her turn her back and re-enter her home, shutting me out, my eyes start to burn.

Flames of pain scorch my insides as I part from the front steps and make my way into my car. My head spins with what I should do as I drive away, glancing at those iron gates through my rearview mirror.

My heart nearly jumps out of my body when my phone pings with a text.

TRENT

Got a hold of Ivy. She got into some special program at Harvard and left early for it. She said she needs some space from everyone here. I'm sure she'll get over being dramatic in a couple of days. Sorry if I freaked you out. We're all good here. Heading to the airport for Antigua in an hour. I'll hit you up when I'm back home.

The same burning sensation continues to build behind my eyes until my vision blurs. I keep trying to call Ivy as I drive, hoping she changed her mind and unblocked me, and we can talk about everything.

I'm considering following through on what I said to Meredith and drive up to Boston and scour every inch of that city for Ivy.

Pulling up to my apartment, my phone rings, and I almost crash into the curb, fumbling to check it. When I see "Courtney" on the screen, my excitement is instantly crushed. Ignoring the call, I move inside, seeing if Uncle Jeff is home.

"Uncle Jeff?" I call out, checking around, but quickly realize I'm alone.

Despair settles around me as I sink into my loneliness. The apartment has more of Uncle Jeff's mark on it than mine, and rightfully so, considering I'm not here much. But I can't fight off this sinking feeling, like my home is becoming uprooted, only this time it's happening so slowly that I couldn't realize it in time.

I'll be moving to Illinois soon to be with the Cobras. I know I'll always have a spot here, but it's not really my home anymore.

And my friends are branching out into their own new worlds.

And Ivy left.

It's just me. Paxton Rhodes, party of one.

I drop down onto the couch. A flash of memories from when Ivy used to come hang out and sit right next to me flickers in my mind. Cradling my face in my palms, I allow the mist in my eyes to freefall.

I don't know how to fix this, but I know that one day I will.

I hope Trent is right and Ivy will have a change of heart in a couple of days, and I'll be able to talk to her.

A hurried knock at my door startles me, making my spine straighten with sudden hope. Quickly wiping my face, I rush to the door, anxiously expecting Ivy to be there like she has been so many times before. Back when she would drop off pictures for Uncle Jeff or just come to spend time here.

Within the few steps it takes me to get to the door, flashes of the past come to the forefront of my mind.

The first time Ivy stopped over.

Ivy in her uniform.

Ivy in a dress after she went to an event with her parents.

Ivy bundled up in a winter coat.

Ivy bringing over a bag of blue Doritos.

My hand twists the knob. "Hey—" I start, but the second I recognize who's on the other side, my optimism takes a nosedive.

"Why aren't you answering my calls?" Courtney puts her hands on her hips, glowering at me.

"Court, I told you already, we're done. I mean it this time." I make sure I'm blocking the entrance so she can't weasel her way in.

"Yeah, okay."

"I'm serious. I should've stopped talking to you back in March, but I was confused by a lot of stuff, and it was a mistake to keep this going for so long."

"Confused about what?"

My gaze drifts off her as I reflect on the past several months. I took a massive step away from Courtney after sleeping with Ivy. We would talk here and there, but nothing like it had been. Then, during my last round of games, Courtney showed up, and I was so wrapped up in being drafted that my triumph dominated any sense of reasoning. I celebrated with Courtney a little too much, and after I realized my blunder, I officially ended things. Or so I thought. "I'm not going to talk in circles," I tell her. "We're done. Please move on."

Courtney opens her mouth to speak, but before she can, I close the door on her and swiftly lock it. Her fist pounds on the wood, demanding I open it, but instead, I sit back down on the couch.

Her tantrum goes on for a little bit longer until I hear her say, "Fuck you, Pax! I hope you stay alone and miserable for the rest of your life!" She stomps away until I can no longer hear her angry footsteps.

A heaviness filled with melancholy weakens my body.

Closing my eyelids, I am greeted by darkness. But soon it morphs into an image of Ivy.

My stomach clenches when I admit to myself that Courtney is probably right. No matter where my career takes me, no matter who I befriend or claim in my mattress—I will be alone and miserable for the rest of my life.

CHAPTER FIFTY-SIX

PRESENT

SHIT.

"You *fucked* my little sister!?" Trent glares at Paxton incredulously, and even though he's dressed prim and proper in his tuxedo on his wedding day, he looks like he's about to gouge Pax's eyeballs out.

"Oh my god, Trent," I interject, playing it cool. "We're all adults. We all know sex is a part of life. It's no big deal."

"It's a big deal when it's you and *him*. You *know* he's a piece of shit when it comes to women. You've *seen* it. The one girlfriend he ever had, he couldn't stop cheating on—and he hasn't had another girlfriend since."

"Yes, and even with that knowledge, I still made a choice. It's no big deal. Plus, we're a little too old for you to be doing this whole big-brother-protector thing."

"He's going to hurt you."

I scoff. "He won't. Trust me."

"Yes, he fucking will!"

Trent has no idea how much I can emotionally handle. Neither of them do.

"I'm fine," I state, anger rising in my voice. "I was fine after he fucked me when I was eighteen, and I'm fine now," I impulsively blurt out.

I bite the inside of my cheek, instantly regretting saying that aloud. Before I can witness either of their reactions, I'm walking away. Each step I take descending to the first floor of the main manor gets quicker as my bones clatter against one another.

Racing into the reception tent, my rose quartz gown brushes over the tops of my feet, my pace continuously picking up. The sound of my heartbeat thunders in my ears, engulfing the celebratory music coming from the band and the jubilant energy pouring out of the guests.

The soft amber glow of the string lights overhead is blinding.

This giant reception is suffocating.

My breaths come out short and shallow.

I know within a matter of minutes, I'll have Pax or Trent or both of them searching for me, and I don't want to talk to either of them. This is over between me and Pax. Today is our expiration date.

I'm not rehashing the past. I'm not. It's over and done with.

Panic laced with grief steals my air, forcing me to take small sips in order to get some flow in my lungs.

I need to get out of here.

It's the end of the night, and everyone's plastered. No one will notice my absence.

I race to my table, grabbing my phone out of my purse to schedule an Uber as soon as possible and book the first flight I can find back to Boston. The action is reminiscent of several months ago when I bolted from my parents' holiday party. But that's what I do best.

Sensing someone's attention on me, I glance up from my phone and make eye contact with Mom from all the way at the other end of the tent. The way she studies me lets me know that she's aware of what I'm doing.

I part my lips to mouth an apology, but I can't form the word "sorry." So instead, I shrug my shoulders in defeat, my eyes immediately watering from the sense of disappointment emanating from her.

Unable to stand in her presence any longer, I dash to the villa where my belongings are and sneak away from the wedding before Mom, Trent, or Pax have the chance to catch me.

My muscles are exhausted as I enter my apartment after taking the red-eye home. Dragging my feet, I push my luggage to the side and collapse on my couch. The moment I'm able to unfold into my solitude, I burst into sobs.

Curling myself up into a fetal position, I feel as if I'm back in high school, crying in my room alone with no one aware of the weight of each teardrop that streams down my face.

I knew when the day of ending things with Pax arrived that it would pain me, but I didn't foresee the night closing the way it did. I thought I'd be able to handle our end. I assumed we'd part amicably, even with the sting of nostalgia in our hearts, but nonetheless, it would be the opportunity for both of us to make peace with our goodbye since we weren't able to last time. It was supposed to be the closure we both longed for.

Yet, here I am, a stupid girl crying over a stupid boy like I once did many years ago.

I thought I was stronger than this.

But underneath my independence and liberation, I'm still the heartbroken teenage girl.

I never gave her a chance to heal. Instead, I covered her up with everything else until she was so small that I could no longer hear her muffled suffering.

My attention is suddenly drawn to the cardboard boxes that have been pushed into the corner of my living room for months. Their presence haunts me, no matter how much I try to avoid them, joke about them being my newest artwork in my home, or pretend that they don't even exist.

I think it's about time I let teenage Ivy heal.

Drifting over to my relics, I take a deep breath before I open the first one.

The *Twilight Saga* books are on top, and I let out a little chuckle at the sight of them.

Oh, how times have changed.

Continuing to allow myself to travel down memory lane, I slowly unpack one box at a time. I make separate piles of things I want to donate, things I can throw out, and a small selection of items I want to keep.

As hours pass by, I don't make much headway because I take the time to hold my memorabilia in my hands, cherishing the stories behind each burned CD, charm bracelet, and sequin purse before letting them go for good.

Through my sentimental tears, I laugh to myself at the silly memories each item harbors.

Opening up another box, a lump forms in my throat when I realize the whole thing is filled with pictures. The nerves in my fingertips are frayed as I continue to connect with the girl I used to be.

Pictures I'd used to hang up on my corkboard, professional ones from my sweet sixteen, stacks and stacks of images from Pax and Trent's hockey games that I'd used to capture on my digital camera. I guess I kept more for myself instead of giving them to Uncle Jeff than I realized.

A loud knock at my door has me jumping out of my skin, ruining this fragile, healing moment.

"Ivy." Pax's powerful voice comes from the other side, causing my stomach to drop. "Ivy, come on."

"The wedding's over, Pax," I shout to him.

"I can't understand you. Just open the door."

I march closer. "I said the wedding is over, which means we are too."

"Still can't make out what you're saying. Open the door so we can talk, please."

"No."

"I still have your key. You might as well unlock your door before I do."

Scowling, I've forgotten I gave him my spare and never got it back from him. Straightening my spine, I stand tall as I turn the lock on the door, intending on having a clear and concise conversation followed by him quickly exiting.

The second I open the door, Pax storms into my space. "We're not done, Ivy."

"Oh, so you were lying and you could hear me," I state, slamming my door shut so my neighbors don't eavesdrop.

"It got me in here, didn't it?"

I watch him glance around at the chaos in my apartment that has unraveled since coming back home from the wedding. He looks exhausted, his eyes with tired circles around them and a thick five o'clock shadow. Drifting my attention downward, I realize he's still in his tux, but it's disheveled and wrinkled.

"You didn't change?"

Pax's focus swings back to me. "No, Ivy. I didn't," he says, with an extra bite to his tone. "I searched the entire wedding reception for you, and when I realized you booked it out of there, I ran after you. I'm assuming you caught an earlier flight than me, but I wouldn't know for sure because you cowardly shut off your phone."

My jaw drops. "I am *not* a coward—"

"This whole fucking arrangement is cowardly, Ivy! Who the fuck runs out of their brother's wedding without saying goodbye? Who turns their phone off so no one can reach them to know they're safe? Who the hell flees the second things get uncomfortable?" Pax exudes anger, an emotion I've seen him colored in before, but never toward me. "Cowards. That's who."

Resentment boils inside me until I burst with fury. "You wanna know who the real coward is in all this, Pax? It's you!"

"Bullshit!"

"Really? Take a look around, Pax." I motion to all my old belongings strewn about the room. "Every single thing I take out of these boxes has memories of you stained on it." I dive my hand into one of the open boxes, grabbing a fistful of whatever is in here and flinging it at him. "You could've fucking had me back then, Pax!" My eyes water even though I keep screaming and throwing our past at his feet. "You could've had me, but you were too scared. Too much of a fucking *coward* to be with me!"

Pax's face pales as he gets hit with my old school uniform.

"I *wish* I could be a coward like you, Pax," I continue, tossing more and more at him until the box is empty and I move on to another one. "I *wish* I could've moved on from you easily. I wish I wasn't hurt by the past. I wish I could be unfazed like you."

Grabbing a handful of photographs, I hurl them toward Pax. They scatter everywhere, an explosion of our history wrecking the room.

As the last few pictures spiral downward, a small white envelope gets caught in the mix, landing directly in front of Pax as if the universe carefully placed it there.

My body freezes as I see "Daisy" written in my handwriting.

My breathing stops, praying he pays no mind to it.

Pax glances at the envelope, then back up at me. All the blood drains from my face as I stand in shock, witnessing him putting the pieces together in his mind.

He carefully crouches down, tenderly picking it up as if he already knows what's inside.

As if in slow motion, Pax rises and takes out the ultrasound.

And looks back at me.

CHAPTER FIFTY-SEVEN

DAISY.

"If you end up having a daughter one day, would you name her Ivy?"

A conversation from our past plays out in my mind as if it were a scene from a movie.

"Definitely not."

"How come?"

"People hate ivy. Sure, it's pretty to look at when it's in someone else's yard, but the second people find it overgrowing in theirs, they complain that it's there and want nothing to do with it."

"I don't hate Ivy."

My heart races.

"You must be the only one. Also, there's poison ivy—I don't want my daughter associated with anything poisonous. If anything, I'd name her the opposite."

"What's the opposite of ivy?"

I can remember every last bit of that exchange. And I know which name she picked.

"Daisy."

I feel everything and nothing all at once as I stare at

the image in my hands, burning a hole through my flesh. An ultrasound with May 2010 marked on top. My mind jumps back in time in a flash, remembering I slept with Ivy shortly after her eighteenth birthday. I'm quick to calculate the timeline.

I look up at Ivy, whose face says it all. She stares back at me with barely any color in her cheeks and her eyelids peeled wide in panic.

My brain turns into a gridlock, swarmed with emotions, thoughts, and questions. "Is this…" My throat is raw. "Is this…"

Real?

Mine?

Ours?

I can't bring myself to form any more words, but Ivy seems to understand what I'm asking. The moment she nods, my gut plummets. A violent sea of nausea takes over my insides. My mouth opens and shuts, trying to say something—anything, at this point—but the words are bottlenecked somewhere behind my current state of shock.

My phone vibrating in my pants pocket brings some awareness back to my pulse, but not entirely.

"What?" I ask Ivy. The only question I'm able to formulate scratches against my vocal cords.

"It was yours," she whispers.

The remnants of that statement will forever echo inside of me.

The room gets flipped upside down as I attempt to absorb what she just said.

"I miscarried a few weeks after the ultrasound," Ivy continues, her voice soft but strong, like she's giving me a gentle lecture on life. "I never got to the point of finding out if it was a girl or a boy, but I pretended it was a girl, and I named her Daisy because of, well, you know." She wipes her cheeks. "I never told anyone about her. Well, aside from Uncle Jeff, sort of."

"Uncle Jeff knew?" Betrayal ruptures my wounded heart.

"He knew I was pregnant. He didn't know it was yours."

"I…I…" My thoughts race so fast, I can't keep up with them. Bile erodes my throat. My feet begin moving on their own, pacing to keep up with everything that's flooding into my mind. Sweat forms at my hairline.

Why would she keep this a secret from me?

Why the fuck would Uncle Jeff keep this from me?

"You're probably going to need some time to process, understandably so," Ivy states. "I'll answer whatever questions you have whenever you're ready."

I nod, adjusting my shirt collar. It feels like it's choking me even though it's been unbuttoned for hours.

"Do you want to sit?" she asks.

"No," I rasp. "I-I need to get some fresh air."

"Okay."

Unsure of what to do with the ultrasound in my hand, I frantically search for where to put it until I finally place it on the top of her couch.

My vision gets spotty as I somehow make it out of her apartment building and onto the street. My head reels, bombarded by emotions as cars whiz past me while I try to find my footing. Unsure of where to focus my thoughts, I end up landing on the bitterness I feel toward Uncle Jeff.

How could he have kept this from me? Even if he didn't know it was mine, he should've at least told me about Ivy—especially because he knew I was upset that we hadn't spoken after some time.

As I continue to walk aimlessly, my thoughts dizzying me, my phone goes off in my pocket again. Taking it out, my pulse stops when I see an incoming call from Massachusetts General Hospital.

"Hello?"

"Is this Paxton Rhodes?" a woman on the other end asks.

"Yes."

"This is Dr. Patel from Mass General Hospital. Your uncle was sent here a little while ago after a housekeeper found him unconscious in his hotel room. He's in the ICU—"

"What room number?" Panic pillages every cell in my body.

"Eight-twelve."

Before she can get out another word, I hang up and start running.

I try to get my bearings, figuring out which roads to take to get to the hospital.

Horns blare, cars swerving around me as I race to get to Uncle Jeff.

All the sounds circle around me. The talking, the honking, my heavy breathing, Ivy's voice, Uncle Jeff's voice. I can hear everything all at once, internally and externally. All of it is consuming me as I race to the hospital, attempting to push it away with every harsh movement of my body.

My feet slam down on the pavement harder and harder with every step, but I barely feel it, running faster and faster.

I need to get to him *now*.

When I reach the hospital, a chill runs up my spine from the air conditioning blasting against my sweaty dress shirt.

I make it to the ICU.

I make it to Uncle Jeff's room.

I stand next to his bedside as the doctors talk to me.

I can't process what they're saying as I struggle to catch my breath. Something about his treatment failing.

They say something about his organs shutting down.

They say something about him being in his final stages.

They tell me he had previously signed a DNR.

Do Not Resuscitate.

They tell me they'll leave me to be alone with him, and if I need anything, to let them know.

They tell me it could take hours.

And then they're gone, and it's just me and Uncle Jeff.

"What the fuck?" I whisper to him even though he's comatose. My vision clouds as I study his colorless face. "Why didn't you tell me your treatment was failing? What the fuck, Uncle Jeff!" I suck in a deep breath, trying to keep my composure. "Why didn't you tell me? Why didn't you tell me about Ivy?" I hope that if I press him enough, he'll somehow wake up and bicker with me. "It was mine. The baby. Ivy said you didn't know it was mine, but you must've. You had to have known, and you didn't tell me. Why?" My voice cracks. "Why didn't you tell me about that, and why didn't you tell me about this?"

I crash onto the chair next to his bed, and, grabbing his hand in mine, I break down and weep. Crying in a way I never have before.

Grieving for him.

Grieving for the baby I just found out about.

Grieving for our life that could've been.

I cry for so long I don't know how much time has passed. I texted Ivy because I didn't know who else to reach out to, and I know she'd want to be here.

Before I know it, Ivy enters the room with watery eyes and a plastic shopping bag. She pulls up a chair on my right side, closer to Uncle Jeff.

"Hey, Uncle Jeff." Her words flow delicately. She waits a couple of seconds, as if expecting a response, and when she doesn't get one, she shifts her attention over to me. "Hey."

"Hey," I rasp.

"I wasn't sure how long we'd be here, and I figured you might get hungry, so I picked us up some snacks." She opens the shopping bag, and I spot two bags of Doritos, one red and one blue.

My lips tip up in a soft smile, and hers do the same. "Thank you."

Time passes by, and Ivy has graciously taken it upon herself to go through the rosters in my and Uncle Jeff's phones to let them know what's happening, so I don't get overwhelmed with the influx of messages.

We talk faintly, here and there. Nurses occasionally pop over, checking in, offering water and ginger ale, and changing out Uncle Jeff's IV bag of pain medicine.

When we're alone again, I glance over at Ivy. "Why did you tell Uncle Jeff and not me?"

She looks a little thrown off by the question and sips in a shallow breath before answering. "He saw me walking out of my doctor's office when I had just found out. I didn't seek him out. Fate just put him in front of me."

I nod in understanding. "And why didn't you tell me?"

Ivy takes a moment to study my features, her sapphire eyes taking in every emotion written on my face. "I debated it for a long time. I had a few different plans, but I was scared. And it would've completely changed your life—"

"I don't care about that."

"Now," she states. "*Now* you would've chosen me

over a career, but do you think twenty-year-old Pax would?"

My shoulders collapse in pure shame. "I'm so sorry, Ivy." My voice wavers. "I'm so sorry I never showed you how much you truly meant to me. I didn't know how to be the person you wanted and needed. But I would've never left your side if I knew you were pregnant. Even me at twenty years old would've realized that."

Her attention falls away from me. "Well, it seemed pointless to tell you once I miscarried."

"God, Ivy, I wish I knew," I whisper in deep regret. "You should've never gone through that alone. I wish I was there to take care of you." I watch as a single teardrop rolls down her face. "I'm so sorry."

Without a second thought, I wrap my arms around her, holding her tighter than ever before. She trembles in my grasp, silently crying.

I kiss the top of her head, allowing myself to weep with her. "I'm so sorry," I whisper into her hair over and over again.

Ivy's arms come around my torso, her hands gripping onto my shirt as we continue to mourn together.

Something she's waited years to do.

Her heart hammers against my body, and I feel everything—her pain, her fears, her anger, her love.

From this day forward, I vow to myself to always be there for her, in whatever capacity she needs.

"Hey." A voice comes from behind us, shifting our attention.

When I spot Trent walking into the room, my forehead scrunches in confusion. "Aren't you supposed to be on your honeymoon?"

"Not until tomorrow. And we can postpone if need be," Trent responds.

"No, don't postpone anything," I state. "How did you get here so fast?"

"Once Ivy texted me, I reached out to a buddy of mine who has a private jet and got here as soon as I could."

Trent puts a chair next to me, on my left, but before he sits down, he places his backpack down and takes a few items out. Then, he adjusts the hospital tray table to be at the foot of Uncle Jeff's bed. He puts his laptop on it and charges it.

"What are you doing?" I ask.

Trent sets up his computer, pulling up YouTube. "We might as well set it up so Uncle Jeff feels like he's at home." He puts on a video of one of my old hockey games, then finally sits down.

I smile, grateful to be sandwiched between the Hartwicks.

"You want anything to eat? We have some snacks," I say, gesturing to the shopping bag.

Trent peers in. "You have any blue Doritos or just the red bag?"

Ivy sighs, passing Trent the Cool Ranch Doritos she had stashed next to her. "Don't eat all of them."

"I'll see what I can do," he responds.

Chuckling, I'm strangely at ease in this moment. Watching a hockey game with Uncle Jeff, Ivy and Trent bickering, sitting around and talking like we used to.

This feels like family.

As the time passes, our conversations morph from laughter to tears and back again.

But as the sun begins to go down, somberness encases the room.

It gets quiet.

Uncle Jeff's blood pressure drops rapidly, and the three of us are aware of what's to come.

Trent plants his hand on my back.

Ivy threads her fingers between mine and rests her head on my shoulder.

And as they fully support me in this moment, we watch Uncle Jeff take his last breath.

Time stands still, yet moves fast as hospital staff enters the room. The sounds of soft voices and sniffles invade my ears.

Minutes pass by, and I'm unsure of how long I've been sitting here.

"We'll give you some time alone with him," Ivy's gentle voice carries throughout the room, and I watch her and Trent leave, along with the staff.

My heart rips open as I witness Uncle Jeff's lifeless body. With tears pouring out of me, I give his hand a squeeze.

I don't know what to do or what to say to him. So I say the first thing that comes to my mind. "I love you, Uncle Jeff. Thank you for everything." I stand up and kiss his forehead. "Take care of Daisy for us."

CHAPTER FIFTY-EIGHT

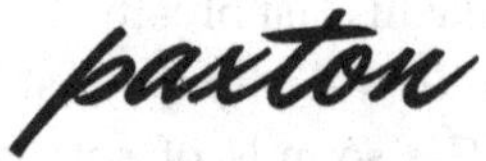

UNSURE OF WHAT we should do, the three of us go back to Ivy's apartment. Exhaustion shrouds all of us, but even though I told Ivy and Trent to go to sleep, neither of them wants to leave me alone.

Trent stretches out on Ivy's recliner, while I settle into her couch. There are piles of Ivy's belongings scattered about, which I'm sure she has organized in her brain in some form. But despite them being arranged in a certain way, she shoves everything back into random boxes, undoing all of her work.

There are some stray photographs haphazardly lying in random places from when she threw them at me earlier this morning.

To think of everything that has transpired in twenty-four hours gives me a piercing headache between my temples.

"Did Jeff ever tell you what he wanted in terms of services?" Trent asks.

"He did. He wants nothing," I state.

"Nothing?" Ivy chimes in, putting the remaining items in the last box.

"Nope. He said he's a simple man and didn't want me to waste any money on a funeral or wake. But it seems kind of wrong not to do anything for him, after all he did for me."

"So let's do something then," Trent says.

"He wouldn't want us to."

"We'll have a small service. Ivy and I will handle it."

"You have a honeymoon to get to," I remind him.

"Already spoke to Lucille. We pushed our plans back," Trent says. I automatically open my mouth to protest, but he holds up his hand and continues, "And before you try telling me no, Lucille suggested it before I even mentioned the possibility, and our travel agent already switched our reservations."

Gratitude pulls my mouth into a smile. "Didn't you want to rip my head off just last night?"

Trent's attention goes to Ivy, watching her as she sits down next to me on the couch. "I'll put that on pause for now," he says, letting me know that he's going to want to have a follow-up conversation at some point. "Jeff saved you this time around."

"Uncle Jeff has saved me many a time," I state with a small grin.

"He was a great man," Ivy says, and both Trent and I nod in agreement. She lets out a woeful sigh but quickly shifts her energy, getting off the couch and heading to her fridge. "Let's spend the night celebrating Uncle Jeff," she says, reappearing with three beer bottles in her hand. She passes one to me and one to Trent. "We'll stay up sharing our favorite Uncle Jeff stories and laugh and cry until the sun comes up." She holds out her bottle. "To Uncle Jeff."

We clink our bottles against hers. "To Uncle Jeff."

The next few days pass by in a blur.

I'm inundated with texts and calls, and I try to respond to them whenever I have the mental capacity to.

Ivy and Trent have been doing most of the legwork for me, packing up Uncle Jeff's hotel room, scheduling a small service at a local church, and arranging the cremation.

By the end of it, the three of us are drained.

Following the service, we go back to Ivy's apartment and order lunch for delivery. As we dive into our meal from O'Donnell's, Ivy's phone pings with a text message.

"Oh crap, I forgot to call Zaina back."

"Who's Zaina?" Trent asks.

"Her best friend," I state. "They met at work."

"Where do you work?" he asks her.

"The Contemporary Art and Lifestyle Museum," I reply.

"You her spokesperson or something?"

"No. I just know a lot about her." Ivy and I exchange glances, fighting back our smiles.

She wipes her hands on her napkin, then rises with her phone in her hand. "I'm gonna call Zaina real quick," she says, stepping toward her bedroom. "Don't steal my fries," she shouts over her shoulder to both of us.

When she's out of earshot, Trent focuses his attention on me. "So you know a lot about her, huh?"

"Trent, I know what you're thinking, but I swear Ivy means more to me than anyone else on this planet."

His eyes pin me in place as he assesses my statement. "Do you love her?"

"I've always loved her."

"Are you *in* love with her?"

I take a deep inhale, then state, "Madly in love with her. I'd marry her today if her stubborn ass would let me."

He chuckles. "Why do you think she wouldn't marry you?"

"I fucked up."

"Did you cheat on her?" His voice automatically sharpens.

"What? No!" I stare at him, flabbergasted. "I just told you I'm madly in love with her."

"Then how did you fuck up?"

"I fucked up in the past, and now she's scared to get too close to me."

He reaches for a french fry off Ivy's plate and mulls over what I shared. I can tell he has more questions, but it might be in his best interest to hold off on asking for more details. After he swipes a few more fries, he clears his throat. "Sounds like you need to win her back."

Immediate relief flows through me. "What?"

"If you say you're madly in love with my sister, then it's about time you step up your game and win her over."

Before I can respond, Ivy walks out of her bedroom. "Sorry, Zaina was just checking in to see how we're all doing and to update me that my exhibit went viral on social media."

"No way!" I burst with pride.

"What's your exhibit about?" Trent asks.

"It explores how the culture and trends of each modern decade shape romance and dating and love."

"Sounds like me and Lucille will have to check it out after our honeymoon."

Ivy smiles. "I'd like that."

When we end our meal, Trent checks the time on his phone, noting that he has to head to the airport soon. He booked a regular flight this time around and didn't need a bougie jet ride back.

"I'm serious, call me if you need anything," Trent says, lingering in the doorway of Ivy's apartment.

"Not a chance in hell that I'd call you on your honeymoon," I say, and he chuckles. "Go have fun."

"Where will you be when I get back?"

"I'm not really sure. I'll have to go to Maryland to go through Uncle Jeff's home eventually, but I think for now I'll just live the nomad life. I'll explore Boston for a little bit longer."

Trent gives me a knowing grin, then gives me and Ivy a hug goodbye.

"Thank you for everything," I say. "Now get the fuck out of here and enjoy being a newlywed."

"Happy honeymoon!" Ivy shouts out to Trent as he drifts down the hallway, toward the elevator.

When the door closes, it's just me and Ivy again.

It was only a few days ago since the last time we were alone in this space, yet everything has changed since then.

"I haven't gotten the chance to thank you for all you've been doing." My voice comes out thick.

"Of course."

"And I don't mean just now, Ivy. I mean all of it. Thank you for showing up at my door after every game Uncle Jeff missed, thank you for always being there for me, thank you for caring about me when I didn't deserve it."

"Pax—"

"I mean it, Ivy." I step in closer, noticing the way her breath slightly catches. "Thank you."

Her eyes get glassy but don't spill over. Gently taking my fingertips, I loop her dark strands of hair around her ear, then drag my touch down her jawline to tilt her chin upward. My lips meet hers in a longing kiss.

Her arms wrap around me at the same time my free hand caresses her lower back.

Her lips are like home. My safe place and my shelter.

The way our tongues graze in a playful manner calls for our hands to roam each other's bodies. We pull the other in closer, not able to get enough of the other. Our passion builds until our sighs get heavy and our grips get stronger. The tips of my fingers sneak under her shirt, eliciting a wake of goose bumps on her soft skin.

I never wanted her more than I do right now. I want to thank her endlessly, pleasuring her in every way imaginable and giving her every last drop of me.

But suddenly, Ivy jumps backward, breaking our connection. "Hold on," she says, out of breath with swollen lips.

"Okay." Confusion ricochets throughout my insides.

"We shouldn't do this." She takes another step back, leery of the magnetic pull between us.

"Why not?"

"We-we just had the most turbulent few days." Ivy's gaze darts around the room as I watch her fears set in. "I don't want us to get wrapped up in each other because we're grieving or emotional or unsure how to process all this. I think we need space and time to reassess everything with a clear head. Let's just be there for each other platonically."

I nod my head, not wanting to fight her on this right now. Because ultimately, I'm going to do exactly what Trent said.

I'm going to win Ivy back.

CHAPTER FIFTY-NINE

ivy

IT'S BEEN two weeks since Uncle Jeff passed.

It's strange how we're supposed to quickly assimilate back into our regular lives when something awful happens. Given a small amount of bereavement days and then expected to return to work as if the few days of mourning were enough.

But if there's one thing I'm good at, it's shoving my trauma in a box so I can continue to move forward.

My shoes clink against the polished floor of the museum as I finish up a morning meeting with our director, Roy. He spent the majority of the time complimenting my work and the success of my exhibit. And to be honest, I'm enjoying the validation.

A wide smile brightens my features as I walk back to my office. But before I can turn down the hall, someone catches my attention.

Pax's strong muscles pull the fabric of his T-shirt as he slowly moves around the memorabilia in my *Journey of Love Through the Ages* exhibit. He's wearing a baseball cap, the same one he was wearing when fate pushed us together on the airplane.

I can't deny the butterflies circling my stomach as I watch him. We've been keeping things platonic, as I suggested, but we still meet up for dinner every couple of days. We text all the time, but as friends helping one another grieve and heal.

My heart flutters as I witness him meticulously reading the signs and examining the items. He's not just casually perusing the exhibit. He's analyzing it as if he wants to imprint the entirety of it in his mind.

"What are you doing here?" I stroll up to him.

Pax spins his attention over to me at the sound of my voice. "I'm a member of the museum. I'm just checking to see if there are any new additions."

"It's the same stuff as the last time you were here."

"Well, then, I guess I love to admire your work." His eyes inadvertently glance over to the 1950s car where we had sex only a few months back.

My cheeks warm up. "You're going to get bored of looking at the same thing over and over again."

"Nope. Every time I look, I discover something new."

"You'll probably be a better tour guide for Trent and Lucille than I will," I tease. Trent kept his word and is coming back here with Lucille after their honeymoon. I'm not sure how long they'll be visiting for. Or if Pax will be going back to Maryland with them. I haven't had the courage to ask him.

"They should be here soon," Pax says. "I'll text you when they are."

"Okay." I take a step backward. "Enjoy the exhibit."

"I always do." He winks.

About twenty minutes later, I get the text from Pax and head to the museum entrance to greet Trent and Lucille. I get a great big hug from my new sister, and she says how overjoyed she is to be here.

"So where should we start?" Trent asks, surveying the museum.

"Pax, you ready to lead them?" I ask with a playful grin.

"I'd be honored," Pax responds with a glimmer in his hazel eyes. "All right, guys, follow me."

He guides the three of us around but bypasses the exhibits we're closest to.

"What are you doing? You're skipping over all of this," I say.

"Yeah, this isn't really my specialty. My forte is on the exhibit upstairs." He cheekily acts as our guide, fully getting into the role as he leads us upstairs. "Ladies and gentlemen—man, I present to you Ivy Hartwick's newest exhibit: *Journey of Love Through the Ages*. It recently became a viral sensation, and the museum extended the display date."

Lucille gasps. "That's incredible, Ivy!"

"Thank you."

"Now, as we travel back in time, please keep in mind that each decade has an interactive element to it, which you're more than welcome to participate in," Pax states.

Suddenly, a small crowd begins to develop, patrons intently listening to Pax's explanation. I cover my mouth, hiding my laughter as more people gather around us. Trent and Lucille exchange glances with me, also trying to hold in their chuckles.

When Pax finally instructs everyone to disperse, the four of us huddle together and quietly laugh.

"You're such an asshole," I say to Pax, not meaning it at all.

He shrugs. "You told me I'd be a better tour guide than you."

"Proved me right."

We move along so Trent and Lucille can experience

what the rest of the patrons are. After several minutes, I hang back to watch everyone enjoying themselves.

Pax sidles up next to me. "I'm proud of you."

"I'm proud of you too. Who knew being a tour guide was your calling?" I give him a small hip-check, and he laughs.

"Does your boss still want you to create a Y2K display?"

"Most likely."

His attention drifts around the space. "What do you think love in the early two-thousands would look like?"

Us.

"I don't know." My voice comes out quiet, uncommitted to my statement.

"What do you think love now would look like?"

My gaze flashes up at him, and he's looking back at me with deep yearning whirling around his irises. "I don't know." My words are barely above a whisper as my heart strums a beautiful melody.

"Excuse me, sir." An elderly woman walks up to Pax. "Could you assist me with the Polaroid camera in the nineties display?"

"Of course." Pax turns to me, saying, "Duty calls." Then he goes off to help her.

I continue to stand on the sidelines, observing. Zaina appears at the far end and is about to walk straight past everyone when I notice Pax stops her. They greet each other, and then he whispers something to her. Zaina's expression lights up, and she nods, then they part ways.

Before Zaina can jet past me, I stop her. "What was that about?"

"What?" She plays dumb.

"Pax whispering to you."

"Don't worry about it." Zaina gleams. She starts to walk away, but spins around to talk again. "Oh, can you stop by my place after work and help me pick out an outfit for a date?"

"I'm supposed to go to dinner with my family."

"It'll be super quick—fifteen minutes tops."

"Okay, sure."

As Zaina rifles through her closet, I chuckle at the incoming text I got from Trent.

"What's so funny?" Zaina asks.

"Trent texted me that they won't be ready for dinner for another hour. The three of them decided to go to the Boston Tea Party Museum."

"That's perfect. I don't have to rush through trying on different outfits."

Zaina does just that, taking her time trying on what seems like a thousand different dresses.

I lay across her bed, watching her groan in the mirror.

"It's been over an hour, and my entire closet, and I hate everything," she states, frowning.

"Wear the yellow maxi dress. That was cute."

"Cute, not hot enough."

"Wear your white wedges with it," I suggest.

"The heel broke off of one of them, and I haven't had time to buy new ones." Zaina gets an incoming text, temporarily distracting her from the task at hand. Once she replies, she refocuses. "Do you have any wedges I can borrow?"

I do a mental recall of my shoe selection. "Yep, I have a pair that you'd like."

"You're amazing."

"I know."

"Can we head over now and grab them?"

"Sure, but then I'll have to meet Trent and Lucille for dinner." I check my phone to see if they have updated me on their latest Bostonian adventure, but they haven't.

Zaina and I swiftly walk from her apartment building to mine. The beaming sunlight hits my arms, heating me up to the point of me being about to break a sweat.

"Why are you walking so fast?" I complain.

"Sorry, just excited," Zaina says as she texts someone.

"About your date?"

"Yep."

When we get to my building and onto the elevator, Zaina impatiently taps her fingers against the strap of her purse. Her restless energy is beginning to impact mine, my heart rate picking up for no reason.

When the elevator dings, I step off but notice she's not next to me. "What are you doing?" I ask.

"Bringing you to your apartment." She hits the Close Door button, and the elevator begins to shut. "Bye!"

As she disappears, I look around me, dumbfounded. There's no one else in the hallway—just me, utterly confused.

Baffled, I walk toward my apartment, anticipating someone to jump out and scare me. When I reach my door, I notice the knob is unlocked. Cautiously pushing it open, I call out and ask if anyone's in here, but I'm stopped by the faint sound of a familiar drumbeat.

Fully entering my apartment, I immediately realize that the cardboard boxes in my living room have been downsized tremendously. Padding closer to the sound of the music, my lips curl upward when I hear "First Date" by Blink-182 playing from my bedroom.

When I enter, I gasp, tears instantly forming.

All of my furniture has been rearranged to mimic the layout of my bedroom at my parents' house. My old cork-board is hanging up, pictures of Pax and me from a lifetime ago are pinned up, and one recent picture is in the center—the Polaroid we took the night my exhibit opened. Next to the corkboard, a crinkled Fall Out Boy poster and a Jack Sparrow poster are also hanging up.

The current reads on my bookshelf have been replaced with my worn favorites, books that I haven't opened up in well over a decade but can exactly remember how they made me feel. My dresser is filled with my near-vintage perfume bottles from Victoria's Secret, stacks of my cherished CDs and DVDs, and a stereo that is playing the nostalgic song. Next to the stereo is the mix CD Pax gave me for my sixteenth birthday, with *"For my Rebel"* written in Sharpie across it. Directly above is my TV silently playing an episode of *Gilmore Girls.*

It's my own personal exhibit of Pax and me, every relic of my past being honored and treasured.

When I turn to look at the other side of my room, my focus immediately lands on Pax. I can't help but laugh when I see him standing there in his old Blink-182 T-shirt, which doesn't fully cover his torso and is bursting at the seams from his athletic build.

"What is all this?" I ask, unable to conceal my teardrops filled with gratitude.

"I want a do-over," Pax says, a hint of nervousness fraying his voice. "I want to go right back to where I left you all those years ago and choose to stay."

My hand goes to clutch my heart. "Pax."

"Trent and Lucille helped me organize everything. We couldn't get it back to exactly how your room was, but I tried my best. I even found a straightener and burned your dresser a little." He points to the dark divot in the wood, and I laugh through my tears, looking at the mark and then the small scar on his hand. "And then I added something a little new." He gestures to my nightstand.

My old Canon digital camera rests on it, next to two picture frames. One is a photograph of Pax, Uncle Jeff, and me that I don't even remember taking, but he must've found it when he was going through everything. The other frame delicately houses the ultrasound of our Daisy.

"This…this is incredible." Love branches out of my vaulted heart, extending out to every fiber of my being.

Pax walks over to me, and with each step, my veins ignite. "Ivy, my biggest regret in life is letting you go back then, and now that I have a second chance, I can't live with another regret of not fighting for you." His hand reaches for mine, his thumb gingerly grazing over my skin. "And I know you're scared. And I know you're independent and are going to be a stubborn pain in my ass about this, but let's give us a real shot. No friends with benefits, no time limit, no letting our careers or families or exes or the fucking Dames getting in the way."

Salty tears hit my lips as my breath flows unevenly. My pulse whirls ferociously as I stand under the loving heat of his gaze.

Since I'm overtaken by emotion, Pax continues, "I asked what love looked like in the two-thousands and what it looks like now. It's us, Ivy. I have loved you since we were young, and I never stopped. I love you."

Nibbling on the inside of my cheek, my mind travels back in time, through all the trends and pastimes and transformations—Pax has always been my constant. Whether I wanted him to be or not.

He's always had my heart.

Since he walked into my room when I was twelve.

Then, out of my room when I was eighteen.

And back into my life now.

"I love you too, Pax."

His hazel eyes become watery. "Holy shit," he chuckles. "I never knew how amazing it would feel to hear you say that to me." A tear drips down his cheek, and I catch it with the pad of my finger. "So what do you say, Rebel? Do we get a do-over?"

"Yeah." I wrap my arms around him and press up on my tippy toes to give him the most loving kiss. "But I don't want to start from right where you left me. I want to start here and now. In our new chapter."

look for

SCARRED HEARTS

Coming soon…

AVAILABLE APRIL 2026

afterward & acknowledgments

The very first person I need to thank is YOU! Thank you for opening up my book, immersing yourself in this fictional world, and taking the ride with Ivy & Pax. I hope you loved their story—even with the bumps in the road.

Thank you to my alpha, beta, and sensitivity readers. I'm forever grateful that you took the time out to help me strengthen my book!

Thank you to Ellie, Kayla, and the whole team at Love N. Books Press! This is my first official trad publication that wasn't a re-release, and I'm forever appreciative for this opportunity.

Lastly, thank you to my husband. We started dating when we were teens, back in 2008, and since then, we've created the most beautiful life together. Thank you for always supporting me and encouraging me to follow my heart!

Until the next book,
Holly

Holly is a new adult & contemporary romance author. Lover of all things steamy and angsty— you're sure to get your fill of these in her books! She also likes to have an underlying message in all of her stories, bringing awareness to bigger issues that are close to her heart.

When she's not reading or writing, you can find her eating an unhealthy amount of bread and cheese, rocking out to emo music, or cherishing wife/mom life

www.hollycasteauthor.com

more trigger info

Hi! If you're back here, you either just finished Ivy & Pax's story (thank you, I hope you enjoyed!), or you're wanting more details about the triggers. I didn't want to include all the information at the beginning of the book to save major plot points. However, I'm aware this is a sensitive topic, and I'd like to be mindful of my different readers and their lived experiences. So here is a more in-depth explanation of the triggers: the story includes a teen pregnancy (18 years old) and a miscarriage. There is also talk of abortion.

If you are still planning on reading, I hope you fall for Ivy & Pax. And I promise they get their happily ever after!

www.ingramcontent.com/pod-product-compliance
Lightning Source LLC
La Vergne TN
LVHW041249110826
845146LV00005BA/1276

* 9 7 9 8 8 9 5 6 7 7 1 1 7 *